W9-AMP-873

THE ROAD TO CARDINAL VALLEY

TITLES BY EARLENE FOWLER

THE SADDLEMAKER'S WIFE
THE ROAD TO CARDINAL VALLEY

LOVE MERCY

Benni Harper Mysteries

FOOL'S PUZZLE
IRISH CHAIN
KANSAS TROUBLES
GOOSE IN THE POND
DOVE IN THE WINDOW
MARINER'S COMPASS
SEVEN SISTERS
ARKANSAS TRAVELER
STEPS TO THE ALTAR
SUNSHINE AND SHADOW
BROKEN DISHES
DELECTABLE MOUNTAINS
TUMBLING BLOCKS
STATE FAIR
SPIDER WEB

THE ROAD TO CARDINAL VALLEY

EARLENE FOWLER

DOUBLEDAY LARGE PRINT HOME LIBRARY EDITION

BERKLEY BOOKS, NEW YORK

This Large Print Edition, prepared especially for Doubleday Large Print Home Library, contains the complete, unabridged text of the original Publisher's Edition.

THE BERKLEY PUBLISHING GROUP
Published by the Penguin Group
Penguin Group (USA) Inc.

Penguin Books Ltd., Registered Offices:
80 Strand, London WC2R 0RL, England

This book is an original publication of
The Berkley Publishing Group.

Cover illustration by Griesbach/Martucci.
Cover design by Jason Gill.

ISBN 978-1-62090-769-6

PRINTED IN THE UNITED STATES OF AMERICA

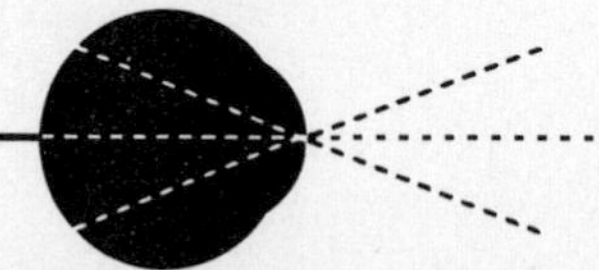

This Large Print Book carries the Seal of Approval of N.A.V.H.

For Charlotte "Bunny" Brown,
Joy Fitzhugh, Bonnie Haskell
and Sally Parker—Ranchwomen
Extraordinaire.
Thanks for your generous help,
enduring friendship and for showing this
city girl how to "cowgirl up."

Acknowledgments

No writer ever truly writes alone. My sincere and humble thanks to:

God the Father, God the Son and God the Holy Spirit—to You be the Glory.

Wonderful and savvy agent: Ellen Geiger.

Delightful and smart editor: Kate Seaver.

Loyal and supportive friends: Tina Davis, Janice Dischner, Jo Ellen Heil, Christine Hill, JoBeth McDaniel, Carolyn Miller, Kay Foster-Pulcini, Lela Satterfield, Kathy Vieira, Kathryn Williams, Laura Ross Wingfield and Marguerite Zechiel.

My much-loved and respected sisters: Mary Kahn, Carol Seaton and Debra Jackson—when the rubber meets the road, we always seem to pull together—Mama and Daddy would be proud.

Dear friends who are also my legal and law enforcement sources: Karen Gray and Pam Munns.

Wonderful friends as well as writing and saddlemaking consultants: Kathy and Richard Vieira and their son, Trajan Vieira, for letting me borrow the name of his company, Mercury Leatherworks.

My cousins, Howard and Ben Nixon (aka Little Buck and Benny): Thanks for taking the time to show me "your" Ajo and for all those crazy childhood times we shared in your hometown—you two are the brothers I never had and I love you both!

Much-appreciated fans from near and far, website and Facebook, city and country, wherever you may be, I have always been blessed by and thankful for your friendship and support.

My beloved husband and best friend, Allen, Forever and Ever, Amen.

THE ROAD TO CARDINAL VALLEY

Prologue

Ajo, Arizona

In the old company town, the copper mine long abandoned, in the always-crowded shelter, the dogs never stopped arriving. They came and they came, all shapes and sizes, with hair as fine as bunny fur and scratchy as old steel wool. They came with tinny yips and frightened howls and dignified baritone barks, the canine equivalent to James Earl Jones. They came with all manner of scars, both physical and mental, the mental less obvious, but ultimately more devastating.

Like people, she thought while bathing them, gently untangling their knotted fur with her fingers. The calming scent of lavender reminded her, for some odd reason, of everything she had thrown away.

They arrived and arrived, legs stiff with fear, eyes round and glowing with desperation. Their identical thoughts could have been written in a cartoon bubble above their heads—*All is lost.*

She understood those feelings. She suspected it was why elderly Dr. Beth who owned the shelter asked her to work with the new ones. She would murmur reassurances in her silky drawl, a voice that hinted of green mountain hollers and gurgling creeks, a place where the air was thick with pollen and ripe with the sound of crickets and bees.

Slowly the dogs comprehended that their suffering was over, that this was the end of the line and that this time it wasn't a bad thing. At the end of this line lay soft old blankets and good food, kind touches and those satiny words, warm and sweet as banana pudding. When no one else was around, she sang to them in her thin soprano—Patsy Cline's broken-heart songs, Kitty Wells and her honky-tonkin' girl and the mournful mountain songs of Hazel Dickens. Like Hazel, she'd grown up with the coal mine knock, knock, knocking at the plate glass windows of the company house, a reality as black as death and just as certain.

It was the only time she sang now. She had long given up the dream whose price had been her family, her dignity, her youth and sometimes she felt, though Father Tomas assured her otherwise, her very soul.

Now she sang to the dogs and wondered about her babies, afraid she would never see them again and just as afraid that she would.

1

Lucas

Lucas McGavin stared at the red ketchup stain on the crown of his new silver gray 10x Stetson and wondered if it was an omen. He'd bought the hat at Walt's Feed and Seed specifically for this trip to the National Finals Rodeo. It was the first new hat he'd purchased in ten years. Before sitting down to eat, he should have taken it off and placed it, like he'd been taught by his grandpa Kitt, crown down on the bench seat of this all-night diner on the Las Vegas Strip. Then the stain would have been on the inside brim rather than right out front for everyone to see.

He contemplated the spot with annoyance. It resembled a child's crude drawing of Florida. The hat had cost him almost two hundred dollars. What a fool he was. Who was he trying to impress?

The ketchup had come from the fork of a hyperactive three-year-old in the next booth. The sorrel-haired boy, waving his fork around like he was leading a marching band, screamed at an unearthly pitch that made Lucas momentarily consider a vasectomy despite being single, only thirty-five and not particularly fond of needles. What was a toddler doing up at one thirty in the dang morning?

"Sorry, buddy." The boy's father caught Lucas's eye and smirked. "He's a pistol. Future bull rider." The father didn't appear to be more than eighteen or nineteen, painfully skinny in that Red Bull-for-breakfast way that reminded Lucas of half the court-appointed cases he'd been assigned years ago as a San Francisco public defender. The guy's accent carried a spongy twang—Oklahoma or East Texas, Lucas would bet, if he were a betting man.

"No worries," Lucas said, though he

was doing exactly that. He moved the hat to the other side of him in case the toddler decided to reload. The boy appeared to be eying the pool of salsa covering his dad's half-eaten huevos rancheros. Where was this kid's mama?

"Here to watch the young guys rodeo?" the young man asked, his smirk stretching a half inch bigger.

Lucas was tempted to prick his smug balloon and say he was *in* the National Finals, that he'd been a champion bull rider since high school, that he'd earned six figures rodeoing last year. He hated that this guy assumed that he was too old to be anything but a spectator.

But he'd never been good at lying.

"I've got a booth at Cowtown Christmas," he finally said.

His inability to bluff was something that proved a problem for him as a public defender when he could not help giving away with his exasperated expression that, most of the time, he thought his client was guilty. Like his two older brothers, Lucas had done a little high school rodeo back in Cardinal. Dad had expected, no, *demanded* their participation.

But Lucas had only tolerated it. Using rodeo skills to actually work cattle, getting the job done with branding and castrating calves was one thing, but the sport of rodeo had always seemed ultimately pointless to him. Too many times it was an eight-second ride right to the hospital's brain trauma unit. Then again, he was not one of those guys addicted to adrenaline.

"That right? What you selling?"

"I'm a saddlemaker."

The guy picked up a used toothpick from his plate and stuck it in his mouth. "You make a lot of money doin' that?"

Lucas studied Mr. Red Bull's face for a moment, taking in the pale freckles, the acne on his chin and his lank, ditchwater brown hair. There was a good chance the young man had saved all year to come to NFR for a few days during these first two weeks of December. He was likely staying in one of the generic motels downtown that still rented rooms for fifty dollars. Maybe he worked at a gas station mini-mart or at one of those thirty-minute oil-change chains. Maybe he once dreamed of being in the NFR. Lucas began to feel a little empathy for Mr. Red Bull with the swaggering words. Why not be honest and tell him the truth? Make him feel less alone.

Lucas pushed back his plate of half-eaten buttermilk pancakes. "I'm . . ." He almost said poor as a church mouse, something his aunt Birch always said, but it made him sound like he was sixty-five rather than thirty-five. "I get by."

"Shoot, why do it if it don't make good money?"

Before Lucas could fire back a snappy reply, the toddler screamed, "Mama, Mama, Mama!"

The child's mother strolled toward them from the direction of the restrooms. She didn't look much older than his niece, Cassie, who just turned eighteen and was graduating from Cardinal High School in June. This skinny girl with black-lined green eyes gave off the same raised-on-Mountain Dew aura as her baby-daddy. She couldn't have weighed more than ninety pounds and looked like one of those undernourished kids seen on a *20/20* special about rural poverty in America. He didn't assume the guy was her husband because, as far as Lucas could tell, no one got married these days before having kids, something his aunt Birch lamented on a regular basis.

An unlit cigarette dangled from the girl's freshly painted bubblegum pink mouth.

"Your boy threw ketchup on this old guy's hat," Mr. Red Bull declared, not even glancing at Lucas.

The old-guy remark felt like a fork to Lucas's heart, a reminder that forty was within buckshot range.

"So why weren't *you* watching him?" the girl snapped, her eyes narrowing with irritation. She glanced at Lucas; her cheeks blushed a lighter shade of pink than her lipstick. "Sorry, sir. He's a jerk. I mean, not my boy . . ."

Lucas brushed away her apology with a calloused hand. "No worries, ma'am. You have a fine-looking son." He smiled, trying to project a sincerity he wished he felt. "He has a prodigious voice. Maybe he'll be a future announcer for the NFR."

"You really think so?" Her eyebrows arched, the obvious delight in his meager compliment told him that she rarely received them about her child.

He nodded, feeling his neck warm at his blatant lie. The toddler was as homely as a mountain goat, but he *was* loud. "I do."

The girl looked over at her baby's father, her expression triumphant. "He probably got that from *my* side."

The young guy snorted, shot Lucas a sour look and hustled his family out of the restaurant.

Lucas was staring at his stained hat when the waitress came back to refill his coffee mug.

"I can so get that out," she said.

He looked up, startled by the richness of her contralto voice. She was a new server. The woman who had brought him his pancakes had been in her sixties with hennaed hair and an Irish lilt. This woman was younger, late twenties maybe, with black hair pulled back in a braid, caramel skin and eyes the color of polished nickels. She wore blue jeans, a faded red Dr Pepper T-shirt and a nametag that read "Sacheen."

She smiled at him. One front tooth

slightly overlapped the other, giving her a tomboyish grin. "Seriously, cowboy, I can clean that spot off your hat. Those folks were a caution." Her laugh was throaty and low, sounding years older than what she appeared. "That's what my grammy Eula would say."

"I'm not a cowboy," he blurted out. *Sacheen.* Why did that name sound familiar?

She filled his empty coffee cup. "Anyone ever tell you that you do not have a poker face? That was a nice thing you said to that girl about her obnoxious baby, but you were lying through your teeth, my friend. Vegas may not be the wisest place for you."

"I don't gamble much. Takes money. Which I don't have." Good move, McGavin, he thought. A pretty woman flirts with you and the first words tumbling out of your mouth are how broke you are.

"You sweet talker," she said, holding out her free hand. The nails were bitten down to slightly swollen fingertips, reminding Lucas of a nervous child. "Don't worry, I'm not going to charge you. Give me that hat."

He handed it to her without comment.

She turned back toward the kitchen. "Finish your pancakes," she called over her shoulder. "Grammy Eula would say you're way too skinny."

He watched her confident stride until she disappeared behind the swinging kitchen door. Her long shiny braid just reached the top of her carved Western belt that inexplicably read "Jonah."

"Better listen to Marie," called the guy behind the grill. "She don't like it when people ignore her advice." His Elvis grin showed a tobacco-stained eyetooth.

Marie? So was Sacheen her last name?

He picked at his pancakes. He wasn't hungry but was just killing time while his roommate, Nate Brody, partied with a girl he'd hooked up with at Cowtown Christmas. Nate was a friend from high school. He played in a country band hired by a Texas clothing company pushing their new cowgirl blue jeans line at the NFR. He and Nate split the cost of a double room at the Motel Vegas Ho!, a relic from the fifties whose name, unfortunately, carried a somewhat different connotation now. The motel was owned by a sober-looking East Indian couple who told Nate and Lucas that the neon sign was too expensive to replace and, besides, they didn't think the motel's name was that odd, despite their customers' frequent jokes.

Lucas realized now that sharing a room with Nate was a mistake. Especially since this foray into marketing his saddlemaking business to a larger audience looked like it might be a bust. So far, he'd sold only one saddle of the five he brought—three to sell, two for display only. Not bad, but not, in his estimation, worth the trip. At least the effort would get his aunt Birch off his back for a while. She was always after him to promote himself.

"Just give me until two a.m.," Nate had begged. "She's here with her girlfriends from Jersey. She's meeting up with them later and says she doesn't want to spend the night with me." Nate gave a chortle. "My kinda girl."

Lucas glanced at the chicken-shaped clock over the food pass-through. In a half hour, he could finally go back to the room and get some sleep. Fatigue made his eyes feel like they were holding up half-pound fishing weights. Only five more days and he could return to Cardinal, resume his normal, if somewhat boring, life.

Even before the unfortunate encounter with the ketchup-tossing toddler, Lucas realized coming to this particular café was a mistake. If he'd been expecting some kind of message from the dead, he was out of luck. Though not much had physically changed in this red and yellow ex-Denny's restaurant, he didn't feel even the tiniest vibration or communication from his dead brother.

The café was the same one where he and Cole had met annually for years, trading stilted catching-up conversation that always left Lucas frustrated and unfulfilled. Then last year, his oldest brother ran his truck off a twisting canyon road outside San Juan Capistrano—a suicide, it appeared—though no one would ever know for sure. Cole's widow, Ruby, had driven into town with his ashes and, in three short weeks, set into motion a series of events that forever changed the McGavin family's story.

Not her fault, he said to himself, taking

out the postcard he'd received from Ruby a week ago. The McGavins had always been prone to drama; they certainly had never needed any outside help with that. It went back all the way to the early twentieth century when his great-grandpa, Jacob McGavin, and his son, Kitteridge, first bought the Circle MG ranch north of Cardinal, located in shadows of the Eastern Sierra Nevada Mountains. It was one of the few working ranches left in Cardinal Valley because great-grandpa Jacob and grandpa Kitt had refused to sell the ranch's water rights to the Department of Water and Power for the burgeoning and thirsty city of Los Angeles, and somehow the DWP had never been able to tap into the McGavins' water. Some envious neighbors had never quite forgiven them for that smart move or their undeserved luck.

The drama continued under Lucas's charismatic dad, Carson, with his roving eye, penchant for underage girls and generally amoral personality. It was culminated by Cole's dramatic exit from this world, though Cole had disappeared from the McGavin family long before that. After his release from prison, no one knew his whereabouts for years, his only contact with the family that annual meeting with Lucas in Las Vegas. Cole had created a completely new life in Southern California, including a wife who had been told that the McGavins were all killed in a tragic auto accident. After Cole died, she inherited one-fourth of the Circle MG, but Ruby didn't care about the ranch or its assets. Earlier this year, before leaving for Nashville, she sold her part back to the family for twenty thousand dollars, a pittance that she didn't want to accept. She'd told Lucas she didn't feel she had a right to any of it.

That was one of the things Lucas found attractive about Ruby. She was a person for whom money and status didn't seem to affect why she did things. She'd only come to Cardinal to return her inheritance and to bring Cole's ashes home. But in the few weeks she'd lived there, she'd become a part of his life.

Then, as abruptly as she arrived, she left.

He pulled the postcard out of his back pocket. It was frayed around the edges from being handled too often, something Lucas hoped no one ever saw. It showed the original *Grand Ole Opry* wooden podium with "WSM Radio" in bold letters down the front.

Dear Lucas,

I'm coming back to Cardinal. Am bringing Nash with me.

He's better, but needs to get away from here. Details when I see you. We hope to arrive before Christmas. I'll call Birch with the exact *date.*

See you soon,
Ruby

She'd left for Nashville last January, eleven months ago. She'd flown back to care for her younger brother, Nash, named for the town where he was trying to make it as a musician. Nash's girlfriend had contacted Ruby and told her that her brother had hepatitis C.

"I'm all he really has," Ruby said. "I have to go."

"What about your father?" he asked, not wanting her to leave.

She just gave him a dispirited look and didn't answer.

Ruby and Nash's father, Joe, was an independent, long-haul trucker, who saw his kids only when he and his fifth wife, Prissy, happened to snag a route through wherever Ruby and Nash lived. Ruby and Nash's mother, Loretta, had left when Ruby was thirteen and Nash was six and was never heard from again.

He tucked the postcard into his shirt pocket. Ruby was coming back to Cardinal. There'd been something special between them, something they had never discussed or resolved. But after he'd driven her car back to Nashville for her, he realized two minutes after he'd arrived that his presence there was a mistake. Her life with Nash was complicated; her relationship with her younger brother, as far as Lucas could tell, was an unsettling combination of sister and mother. Nash was an alcoholic, and the crazy lifestyle of a musician didn't encourage sobriety. Though he appeared to be sober when

Ruby arrived, scared by the hepatitis and his girlfriend's dire warnings that she couldn't take much more, Lucas had his doubts about Nash's desire to get clean. It appeared to Lucas that Nash wasn't as committed to his sobriety as Ruby and Nash's long-suffering girlfriend were.

Lucas was experienced with the promises of alcoholics and drug addicts from living with his dad as well as his time serving as a public defender. Addicts were adept at subterfuge and could often charm the boots off you. The only thing that was always true was that no one could make them stay clean. Getting sober and staying sober had to be their decision. Lucas could tell that Ruby wasn't ready to accept that yet. She still held the illusion of many enablers, that she could somehow orchestrate her brother's recovery.

They'd all spent a few uncomfortable days in her brother and his girlfriend's cramped, shabby apartment before Lucas bought a Greyhound bus ticket back to Cardinal. On the long trip across the Midwest, he contemplated his feelings for Ruby, trying to decide whether it was totally whacked to have fallen partially in love with his late brother's wife.

Yes, he'd decided somewhere around Kingman, Arizona, it was whacked and bizarre and yet he couldn't help what he felt.

"I should just tell her how I feel," Lucas said to his friend Ely Grey the first night he was back from Nashville. They were drinking in the Red Coyote. After three beers, Lucas confessed to his friend of his mixed feelings about his brother's widow. "Or how I think I feel. No, maybe not. It'd freak her out. It kind of freaks me out. What do you think?"

"I think you worry things like an old woman," Ely said, black eyes amused. He wore a navy long-sleeve T-shirt that showed a stylized Indian chief's head and stated, "Making Thanksgiving Possible Since 1619—Regretting it Ever Since."

"Birch would nail your hide to that wall if she heard you say such a sexist statement," Lucas said, looking across the table at his friend. Ely's thick dark eyebrows seemed to blur into one long black line.

Ely gave the cocky white grin that never

failed to endear him to women from age five to eighty-five. "She would, but she'd agree with me, too. Birch would likely say you need to chill out."

Lucas looked for answers in his half-empty beer. "I need a life, man."

Ely had laughed and lifted a hand to signal the cocktail waitress. "What you need is a cheeseburger and a good night's sleep. You've got a life, partner, and it ain't all that bad."

"Here you go, cowboy," Marie-Sacheen said, bringing Lucas back to the brightly lit café. She held out his hat. The ketchup stain was gone, replaced by only a faint wet spot.

"Wow," Lucas said, peering closer.

She grinned and shot a finger pistol at him. "You're welcome."

He ducked his head, embarrassed. "I'm sorry. Thank you. It's . . . amazing. How did you . . . ?"

"Old Paiute secret learned from my grammy. If I told you, I'd . . ."

"Have to kill me?"

"I was going to say scalp you. More descriptive. I'm an English major. Creative writing, actually. No master's degree though. Couldn't afford that. So I have a degree that qualifies me to . . ." She held out her hands as if presenting him with the fluorescent-bright diner.

"Oh." He studied her animated face, his eyes dropping briefly to her nametag. "Sacheen Littlefeather! I get it now. The Indian woman who refused Marlon Brando's Oscar for *The Godfather* in 1973."

She grinned, jutting out a nicely rounded hip. "You're too young to remember that. What are you, thirty-three, thirty-four?"

"Thirty-five. But my dad was a huge Marlon Brando fan. He must have told that story a million times. He was royally pissed at Marlon for turning down the Oscar for what he considered a stupid reason. My dad was a major bigot. The woman's real name was Marie."

She nodded. "Yes, I know."

"That's your real name. I mean, that's what the cook called you." He glanced toward the kitchen. "But, you probably weren't even born when . . ."

"Nope," she said cheerfully. "I'm twenty-nine, but my grammy's a Brando fan, too. Well, early Brando. When he was skinny. She thought it was great when he refused the award. Tells the story like it happened yesterday."

"Small world." Now, there was an original remark. He felt like an idiot and wished he'd just gone to McDonald's to wait out his friend's late-night date.

After an awkward pause, she pulled his bill from the back of her order pad and slipped it under his plate. "I'll make sure Audrey gets her tip. She left early. You take care. Try to stay away from toddlers armed with ketchup-filled trajectories."

He touched the faint watermark on his hat before placing it on his head.

"Thanks, Marie-Sacheen. This was the nicest thing that has happened to me since coming to Vegas."

"Sorry to hear that, cowboy. Hope things get better before you head home." With that, she turned and strode toward the front where a group of young men in brightly colored cowboy shirts and black cowboy hats were taking over two booths.

"Look, boys, I can already tell you're gonna be trouble," she said. "My tip better be more than spare change and pocket lint." The men laughed, nudging each other, delighted by her teasing.

Lucas slipped two tens under the five-dollar-and-ninety-cent bill, hoping that Marie would guess some of the extravagant tip was for her. Maybe he should write his intention on the bill. He patted his front pockets, hunting a pen or pencil. Of course he didn't have one.

He found one of the business cards he had printed for this trip in his back pocket. *Cardinal Custom Saddlery, Lucas McGavin, Cardinal, California* and his phone for the shop on Main Street. It had a reddish stain on it. Barbecue sauce? How had that happened? She was going to think he was the biggest slob on earth. He hesitated, then slipped the card back in his pocket. Truth was, she lived in Las Vegas. And, despite how undeniably cute she was, he really wasn't looking for a relationship right now.

But mostly there was Ruby. Whatever there was between them had to be addressed. He slid out of the booth and headed for the door.

It was freezing outside, but it was a dry

cold that was similar to the air in Cardinal. Though located in the lower desert, Las Vegas's winter temperatures felt like the high desert plain of his hometown. The biggest difference was Cardinal's perpetual dusky-sweet scent of sagebrush. Here on the Strip, all he could smell was a grimy, rubbery odor with a deep-fried undertone. If it were a perfume, he would have named it *Despair*.

It was past two a.m. He climbed into his rusty 1972 Ford pickup, held together by baling twine, duct tape and Ely Grey's miraculous mechanical talent, and drove back to Motel Vegas Ho! Only five more days of these headache-inducing neon lights, five more days of trying to sell himself to rich Texas ranchers, wealthy New York stockbrokers and affluent Florida horsewomen. Five more days and he could drive back to Cardinal, the place where he grew up, ran away from and ran back to when he realized that he'd never be completely happy anywhere else.

In the motel parking lot, he pulled out his cell phone and dialed Nate. Ten seconds later, his friend answered.

"Hey, Lucas," Nate whispered. "Look, she's taking a shower and she's decided to stay the night and . . ."

Lucas groaned out loud, knowing what was coming.

"Sorry, buddy. Really, but . . ." Nate's voice was cajoling. "Look, I'll try to rent you another room . . . I'll . . ."

Lucas sighed audibly. "Forget it. I'll just bunk down here in my truck. Won't be the first time. Wake me when it's time for breakfast."

"Really, it's . . . I'm . . ."

"No worries, Nate. But you owe me."

"You bet. I won't forget this. I'd do it for you, you know."

"Sure," Lucas replied, knowing he'd never be the type to ask.

He pulled his truck around the back of the motel so the staff would be less likely to notice and call the cops. He found an old wool camp blanket behind the seat, folded it into a makeshift pillow and laid it against the passenger door. Then he stretched out across the worn bench seat. After pulling his wool-lined Carhartt barn jacket around him, he covered his face with his expensive hat—a cowboy's single room, his grandpa Kitt used to call it—and settled in. He knew by morning he'd be stiff, cranky and annoyed at himself for not insisting Nate take the girl back to her own hotel. But, Nate was his friend—sort of—and Lucas had so few of those these days.

Only five more days and he would be home. Only five more days and he'd be sleeping in his own bed in the apartment above his aunt Birch's garage. Only five more days and maybe he'd see Ruby again.

2

Ruby

"Are you hungry?" Ruby asked her brother again.

"Not really." Nash shifted in the passenger seat of her old green Honda, pulling out his shoulder belt and holding it a second like it was keeping him hostage.

They'd left Gallup, New Mexico, early this morning. The rising sun had painted the desert sky salmon and gold as they barreled across Interstate 40 toward California. Nash had slept, missing the show, his head propped against the cold window glass. His complexion, still tinged a pale buttery color, worried Ruby.

Last night he had left the Motel 6 double room they'd shared with the excuse he needed some exercise. He hadn't fooled her. There was a bar across the highway. But she was exhausted from doing all the driving—he'd lost his license a year ago—so she fell asleep shortly before eight p.m. He was in the other bed the next morning, still in his clothes, but she had no idea what time he got in.

She glanced over at him, started to say something, then quelled her urge. There was no use getting in an argument on the road when they had to spend so many hours together in the small car. She'd bring it up when they got to Cardinal.

"You really need to eat more," she finally said. They'd stopped for lunch in Flagstaff and he only ordered iced tea and nibbled at a slice of her cornbread. "Nutrition is important." She sighed silently, hating how nagging her words sounded.

Nash grunted a noncommittal reply and turned his head to stare back out his window. They stopped briefly outside of Hesperia, where Ruby filled the gas tank, anticipating this long stretch of California's Highway 395 that would eventually lead them to Cardinal, elevation 4,300 feet, population 3,259. Plus, she hoped, two more lost souls. The route she'd taken wasn't the quickest from Gallup to Cardinal according to the map, but it was familiar to her, and right now, familiar beat efficient. Joshua trees flashed by them at seventy miles an hour, their spidery arms reaching into the stark blue desert sky. Their shadows were long and gangly in the late-afternoon light, reminding Ruby of Christmas scarves crocheted by someone's crazy aunt.

On their left was Manzanar, the former Japanese internment camp that was now a national historic site and museum. She'd stopped there the first time she'd come to Cardinal a year ago, an excuse to delay her entry into her late husband, Cole's, hometown. Today she felt the opposite. She couldn't wait to get to Cardinal. Like Dorothy's hope for the Wizard of Oz, Ruby's hopes were pinned on this small town in the foothills of the Eastern Sierra Nevada. The town, once a prosperous ranching and mining town and now dependent almost completely on tourists, was the closest thing she'd ever felt to home.

"That's Manzanar," she said, nodding at the park's entrance sign. "Thousands of Japanese Americans were imprisoned there during World War II. They prospered despite losing everything. They even had an orchestra."

"Awesome," he said. He didn't even turn his head.

She sighed. "We'll be there in a few hours. Birch has rooms waiting for us. You'll like the Tokopah Lodge. The rooms are decorated to match famous Western stars. South of Cardinal, there are dozens of places where they filmed old cowboy movies in the twenties and thirties. There's a new Western Film and History Museum on the edge of town. Really nice."

His answer was another grunt. Nash had been like this since they'd left Tennessee, doling out words like precious gems. About two hours after they left Nashville, he decided he was pissed about coming with her, though he'd reluctantly agreed that leaving Nashville for a few months might be the best thing for now. His girlfriend, Angela, an LVN at a fancy retirement home, had stuck with him throughout his many alcoholic benders and the worst part of his illness. But during the last six months, with his numerous setbacks and relapses into drinking, she had quietly fallen out of love with Nash. A month ago, Angela moved out of the two-bedroom apartment where she, Nash and Ruby had lived since January.

"I'm so sorry," she said to Ruby with tears in her eyes. "I wish . . ."

"I understand," Ruby said, hugging her, wishing she could beg her to stay. "It's not your fault." She couldn't really blame her. Nash was talented, boyishly handsome and could be charming when he wasn't pouting, but his drinking and health problems proved to be too much for Angela, who simply wanted a stable life that included marriage and children. One good thing that came from their breakup was it helped Ruby convince Nash to come to Cardinal. The promise of a part-time gig at the Red Coyote, thanks to Ely's connections, had also helped. The unspoken truth was Nash had nowhere else to go. He had burned too many bridges in Nashville, both in his restaurant jobs and his music gigs. Drinking was tolerated in the music world, but unless you were a superstar, missing gigs wasn't. There were too many other musicians in the wings waiting to step into your spot.

Secretly Ruby was glad the situation forced Nash into leaving Nashville and access to the life that had certainly contributed to him contracting hepatitis. They had never discussed whether he'd ever used drugs, but Ruby wasn't naïve. She dated too many musicians in her twenties. But Nash had been clean for two months straight, and while they were packing their meager possessions for the move west, Ruby felt a small swelling of hope in her chest.

Until last night. Was it the stress of moving that set him back? She felt a stab of guilt. But it was unthinkable to just leave him in Nashville to fend for himself and she had no desire to make Nashville her home.

"Bring him back to Cardinal," Birch had said during one of their long phone conversations. "We'll make sure he has work.

People miss you, Ruby." There was a moment's pause. "I miss you, sweetie."

"Thank you," Ruby replied, her voice catching slightly. Those two words couldn't convey the love and gratitude she felt for this woman.

The thought that there was a place where people cared about her was still so new to Ruby, so precious, that she savored Birch's words like the long-anticipated taste of ice cream on a hot summer day.

"Even though I miss it, coming back to Cardinal feels strange," she told Ely Grey on the phone her last night in Tennessee.

"I bet it does," Ely said.

When she left Cardinal last January, Ely, Lucas's best friend, told her he'd call her occasionally to see how her car was doing. He'd made certain her old Honda was fit for the long drive cross-country. She was grateful for that, but, surprisingly, even more grateful for his phone calls. Despite her love for most of the McGavin family, she felt slightly embarrassed by her brother's problems with alcohol. Maybe because of Ely's time in prison and his own troubled past, as well as his one-time friendship with her late husband, she felt freer talking to him about Nash. Though she loved Lucas, Birch and Sueann, the three people she'd become closest to in Cardinal, she was afraid of what they would think if they knew too much about Nash's failings. She'd seen the look of disgust on Lucas's face the first night he'd arrived in Nashville when Nash came home from a gig and passed out drunk on the kitchen floor.

"I can't wait to see everyone, but it's hard. And weird."

Ely was quiet, letting her speak when she felt like it. The long silences between them never felt awkward. She liked that about him, his ability to wait. She understood why Lucas valued his friendship.

Though Ely grew up in Cardinal, he'd left town as a young man, a high school dropout. He lived through his own share of troubles, most, he candidly admitted, of his own doing. He'd gone to prison for stealing a car and eventually connected with Cole when they ended up being roommates in the same halfway house in

LA. Cole had even been his AA sponsor for a while.

Ely now owned The Novel Experience, the town's only bookstore, and Holy Grounds, a popular coffeehouse. He inherited both businesses from his friend, Lincoln Holyoke, who died last New Year's Eve in the same car accident that put Birch's husband, Bobby Hernandez, and Sueann McGavin in the hospital.

"How's the Lone Pine doing?" she asked. "Is Sueann keeping everyone on the straight and narrow?" Sueann owned and ran the Lone Pine Café. "What color is Cassie's hair this week?"

Cassie, Sueann's daughter, worked at the café and had been Ruby's first acquaintance in Cardinal. When Ruby first met Cassie, the teenager's shaggy hair was toilet bowl cleaner blue, but according to Sueann, it was now dyed solid black with one white streak.

"Still black and white. Sueann says Cassie looks like a skunk, but she's graduating Cardinal High with honors, so how can Sueann complain?" Ely's deep laugh brought his face to Ruby's mind—dark toffee-colored skin and angular cheekbones, the hollows slightly scarred by adolescent acne, a wiry, restless body that always seemed to be either in quick, efficient motion or completely still. His physical looks declared an Indian heritage that, at least to her, he never spoke about.

"We plan on arriving this weekend," Ruby said.

"In time for the wassail party on Saturday? It's early this year."

Every year the Tokopah Lodge, owned by Birch and Bobby Hernandez, hosted the annual holiday get-together for their guests and friends. Ruby hesitated, remembering last year when she had been new to town herself, how overwhelming all the unfamiliar faces had been.

"No. We'll probably get into town Sunday evening. I think a quiet entrance into Cardinal life might be better for Nash."

"Might be. How's he holding up?"

"Upset about Angela, but he seems to be doing okay. At least for today."

"Day at a time," Ely said, his voice calm.

"That's what they say." Her words were clipped, exasperated.

"They could be right."

"I'm sorry, Ely. That didn't come out right."

"It's okay." She could hear his breathing through the phone line.

"I'll see you soon," she said.

"I'll keep the coffee hot."

In a few hours, she and Nash would drive into Cardinal. The town where a year ago she'd come to merely drop off Cole's ashes and give back her inherited share of the Circle MG ranch. Give the McGavins back their son and their ranch land, then leave. Instead, she'd somehow become a tiny part of the community; she'd made friends. Friends who now seemed willing to help her with her troubled brother. The possibility of making Cardinal a real home, a place where she might live out her years, die among people who knew her name, was a desire so strong she was certain the world could see it like an actual mark on her forehead.

She was back. Not really a prodigal daughter, since prodigal implied some kind of genetic claim. She was back, carrying her problems like a homeless person's overflowing shopping cart, the burden of her broken brother, her still grieving heart and her unspoken fear of something—she didn't know what. She was back and she knew she should feel happy, relieved, at peace. For the second time, she was driving into Cardinal filled with apprehension and doubt. The only difference this time was there was a tinge of hope, too.

See, she thought. There's progress for you right there. It was something Bobby Hernandez might say. She could almost hear his voice, distant and strong, like the rumble of the earth moving beneath her feet.

She pushed down on the Honda's accelerator, causing it to whine a moment before kicking into a higher speed. Nash didn't even flinch, his face still turned away from her, searching, it appeared to Ruby, for some mysterious something in the stark, unforgiving high desert plain.

3

Lucas

The next morning, it took three cups of black coffee and one giant cinnamon roll before Lucas felt human again. Though he'd awakened at nine fifteen—Nate had obviously forgotten his promise to wake Lucas up for the motel's free continental breakfast—he'd made it to the booth that he shared with Maddie Silverhorse by ten. Maddie was already ringing up her first four-hundred-dollar sale. Lucas thought she was as nutty as a PayDay candy bar, but he liked her the moment they met. She designed and made glass bead and silver jewelry that had become one of the minor hits of Cowtown Christmas. She was also from Cardinal, a friend of Ely's. She worked part time at Cardinal General Hospital as a psychiatrist, having retired three years ago from a full-time practice in Pasadena. She claimed to be fifty-something, but Lucas surmised she was probably ten years older than that. Why would a psychiatrist lie about her age? he wondered. Isn't that a thing she would have psychologically worked out? She told him when they were setting up the booth that her real name was Margaret Collins.

"Maddie Silverhorse sells significantly more jewelry than Margaret Collins," she'd said. "It has that Native American flare. People eat that stuff up. Besides, I'm sure I must have a Cherokee great-grandmother in my background somewhere." She grinned at him with horsy teeth. "Doesn't everyone?"

She'd shared her space with him out of pity not need and because, like so many other women in Cardinal, she adored Ely Grey. She was "roughing it," as she called it, in a shiny new Airstream trailer whose cowgirl décor looked like something out of a *Cowboys & Indians* magazine spread.

"Lucas McGavin, you look like a bowl of fresh horse manure," she said cheerfully, scratching her frizzy white hair with the tip of a gold Cross pen. "Hope the lady was worth it."

"No lady," he replied, gulping the last of his coffee.

She arched her penciled-in eyebrows. "What happens at the Vegas Ho stays at the Vegas Ho?"

He tossed the paper cup in the trash can hidden behind one of his show saddles. "I mean, there was no lady. At least for me. Nate had company last night who didn't want to leave so I slept in my truck."

He sat down hard on the chair next to the five sample saddles he'd brought with him, two to display and three to sell. The one he already sold would be picked up on the last day of Cowtown Christmas. He needed to sell another finished saddle or at least take an order for a saddle to justify the expense of this trip. His sample saddles showed his range of work, from basic to fancy. They went from a plain saddle for three thousand six hundred dollars to a basket stamped for four thousand five hundred dollars to full flower carved for six thousand five hundred dollars.

His stand-out saddle, one that always made people pause at the booth, was a full-carved saddle he'd built for Cassie when she was twelve. She had loved hearts and flowers, so he'd carved hearts and flowers native to Tokopah county—lupine, Indian paintbrush, columbine, shooting star, blue sky pilots, yarrow—intertwining them in the design. On the fenders, he carved mirror images of her feeding an apple to her horse under the cottonwood tree at Clear Creek. That one wasn't for sale, but it gave people an idea of his style.

The other one he'd brought just for show was a full-flowered Sheridan-style he borrowed from a local cowboy who'd won All Around Cowboy at last year's Eastern Sierra Wild Mustang Days Rodeo. Lucas had been paid fifteen thousand dollars for that saddle and another for All Around Cowgirl. The saddle he brought to display showed some of his best carving and featured silver conchos by Bruce Haener in Atascadero. Getting that commission from the Mustang Days board had really helped Lucas, even though he suspected his mom, June, had probably paid for half the saddles or talked her affluent gentleman friend (as she called him), Walt Creston, to spring for them.

Maddie shook her head, her silver bead and red crystal earrings swinging like tiny chandeliers. "What did we discuss the other day about boundaries?"

He leaned back in his chair and closed his eyes. "I've slept in my truck a million times. I don't remember it ever feeling this bad."

"Well, you're not a spring buck anymore and quit avoiding my question."

He opened his eyes in time to see her pop a red grape into her mouth. She wore another vaguely Native American outfit today—a black velvet skirt that was kind of layered, and a red puffed-sleeved blouse with black embroidered flowers around the neckline. One of her popular necklaces, this one made with red, black and silver beads, hung around her age-spotted neck. He had considered buying one of her hammered silver and green turquoise bracelets for Ruby, but he wasn't sure if it was something Ruby would wear.

"The cliché would be spring chicken," he pointed out. "Or young buck. Pick one."

She shrugged, picked off another grape. "Boundaries, my dear boy. Lack of them. That'll be your downfall."

"How did dinner with the silversmith dentist go last night?"

She wiggled her fingers at him. "Still evading the issue, my little kumquat. You know I'm not through with you. People used to pay two hundred fifty dollars an hour for my advice. You're getting a bargain."

"Yes, ma'am." He sat forward and touched a finger to the rim of his hat. "And I'm mighty grateful. Mighty, mighty, mighty grateful."

She snorted and threw a grape at him. "Bull palooka. And dinner was actually quite lovely. We have absolutely nothing in common but our mutual love for .9995 fine silver and deep-fried prairie oysters, but it was nice to have a man help me with my jacket and pull out my chair for me."

"Did you tell him what you do for a living?"

"I told him I'm the brokenhearted widow of a proctologist who is living her dream of a second life as a jewelry designer in beautiful Cardinal, California." Her lips turned up in a wicked smile. "None of which is an actual lie."

Lucas couldn't help smiling back. "A sin of omission. You're a bad girl."

"Thank you, kind sir. Another thing to check off my very eclectic bucket list."

Lucas had to admit that Ely had been right when he assured Lucas he'd enjoy sharing a booth with Dr. Collins. Though he and the doctor agreed on very little, especially concerning politics, he found her easy to talk to and generous with laughter, two things he appreciated more in women the older he became.

"Only five more days and I get to sleep in my own bed," Lucas said out of the side of his mouth. He smiled and nodded at a sixtyish couple who picked up one of his brochures. "Any questions, folks?"

They were dressed plainly in matching blue cowboy shirts and new knife-pressed Wranglers. Compared to a lot of the sparkly Western wear popular at the NFR, they looked like sparrows among a flock of peacocks. But Lucas knew that clothes didn't always tell a person's real worth. They could be multimillionaires or they could be tire kickers.

"Be my guest," he always politely told the tire kickers, who often had the nerve to proudly boast that they could likely find a saddle just like his on the Internet for a much cheaper price. "That's certainly an option for you, but mine are a little different." They aren't assembly-line shit, was what he was thinking.

He suspected this humble-looking couple weren't the latter. The huge diamond wedding ring set on the woman's left finger gave them away. These folks had some means.

He was right, and before he knew it, he'd made his second sale—an eight-thousand-dollar custom order for their ten-year-old granddaughter who adored hearts and tulips because her grandparents were from Holland. They'd even discussed the possibility of windmills on the saddle fenders. He asked general questions, like if they wanted semi quarter bars on the tree for a narrower horse or full quarter horse bars, whether the horse was high withered or flat backed and the approximate height and weight of their granddaughter. They were very knowledgeable and even had the measurements of their granddaughter's five-year-old gelding.

"Chrissy is here with us," said the woman, Mrs. Beumers, in a soft voice tinged with a slight accent. "She's at Mandalay Bay's shark exhibit with her parents. We'll bring her by later to meet you."

"Good job," Maddie said, after they left. "Things are looking up."

Lucas looked at the man's card before putting it in his wallet. Peter Beumers, CEO, Carolina Investments—Charlotte, North Carolina, and Newport Beach, California. They'd told Lucas they owned a second home in California, so coming for a fitting at his shop on their way to Mammoth wouldn't be a problem.

For the next few days things did improve. Nate took his amorous adventures elsewhere and Lucas was able to actually sleep in a bed. That made him much more amiable in the booth, which, Maddie declared, attracted more business. She might have been right, because he sold one more finished saddle and took an order for another custom saddle. It was enough work to keep him solvent for a while. But eventually he'd have to make some kind of decision about whether he could continue to work solely as a saddle maker or whether he needed to find another way to bring in a more dependable income. With Ruby on her way back to Cardinal, he needed to make some decisions about his life.

On the last day of Cowtown Christmas, the Sunday after NFR's final Saturday-night round, most of the vendors were looking frazzled. Even Maddie, one of the most energetic people Lucas had ever met, seemed snappish and irritable. At eleven a.m., there were still a good number of folks wandering the aisles, though no one seemed to want to spend any money. It appeared the only people left were those killing time before driving or flying back home. Though most of the vendors would have loved to close up shop right then, it was in their contracts that they had to stay open until five p.m. sharp.

"It's been a blast hanging out with you," Maddie told Lucas. "But I'm ready to head back to my little bungalow. Let's stay in touch. Have lunch or dinner occasionally."

He held up his umpteenth cup of bitter convention center coffee. "Name the place and day." He meant it. Though he knew hundreds of people in Cardinal to speak to, he didn't have many actual friends. He liked Dr. Maddie "Silverhorse" Collins.

She glanced down the aisle filled with exhausted-looking people. "You aren't going to sell a checkbook cover, much less a saddle, to any of this crowd. Why don't you take a break? The dentist gave me tickets to the shark exhibit at Mandalay Bay. He said it was awesome." She tsked under her breath. "I think the *Oxford English Dictionary* should retire that word. It'll do you good. You need to have some fun. You act like you're seventy, not thirty-five. I can call you on your cell if an interested buyer happens by. Shoot, you might learn something."

Lucas stood up and stretched. "Sure, why not? I don't have anything better to do." His two sold saddles had already been picked up by their new owners and now he was just killing time.

The line at the shark exhibit was about thirty people long, so Lucas almost left. But that would mean going back to the booth and listening to Maddie deride him for being stodgy. A half hour later, he handed the ticket to the young woman at the entrance and walked down the curving hallway into the exhibit. He waved off having his photo taken in front of a green screen that would likely show up as a background of cartoony sharks that the exhibit was hoping people would pony up forty bucks to purchase at the end of their visit. A green screen. That's what he needed for his life. The question that Maddie would have likely asked was what would he want inserted into the background picture? He really couldn't tell her.

He stopped to read a plaque hanging at the entrance.

"Ninety percent of all large predator fish have been removed from our oceans. If current trends continue, the entire edible seafood supply will be depleted in forty years."

He wondered what his mother, June, who adored shrimp and lobster, would say to that. He stared at the photo of the gray reef shark and thought he saw more than a passing resemblance to June when she wanted something. Like, for example, Clear Creek, the pastureland that Lucas currently used for his motley crew of rescued horses.

His use of the prime ranch property north of the Circle MG had always been an uneasy subject between Lucas, his mom, June and his other older brother, Derek. Years ago, Lucas agreed to go along with whatever they wanted to do with the rest of the ranch as long as he could use this piece of land. That it happened to be the best land they owned with a year-round creek running through it was a source of animosity between them. In the always parched Eastern Sierras, any consistent source of water was more valuable than a gold mine. June received offers for the property often, which she always sent on to Lucas, trying to tempt him into changing his mind. He stacked them, unread, in a corner of his saddlemaking shop, using for a paperweight a large Mexican silver inlay spur made by G. S. Garcia that once belonged to his great-grandfather.

He walked deeper into the exhibit, feeling a bit claustrophobic as the air became thicker, more humid. If they were trying to make visitors feel as if they were slowly going underwater, they succeeded. Then it started to feel cooler, as if he were indeed sinking into the ocean. Around him, jungle sounds echoed and mingled with the screams and laughter of children. He stopped in front of the golden crocodile exhibit. The reptile blended so well into the artificial jungle that he really had to search for her. But there she was—for some reason Lucas thought of it as a female—waiting. For what? Dinner most likely, he thought, smiling to himself.

The crocodile stirred, causing nervous giggles to ripple through the group of children bunched in front of Lucas. They wore identical green T-shirts printed with "Miller Day Camp" on the back.

"Look," said the cute young woman with blond braids who obviously was their counselor. She pointed to the display blurb, reading it aloud to the restless kids. "Did you know that crocodiles are good parents?" She caught Lucas's eye and gave him a crooked smile and a shrug, as if to say, *Who knew?*

He nodded at her, silently wondering what the statement meant. It didn't say why crocodiles were good parents. What constituted a good parent? Who decided on the criteria for animals or humans? His mother, if asked, would vehemently declare herself to be an excellent parent. She had fed, clothed, educated and was physically present for her three boys every step of their lives. She would be the first to point out she had attended every football and basketball game, every high school rodeo and every open house and parent-teacher conference. Did just showing up make a good parent? Maybe he and his brothers would have been better off if she'd been a little less invested in their lives. Maybe if she hadn't been so invested in their lives, she would have been less disappointed with their decisions, something she was not shy about bringing up again and again.

"Derek's divorced and seems to be content with dating every cheap tramp in Tokopah County," she said the last time she and Lucas had dinner at a new steakhouse downtown. Five gold bangle bracelets clinked softly as she brought a forkful of rare steak to her mouth. "I'm beginning to think it might have been better if he and Sueann had stayed married."

Lucas stared down at the melting garlic butter and sour cream on his baked potato, feeling like he was fourteen.

"And you," she'd continued. "After I spent thousands of dollars on your law degree, here you are, back in Cardinal, living over your aunt's garage, playing with leather and barely making ends meet." She pointed her sharp steak knife at him. "You've wasted your life and my money."

He stabbed his fork into the baked potato, knowing from experience it was best to let June spout off, not interrupt the lava flow. It only made the tirade last longer if you tried to argue or defend yourself. That was only one of the things his oldest brother, Cole, had taught him.

"And then there's Cole." She spat his

name as if it was bitter seed in her mouth. "What can we say about him?"

Lucas looked at her, feeling the heat in his chest rise to his throat.

"I can say I miss him. Don't you?"

His blunt words shocked her silent for a moment.

"Sometimes," she said, looking straight into his eyes.

He thought he detected a flicker of sadness. Then, as quickly as a Cardinal Valley summer rainstorm, it was gone.

"He made his choice," she'd said, giving her steak the evil eye. "This beef is as tender as jerky. Did you read that last offer we got for the Clear Creek? We cannot support those broken-down horses of yours forever. The ranch needs the money."

He came to the end of the shark exhibit before he realized it, and if he'd been given a pop quiz about sharks, he would have scored a zero. On the way back to Cowtown Christmas, he thought about how lucky it was he wasn't trying cases any longer. Some poor dude who'd been arrested for shoplifting beer would probably end up with life plus twenty simply because Lucas couldn't seem to focus on anything longer than a minute.

The convention room's aisles were now almost empty of customers. He glanced at his watch. Three p.m. Still two more hours until they could close up their booth. He didn't have much to pack, just the sample saddle that hadn't sold, the two display saddles, his brochures and business cards and the sign Cassie had made for him with Photoshop. But he'd help Maddie pack her jewelry and display items and haul them to her trailer. It was the least he could do since she refused to take one cent from him for sharing her booth.

He wandered the brightly lit aisles, glancing at the myriad products people had brought to sell—deerskin gloves, Black Hills gold jewelry, milk can barstools sporting old tractor seats, Heel-O-Matic battery-powered calves to practice roping, braided horsehair hat bands and key rings, wooden canes with handles carved into the shape of horse heads, Western plates, mugs, silverware, tea towels and bottle openers. Whatever product a person could slap the image of a horseshoe, barbed wire, galloping Mustang or cowboy boot on, it was sold here.

He paused for a second in front of a booth selling custom saddles and boots, Mercury Leatherworks, from Cody, Wyoming. It was a small, but prestigious three-generation family operation—the Vieiras. He'd read about them in *Cowboys & Indians* magazine. Like Bohlin, they catered to very high-end buyers and their booth showed it. They displayed six saddles, all without price tags, which told you something right there, and all bearing "sold" signs. In the center was a saddle custom made for some Saudi prince. According to the display card, it was insured for one million dollars and would be on its way to Dubai on a private jet right after the show. The saddle was incredible; Lucas had to give them that. The silver and gold alone could have bought a mansion in some parts of the country.

"Lookin' to buy a saddle, young man?" called a dapper-looking man with a salt-and-pepper mustache sitting behind the fancy-carved oak desk. He wore an obviously expensive black cowboy hat with a cattleman's crease and a string tie made from a jagged chunk of obsidian. His dark, twinkly eyes were set in a noble, sun-creased face. He started to stand up.

Lucas gestured at the man to stay where he was. "Just killing time, lookin' at stuff I can't afford. Thanks, anyway."

"Ain't we all?" the man said, a huge sigh inflating his chest. He pointed over at the large poster of a big-haired Miss Rodeo America. "I've been staring at that for two long weeks." A few seconds later, two ginger-haired little girls dressed in matching lavender plaid shirts came running up yelling, "Grampa, Grampa." The man grinned at Lucas. "Forget gorgeous Miss Rodeo. This is really what life is all about."

"Yes, sir," Lucas said, touching his finger to his hat rim.

He ended up at the food court, vaguely hungry. Breakfast at eight a.m. had been his last meal, and even the burnt-rubber scent of the convention center's hamburgers was beginning to smell good. But, after gazing over the gray meat patties floating in grease, he settled on a plate of nachos, extra jalapeños, and a Jack Daniel's with ice. His meager lunch cost him an irritating seventeen dollars and fifty cents. He took his food and whiskey to a bench outside the dining area. Before he could take his first sip, his cell phone buzzed in his pocket. The screen showed June McGavin. For a split second, he considered not answering. But, there might be an emergency at the ranch or with one of his rescue horses. The responsible part of his personality couldn't ignore her.

"Hey, Mom." He sipped his whiskey, contemplating just knocking it back. But at nine dollars and fifty cents a pop, he wanted to savor it.

"There's a stack of legal papers I want you to look over. I don't trust Will Wagner's boy. Why in the world did Will have to retire?"

"Mr. Wagner *is* eighty-two," he said. "And Jake's a good lawyer. You can trust him."

"Still, he's not his father. When are you coming home?"

"Today's the final day. I'll be coming home tonight." He was anxious to get back to Cardinal. It was only about a seven-hour drive and speeding through the desert at night was something he enjoyed.

"Sooner the better. There is a lot of work at the ranch. Derek can't do it all. The Gonzales brothers quit this week. Just up and left without even a how-do-you-do." She made a disgusted sound deep in her throat. "They are the laziest—"

"I'll come by after I've taken a nap," Lucas interrupted, not wanting to hear one of her rants. Frankly, Lucas was amazed any ranch hand stayed longer than a week. Gil and Joey Gonzales lasted for three months. It wasn't easy working for Derek or June. How well Lucas knew that.

June hung up without saying good-bye.

"Drive safely," he said into the phone. "Don't pick up any hitchhikers. Be careful, son." He shook his head and slipped his phone into his shirt pocket. Too bad you can't quit your family.

Like that first jolt of Jack Daniel's, a pang hit his gut. In a way, quitting them was exactly what Cole did when he left so many years ago. Then he permanently quit on everyone when he drove his truck off that highway.

He drained the rest of the whiskey. That was it with booze. He'd better start drinking coffee or Red Bull if he wanted to get back to Cardinal in one piece.

He set the plastic cup on the floor and settled back on the wooden bench, holding the paper plate of nachos in his left hand. His bench faced a small stage where a thin-haired man with an old Fender guitar was tuning up, getting ready to play for shoppers slipping gratefully into the folding chairs. The musician looked to be in his early fifties, way past the age where some record company would want to make him a star. Lucas would bet he played small-town honky-tonks and conventions like this or sang background music at the occasional affluent middle-aged man's Western-themed birthday party.

Without looking up, the man started singing a Randy Travis song, one that Lucas's aunt Birch was always humming—"Forever and Ever, Amen." He had a decent baritone and knew his way around the guitar as far as Lucas could see, but that was it. He'd forever be a side act just like Lucas would forever be a once adequate public defender and a pretty decent saddle maker. He wondered if this musician still dreamed of platinum records and beautiful women hanging on his arm. Did he imagine screaming crowds, long lines of fans wanting autographs, meeting the president, seeing his name in the Country Music Hall of Fame?

The man barely let the last note of the song end before he segued into another song—"Are You Sure Hank Done It This Way?" It felt like he looked straight through the crowd and focused his eyes directly on Lucas. In the middle of the song, Lucas stood up, tossed his half-eaten nachos in the trash. He walked up the short aisle toward the man and, as the last note of the song faded away, he tossed a twenty-dollar bill he couldn't afford into the man's open guitar case.

"God bless you, buddy," the man said, without interrupting his picking. "That'll get me halfway home to my sweetheart."

Lucas nodded, feeling good for a split second. It reminded him of something Ely told him one evening in the Red Coyote. Cheap grace, Ely had called it.

"Cheap in terms of cost to me," Ely had said, when he over-tipped their cocktail waitress who'd just been harassed by a drunk patron. "At this moment that twenty-dollar bill means more to her than me. So I have directly improved someone's life, if only for a moment."

Lucas looked suspiciously at his friend, waiting for some kind of spiritual punch line. Since Ely had inherited the coffeehouse and bookstore from that minister, Linc Holyoke, Lucas had noticed a change in Ely, a seriousness that was sometimes disconcerting. Ely had once been one of Cardinal High School's most notorious bad kids and had an adult history that wasn't all that pristine. Was he going all crazy-good on Lucas now?

Ely gave his familiar kiss-my-ass smile that used to drive teachers crazy and made women always look twice, desire lighting their eyes like little Coleman lanterns. "You can wipe that, 'oh, shit, he's going to try and convert me' look off your face, partner. I did it as much for myself as for her. Just sayin' it's a good kind of addiction, this giving-back stuff. Hey, I'm going to take a leak. Get me another beer."

Ely was right, Lucas thought, walking back through the convention center to their booth. It felt good to think his small gesture might have made life easier for another human being. He spent the rest of the time until five p.m. trading jokes with Maddie. Once Cowtown Christmas officially closed, he helped her pack up her jewelry and carry the boxes to her trailer.

"You be careful driving across that desert tonight, kiddo," Maddie said, giving him an unexpected hug. "You're part of my life now and I don't like losing things I care about."

"A thing?" Lucas laughed and hugged her back. "Is that all I am? One of your things?"

She pulled away and looked up at him, her face serious. "Stay safe, Lucas. I mean it. Godspeed to you, son."

"I'll call you next week," he said, feeling embarrassed, but warmed by her unexpected emotion. "Meet you for coffee at the Grounds, as my niece Cassie calls it. I'll buy you a Cup of Gino." He used the nickname Maddie had given to the ubiquitous cappuccinos she loved.

"You've got a date," she said.

It was eight p.m. when he finally hit the road. With no traffic, depending on how fast he drove, he could be back in Cardinal by two or three a.m. At ten o'clock, his cell phone buzzed. He pulled it out of his pocket and looked at the screen. His heart started thumping hard. Ruby.

He took a deep breath and answered. "Are you and Nash in Cardinal yet?" He listened for a moment. "You're kidding me. She is? Well, tell me everything. Take your time. I've got all night."

4

Etta

"Bless me, Father, for I have sinned. It's been twenty minutes since I last cussed some fool out in my head."

Etta finger-combed her short, silver-laced dark hair before sitting down at the metal table across from the elderly priest. It was Tamale Sunday at Marcela's Café & Bakery, one of her favorite restaurants in Ajo. The December sun had warmed the air enough for Father Tomas to choose an outside patio table. It was three p.m. and they were alone, in between the lunch and dinner crowd.

"A new guest at the shelter?" the priest

asked. He knew the only thing that could make Etta curse these days were people who had abused a dog.

She took a long drink from the Diet Coke he'd ordered her. They had shared Tamale Sunday lunches for the last three years, so he knew her drink of choice. Though she wasn't officially Catholic, Father Tomas had been her confessor on more than one occasion since, after years of wandering, she landed in this town five years ago. They'd developed an unlikely friendship—a woman in her late fifties raised Southern Baptist but long backslidden, and a seventy-five-year-old priest sent to minister to the disparate flock in this once thriving copper mining town on the edge of the Tohono O'odham Indian reservation.

"A terrier–cattle dog mix someone left chained up in an abandoned trailer out past Coyote Wells. One of the Border Patrol officers found her. That new redheaded one. Jed, I think his name was. Thank God that boy has the hearing of a bat. Poor little thing was hiding under a bed, practically dead. But she squeaked when he walked by. Dr. Beth said one more day and she would likely have died of dehydration."

Father Tomas stirred his iced tea, his oval brown face thoughtful. "I'll pray for her recovery. And for those who left her. For a change of heart. So they feel compassion for God's creatures."

Her gray eyes darkened. "Pray they get lost in the desert without water for a week or two. See how they like it."

Father Tomas reached across the table and patted her hand. "What have you named her?"

"Still working on that. She's a hard one. Sad little ice blue eyes." She rested her strong, wiry arms on the table, interlocking her fingers as if in prayer. "She's black-and-white speckled, like an Appaloosa's butt. She needs a happy name." She gave a half smile. "Maybe I'll call her Appy."

"I like it," Father Tomas said with the same even-tempered voice he used when assuring her that God has forgiven her, continually forgives her, that the one holding the grudge against Etta is the face she sees every morning in the mirror.

Etta nodded, staring down at her

clasped hands. "I get so mad at these stupid, uncaring people." She looked back up into the priest's weathered face. "Then I feel like shit." Who was she to point a finger? She was no better than the people who'd abandoned that dog. Truth was, she was worse.

She didn't say why. She didn't have to. Etta and Father Tomas had talked many times about how she'd walked away from her children twenty-three years ago searching for a dream and finding only a cruel man who had dragged her down with him into a nightmare that was burned into her brain like a psychic brand. It was the reason she had never contacted Ruby and Nash. After what she did, she didn't deserve to be a mother. They were better off without her.

"God is merciful to those who show mercy," the priest said.

Before she could answer, their waitress brought their tamales. Chicken for the priest; green chile and cheese for Etta. The first bite was heaven. Etta didn't know what they put in the cornmeal, but it was something magical. She'd never tasted tamales as good as Marcela's.

"Some people don't deserve mercy," she said a few minutes later. Their conversations often went like this, with long pauses between remarks.

Tilting his head to one side, Father Tomas considered her comment. "We can't decide for God. He shows mercy to whom He pleases." He smiled, his black eyes disappearing into a thousand wrinkles. "And it pleases Him to show mercy to whomever asks."

She shrugged. She didn't mince words with the priest. She never had. But she didn't want to ruin their meal with an argument, even a good-natured one. He knew every bad thing about her and would still break bread with her. That was a mercy she didn't deserve, but she treasured. Sometimes, with all she'd seen of the world, she wasn't all that sure she believed in God, but without a doubt, she was sure as heck certain she believed in Father Tomas.

5

Birch

"What time is it?" Birch McGavin Hernandez asked her husband, Bobby. "We either need to get that old clock fixed or give it to All Saints' thrift store. Honestly, I'm sick of things not working around this place." She glared at the antique rosewood mantle clock that had presided over the Tokopah Lodge's huge natural smooth-stone fireplace since they bought the place forty-two years ago.

The oak mantle was one of the newer pieces in the hotel's lobby, carved by a local artisan back in the '60s, when they had some extra money to spend. It was popular with birders who came to Tokopah County to add to their bird counts. There were twenty-three local birds represented on the mantle and the birders loved naming them out loud—California quail, cattle egret, Cooper's hawk, killdeer, black-bellied plover, Wilson's snipe, willow flycatcher and on and on. It made Birch smile every time a guest singsonged the bird names. It reminded her of her former elementary school students reciting multiplication tables.

"That clock has never worked, my love," Bobby said from behind the knotty pine counter draped with silver and green tinsel. "And it's five minutes later than when you asked me five minutes ago." His tone was teasing, the expression on his coppery, finely wrinkled face gentle.

"Well, excuse me for being concerned." Fists ready to do battle rested on each hip. She gave a small laugh. "I'm acting crazy, aren't I?"

She turned to gaze over the lodge's spacious lobby. It was crowded with people who chose to spend the night here in Cardinal before driving the extra fifty miles to the Mammoth ski slopes. Guests frequently fell in love with the lodge and its cowboy movie history and decided to stay, commuting every day to the slopes. They were charmed by the vintage Pendleton wool sofas ("They weren't vintage when we bought them," Bobby always told guests with a laugh) and by the photographs of Clark Gable, John Wayne and Jean Harlow, who'd stayed here in the '30s and '40s. Birch and Bobby counted on the lodge's unique history and their natural friendliness to convince people the Tokopah Lodge was a better lodging choice than one of the town's more modern motels.

The lodge was especially popular in December when they went all-out with Christmas decorating, from their twelve-foot Douglas fir tree trimmed with Western and Indian ornaments, many bought at the Cardinal Valley Paiute-Shoshone reservation gift shop, to the fresh pine wreaths with red and white gingham ribbons on every guest room door.

"Not crazy," Bobby said, standing up slowly, gripping the counter for support. Since the car accident that almost killed him last January, he didn't do anything fast. "Just being your concerned, mother-hen self."

"It's a long drive from Tennessee," Birch said, straightening a pile of brochures. "Ruby said she'll be doing all the driving. She says Nash doesn't have much stamina." The fresh pine bough and red rose arrangement on the counter gave off an odd but pleasing scent of sharp and sweet. It was one of her great-niece Cassie's practice pieces. She was working part time at Loreen's Floral Boutique, a new business in town. Loreen let Cassie experiment with the flowers too past their prime to sell. The Tokopah Lodge and the Lone Pine Café, owned by Cassie's mom, Sueann, were the lucky recipients of Cassie's creativity.

"Ruby's young and strong," Bobby said, arching one thick eyebrow. "Remember when we were in our thirties? We could party all night and still feed the chickens at five a.m."

Her white eyebrows arched over aqua blue eyes. "We've never owned chickens."

He chuckled. "She'll be fine. Ruby

doesn't have a foolish bone in her body. She won't drive when she's tired."

Birch reached across the counter and took one of Bobby's large warm hands. There were still times when her heart froze for a moment, remembering how she almost lost this man who she loved more than anyone on earth. In March, they would be married forty-five years, more than twice the number of years they were when she defied her father and married twenty-one-year-old Roberto Domingo Luis Hernandez, a beautiful amalgamation of Mexican, Paiute, Shoshone, Navajo, Scotch-Irish and, he claimed, a Chinese great-great-great-something-or-other. He'd been one of her father's ranch hands. The price of their love was her part of the Circle MG ranch and her father's acceptance.

"You marry that Indian and you are no longer my daughter," Kitteridge McGavin had said. Behind him, her older brother and only sibling, Carson, smirked at her dilemma.

She had crossed her arms over her chest, her legs wide apart in a solid stance she'd learned from Kitteridge himself. "I love Bobby."

Her father turned his head away, sealing her fate. A man who was a stickler for keeping his word, he never spoke to his only daughter again, not even on the day he died.

Glancing at her husband, his full lips, his waist-length silver braid, his thick, deep-chested body and, most of all, his kind and generous heart, she never regretted her decision for a moment. Not one single moment.

"So much has happened this last year," Birch said, going over to one of the long narrow windows that bookended the lodge's double front doors. She pressed her face so close to the wavy old glass her breath made a small uneven circle of condensation. It was almost four o'clock and the winter sky was turning a dusky lavender. "Their rooms are ready, aren't they?"

"Yes, Mama," Bobby said, coming around the counter, limping heavily. "The nests for your wayward chicks are filled with fresh straw and there is clean water in their bowls. When did she last call?"

"Hours ago. They stopped in Flagstaff for lunch but she said he barely ate anything, that he's just living on iced tea. That's not good for someone with his condition."

"I bet they're here within the hour."

"Sueann said we'd better bring them over to the Lone Pine for dinner. She's had Carlos make white enchiladas, one of Ruby's favorites."

"Mine, too," Bobby said.

She grabbed his wrist to look at his watch. "I'm going to check their rooms one more time. I want to make sure everything's perfect." She went up the wooden stairs, her voice trailing after her. "I hope Nash likes the Gene Autry room. It's got the best view of the back gardens."

"I know," Bobby called, chuckling at his wife's excitement.

Ten minutes later, Birch was coming back down the stairs when she heard Ruby's voice. Wouldn't you know, she thought, taking the steps as fast as she could. She overstepped and missed the last one, coming down hard on one heel.

"Ruby!" Birch cried, holding out her arms as she crossed the crowded room. "Sweetie, you are a sight for these sore old eyes." She pulled her into a hug, tears burning her eyes. "I've missed you so much."

"Me, too," Ruby said, hugging her back. "It's so good to be back." After a moment, she pulled away and turned to the lanky young man standing next to the counter. "Birch, this is my brother, Nash. Nash, this is Birch and Bobby Hernandez. They are dear friends of mine."

The pale young man nodded, flicking his gray eyes from Ruby to Birch. He towered over his sister's five feet six. He had a handsome face, though he was extremely thin—skinny as a barn cat, Birch's mother would have said—with cheekbones that seemed ready to burst through his skin. Unlike Ruby's thick chestnut hair, his was a sandy blond. It hung shaggy to his shoulders. If you met these two on the street, Birch thought, you might not guess they were siblings. Except for their eyes. Nash had the same black-flecked granite eyes as Ruby.

Birch walked over to him, holding out

her hand. "It's so nice to meet you, Nash. It feels like we already know you."

"Nice to meet you, ma'am," he murmured, his voice a pleasant baritone with a tinge of a drawl. His narrowed eyes caught Birch's for a brief second, and then darted beyond her again. The faint yellow tinge to his skin verified what Ruby had told her on the phone, the hepatitis had not been completely beaten. It was the reason she'd encouraged Ruby to bring Nash to Cardinal.

"Tell him there are places to play music here," Birch had said a month ago. "We want you to come home."

"Are there really any jobs for him?"

"There will be," Birch said firmly. "I'll talk to Ely. He has a lot of contacts here in Cardinal and in Mammoth."

"Well," Ruby said doubtfully. "He can't get work here. Maybe that will convince him."

After giving the bar owners a CD Ruby sent him of Nash's work, Ely had arranged a two-night-a-week gig with the house band at the Red Coyote and one night a week at a roadhouse on the way to Mammoth. Nash would be playing his bass guitar with the house band and doing a two-hour set with his acoustic guitar at the roadhouse called Mamie's Mountain Inn. And Ely said Nash could play for tips at Holy Grounds like many Tokopah County musicians did. Reluctantly, Nash agreed to try it out.

"I hear you'll be working at the bookstore," Birch told Ruby.

"Yes, Ely was kind enough to hire me for twenty hours a week. I'll try to get something else, too, though I've been able to save a little of the money I received for the Circle MG."

"Sueann would kill to have you back even part time," Birch had told her. "It'll all work out, Ruby. Just come back to Cardinal."

So, with everyone's encouragement, Ruby managed to talk Nash into coming to Cardinal and now here they were. Though Ruby didn't know it, Birch did not intend to let her ever leave Cardinal again. Not if she had anything to do with it.

"You two must be exhausted," Birch said. "Let me show you your rooms. I have found the cutest little house for you to rent. It will be vacant right before

Christmas. Until then, you'll stay here at the lodge."

Ruby and Nash followed Birch to the Gene Autry room up on the second floor. Birch was a little disappointed when Nash set his guitar case and duffle bag down on the clean oak floor without a comment about the room. It was one of the lodge's most requested and they were losing money by not booking it for a couple of weeks. The dove gray walls were decorated with black-and-white photographs of the famous singing cowboy as well as framed sheet music from his records. The antique music stand held a replica of Gene's actual playlist of songs. Birch had hoped the music motif would appeal to Ruby's brother.

"We'll be heading to dinner at the Lone Pine at seven o'clock," Birch said.

"Thanks, Mrs. Sanchez," Nash said, nonchalantly flopping down on the bed.

Now let it go, love, she heard Bobby's voice whisper inside her head. Give the boy some room to get used to his new surroundings. "You're welcome. And, please, call me Birch."

Ruby practically skipped ahead of

Birch down the hall toward the Dale Evans room. She threw open the door and stood in the threshold, clasping her hands like a girl. "I've missed this room."

The Dale Evans room was reserved for family and friends. The décor was rodeo queen chic with a lodge pole pine bed, fringed, Western-style pillows, the chenille bedspread showing Dale Evans and her horse, Buttercup, Western bric-a-brac from the '40s and '50s and pictures of cowgirls from Dale Evans to Pee Wee Burge to Bobby's revered signed photo of Patsy Cline dressed in one of her famous fringed cowgirl outfits.

Birch's hurt feelings softened. "This sure beats the first reaction you had to this room."

Ruby sat on the bed and smiled up at Birch. "I was scared as a rabbit that day. But once you showed me this room, I wanted to stay forever. I felt . . ." She thought for a moment. "Safe."

Birch's cheeks flushed with pleasure. "Exactly the feeling we wanted you to have." She sat down next to her on the bed. "I hope you feel safe again."

Ruby took her hand. "I cannot tell you

how grateful I am to be back. Please, forgive how . . . Nash . . . He doesn't." She stopped and took a deep breath. "He's a sweet guy once you get to know him. I think he's overwhelmed. He reacts to new situations by acting like he doesn't care. He's been like that ever since our mother . . . well, ever since he was a kid."

Ruby's pleading expression broke Birch's heart. She knew the guilt Ruby carried, unwarranted though it was, of the years that her brother spent in foster care. When Ruby was in Nashville, she and Birch had talked about it on the phone.

"I was seventeen when Daddy lost custody of us," Ruby had told her. "The couple they placed me with was kind and they tried hard to make me feel comfortable. It was hard, but I could really take care of myself. But Nash was only eleven and at first, when he was placed with his friend's family, he seemed to be okay. I tried calling him every week. Then his friend's family moved out of state and Nash was back in the system. He changed foster homes three times. There were weeks when we lost track of each other.

Daddy sometimes sent money and postcards, but he was always on the road and we hardly ever saw him." Birch noticed that Ruby never mentioned their runaway mother.

Though Birch had never met their father, Joe Stoddard, she felt anger so strong she thought she'd slap his face if they ever came face-to-face. And that mother of theirs? What kind of mother just up and leaves her children? Birch couldn't help thinking of her and Bobby's infant daughter, Emily Robertina. She died a month before she was born. Birch and Bobby had never been able to conceive again. Why were irresponsible people like Ruby's parents given the gift of children and she and Bobby denied it? A mystery, Father Antonio always told Bobby. We can't know God's eternal plan, a succession of her own Methodist pastors would say. She wished their answers gave her more comfort.

She patted the top of Ruby's hand. "Don't you worry. He'll be fine once he gets to know us."

Relief washed over Ruby's face, assuring Birch that she'd said the words with enough sincerity that Ruby bought it. The truth was Birch wasn't all that certain. She'd been an elementary school teacher for forty-one years before retiring, and over the years, she'd almost given up believing people could overcome their childhood traumas. She had watched too many kids take the easy route and follow their family's destructive path—to dependence on welfare, to gangs, to alcohol and drugs, to apathy and ignorance. Still, the optimistic angel perched on her right shoulder argued there were always exceptions.

"Get some rest," Birch said, standing up. "I'll call you a little before seven. The dinner rush at the Lone Pine should be over by then."

Ruby smiled. "Gosh, it'll be good to see Sueann again."

Birch touched Ruby's cheek with her fingertips. "She's thrilled you're back. She and Cassie can't wait to see you."

Back down in the lobby, Birch surveyed the thinning crowd. It was close to six p.m. so most guests were out having supper and, hopefully, spending money in the local shops open late for the Christmas holiday. It had been a hard year economically for Cardinal, never an extremely prosperous town even in its boom years when agriculture and the mines dominated the local economy. Now the community and local businesses depended on affluent tourists and their fickle generosity. However, they weren't alone. Times were hard all over the country and relief didn't appear to be on the horizon. Still, it looked like the lodge would make a tiny profit this year. That was something for which to be thankful.

"Bobby said to tell you he's gone home for a bit," said the pretty young woman minding the counter. Rodeo was twenty-two, smart, perky and eager to please, which Birch knew meant she'd eventually find a better job. She was a new hire, one of Bobby's cousin's children. Her family lived outside of Reno. Bobby had hired her three weeks earlier and she was staying with yet another cousin across town on the reservation.

"Who on earth names their child Rodeo?" Birch had asked Bobby, reading the letter from his cousin asking if Rodeo could work there a few months to get some experience.

"It's pronounced Ro-day-oh," he said, laughing. "Like the fancy street in Beverly Hills. My cousin's wife thought it sounded chic."

"Pardon me," she replied, touching her chest and laughing. "Whatever happened to the good old dependable easy-to-pronounce names like Judy and Polly and Susan?"

"They'll be back. Everything is a circle."

"A bit of Paiute-Shoshone-Mexican-Chinese wisdom?" she teased.

He raised his dark eyebrows in amusement. "Nah. I think I read it on the back of a Wheaties box."

6

Ruby

"Let me see what's taking him," Ruby said an hour later. The short nap had done her wonders; she felt human again. She'd come down to the lobby to walk with Birch and Bobby over to the Lone Pine Café for Sueann's welcome-home dinner. But it was ten past seven and Nash still hadn't appeared. "You two go on ahead. We'll catch up."

"No, we'll wait . . ." Birch started.

"She's right," Bobby said. "Takes me a bit longer to mosey on down there anyway. I need a head start."

Ruby flashed him a grateful look.

"All right," Birch said reluctantly, turning to Rodeo. "Are you going to be all right alone here, sweetie?"

"We're only going to be three blocks away, Birch," Bobby said.

"I'll be fine," Rodeo said in a chirpy voice. "Everyone who had reservations is already checked in and I can handle any walk-ins. I'll call you if I have any questions."

"We'll be right behind you," Ruby said, kissing Birch's cheek. "Just don't eat all the white enchiladas."

"No promises," Bobby said, leaning on his cane.

"Who told you what Sueann was making?" Birch shook a mock angry fist at her husband. "It was supposed to be a surprise."

"Wasn't me, I swear." Bobby held a palm up in protest.

Ruby laughed. "Don't blame Bobby. It was a lucky guess. Sueann knows it's my favorite dish at the Lone Pine."

"Okay," Birch said, taking Bobby's outstretched arm. "We'll see you two in a few minutes."

Behind Nash's closed door, Ruby heard

the guitar's soft strumming. She knocked lightly. When no one answered, she rapped harder and called his name.

"Unlocked," Nash called.

He sat on the floor, his battered acoustic guitar lying across his lap. His duffle bag was in the same spot where he dropped it. Without looking up, he fingered a bluesy melody full of mournful sharps and flats and hummed under his breath.

"That's nice," she said.

"A song I'm working on." He played a riff that, for some odd reason, reminded Ruby of the sound of water tumbling over rocks. "'Cardinal Valley Blues.'"

She didn't know what to answer. Was he being sarcastic? In the eleven months they'd lived together, she realized that the boy she knew growing up had disappeared somewhere inside this complex, troubled man. "Are you ready for dinner? You'll love the Lone Pine. It's—"

"Not hungry."

A small throbbing started in her left temple. They'd been through this scenario countless times in the last year.

"You need to eat," Ruby said, rubbing her forehead.

He stopped the vibrating guitar's strings with the flat of his hand. "Not hungry, the man says for the second time."

"My friends are waiting. Sueann and her cook, Carlos, prepared a special meal for us. Birch and Bobby are already—"

"The key word in that sentence being *your*. Look, Ruby, I'm tired. I don't feel like making conversation with strangers." He gave her a beseeching look. In that brief moment, she saw the vestiges of that eleven-year-old boy pulled from her arms by a well-meaning but overworked social worker who had done her best to keep them together. At the group home, where they initially went while waiting for foster homes, boys and girls slept in different buildings.

"Don't let them take me, Ruby," he'd cried. "Please, please! Tell them I'll be good. Please don't let them take me."

It remained one of the most horrific moments of her life.

It had been a small consolation that, in a few days, Nash was taken in by a school friend's parents. A year later, they'd returned him to Child Protective Services when the man's job was transferred to another state. Ruby was eighteen by then and still living with the couple who originally took her in. Despite her asking—begging, really—they explained that they didn't feel capable of raising a young boy. Shortly after that, she left their home, grateful they had been kind to her, but determined to try to gain custody of her brother. But they thought she was too inexperienced and didn't have the ability to make enough money to convince CPS she could care for Nash. During that second year, he went through three foster homes mostly because of his inability to follow the foster parents' rules.

"Like a rental car," he had said many times over the years, always with a bitter laugh. "People kept turning me in like I was a damn rental car."

She dropped down to the floor to sit next to him. "I know it's hard, Nash, but they want to be your friends, too. Besides, you need to eat. You know what the doctor said about how important nutrition was to someone in your condition."

"Stop it!" he said, shoving his guitar aside. "My condition! That's all we've talked about for the last year. My freakin' condition. I'm sick of it. Can't you just leave me alone?" He jumped up and started pacing back and forth across the blue and white braided rug.

"Shhh," Ruby said, standing up. "There are other people staying here. I don't care if you go tonight . . . Well, I do care, but I understand—"

He interrupted her, a frown darkening his face. "No, you don't."

"I think I do."

"If you did, you'd leave me alone."

She wished in that moment that she could do just that, leave him totally alone. Like she had for so many years. Except when he was alone was also when he reached for a drink. Being alone too much was what got him in this situation to begin with. Leaving each other alone was what the Stoddard family did best. That was their whole problem. She would always wonder if she'd given up too quickly when she tried to get custody of him. But she'd been so young and so broken herself.

"You don't have to come tonight," she

said. "But you're going to have to talk to people eventually. You've got gigs here. People will want to know you."

"I can play music without becoming best friends with everyone. Really, people like it better that way even though they don't realize it. People don't really want to know the ugly realities about the people who entertain them. They like their illusions."

His comment caused her to pause in startled shock. Was he right? He would know about that better than Ruby. He'd been a professional musician for almost eleven years, ever since he aged out of California's foster care system. Music was always there for him, he told her once. He'd discovered his love for it at ten when one of their neighbors, at the complex where they lived with their dad, gave him a battered acoustic guitar and taught him a few chords.

Though she wasn't able to break him out of foster care, Ruby did manage to buy Nash his first good Fender guitar for his sixteenth birthday. She worked two waitressing jobs, sixteen hours a day, and it cost her a year's worth of tips, but she did it.

"Don't you want to know people better?" she asked. "I mean, at some point?"

He stared at her with the same distrustful expression that she was sure had colored her own face many times. An expression that she likely wore when she walked into this very lodge last January. "So that it's easier for them to turn their back on me and walk away when I least expect it?"

She held his gaze, her heart thumping in her chest. He was talking about Angela, of course. And probably their parents. Maybe even her.

"They don't always," she said softly. "I felt the same way you did. But then I found—"

"Yeah, yeah . . . you found these great people in Cardinal who are like family to you. Seriously, Ruby, I guess Cole was better than most the guys you hooked up with. I mean, he did marry you. But in the end, he left you. You can't deny that. These people are his friends and family, the people he never told you existed until after he killed himself. Why would you trust them? He apparently didn't."

His words were like an ice pick in her gut. Then the temper that had seen her through many tough times flared like a firecracker. "You selfish little brat. You wouldn't know a decent person if they advertised on a billboard across your forehead. What friends have you had? Bar owners who pay you in beer? Your musician buddies? Your so-called fans who come to hear you play? Where were all of them when you were sick and needed money? Where were they when you were puking blood in the emergency room? They scattered like cockroaches. The people I've met here in Cardinal are there for their family and friends. They are trying to welcome you and you are practically spitting in their faces. My whole life this last eleven months has been all about you. And you repay me by . . ." But she'd run out of words; all that was left was an unreleased sob, stuck deep behind her breastbone.

Instead of feeding his anger, her words seemed to calm him, straighten out the agonized lines in his forehead. "I am selfish, Ruby. Why does that surprise you? Why didn't you just let me stay in Nashville? You know, I did okay all those years you weren't there." He gave her a ghost of a childhood smile. "Like with Dad, I think we probably get along better when there are some miles between us, don't you?"

She narrowed her eyes. "That's not a relationship, Nash. We got along because we spent ten minutes on the phone once a month. Not a lot of responsibility there."

He stuck his hands deep into his jeans pockets. "Responsibility sucks."

"Sometimes, but it's what grown-ups do, be responsible for each other. Just because our parents were flakes doesn't mean we have to be."

"So, it's better living here in Happy Valley where everyone gets along?"

She frowned. "People struggle here, too. But they don't run away every time there's a problem."

In a heartbeat, she realized the irony of her statement. Running away was exactly what Cole had done. But he'd had a good reason. Still, she wondered if he and the McGavin family might have been better eventually if he had stayed and faced his demons. Maybe he could have made a life here in the valley he loved. Of course, then she would have never met him. She likely would never be having this conversation with her brother.

Fortunately, Nash didn't seem to feel compelled to point out the obvious. He leaned against the wall and crossed his arms over his chest. "Ruby, what did you really expect would happen by bringing me here? That we'd somehow get to redo our lives? That ain't gonna happen, big sis. We are who we are. We have what we've been given."

"Not necessarily. We have some control about what we'll do with our lives. We aren't just our genetics."

He shrugged again and she fought the urge to stride across the room and smack his upper shoulder like she did when he was a boy.

Instead, she softened her voice. "So, will you come to dinner tonight? Meet Sueann and some of the other people who helped me when I was down. Please? For me?"

He sighed deeply. "It's all just too

much, Ruby. I need a little time to myself. Then I'll try. I promise."

She walked across the room to him and wrapped her arms around his thin frame. "Okay, I'll quit pushing. I'll let you do this in your own time. Just promise me two things, okay?"

He gently wiggled out of her embrace, impatient as a ten-year-old with her affection. "What?"

"Eat something tonight. At least an energy bar."

"No problem. Got one in my luggage." He grinned at her. "Thanks to an obsessive-compulsive older sister who is obsessively compulsive about my calorie consumption."

This time she did slap him gently on his upper shoulder. "Humor me. Please, let's make a pact not to lie to each other. There have been enough lies and broken promises." She left the word *parents* unsaid.

He looked away, his expression suddenly guilty. "Man, Ruby Tuesday, I wish you hadn't said that."

A cold chill traveled up her arms. "Nash, what have you done?"

His expression was an odd mixture of sheepish embarrassment and, it seemed to her, cruel pleasure when he blurted out the last words in the world she ever expected to hear.

"I know where mom is."

7

Birch

"Do you think I should call her?" Birch asked Sueann while helping her and Ely carry dishes of guacamole, warm flour tortillas and salsa verde to the big round table in the middle of the Lone Pine Café. The table was set with the café's signature Western brand–covered dinnerware. In the middle of the table was an old King Arthur Flour tin filled with red carnations and two sunflowers. Platters of white enchiladas made with sour cream, green chile and chicken, spicy Spanish rice and nutty-smelling pinto beans covered the table. "It's seven thirty . . ."

"She's here," Sueann said, her voice low. "Alone."

"Oh, dear," Birch said. "What do you think is wrong?"

"Try not to make too much of it," Ely said, setting down a basket of tortilla chips. "Don't forget, he's been sick. Not to mention, we're all strangers to him."

Birch nodded, but wasn't comforted by Ely's words. She'd wanted everything to be perfect tonight. An uneasy feeling about Nash Stoddard niggled at Birch.

Cassie came through the swinging doors that led to the kitchen. "Hey, Ruby, where's this totally wicked guitar-playing brother you were always texting me about?"

"Come here, you," Ruby said, hugging the teenage girl. "I've missed you so much. Your texts for the last year were great. They could always make me laugh when I was having a bad day. And, believe me, I had lots of bad days."

"No prob," Cassie said. "Where's Nash?"

"He's not feeling well," Ruby said, not looking at Birch. "I think he might have eaten something bad along the road." She gazed around the café, as if seeing the old spurs and brands, the photos of Roy Rogers and Hopalong Cassidy and Judy Canova, for the first time. "I've missed this place."

"That sucks," Cassie said. "I mean, Nash being sick."

"Such an advanced vocabulary for someone who got six-fifty in her verbal SATs," said Sueann.

Cassie grinned at Ruby and wagged her hand as if it were a duck quacking. "As you can see, some things never change. Mom's still the Queen of Naglo-nia. When will I get to meet him?"

Ruby playfully patted Cassie's cheek. "Soon, I promise."

"Who's hungry?" Carlos said, carrying two platters, one of steaming tamales, the other of chicken verde.

After everyone found a seat, Birch looked around at the people who'd come for Ruby's homecoming dinner—Ely, Sueann and Cassie, Bobby, and even Derek, who came a few minutes late, his latest girlfriend on his arm. Birch was happy to see her second nephew tentatively hug his older brother's widow, asking after her brother, trading teasing remarks with Sueann and Cassie.

"Where's Lucas?" Derek asked.

"On his way back from the NFR," Birch replied. "He won't be here until early tomorrow morning."

"How were sales?" Derek's words weren't sarcastic. Birch could tell he'd mellowed in the last year, which gave her hope that maybe, someday, June would also.

"He said he sold enough saddles to keep him busy a good while," Birch replied.

Derek nodded, his face neutral. Everyone knew that he would have been happier if Lucas hadn't made a single sale. Then it might force him to close up his saddlemaking shop and come back to work full time at the Circle MG.

"Ruby," Derek said, looking down at his plate. "Mom had a meeting she couldn't reschedule. Said she'd see you soon. Uh, lunch or something." He shoveled a huge bite of enchilada into his mouth, flinching slightly at the unexpected heat.

Birch watched her nephew's embarrassed expression. They all knew his mother had no intention of going to lunch with her oldest son's widow.

Ruby just smiled politely. "Please, give her my regards."

During the lively meal, Birch noticed Ruby's eyes glancing occasionally at the café's front door. For a split second, Birch regretted encouraging Ruby to bring her brother back with her to Cardinal. She'd been looking forward to Ruby's return, secretly hoping that maybe Ruby and Lucas would end up dating, marrying, having some babies. But with Ruby's difficult brother occupying her thoughts and time, would there be any room for Lucas?

Birch chided herself at her fantasies. Look at you, planning a wedding and a baby shower. How about letting Ruby unpack her suitcase?

"Everything copacetic?" Bobby whispered to her.

"I'm fine," she whispered back. "Does Ruby seem sad to you?"

"She just made a cross-country trip," he said, squeezing her hand. "I think she's just tired."

Sueann stood up. "Fortune cookie time!"

The Lone Pine Café had a long-standing tradition of giving customers a fortune cookie with their meal. It hearkened back to the restaurant's long and myriad history. Before Sueann changed it to an old-fashioned diner, it had been a Chinese restaurant. When Sueann bought the café with her divorce settlement from Derek, she sold or tossed most of the former owner's Chinese condiments and decorations. But she couldn't bear to throw away the case of fortune cookies, so she started handing them out with her Denver omelets and chicken fried steaks. They were an instant hit, with the funniest ones posted on the community bulletin board at the café's entrance. She eventually ran out and had to find a vendor to supply her with more.

"You are my guinea pigs," she said, handing out the cellophane-wrapped cookies. "My new supplier in San Jose is a young man who inherited his dad's fortune cookie company. He decided to think outside the cookie."

"What does that mean?" Ruby asked.

"Just read your fortunes," Sueann said, grinning. "This is his twenty-first-century collection."

Bobby was the first to find his fortune. He cleared his throat and read it aloud. "'A totally mysterious text will change your life soon.'" He shook his head, giving them a big smile. "Like, I don't even have a cell phone, dude."

Everyone laughed and eagerly tore open their cookies.

"Hey, listen to mine," said Carlos. "'You are for sure the most rad-looking dude at the table.'" He high-fived Cassie. "So totally true!"

"Look to your Mac for inspiration about an important decision," read Birch's fortune.

"But we have a PC," she said, shaking her head.

After they'd all read their crazy fortunes, Sueann collected them and went over to the bulletin board, where she'd made a special spot for them.

"This feels so right," Ruby said to Birch

later as they helped clean off the table. It was getting close to ten p.m. "I missed all of you so much."

Birch stacked dinner plates and nodded her agreement, still worried by the strained look around Ruby's downcast eyes. "Have you talked to Lucas recently?"

Ruby wiped up a smear of enchilada sauce off the table with a paper napkin. "We talked about two weeks ago. I sent him a postcard telling him I was coming back to Cardinal. I hope he got it before he left for Las Vegas."

"He did." Birch had seen it before Lucas since his mail came to her house. She felt a little guilty for reading it, but assumed that it couldn't be too personal if Ruby wrote it on a postcard. That, alone, made her wonder if anything romantic was blossoming between Ruby and Lucas. If there were, surely they would be sending private letters or e-mails, not postcards.

"I'll see him soon," Ruby said, stacking glasses and carrying them to the kitchen.

The walk back to the lodge was slow because of Bobby's bad leg. Ely, who had been relatively quiet throughout the meal, joined them.

"Sorry old gimpy here is slowing down the parade," Bobby said, his complexion shining with a patina of fatigue.

"Stop it," Ruby said, taking his arm. "It just gives me that much longer to see Cardinal. I really missed this old street when I was in Nashville."

They passed Holy Grounds Coffeehouse, where they could see through the plate glass window. About twenty people were listening to a woman playing a mandolin. A poster in the window advertised that the coffeehouse was participating in the upcoming First Night celebration on New Year's Eve. Free rides home would be offered in the coffeehouse's old wood-paneled station wagon.

"Hey, Mr. Grey, how do you like being one of Cardinal's up-and-coming young businessmen?" Ruby teased Ely. "What's next? Running for mayor?"

Birch glanced over at Ely to see how he'd react to Ruby's playful words.

Dressed, as always, in a flannel shirt and faded jeans, he just smiled and raised one black eyebrow. "You never know."

Birch knew he was sensitive about his new role in the community. Many folks had snickered behind their hands when the town's beloved and respected minister, Lincoln Holyoke, left all his worldly possessions, including the coffeehouse and the town's only bookstore, The Novel Experience, to Ely Grey, an ex-con, recovering alcoholic and one of Cardinal's infamous bad boys. The tales of his high school escapades in the early '80s, including an alleged affair with a fresh-out-of-college biology teacher, were still talked about at local teachers' reunions. He'd been on many Cardinal High School teachers' life list of "Worst Students I've Ever Taught."

As a grade school teacher, Birch taught fractions and penmanship to Ely and a good many other people in this town. She remembered the sullen, dark-eyed boy who sat in the back row, his arms defiantly crossed over his undernourished chest. His mother, a thin, high-strung Anglo woman who Ely didn't resemble at all, never showed up to any scheduled parent-teacher conference and attended only one open house. At the open house, her dyed black hair piled on top of her head in a scraggly bun, she stared at her son's artwork, a painting of a blue and green pinto pony jumping over a bright orange moon. Below the moon, a red and white cow with shiny black eyes looked up at the pony. She said with a soft slur to her words, "That is one crazy-ass picture you drew, kid. That's gotta be from your daddy's side." She laughed loudly, causing other parents to slip each other uneasy glances.

"I think Ely's choice of colors is highly creative," Birch had replied.

"I guess," his mother said, shrugging. She pulled out a package of Salem cigarettes, hitting it sharply against the top of her hand.

"I'm sorry, Mrs. Grey," Birch said softly, not wanting to embarrass Ely. "There's no smoking allowed in my classroom."

"Well, shit," she'd said, fixing Birch with a hard look. Then she shrugged again. "Who needs this?" She strutted out of the room without a backward glance, leaving her son standing next to his painting.

"Ely," Birch said, touching his thin shoulder with her fingertips. She remembered how he seemed to vibrate under her touch, like an animal caught in a trap. The expression on his young face was undecipherable. He jerked away and dashed out of the classroom into the dark street. The next day when each child was given his work to take home, she watched Ely Grey take his painting, fold it up neatly until it was the size of a wallet, then drop it in the trash can on his way out the door. After he left, she retrieved the painting, smoothing out the folds, her heart aching for him.

She looked over at the lanky man walking next to Ruby. His cheekbones, sharp as chipped granite, gave no hint of the round-faced boy who'd spurned her sympathy.

Though she'd heard many rumors about his father, no one actually knew who he was. His mother had come to Cardinal when Ely was a toddler and worked off and on as a barmaid at the Red Coyote. Because of his looks, everyone assumed his father was Native American or perhaps one of Cardinal Valley's itinerant Mexican cowboys, though she'd never heard Ely claim either Native American or Mexican heritage. He wore his straight, black hair in a long braid. His skin was the color of an old penny. After he'd served time in prison for armed robbery, he'd come back to town and kept himself clean. Though she'd initially been nervous about him and Lucas becoming friends, after she heard how kind he'd been to Cole when they shared a room at the halfway house in Los Angeles, she relaxed. She'd come to know Ely better and they'd had some fine conversations about books they'd read. One of his favorites was *The Great Gatsby*. She still remembered the spirited discussion they'd had about the book and whether the green light represented hope and renewal or just signaled change.

"Frankly, Mrs. Hernandez," he said, lapsing into her teaching name whenever they discussed books. "I think old Scotty F. was just messin' with people's minds. Maybe it didn't mean anything." Then he'd flash her that devastating smile. She understood why Cassie teasingly called him Professor Ely.

When they reached the street where Birch and Bobby lived. Birch paused, hesitating. It was still two more blocks to the lodge. "Ruby, it's late, so I'll just walk you—"

"Don't worry, Birch," Ely said. "I'll walk Ruby to the lodge."

"Oh, you two. I'm perfectly capable of walking myself two blocks," Ruby said.

"Let the boy be a gentleman," Bobby said, settling it. "Now give us a hug."

"Thank you," she said, hugging him, then Birch. "Both of you."

"I'll see you tomorrow," Birch said. "We can have a nice, long visit. Just call me whenever you are up and about."

"I will."

Birch watched Ruby and Ely for a few seconds as they walked down Main Street toward the Tokopah Lodge. "Against all odds, Ely has turned into a really fine young man."

Bobby draped his arm over her shoulders, making her feel young as the day they'd met. "Did you ever think that we'd get old enough to consider forty-one young?"

She gave a high girlish laugh, the same laugh he fell in love with so many years ago. She sighed when they reached their driveway, glancing up at the dark apartment above the garage. "I'm glad Lucas will be home soon. I've missed looking out of the kitchen window at the light in his apartment."

"You do know he's not going to live there forever," Bobby said.

"I know, but I'm enjoying it while I can."

Bobby looked up into the clear night sky, his genial face troubled.

"What is it, Chief?" Birch said, her hands suddenly cold as popsicles.

He inhaled deeply, his chest inflating with the cold winter air. He pointed up at the sky to the constellation Lepus. "Look, your bunny is out tonight."

"It's beautiful," she said, knowing that wasn't what he was thinking. She'd known her husband almost half a century. His face was like a well-thumbed atlas, the wrinkles like familiar roads she'd traveled many times.

"You're worried, too, aren't you?" she asked.

He patted her back and opened the front door. "Whatever comes, comes."

Comes, she thought. Something wicked this way comes. It was from *Mac-*

beth and also the title of a Ray Bradbury book, one of her favorites. She'd heard the author speak a few years ago at a teacher's conference in Bakersfield. He was old even then, his hair the color of new cotton balls. They carefully wheeled him up to the podium and she'd wondered if they'd even be able to hear a voice that had to be as feeble as he looked. But when he started talking, his enthusiasm and the power of his words made the wheelchair and his age disappear. His love for the written word was like a drug that seemed to revitalize him.

Well, maybe something wicked isn't coming, she thought, helping her husband over the threshold of their house. That's a bit dramatic. Still, there was a feeling of change in the air, like they were on the cusp of a shift. Was it just a chimera? Like her dreams for perfect lives for everyone she loved, was it just an illusion? Whatever it was, she couldn't help feeling an unexpected relief when she closed and locked the solid oak door behind them.

8

Lucas

It was three a.m. when Lucas drove down Main Street. The old-fashioned iron streetlights cast a golden glow on the snow-lined street he knew as well as he did the fence lines of the Circle MG. He'd roamed this mile-long street as a boy when he stayed in town with his aunt Birch and uncle Bobby; cruised it with his first pickup truck when he was a teenager; drove slowly back into town on it when his marriage and job failed and he'd come back home.

It had taken him a little while, but he'd finally realized that Cardinal was the only place where he could be happy, though true joy had somehow eluded him since he'd come back. Still, he'd always felt if he were to find happiness, it would be somewhere in this valley, in this town, among these people. Maybe all this time he'd simply been waiting for Ruby to arrive.

He'd decided to stop by the saddle shop first, catch a quick nap on his cot in the back. He didn't want to disturb his aunt and uncle by pulling into their driveway so early. At sixty-five years of age, his aunt Birch still had the hearing of teenager, or rather, the parent of a teenager. He'd catch heck for it, of course. She would scold him, saying he should have called her the minute he drove into Cardinal city limits. Though he teased her about her hypervigilant desire to know the whereabouts of everyone she cared about, he understood her anxiety and loved her for it. When Cole disappeared for so many years, not telling any of them where he lived, what his life was about, that changed something in all of them. Though Birch would be horrified to be compared to his mother, June, they both had something in common—a need to control the young men they loved.

Well, *love* might be exaggerating a bit for June, though Lucas assumed that, in her own way, she loved her sons. Right now, Derek was the one she really controlled since he was left with the ranch's daily operations.

Not left with, he reminded himself, *chose*. Derek liked to complain that Cole and Lucas had dumped all the responsibility of the ranch on him but, truth was, Derek wanted it that way. He loved being a rancher, didn't know anything else, didn't want anything else. Of course, June came with the ranch. That part, Lucas was sure, Derek would have given half their land to relinquish. However, those were the terms. If you got the ranch, you got June.

That's why Lucas had studied law and when that didn't work out, he learned to build saddles. He helped with the ranch when it was necessary, but he never wanted to depend on it for his living.

He parked his truck in front of his shop, flexing his fingers on the frigid steering wheel. Maybe someday he would make enough money to afford a truck with a decent heater. He contemplated the square, shiplap wooden building painted a dark brown with red trim and matching front door. The Christmas wreath complete with perky leather bow was his aunt's suggestion and, he had to admit, it gave the small building a jaunty, almost prosperous air.

Inside the building, it felt colder than out on the sidewalk, but the scent of neat's-foot oil and new leather relaxed his stiff spine. He looked at the thermostat—thirty-seven degrees. What was he thinking? He liked chilly air, but it was not conducive to sleep. He flipped on the furnace so that in a few hours the two small rooms would be bearable for possible customers, and stepped back outside. It was only a few blocks to his apartment above his aunt and uncle's garage. He'd walk there so his truck wouldn't wake his aunt. After sleeping a few hours, he'd meander over to the house and cajole her to make him buttermilk pancakes and maple bacon. He smiled, knowing that all he had to do was ask.

He walked carefully down the deserted

Main Street, the hard-packed snow slippery under his leather boots. Streetlights illuminated the frozen snow, turning it an odd shade of golden gray. His thoughts returned to the bombshell Ruby dropped when she called him on the road last night.

"After all these years, Lucas, I know where she is," she said. He could hear a soft hiccup in her voice. "My mother lives in Arizona. In an old copper mining town. Ajo? I looked it up on a map. It's spelled A-J-O. Took me a while to find it. I was spelling it how it sounded, Ah-hoe."

"Ajo is Spanish for garlic." He had no idea how he knew that since his Spanish was rudimentary. Why would a copper mining town name itself after garlic?

"Nash said that he's known for almost a year. I could just kill him! That's all he would tell me. I don't even know how he found out. He refused to tell me any more."

"He knew the whole time you were living in Nashville." Lucas was just stating the obvious, but he didn't know what else to say.

"He drops this information on me two

minutes before I'm supposed to go to Sueann's welcome-home dinner tonight at the café, which he wouldn't even attend. When I got back, he wouldn't answer his door. If it wasn't for the other guests, I would have screamed like Stanley Kowalski until he let me in." Her voice grew lower and softer, losing some of its agitation, like the air seeping out of a balloon. "How could he keep something like that from me?"

Lucas wished he could think of something wise or comforting to say. Why had Nash kept this from Ruby? It reminded Lucas of his family and their determination to hide the truth from each other. Ruby and Nash's mother left when they were just kids. To have her suddenly reappear now . . . Lucas couldn't imagine what he would do if he were Ruby.

So he just listened. As he drove across the dark desert toward Cardinal, he listened as she repeated over and over her hurt, her anger and, finally, her determination to find out why her mother left so many years ago.

"I'm going to contact her," she said.

"You're going to Arizona?" he said, not

really surprised. That was Ruby. She faced things head-on, with the power of a bullet train, or more accurately, the persistence of an ant carrying a load twenty times its body weight. She just kept on pushing until she figured things out. It was the trait that enabled her to come into Cardinal a year ago carrying his brother's ashes and a will stating she owned one-quarter of the Circle MG ranch. Because of her, his family was forced to face some painful secrets. Because of her, Lucas felt, Cole was able to rest in peace.

"Maybe I'll go there, maybe I'll call. I don't know yet. First, I have to find out exactly what Nash knows. He can't avoid me forever." She yawned into the phone. "I'm sorry, Lucas. What a bunch of crap for you to listen to on your way home from Las Vegas. I didn't even ask you how things went. I'm the most selfish person on earth."

He laughed softly. "Not even close. But, no worries. Things went great in Vegas. Made some sales. Had a good time. My booth partner was a new lady in town."

"Maddie Silverhorse," she said, giving

a small laugh. "Dr. Margaret Collins to the real world."

"How did you know that?" he asked.

"Ely told me. Said you and she would get along like two apples in a barrel."

"We did." He felt an irrational pinprick of annoyance hearing that Ely had discussed him with Ruby.

"After you've rested, call me at the lodge. We can meet for coffee or something. I'll have found out more about my mother, I'm sure."

"Sure," he said, keeping his voice light.

"Drive safe, Lucas. I don't want to lose two McGavin boys."

"Right. Then you'd be stuck with Derek."

She made a pretend gagging sound. "See you soon."

It had been near midnight when Lucas and Ruby ended their phone call. He was somewhere in the desert near Beatty Junction. Though he was flattered that she'd confided in him, giving him hope that a relationship between them was possible, her last comment reminded him that the specter of his dead brother still loomed between them.

As he walked down the empty street toward his aunt's house, he replayed their conversation in his head, trying to find some kind of hint that she might be interested in more than a friendship. He could understand her reluctance. It was embarrassingly biblical, he being Cole's youngest brother. But Lucas had been attracted to her from the moment he looked out of his shop window last December and watched her kick the crap out of her Honda's door. He hadn't known then that she was Cole's widow.

Cole. Even after a year, he missed his older brother as if he'd lost him yesterday. At times, it was an actual ache in his gut. He missed him in a way he'd never missed their father. Relief was all he'd felt when his dad died. Relief and, maybe, a little regret. Regret that Carson McGavin hadn't been a father who could be missed. But Cole. Missing him was like a pain in his chest that never stopped. Sometimes, Lucas had a strange feeling that Cole was still out there, that he wasn't dead, just gone for a while. Like he'd been for so many years. It was ridiculous, of course. Ruby had identified his body, had arranged for his cremation. They scattered part of his ashes at the foot of the cottonwood tree at Clear Creek; the other half were buried in a grave in Cardinal cemetery with a proper marble headstone. Cole was gone.

He stuck his hand deep into the pockets of his Carhartt barn coat. The temperature sign over Cardinal Valley Bank flashed twenty-four degrees. He hoped Ely kept his promise and took grain out to the rescue horses and made sure the barn door was open so they could escape the cold. Of course, he would. Ely was not the kind of guy who'd say he'd do something and not do it. If Cole had trusted him while they were in the halfway house together, Lucas should, too.

He walked past Holy Grounds, where he could see a light on in the kitchen. Ely's baker, Naomi Lewis, was likely on the job. She was famous in town for her baking, especially her fry bread, which she baked only to sell at powwows, the occasional fund-raiser for the Cardinal Valley Paiute-Shoshone reservation or one of her grandkids' soccer, baseball, dance or cheer teams. Now that she worked for Ely at the coffeehouse, she was giving the town's other famous baker, Maxie, of Maxie's Bavarian Bakery, a run for the best cinnamon rolls in Cardinal Valley. It had become sort of a personal marker as to whose rolls a local preferred. (No one cared what the tourists thought.) Since Maxie and Naomi were old friends, both graduating from Cardinal High School in 1942, it was all in good-natured fun. Lucas, never one to take sides if he could possibly avoid it, always told them this was the one area he was bipartisan; he loved their rolls equally.

"Coward," Maxie said, shaking a perpetually flour-dusted fist at him. "Fence-sitter."

Naomi would just give him a small, secretive smile, her raisin eyes sparkling, telling him she suspected that he preferred hers.

When he glanced a second time, looking to wave at Naomi, he saw Ely's dark head rather than Naomi's gray braids. He knocked on the front door glass. Ely's head popped up, eyes narrowing a moment as he peered through the pass-through. When he saw it was Lucas, he came out of the kitchen, wiping his wide brown hands on his white apron.

"Hey, partner," Ely said, opening the front door. "When did you get back?"

"Fifteen minutes ago. Afraid my truck would wake Birch so I was going to sleep in the saddle shop. But it was too dang cold so thought I'd slip into my apartment quietly. Where's Naomi?"

"Grandson had to be taken into emergency. Burnt his hand playing with matches."

"Which grandson? Was it bad?"

"I think it was Richie's youngest. She's been watching the kids since his wife left and he works the night shift at the Shell station." Ely shook his flour-dusty hands. "Wasn't real bad, but there'll be some scarring. His sister was supposed to be home watching him, but she's sixteen and snuck out to see her boyfriend. Thought her brothers were asleep."

"What time did all this happen?"

He glanced over at the clock above the pass-through—three forty-five a.m. "About an hour ago. Thank the Good Lord, Naomi had already finished the croissants. I can make the turnovers and the cinnamon rolls, but the croissants kick my ass every time."

Lucas laughed, shaking his head. "Man, I wish I had a picture of you. Former lady-killer of Cardinal making cinnamon rolls. Irony, thy name is Ely Grey."

Ely shrugged, gestured at Lucas to follow him into the kitchen. "How was Vegas? If you didn't sell anything, I can always use another barista."

"Did okay. Sold enough to keep me in beans for a while. But I'll keep your offer in mind."

Ely went back to the yard-long log of dough he was slicing for cinnamon rolls. "Talk to Ruby?"

Lucas sniffed the warm, spicy air. "Any of those cinnamon rolls done yet?"

Ely nodded over his shoulder. "Behind me. They aren't iced."

Lucas walked over to the large pan of warm rolls. "Want me to ice them?"

"Appreciate it. Icing is in the fridge."

"I get the first one."

"All yours, partner. I'll only charge you half price. Wash your hands."

"Perfectionist," Lucas said, shedding his jacket and rolling up his sleeves.

While Lucas iced the rolls, he told Ely about Ruby calling him on the road. He didn't seem surprised when he heard that her mother had been found.

"It was only a matter of time," Ely said.

Lucas looked over the pan of rolls. "Why so?"

"I think Ruby would have eventually looked for her anyway. Maybe when she had a child of her own." He cut a roll, flipped it onto the baking tray, then cut another. His rhythm surprised Lucas, more used to seeing his friend working on the engine of someone's truck. "Or maybe when she was tired of being angry."

"And you base that opinion on what?" Lucas said, going back to smearing icing over the rolls.

Ely kept slapping down cinnamon rolls. His black braid swung back and forth across his broad back. "Nothing, I guess. Might be what I'd do."

"I can't imagine what a mother would say to her children after deserting them all those years ago. If I was Ruby, I think I'd tell her to kiss my ass."

Ely laughed, rearranged a few rolls so

he could fit the last one in. “Maybe that’s why Ruby wants to see her.”

After Ely slid the last of the rolls in the big commercial oven, he poured two mugs of coffee and they sat on wooden stools in the kitchen, eating hot cinnamon rolls and catching up on what had happened in Cardinal for the two weeks Lucas was gone.

“You were right,” Lucas said. “I liked Dr. Maddie a lot.”

“Yeah, she’s a pistol. Not a bad person to have in your corner.”

At six a.m. Lucas finally said good-bye, promising the notebook Ely ordered for Naomi would be finished in time for Christmas. Lucas was carving a leather notebook with the picture of a Paiute woman weaving a basket on the front. Naomi was taking an oral history class at the community college and was trying to write down her grandmother’s stories for her own grandkids.

“Where are you spending Christmas this year?” Lucas asked, knowing that with Linc gone, Ely would likely be alone. Many folks in Cardinal were dreading this first Christmas without Lincoln Holyoke, who had made his coffeehouse a refuge for any of the county's lonely or disenfranchised people who needed a place to go on the holiday.

"Keeping the dream alive," Ely said, resting his hands on his hips. "The Grounds will be open on Christmas Eve and Christmas Day, just like the Tokopah. Those who don't feel like going to the lodge can come here. Everything on the house."

"You can afford that?"

"I can."

On the walk back to his aunt's house, carrying a package of fresh cinnamon rolls, Lucas thought about Ely. Though Lucas knew at least half the people in this town to speak to, having lived the majority of his life here, he would venture to say that Ely was his only real friend. Lucas could shoot the breeze with anyone, find common ground for casual conversation, but it was only around Ely that he didn't feel as if he had to watch every single word that came out of his mouth. It was an unexpected, though much-appreciated, friendship.

It was almost six thirty when he opened

the back door to his aunt's house and entered the warm kitchen. Birch turned around, her pale blue eyes lighting up at the sight of him. She wore a fuzzy robe decorated with red and black vaguely Indian symbols. It reminded Lucas of the lodge's Pendleton sofas.

"Lucas! When did you get home? Where is your truck?" She wiped her hands on an embroidered tea towel and came over to hug him.

He set the box of cinnamon rolls on the kitchen table and hugged her back. "Few hours ago. Didn't want to wake you and Uncle Bobby. Happened to see Ely working in the back of Holy Grounds and I helped him."

"Naomi's grandson is fine," Birch said, turning back to the coffeemaker. "But that granddaughter of hers." Birch shook her head. "She'll be pregnant by seventeen, no doubt."

"How *do* you find out all this stuff so quickly?" He laughed, pulling off his coat and hanging it over a green ladder-back chair.

"Appaloosa Express," she said, using the same explanation she'd been giving him since he was a boy. She set a platter of scrambled eggs in the center of the kitchen table. "Have you seen Ruby yet?"

He concentrated on taking the cinnamon rolls out of the pink bakery box and placing them on a platter. "Not yet." He wasn't actually lying. He hadn't *seen* her.

"She's already having problems with that brother of hers. He's a nice-looking boy, and polite and all. But, I can tell already, he's trouble on a stick."

He took three coffee mugs off the wooden tree and set them next to the coffeemaker. He could hear Bobby rustling around upstairs, the creak of the old house's wooden floor. The scent of the brewing coffee reminded him of early court mornings when he was a public defender and lived on coffee and peanut butter energy bars he bought by the case from Whole Foods.

He'd been thinking a lot lately about his time in San Francisco. Did he miss it? Maybe a little. He missed the rhythm of court and the detail of law, how the dialog of the judge and the bailiff and the prosecutor was almost always the same, almost always predictable. He missed how each case was like a story with a beginning, middle and end. How you could sometimes predict what would happen, but how, sometimes, you were completely surprised. What he didn't miss was the petty evil of the average person. He didn't miss how often the bad guy got away with his crime. And he definitely didn't miss his cheating ex-wife.

"So," he said, pouring his aunt a cup of coffee and pulling out her chair, "tell me what's been going on in our little corner of the universe."

9

Ruby

At eight a.m. the next morning, Ruby walked down the carpeted hallway to her brother's room, preparing herself for a confrontation. She imagined herself softly beseeching Nash through the closed door to let her in, trying to keep her voice low so she wouldn't disturb the Tokopah's guests. She would stay there until he let her in, no matter how long it took. He could not drop a bomb like that and avoid her forever.

He answered the door on her first knock. That was Nash for you. Just when you thought you had him figured out, he threw a curve ball. He was dressed in faded Levi's and a red T-shirt advertising the last place he worked—Café Oz, Nashville. His eyes were clearer than yesterday and the expression on his face calm. In fact, he looked more relaxed than she'd seen him in months. He was so calm that she instantly became suspicious. Had he had a drink this early in the day? Was he taking drugs? She took a deep breath and pushed away her suspicions, wanting to give him the benefit of the doubt.

"We need to talk about Mom," he said, before she could say a word. "But not here. We need privacy."

She nodded, relieved she didn't have to beg. "I know someplace private we can go. Let's drive through McDonald's for breakfast."

Fortunately, the Tokopah's lobby was crowded with guests either waiting for a table in the breakfast room or gathering their gear and groups together to head up the mountain to the Mammoth ski slopes. Bobby and Birch were nowhere to be seen so Ruby and Nash were able to slip out the front door and into her car without speaking to a soul.

On the outskirts of town, Ruby pulled into the McDonald's drive-through. After they'd bought breakfast, Ruby drove back out on the highway and headed north toward Mammoth.

"Where're we going?" Nash asked, unwrapping an Egg McMuffin and handing it to her.

"Clear Creek. It's where Lucas keeps his rescue horses and where we sprinkled some of Cole's ashes."

In about ten minutes, she turned off on the road that led to the Circle MG, but at the fork, she went left not right. During the drive to Clear Creek, Ruby was tempted to demand an explanation right away, but she held herself in check. She didn't want to fight. She'd hear Nash's explanation first.

When they pulled up the dirt road to the Clear Creek pasture, Nash let out a soft "wow." She parked with the Honda's front bumper almost touching the pasture's locked aluminum gate. In the distance, she could see the ramshackle old barn, the cottonwood tree Cole had loved, the outline of Lucas's rescue horses. Behind all that lay the majestic Sierra Nevada

Mountains, jagged and a million shades of blue gray, topped now with pristine snow like icing on a cake.

In the crisp, clean air, the sound of a whinny echoed across the deep pasture. The horses knew they were there. She couldn't remember all their names, but she knew the sorrel mare was called Greta, because she didn't care to be around people, like the long-ago actress. Another was named for a blues singer . . . something about water?

"Whose horses?" Nash asked.

"Muddy Waters," she blurted out.

He turned to her, his eyes quizzical. "Say what?"

She gave a small shrug. "That brown one with the black mane is called Muddy Waters. The sorrel mare is Greta, as in Garbo. The others I've forgotten. Lucas could tell you. They're his horses. He rescued them." She opened the car door, gasping at the cold air, and started walking toward the fence.

She stopped at the fence, watching the horses amble toward them. She remembered now: They associated people with treats. She was sorry she'd forgotten to bring carrots or apples. She took a deep breath and turned to look at her brother. He stood next to her, resting his forearms on the top rail of the fence. "Okay, Nashville Stoddard, I'm not driving you back until you tell me everything. Start talking."

"Look out, she's serious," he said, trying to charm her. "Using my full given name."

"Mama was crazy naming you that. Talk about pressure . . . or rather living out *her* dream."

"Bitterness will give you wrinkles, sis."

She gripped a rung of the metal fence with one hand, willing herself not to say another accusing word despite what she felt. Above them, a crow squawked a warning. "Just tell me how you found her."

He glanced up at the noisy bird. "Wasn't nothin' I did. Dad told me when he and Prissy blew through Nashville last year. Right before you came out. He and I was drinking and, well, it just came out. He's known where she was for a while."

It felt like a chunk of ice appeared from nowhere and lodged in the middle of Ruby's chest. "How long?" she whispered.

Nash studied his hands, refusing to make eye contact. "Dad got a phone call from her out of the blue. She needed money. Not much and she said she'd get it right back to him. He sent her five hundred bucks and she eventually paid it back. That's it."

"How long, Nash? How long has Dad known where she is?"

"He said a few years ago. That's all I really remember. We were pretty wasted, Ruby. I'm amazed I even remembered he told me."

Anger started melting the chunk of ice in her gut. "Why wouldn't he tell *me*?"

Nash picked at a hangnail. "Shoot, Ruby, I don't think he *meant* to tell me. We got drunk. He told me not to tell you or to get in touch with Mama. Said she didn't want to be found by anyone. Made him promise he wouldn't even call her brother in Tennessee."

She just stared at him, not knowing what to say. Since she was thirteen, she'd wondered how she'd react if she ever found out where her mother was. Now that it was a reality, all she could think was—why didn't Dad tell *me*?

"Someone should call Uncle Burr," she said.

"Think he would even care? I don't."

Ruby stared at the back of her hands. He was probably right. Their uncle had not even cared enough when Ruby and Nash were kids to see if they were doing all right when Mama walked away. They'd only met him once, long before Mama left, when Ruby was ten years old. Uncle Burr and Aunt Wilma came out to California to take their son, Jared, to Disneyland. They'd spent one night with them in Bakersfield before going down to Orange County. Dad and Uncle Burr had smoked cigarettes and argued about politics. Aunt Wilma made lemonade from the lemons she picked from their backyard tree. It tickled Mama that Aunt Wilma raved on and on about that tree.

"Honestly, Ruby," she'd said after they left. "The kind from the can tastes better. Wilma's loco." She circled her finger around her temple, making Ruby giggle because a grown-up making fun of another grown-up seemed so exotic and thrilling.

I can count the things I remember about my mother on my ten fingers, she thought.

Nash waited for her to speak. He'd always had an uncanny ability to simply wait and wait, not moving a muscle, not giving any hint to what he was feeling. All those years waiting in social services offices, she thought. All those years waiting for someone to take him home.

"Did you try to contact her?" she finally asked.

He shook his head. "Why would I?"

"Well," Ruby said slowly, drawing out the word. "Maybe to ask why she left? Where she's been? What in the world possessed her to desert her *children*?"

He took a deep breath and faced her, his back to the gate. "Those are your questions, Ruby. I really don't care. What does it matter now?"

She cocked her head, amazed that they were two people who'd experienced the same abandonment and yet felt so different about it. "It matters. It will always matter."

"To you."

She sighed, suddenly weary of this conversation. "Did he give you an address or phone number?"

"Are you going to contact her?" His face looked alarmed.

"What does it matter?" she mocked softly.

"Touché. Look, I don't have either and I don't care. Just leave me out of it, okay?"

"Deal."

Above them, the crow let off a loud *caw* and took flight, catching an air current and gliding over the horses. A small light-colored horse that Ruby didn't remember reached the fence first, blowing air, announcing its appearance.

The unfamiliar sound behind Nash caused him to jump and turn around. He backed up quickly, laughing nervously. "Whoa, back off, large mammal."

Ruby laughed, recognizing the same discomfort she'd felt when she first encountered these horses. Hard as it was for rural people to understand, most kids raised in the city were more familiar with bicycles and buses than horses and cattle.

"She won't bite," Ruby said, reaching

out her hand to the horse. "Hard, anyway."

"Har, har," Nash replied. "So, have you ever ridden any of these nags?"

She let her hand hang in the air near the horse's nostril so it could pick up her scent. In seconds, the horse pushed its nose into her palm, searching for a treat. She smiled at the warm air and feel of its soft and scratchy nose. "That's not why Lucas keeps them. They were all abused in some way. They are here living out their life without hassle."

Nash narrowed his eyes, turning back to study the horses. Six of them were at the fence now; Greta lingered behind the others, still shy. "Lucky them."

"Nash, do you know how to contact Mama?"

He shoved his hands deep into the pockets of his jeans. She could see his shoulders slump slightly. She fought the urge to go over and rub circles on his back the way she did when he was a little boy and couldn't sleep. "He said she went by Etta now."

"Etta?"

"Etta Walker. She's gone back to her

maiden name. That's all I know except that she lives in Ajo, Arizona."

"Etta Walker from Ajo," Ruby repeated. It sounded like a stranger.

Loretta Stoddard to Etta Walker. With a pen stroke, her mother was gone. Ruby couldn't help feeling angry. And sad. It felt like her mother was erasing what little connection she had with them.

The horses started at something, a sound on a level that was inaudible to Ruby and Nash. They turned and darted away, kicking up small dust clouds. Only the buckskin gelding remained, unafraid, hopeful. What was his story?

She turned back to Nash. "That's it?"

"All I know is what I told you. If you want to know more, you'll have to call Dad." He shrugged and started back to the car. "Are we done here? I'm cold."

"I will," Ruby called after him. "I'll call Dad." If he wouldn't tell her more, maybe Prissy would.

"Whatever," Nash said, climbing into the car and closing the door behind him.

10

Etta

Eventually, Etta told old Dr. Beth everything. About her desperation to escape the poverty of her Tennessee childhood. About her quickie wedding to a man named Joe Stoddard whom she'd met at a Las Vegas blackjack table and known only three days. About her impossible dream of becoming a country singing star. And about the second-worst thing she had ever done in her life—walk away from her children. The worst thing she still couldn't put into words, still afraid that if Etta told her, even kind Dr. Beth's sun-creased, seventy-five-year-old face, so patient and accepting of all human and animal foibles, would freeze with disgust, draw back from Etta with revulsion. Etta told her everything but that.

Dr. Beth never uttered one judgmental word, something Etta still found amazing. The old veterinarian just listened and nodded as Etta talked and talked. Gradually Etta found out Dr. Beth's own story, how she'd come to live in this once prosperous copper mining town that was now a combination artist colony, snowbird sanctuary and inexpensive retirement community.

"I was a horrible mother," Dr. Beth said, her trilling laugh echoing as she and Etta walked through the air-conditioned rows of cages. The rotating fifty or so dogs who lived at All Good Dogs Animal Rescue barked joyously and wiggled their rumps at the sound of her laugh. They knew it meant playtime, snack time or cuddle time.

"I don't believe that," Etta murmured, walking behind her, reaching out every so often to caress a cold nose poking through the chain- link fencing.

"Oh, I was, my dear. The worst mother

you could imagine. Fortunately, my kids became decent human beings in spite of me and Phil."

Phillip Harvey was her long dead husband, a stockbroker who had made millions during the early years of computers. "I cared more about going to vet school and rescuing dogs than my own poor little children." She looked back at Etta, her face sad. "I wasn't mean. I didn't beat or abuse them. I just forgot too many times that they existed. All I could think about was my rescue dogs." She sighed. "Fortunately, they had wonderful nannies, because Phil was an equally absent father."

Etta nodded, understanding what it was to be consumed by ambition or desire so strong and overwhelming that nothing else existed. First, it was the music. Then the drinking. Both she'd quit years ago. For the drinking, she had AA. The music, she just let go. There was no twelve-step program for that.

When she finally became sober, her daughter would have been twenty-five, her son, nineteen. Too late to go back. Too late to erase what had happened. Besides, she didn't deserve them. She knew by leaving them, she did a wrong that was unforgivable. She wondered if being regretful for her actions meant anything. Was that just a tiny bit better than not recognizing she screwed up at all?

"They're just happy now that I'm no trouble to them," Dr. Beth said cheerfully. "I have Phil's money to pay for this place and keep us all in kibble and Metacam. And my kids always know what to give me for Christmas and birthdays: gift certificates to pet supply catalogs."

Her children still lived in the San Francisco Bay Area; both inherited trust funds when their father died. They had become successful in their own right—her son a tax attorney, her daughter a well-known interior designer. In the years Etta had lived in Ajo and worked for Dr. Beth, she'd never met either child, had not even seen a photo of them.

Everyone truly does have their own sorrows, she thought, after hearing Dr. Beth's story. She had assumed the veterinarian's life had been idyllic.

Late at night, Etta sat out on the back patio of the old company house that she rented from Dr. Beth. The vet had bought a dozen of them when she moved to Ajo years ago and rented them to myriad artists and hard-up folks. Etta had become fascinated by the constellations, had gotten a book from Ajo's small library and learned to identify them according to the seasons. December was one of her favorite months when Eridanus, Cetus and Triangulum were especially easy to spot. She never tired of finding Canis Major and Canis Minor. Lepus's name always made her smile. Leaping Lepus, she would say to herself. It helped her remember it was the rabbit. She liked how the constellations were as sure as anything on earth was. Dependable. Eternal.

Etta would lay back in the old green and white webbed lounge chair that she'd bought at a yard sale, wrapped in the one quilt of her mama's that she'd managed to save through all her wanderings. It was a red and black Drunkard's Path pattern, an odd pattern for her teetotaling mother to choose. Ironic now, considering Etta's own life.

"Oh, Loretta," her mama used to say. "You got the wandering gene. I can see it in your face. Baby, you ain't never gonna be happy in this world. You're always gonna be a'lookin' and hopin' for something over that next mountain."

Etta stared at that face every morning while brushing her teeth, combing her dark hair. Silver strands laced it now, bringing out her pewter eyes. She studied her aging skin for a moment, then inhaled deeply. The wandering and looking parts had come true, but the hoping? No, that's where Mama read it wrong. Etta had stopped hoping a long time ago.

11

Birch

"Have you seen Ruby this morning?" Birch asked Ely. They were setting out plastic glasses, chocolate-chip scones, pitchers of lemonade and a variety of sandwiches in The Novel Experience's back room in preparation for the Cardinal Valley Story Jam committee meeting scheduled for noon.

"No, ma'am," he said.

"Her car was gone before I got to the lodge this morning at nine a.m. Nash was gone, too."

"Maybe they went to breakfast."

She gave a small frown. “We serve breakfast at the lodge.”

Ely raised an eyebrow. “Privacy?”

She sighed, shifting the glasses to the far side of the table. “I know I’m an interfering old woman, but there’s something bothering Ruby, I can tell. I’m worried and I’m just . . . I just . . .”

“Want to help. Nothing bad about that. I’d venture to say not enough people have worried about helping Ruby most her life.” His black eyes were opaque and unreadable.

She smiled at Ely. “Mr. Grey, you are rapidly turning into one astute and wise old man.”

“Old?”

His face didn’t change expression and she wondered if he thought she was making fun of him. “Beats the alternative, sweetie.”

His smile came slowly, but it did reach his eyes. “So I’ve been told.”

Behind her, she could hear the booming voices of teenagers. They burst into the room, filling it with the smells of baby-powder-scented cologne, raspberry bubble gum and that particular pungent odor that Birch had always labeled in her head as *adolescent male looking for trouble*. In the lead was her great-niece, Cassie McGavin, a senior this year, bound for college in the fall. This story jam had been her idea, born from a discussion in her American history class about the value of oral history, the stories of everyday folks.

"I thought about all the different kinds of people here in Tokopah County," she'd explained to Birch and Sueann one night at the café, "and what they'd seen and went through, like with Manzanar and the Indians and the miners and all the stuff about water and cowboys, and how kids my age we don't even *think* about all that 'cause we're so self-involved and I needed this senior project and kids need to know about their history and, well, I thought, story jam!"

"Forgive your uneducated mother here," Sueann had said. "But what exactly is a story jam?"

"Well, it's like with musicians. Jamming is free form; it means you can kind of make it up on the spot. My history teacher, Mr. Lindquist, and my English teacher, Ms. Portillo, think it's great. I just have to get tons of people involved, like, all kinds of people. Then it would give the whole Cardinal Valley experience to people. It would give everyone who lives here a voice."

Birch looked at her niece, amazed at the change in her in the last year. She'd gone through some painful things since last December, but instead of sending her barreling down a path of trouble, Cassie had emerged stronger, more mature. It was hard to believe by this time next year she'd be eighteen, away at college. Birch had always known this day would come, but it still seemed surprising. She felt that way whenever she saw one of her students walking down the street holding a baby or maneuvering a toddler or coming back to see her with tales of jobs in the city.

"I think it sounds wonderful," Birch had said. "How can I help?"

Which was why she was sitting in the room right now with six chattering teenagers, Ely Grey and Dr. Maddie Collins, whom Ely also finagled into joining the committee. Maddie, who'd come in right after the kids, was trying to get everyone to quiet down.

"Take a seat, you crazy bunch of Tater Tots," she yelled in a voice that reminded Birch of the boom of those old stereos teenagers used to lug around on their shoulders before iPods became all the rage. "We have a cruise ship load of stuff on the agenda and not much time."

The kids were given special permission to be off school campus for the noon meeting, but they had only an hour.

"Grab yourself a sandwich, a scone and something to drink and scurry back to your seat," she continued, a huge smile on her face. She was obviously enjoying herself.

Birch and Ely had agreed to let Maddie take charge of the committee.

"You may as well let me run it," she'd said the first time the three of them met to discuss the event. "I'll end up doing it anyway and annoy the heck out of everyone. However, I'll be honest, I do love to delegate, so you all will have plenty to do. Nevertheless, I'll be happy to take the brunt of any and all screwups. I understand it comes with the privilege of telling everyone what to do. I'm also really adept at convincing people to pitch in and help.

We'll make this the best darn story jam this town has ever seen."

"Fine with me. I'm just here to move chairs and put together tables," Ely said.

"Oh, Maddie, you do whatever you want and we'll help," Birch said. "We just want this to be nice for the kids."

"Well, I'm all for making the kids do most the work," Maddie said.

"Sounds right to me," Ely had said.

Maddie clapped her hands again. The kids kept chattering, so she put two fingers in her mouth and let out a shrill whistle. The kids instantly fell silent and came to attention, like a bunch of trained hunting dogs.

"Thank you," she said sweetly. "Now, you may quietly get something to eat and drink because I don't want to be accused of causing anyone to collapse from low blood sugar, but you all need to listen while you do so."

She put on her rhinestone-dappled half glasses and read from her purple leather notebook. "We've already got fifteen sign-ups from the senior center, which means we now have fifteen entries." She peered at the kids over her glasses. "You all need to get some young folks to sign up, otherwise we're going to be hearing nothing but odes to Depends and sonnets about our screwed-up Social Security system."

A small titter of laughter ran through the crowd.

"Seriously, kids," she said. "This is about showing all the viewpoints in Tokopah County. Get out there and beat the bushes."

"Can I say something?" Cassie asked, standing up.

"The floor is yours, Ms. McGavin," she said. "It is not lost on me that this whole thing was your idea."

"Right," she said, nodding her thanks. Then she turned to face her peers. "Look, what we want is not just stories from people our age, but also the stories and memories of your parents, your grandparents, whoever. And they don't actually have to be told with words. Like, I mean, you can do it with photographs or art or music. All we want is for people to tell their stories about Cardinal and this area.

However they want to tell it. It doesn't matter if it's totally opposite of someone else's story."

"Like telling about a battle from both the Indian and white man's side," one kid said. He wore a black T-shirt that said "Paiute Power On!"

"Yeah, like that. We have lots of things in this county that people disagree on, but hearing other people's stories can, like, help illuminate and, uh . . ." She stumbled a bit, glancing around the room as if the answer were hanging in the air somewhere.

"Promote empathy," Ely said.

She shot him a grateful smile. "Exactly. Like Ely said. Empathy." She looked around at the other kids. "The reason I asked you guys to be a part of the committee is because of your backgrounds. Each of you comes from a different part of our town's heritage. I want you to be like the . . ." She thought for a moment. "Point men . . . and women. Be the person who goes out there first. Okay, that's all I have to say." She sat down quickly, her face flushed.

"Thank you, Cassie, that definitely

helps clarify our mission," Maddie said. "Now, I have an important topic we all need to discuss and vote on. It has to do with the date of the jam. I know we'd talked about having it in February and using the school auditorium. But the more I heard about this, the more I thought it was something that more people should see and experience. So, using my somewhat dubious connections, and also dropping Mrs. Hernandez's name, which goes very far in this town"—she smiled over at Birch—"the city council and the board members of the Cardinal Valley Western Film Museum have agreed to not only let us use the museum's auditorium, they've also agreed to include it in the museum's first anniversary. In fact, it'll be the entire Friday night entertainment. It'll start the week's activities marking the museum's anniversary."

"Cool!" Cassie called out, her friends echoing her enthusiasm.

"Now keep in mind, that's the second Friday in January," Maddie said. "So that doesn't give you a huge amount of time and you'll likely be working through some of your winter break. But when we meet back in a week, I expect to have a report of whom you have lined up. Troops dismissed!"

"That went well," Birch said after the kids had left, taking almost every bit of food with them.

"Thank you," Maddie said. "I mean it . . . thank *you*. I know you ran interference for the kids to get them that opening night. Those old farts on the city council weren't exactly thrilled about giving up the Friday-night spot to something that has never been tried before."

"Sometimes this town can be a bit stuck in the mud," Birch said. "We were just lucky that four of the six council members learned how to diagram sentences from me."

Ely contemplated the empty platters. "Locusts would have left more."

"Teenagers. Gotta love 'em," Maddie said. "Or else you gotta strangle 'em. No in between. Walk me out, Birch?"

Out on the sidewalk, Maddie didn't beat around the bushes. "Had a real good time with Lucas in Las Vegas. He is a sharp young man and I like him a lot."

Birch smiled. "I'm a bit partial to him myself."

She had not known Margaret Collins—Maddie—long, but she liked her. Birch had come to an age when someone who just laid it all out there was so much easier to be around than someone who was always making you guess about what they thought or felt. Transparency in a person was a relief and a delight.

"But, you know, he needs to fish or get off the pot. He's too smart and too talented not to be giving his all to something . . . anything. What does it take to light a fire under that boy?"

Birch was dumbstruck for a moment, taken aback by the same bluntness she thought she had liked about this woman. Who was *she* to be making that kind of judgment about Lucas? Why, she'd only known him a few weeks.

"Oh, dear, my big mouth does it again," Maddie said, her expression a combination of distressed and amused. "I'm so sorry, Birch. I'm really overstepping, aren't I? Please forgive an old psychiatrist who can't help but stick her nose in to someone else's psyche. If it makes any difference, these days I tend to do it only with people I care about. And I truly do like your nephew. He's one of the nicest men I've ever met. He'll find his way, I'm sure."

Birch felt her anger dissipate. How could you not like someone who was as self-censoring as Maddie Collins? "It's all right. I do understand what you are saying and I agree. He just seems to be stuck. I've nagged him to the point where I fear if I say one more thing he'll never speak to me again." She laughed at the absurdity of Lucas being that dramatic.

"Never happen. But, you're right, nagging or as I like to refer to it, concerned cajoling, usually doesn't help. Sometimes all you can do is just let a person be. I don't know why I even brought it up to you. I know better."

Birch reached over and put a hand on the woman's arm. "You care about him. I understand that completely. You're right, he's a nice man. He deserves more . . . I want to say happiness. But most of the time he seems perfectly happy."

"Maybe we need to concentrate on

something else," Maddie agreed. "A couple of old women who, as they say, need to get a life."

"Oh, Lord, I have plenty of life," Birch said, laughing. "Too much, I think sometimes."

Back at the lodge, the lobby had quieted down. Only a gray-haired man wearing a red ski sweater reading a book sat on one of the Pendleton sofas. This lull during the middle of the day was common during ski season when most of their guests were either up at the Mammoth slopes or snowshoeing or cross-country skiing in the local area. The snow had been abundant so far this year so bookings were good. Even letting Ruby and Nash stay in rooms for free wouldn't hurt them too much. But, she needed to call Julie over at Parker Real Estate and see when that little house on Maple Street would be ready for Ruby and Nash to move in. She was certain that Ruby, as much as she liked the Dale Evans room, would feel more relaxed once she was in her own home.

Bobby sat behind the counter, a frown on his normally genial face.

"What's wrong?" Birch asked, coming around to stand next to him.

"There's money missing from petty cash."

"Oh, no. How much?"

"Forty dollars."

One-fifth of their petty cash. It wasn't much, but enough that they couldn't chalk it up to miscounting or giving a guest too much change.

"What are you going to do?" she asked.

He closed the lid on the gray metal box. "I don't know. Pretty much everyone who works here knows where the key to this box is located." He placed the box back into the drawer, locked it and stuck the key in an adjacent drawer.

"Maybe we should raise our security level a bit," she said, giving a wry smile.

"Whoever works the desk needs to be able to get to the cash." He didn't mention Rodeo's name so Birch didn't, either. They both knew she was their only new employee.

"Well, let's think on it a bit before doing anything."

He nodded, his face still troubled. Bobby had the kindest, most generous heart of anyone she'd ever known. It was the reason they had a never-ending succession of his nieces, nephews, children of friends, first, second and third cousins, all working off and on at the Tokopah Lodge when they needed job experience, a little extra money or both.

But they'd never had anyone steal from them.

The times they are a'changin', she thought, going into the back office to find Julie's business card. People just didn't raise their kids with any sort of morals anymore. And thank-you notes! You can forget that. If you did something nice or gave a gift to anyone under forty these days, you were lucky to get a text message, much less a handwritten note. Then again, she'd read recently that some schools were contemplating not even teaching penmanship any longer. What kind of world would it be if people couldn't handwrite a letter? She treasured her mother's and grandmother's handwritten letters. When she held them, she was always a bit awed knowing that their DNA was still embedded in the fragile paper.

She dialed the number for Parker Real

Estate and Julie answered in a perky, cartoon-character voice that belied her master's degree in economics from UCLA. She'd come to Cardinal to care for her ailing, widowed dad and made a life for herself in this small town by falling in love with a local boy, marrying and having two children ten months apart.

"Hey, Birch," she said. "I was just going to call you. The house is all ready for Ruby and Nash, though it needs a good cleaning. Someone needs to just come by and pick up the key. Or I could drop it off. I've got a craving for the lodge's peach turnovers."

"No, you've done enough already. I'll send someone over to pick it up and I'll send some turnovers along with them."

"Aren't you the sweetest thing in Cardinal Valley? The office will be open until five. I'll be here all day except for an appointment I have with the film commissioner and a film scout at two. They're planning to do some filming at the fairgrounds for a new cable movie about rodeo cowboys in the fifties and the unnamed star has demanded a house with at least four bathrooms, two freezers, an outside Jacuzzi and an old-fashioned windmill. They didn't say why the star absolutely needed a windmill and I don't think I'm going to ask." Her high-pitched laugh sounded like a loon, which made Birch smile.

"Another movie? That's always good news for local business."

Just like in the '40s and '50s, when movie and television crews from Los Angeles filmed many Westerns in Cardinal Valley, this area had again become economically attractive to cash-strapped studios. It was only six hours to the LA metro area. Some popular movies and commercials had been shot in the arid hills and high plateaus.

"They are also contemplating a commercial," Julie said. "They're looking for an adobe-type home to film a spot about salsa."

"Well, thanks for taking the time to help me find a house for Ruby and her brother."

"No problem. It's always my pleasure."

Birch walked back into the lobby and found the front desk empty. "And we wonder why there's money missing," she murmured to herself. Except for the man reading, the lobby was empty. She straightened up the counter, refilled the Christmas candy bowl and checked the register. There were no arrivals today because they had a full house. For that, she was thankful. There'd been many Christmases where their annual free Christmas Eve dinner had more beans than turkey on the menu. Things were good now, but like a true ranch-raised Western woman, she knew that lean times always, always lurked around the corner.

But for now, their coffers were full, there'd be plenty of turkey this year, all her family was alive and well, and even though there was this troubling theft, she was even certain that would work out. Best of all, Ruby had come back to Cardinal. Yes, there was Ruby's brother, but Birch was optimistic about that, too. It would be a good Christmas and, God willing, a prosperous and happy New Year. Birch just wouldn't settle for anything less.

12

Lucas

It was early afternoon before Lucas made it out to Clear Creek to check on the horses. He leaned against the door of his truck, enjoying the weak warmth of the winter sun and watched his herd. Ely had taken good care of them. Lucas didn't know why he doubted his friend. Lord, he supposed he was getting more like his aunt Birch as he got older . . . good-naturedly assuming no one could do a better job at something than he did.

He counted bodies—Muddy Waters, Beau, Eddie, Spike, shy Greta, who in the last year had finally started letting him hand feed her carrots, and the latest, Chico, the buckskin gelding he'd named after the character played by Freddie Prinze in that '70s television show *Chico and the Man*. He'd called the horse this because "The Man" had given the gelding to him. That is, a local sheriff's deputy, Gordon Vieira. Gordon found the horse at another abandoned meth-lab house outside of Cardinal, labs that were getting as prolific as tumbleweeds.

Chico had been half starved, jumpy as a wild cat, and so filthy that his color was not apparent until Lucas washed him off at the ranch. His coat gradually emerged, the color turning out to be a shade of buckskin that reminded Lucas of the silver gray hills outside of Cardinal right before the first snow, which made Lucas guess the horse might be a grulla, a rare color in buckskins.

He looked over at the horses meandering toward the gate, knowing his presence signaled pieces of sweet apple, carrots and, sometimes, sugar cubes. Giving them sugar cubes was as healthy as giving suckers to children, but he loved the sound of the crunch between their flat, strong teeth and how their ears would flicker in appreciation and, he thought, maybe joy.

His cell phone rang—"Send in the Clowns"—a ringtone that Cassie set up as a joke when he first bought the phone and he never bothered changing. He was surprised it reached out here when there were places in town where people did crazy dances trying to find a signal. The Cell Phone Polka his uncle Bobby called it.

It was Ruby.

"Hey," he said. "What's up?" He was tempted to say, *Where have you been for the last eight hours?* but held back. It really wasn't any of his business.

"Oh, Lucas, I'm sorry. I truly haven't been avoiding you. I was just tied up all morning talking to Nash. He finally opened up to me about our mother. Well, if you can call the meager information he gave me opening up."

"What did he say?" He held out his palm, giving Chico the last sugar cube. The other horses tried to edge the gelding aside and steal his treat. Lucas cradled the phone against his shoulder and used his arm to push them away. "Get back, you selfish beasts. Give him a chance."

"What?"

"Talking to the horses. I'm out at Clear Creek."

"Oh, we were just there. You have a new one."

Lucas was silent a moment. "When were you here?"

"This morning. Nash and I needed a quiet place to talk. And I wanted to see the horses again. What's the new one's name?"

For some reason it irritated him that she came out here with her brother. Then he mentally cuffed himself. She had as much right as anyone to visit Clear Creek. Part of Cole's ashes was mixed with the soil at the base of the cottonwood tree.

"Chico. Another meth-house horse. Greta is getting as pissy and stuck up as the others now that she's not the new kid on the block. How quickly they forget. Poor little Chico is still trying to fit in."

"It is hard being the new one," she said softly.

"Thinking about Nash?"

"I just hope he can make some friends, maybe find some peace here."

Lucas didn't answer. After the days he'd spent with them in Nashville a year ago, he seriously doubted that her brother would be happy anywhere except maybe a bar. There was a restlessness about him, a dissatisfaction that Ruby, in her blind love, didn't seem to notice.

"What else did Nash tell you about your mom?" he asked, holding up an empty palm to show the horses he had nothing left. White air blew from their noses, their nostrils fluttering in the cold. He started back to the truck to finish the call inside the cab.

She repeated what Nash told her a few hours earlier. "It's not much, but, you know, I'm trying to decide when I should call my dad. I hope he has her phone number. Maybe I'll go see her."

"Soon?" he said, already mentally rearranging his schedule so he could drive with her to Arizona.

"Well, not today," she said, giving a small laugh. "I'm tempted, but I just got here and there's the house Birch rented for us and the job Ely has for me. And Christmas and New Year's. Besides, I need to think about what I want to say to her. January might be a better month to go."

Relief washed over Lucas, though he wasn't sure why.

"Have you told Birch yet?" He was sure his aunt wouldn't take the news well. Though she thought she hid her feelings well, it was obvious to everyone that she had emotionally adopted Ruby. Aunt Birch was not likely to feel happy about Ruby reconnecting with her long lost mother.

"Not yet. I'm back at the lodge now. Nash went up to his room to rest and I'm waiting for her to finish a meeting about a story festival or something."

"The first annual Cardinal Valley Story Jam," Lucas said.

"The what?"

"Cassie's senior project. She'll be glad to tell you all about it. Look, are you free for dinner?"

"Sure, want to meet me at the Lone Pine at six? I'm dying for one of Carlos's green chile cheeseburgers."

He wanted to say no, he meant dinner

at a real restaurant like a real *date*. Someplace where they could be alone. At the Lone Pine, they might as well shout their conversation from the top of Mount Whitney. But he didn't. Because he still didn't know if the feelings he had for her were reciprocated. At some point, he knew, he'd just have to jump off that cliff and ask her.

But not tonight.

"I'll be there," he said. He sat in the truck's cab and stared at his motley band of horses until they wandered to the back of the pasture and were lost from sight.

13

Ruby

Ruby and Nash moved into the house Birch found for them a week and a half later, on Christmas Eve. Ruby stood in front of the gray and white clapboard house not quite believing her good fortune. On the dark red front door hung a fresh pine wreath tied with a white and silver ribbon. She knew that Birch had hung it there, just as she had supplied their furniture, dishes and flatware, pots and pans. She had arranged everything, assuring Ruby that it hadn't cost her a penny, that almost all of household goods were things they had in storage.

"In forty-five years of marriage, you acquire a lot of stuff," she told Ruby this morning while she helped Ruby pack. "If we didn't use it, it'd end up sitting in our attic or the storage building behind the lodge until it disintegrated."

"Thank you," Ruby said, knowing the words didn't convey all emotions she was feeling. Was this what it felt like to have a real mother? Though she didn't quite trust her good fortune, for a moment, she let herself bask in the comfort of Birch's nurturing.

"You and Nash go on and get settled," Birch said, folding one of Ruby's sweaters. First thing this morning she had put the keys to the house on Ruby's breakfast tray next to a fresh scone and hot coffee. "Don't forget Christmas Eve supper at seven p.m."

Ruby had turned back to the bird's eye maple bureau in the Dale Evans room, tears burning in her eyes. "I won't."

A few hours later, Ruby unlocked the front door and she stepped into the compact living room. Nash was two steps behind her.

"Sweet," he said, heading down the hallway. "Do I get my own room?"

"Birch says it has two bedrooms," Ruby called after him.

After a quick investigation of the house, they met back in the cheery yellow and white kitchen.

"Dibs on the back bedroom," Nash said. He threw his backpack down on the linoleum floor. "The one with the back door."

"Since there are only two bedrooms and only one is in the back and only one has an outside door, I think I know which one you mean," Ruby said, laughing. "I wanted the front bedroom anyway." That bedroom looked out on the wide front porch and faced east, catching the morning sun.

"So, what's for dinner, Ma?" he teased when they went back into the living room. He flopped down on the gray and green plaid sofa. Though there had been some uncomfortable moments between them since he told her about their mother, she'd been trying to get past her feelings of betrayal.

"Whatever you want to cook?" she retorted.

"Domino's pizza, it is," he said, grinning.

For a moment, it felt like when they were kids, before social services discovered they were essentially on their own, their father gone for weeks at a time. They'd eaten Domino's pepperoni pizza at least four times a week back then, though she had tried to make Nash eat a salad once or twice a week. She looked at his thin frame now and worried about the poor nutrition he'd had as a boy. She felt a pang of guilt. She should have done better.

"Actually, dinner is at the lodge," she said. "You'll love Bobby's Christmas Eve chili."

"C'mon, Ruby, again?" They'd eaten dinner at Birch and Bobby's house twice in the last week and met them for dinner at the Lone Pine once. "I was going over to the Red Coyote, practice with the band." His first gig was on New Year's Eve.

She frowned. "It'll only be a few hours. Besides, a bar isn't the proper place to be on Christmas Eve."

"Yeah, like we're such a proper family," he said, with a snort. "Let's hang the stockings by the fireplace and wait for Santa." He stood up and walked down the small hallway to his bedroom. "I love ya, Ruby Tuesday, but you ain't my mother."

She didn't answer, just watched him close the door.

Their mother. For a week and a half now, she had known about Loretta's whereabouts. Or rather Etta. Ruby knew the day was coming when she'd contact her mother, but she wasn't ready. Not yet.

On Ruby's second day in Cardinal, before she'd had dinner with Lucas, she found Birch and told her that she knew where her mother lived. They sat in Birch and Bobby's airy blue and white kitchen, the afternoon sun streaming through the lacy white curtains, drinking hot peppermint tea. Birch's face remained calm while Ruby quietly told how her father and brother had known about her mother and kept it from her. She interlaced her fingers and stared at them while she talked, watching her thumb knuckles turn white.

When Ruby was finished, feeling as drained as if she'd run a marathon, Birch said, "May I rant for you?"

Ruby nodded mutely, glad that they'd chosen to have this conversation in Birch's kitchen so no one could overhear them.

"I could just smack those two men silly!" she declared, slamming her palm down on the wood kitchen table, causing the wooden lazy Susan filled with Christmas candy and unshelled nuts to quiver. "After all you've been through, after all you've done for them. This is how they treat you? Oh, isn't that just like a couple of men. I'm so mad I could spit cherry pits. You had every right to know about your mama the minute she got back in touch with your daddy."

Her remark made Ruby crack a small smile. "Oh, Birch, thank you. I felt mean thinking those exact things. Now I don't feel so petty."

Birch reached over and patted Ruby's arm. "You are not petty. Not even close. What are you going to do?"

Ruby inhaled deeply and stared over Birch's shoulder at the hutch behind her that held Birch's collection of beaded Paiute pottery. "I don't know. I have to confront her, right? For, I don't know, closure?" She unclasped her hands, staring at her long fingers. Did her hands look like her mother's hands? What was her mother doing in that small desert town? "Or maybe it doesn't matter. She left and that's that."

Birch thought for a moment, her eyes never leaving Ruby's face. "Of course it matters. I can't tell you what to do, of course. But, I do know this. It matters. It matters what you feel and whatever you decide to do. It matters because . . ." She paused a moment, hesitating about her next words.

"What?" Ruby said.

Birch took one of Ruby's hands in both of hers. Ruby could feel the warmth seeping into her cold skin, feel the papery texture of Birch's dry palms. "Because it'll help you form who you'll be as a mother.

Whatever happens between you and your mother will influence your relationship with your own children someday."

Ruby's stomach felt like someone had wrapped it in barbed wire. "Maybe that's why I want to think before jumping into it. I'll decide after the holidays, once Nash and I have settled in."

Birch squeezed Ruby's hands. "A wise decision. Your heart will tell you when the time is right."

"Lucas agrees with you. You two are like those two little peas."

"He's a good boy," Birch had said, getting up to refill their coffee cups. "A good *man*."

Ruby had nodded silently, knowing what Birch was implying. Lucas was a good man. Don't pass up this opportunity. Ruby had felt both Lucas's and Birch's longings even back in Nashville, this expectation that she'd just slide into a romantic relationship with her late husband's brother and become the daughter that Birch had never had. She sensed their desire for her to fill the empty place that Cole had left in their lives.

She wished she could tell them it

wasn't that simple. She loved them for their kindness, their acceptance, their willingness to welcome her into their world, their family. But they didn't know that whenever she looked too long in Lucas's face, her sorrow for Cole and her love for him, the first she'd ever had for a man, was overwhelming. When she remembered Cole and their brief, joyful time together, time did funny things, memories swirled around in her head like a heady mixture of sweet and bitter. It was only a year since he died. It felt like both a lifetime and a minute.

Ruby stood in the doorway of her bedroom. The sparseness of the room gave her an odd sort of comfort. She studied each piece of furniture—the double bed with a white, wrought-iron headboard, a bird's eye maple chest of drawers—the twin to the one in the Dale Evans room—a white bedside table holding a lamp made from elk horns and, best of all, an old-fashioned maple rocker in the corner with a red and white quilt thrown over the back. The bedspread was white cotton, but at the foot of the bed rested a red and black Pendleton lap blanket showing a cowgirl on a rearing horse. A framed photograph of three horses in a lupine-dotted pasture under a snow-capped Mount Whitney hung over the bed. A note was propped up against the two embroidered pillowcases. Ruby recognized Birch's precise, flowing handwriting.

Hope you like the house. The furniture is hit and miss, I know, but it'll do. The Pendleton blanket is an early Christmas present from Bobby and me. Nash has one, too.

Love, Birch.

Ruby ran her hand over the heavy wool blanket.

"Hey, Ruby, did you see this?" Nash came into her room carrying an almost duplicate blanket, his depicting a cowboy. "Your friend, the lady from the lodge, gave it to me."

"Birch," she said. "Like the tree."

He grinned at her, looking again like he was eleven. "Hope I don't forget and call her oak or elm or eucalyptus."

She shook her head and laughed. "Please, try to be nice to everyone."

He came over and sat next to her on the bed, still clutching his blanket. "I'll try, Ruby Tuesday. It's just . . ." He hesitated, his face taut with doubt. "You know, people, you can't always . . . well . . . They have agendas, Ruby. Just remember, everyone has an agenda."

She took his long-fingered hand, too thin for a young man his size. His knuckles felt like little doorknobs, dollhouse knobs. "I understand what you're saying, but I promise, these people don't have anything to gain by being nice to me . . . to *us.* They're my friends. And they want to be your friend, too."

His face wasn't convinced. He pulled his hand away, brushed the long blond hair from his face. Eyes the exact pebbled gray as hers stared back at her. "Whatever gets you through the night, Ruby."

She stood up, irritated now. "I don't understand how you can be so cynical."

He interrupted her. "No, you don't understand, Ruby. There's a whole bunch of my life you don't understand because you weren't there. I know you're all into playing house now, pretending like we are some kind of family. But, this is your baby brother you're trying to fool. We aren't a family, we never have been. You and I . . . well, we had something. When we were young. But we've lived separate lives for a long, long time. This is your thing, and I guess it's cool, even though I don't think it'll last. When you disappoint them, they'll throw you away. How is it any different than any of those foster parents I had? Pity is all this feels like to me. I'll stay here awhile, but not forever. You gotta understand that when I'm ready to go, I'm out of here."

It was the longest speech she'd ever heard him make. And the most honest. She put her face in her hands, suddenly sickened by her own stupidity, her own neediness, her own pathetic longing. But no tears came. It felt like she had no tears left in her body. She'd cried them all out for Cole and, in the last year, for Nash.

"Hey, don't," he said softly, touching her forearm in that way he used to wake her up when they were kids and he was scared by some sound in the dark. "I'm sorry, Ruby. I didn't mean to screw this up for you. I . . ."

She lifted her head so he could see she wasn't crying. "No, you may be right about the people here. I guess time will tell. But it's a place for me to stay and I understand if you need to eventually move on. But, just promise me you'll try it for a few months. I just want to make sure you're healthy. Please, just do that for me."

"Sure," he said, always accommodating. Like he was as a boy. Telling people what they wanted to hear until he simply disappeared. "I bet you ten bucks that you can't take one more month of me."

"Sucker bet," she said. "Now, get out of my room. You're taking up all the air." It was something she used to say to him when they were kids, when she was weary of him hanging around in her room, chattering about his day at school.

"Say, don't we have a party to go to?" he asked, standing up.

She smiled at him. He was at least trying. "Wait'll you taste Bobby's chili. And he dresses up like Santa. Then we all stand around the piano and sing Christmas carols."

"Wow," Nash said, wrapping his Pendleton blanket around his shoulders like shawl. "These people are radically intense about their holidays, aren't they?"

14

Ruby

"Wondered when you'd get here," Sueann said, when Ruby and Nash walked through the lodge doors a few hours later. She gave Ruby an enthusiastic hug. "You've been here two whole weeks and we've barely gotten to talk." She nodded at Nash. "Nice to see you again."

He gave her a wide smile. "Good seeing you, too. Love your Western omelets. Best I've ever eaten."

Sueann beamed. "Thanks!"

"I'm going to get some food," Nash said. "See you two later."

"I'm sorry," Ruby said, watching Nash

head toward the crystal bowl of eggnog. "I've sort of hit the ground running since I got here."

She set down a green plaid vinyl bag filled with gifts. Most were books, bought last minute at The Novel Experience. She'd spent more than she'd made working as a part-time clerk at the bookstore this last week, but she couldn't come to the party empty-handed. "I need to put these under the tree. There are gifts for you and Cassie." She unwrapped her red wool scarf.

"Thanks, I'll open mine tomorrow at the café. It'll make my Christmas day bearable." Sueann's divorce agreement with Derek stated that Cassie, in exchange for living with Sueann during the school year, would spend every Christmas Eve and Day until she turned eighteen at the McGavin ranch. "This is the *final* year Cassie is required to spend Christmas at the ranch." Sueann clapped her hands like a child, her freckled cheeks pink with emotion. "Hallelujah. Of course, next year she'll be off at college and probably won't even come home." She sighed and picked up Ruby's bag of gifts. "June

McGavin wins again. Because of her, I missed most of my girl's Christmas mornings."

Ruby hung up her jacket and scarf on a wooden coat rack next to the double doors. "You know, despite being here two weeks, I haven't even seen June yet."

"Oh, the wicked witch of Cardinal Valley is still flying around on her broomstick," Sueann said, rolling her translucent green eyes. "Derek says she's just been up to her diamond-studded ears in real estate negotiations. I guess the ranch needs some quick cash so they're trying to sell the pasture that borders Clear Creek. That property they tried to develop last year fell through. Drilled for water and came up dry."

"Does Lucas know about that? Who's buying it?"

"To answer your second question first, I don't know. I never have been privy to McGavin family business even when I was technically part of the family. And I assume Lucas knows. Why wouldn't he?"

"If they plan on developing it, he'll be angry. It'll ruin Clear Creek."

"No doubt."

Ruby knew Lucas would be upset about the sale not just because he boarded his rescue horses at Clear Creek, but also because that piece of land was special. It was where he and Cole used to camp when they were boys. Selling the land bordering Clear Creek likely meant the construction of fancy log houses owned by people who built them as investments. Many would become rentals that often meant loud, late-night parties and drunks tearing up the pristine landscape with their off-road vehicles and snowmobiles.

"You know June," Sueann said. "She's all about keeping up the façade that the McGavins still have money and power in this county." She held up Ruby's bag of gifts. "I'll put this in the office. Birch decorated a special tree for the family. We're going to open a few gifts later, after the public party."

"Okay," Ruby said, glancing around for Nash.

"Not even rum in the eggnog?" he'd said when she told him earlier that Birch and Bobby didn't serve alcohol at their party. The lodge didn't have a liquor permit and, besides, Birch said, there are enough places for people to drink in Cardinal.

"What does it matter?" she'd answered. "You're not supposed to be drinking."

He'd refused to meet her eyes.

"He's over by the dessert table with Cassie," Sueann said, poking Ruby's shoulder. "Quit being such a mother hen." Her voice went low. "You know there's no alcohol here."

"Right," Ruby said, feeling a little foolish. "Who's the guy with them?" The dark-haired young man had long sideburns past his earlobes like her father used to wear in the '70s. He wore faded blue jeans, a green plaid cowboy shirt and a light brown fedora-type hat.

Sueann fingered one of her long, reddish blond braids. "Cassie's latest love. Shoot, that girl might be book smart, but her man-Q is subpar. He's another musician. You'd have thought she'd learned with the last one." Sueann brought a hand to her mouth. "Oh, man, hit me with a wet noodle. I'm sorry. I forgot Nash was a musician."

"No offense taken. You're right. Musicians aren't the most stable people on earth." Ruby nodded at Mr. Fedora. "At least this one isn't dressed like he's going to a funeral every day."

"Amen to that, sister. Thank goodness the Goth look is so last year, at least with Cassie."

Nash, Cassie and her boyfriend seemed to be engaged in a spirited conversation about something. Rodeo, the young girl who was a niece or cousin's niece or something to Bobby, was looking at Nash with the same adoring gaze Ruby had seen too many times since Nash had been a teenager.

"Yeah," Sueann said, grabbing a candy cane from a wooden dish made from a duck decoy. "Although Chad seems slightly better than that last loser, in my opinion, he's still too old for her." She tore the wrapper from the candy and licked it. "He's twenty-one. But my darling daughter informed me that she is now eighteen and who she dates is *legally* none of my business."

Ruby cocked her head. "Really?"

"I know. Irritating as panty hose, but

technically she's right. I can't stop her, but I've also informed her that she can now officially go to big-girl's prison." Sueann gave a wicked grin. "As if that scares anyone below the age of twenty-five. Wouldn't have me. Anyway, his dad is the new manager of the Cardinal Valley Bank. They moved here just a little while after you left. He plays the banjo, goes to school online studying to be a . . . get this . . . *writer*. And, according to Cassie, he writes *awesome* poetry."

Ruby smiled. "That and five bucks will buy you lunch at McDonald's."

Sueann lifted one shoulder. "I can only hope that it fizzles out come September when she goes away to college. Look out, it appears Santa has you in his eye-sight. See you round the punch bowl."

Ruby looked up to see Santa Claus limping toward her, using a cane painted to look like a red and white peppermint stick. His black eyes sparkled behind his fake beard. "Miss Ruby, I've been looking for you."

Ruby hugged Bobby Hernandez. His Santa suit smelled of freshly laundered cotton. "Hey, Santa! You feel like you've been eating a few too many sugar cookies. Or is that padding?"

"Don't tell Birch," he whispered. "But I didn't need the extra padding this year. If she finds out, she'll put me on a starvation diet."

"Mum's the word," Ruby said, laughing, knowing that Birch likely knew his weight to the ounce. "Why don't we sit down? You're Santa. Everyone should be coming to *you*."

"I do believe I will," he said, allowing her to take his arm. "We'll be passing out presents to the kids soon. Want to be one of my elves?"

"I'd be honored," she said, picking up the needlepoint Christmas tree pillow from the overstuffed chair and setting it to the side. "Would you like anything to drink or eat?"

He waved his hand. "No, thanks. I've been sampling for the last hour. I'm full as a tick. But you go on and get yourself something. Try the chili. I'm told it's the best in Tokopah County."

"I've heard that exact same thing. Maybe I'll just sit here next to you for a moment." She pulled up a small footstool and sat down. "My feet are screaming for a break."

"Ely said business at the bookstore is really picking up these days. Said you came on staff at the perfect time."

Ruby shrugged. "He's just being nice. I needed the job more than he needed me."

Bobby tilted his head, his wide, copper face thoughtful. "Ely's not prone to exaggeration."

Ruby looked away, warmed by the praise but also embarrassed. She knew there were plenty of people Ely could have hired. She glanced over at the long tables where Birch stood guard over the chili, cornbread, tamales and other casseroles brought by friends and neighbors. She held a bright red spatula and wore one of her many Christmas sweaters. This one depicted a Christmas tree made of acrobatic reindeer. Rudolph was, of course, the angel on top. Their eyes met and Birch waved the kitchen utensil at Ruby, then waved it over the food like a snowy-haired Christmas fairy.

Ruby held up an index finger indicating she would be there in a moment. She turned back to Bobby. "Thank you for the

Pendleton blanket . . . blankets. I love mine and I know Nash loves his, too."

Bobby patted her hand, the warmth from his palm like a miniature heater. "You're welcome. It was a two-fold good deed. The Western Film Museum gift shop was having a slow month, so we did most of our Christmas shopping there."

"I love it doubly, then. Keep that money circulating here in Cardinal."

"That's the idea," he said, nodding. A trio of girls with black braids and glittering button eyes sidled up to Bobby. They looked to be about six or seven. The tallest one giggled, causing the other two to follow suit.

"Go on," encouraged a young woman sporting two similar braids tied with red and green ribbon. "Tell Santa what you want him to put in your stockings."

"Ho, ho, ho," Bobby said, leaning forward, his white smile almost the same color as his fake beard. "What can I bring you lovely young ladies?"

Ruby stood up. "Looks like you've got business to attend to, Santa. I think I'll mosey over to the buffet."

"Candy cane?" Bobby said to the girls. "They're cotton-candy flavored. Freshly made last night by my industrious elves." He winked at Ruby.

Ruby was standing in the food line when a raspy voice behind her said, "I heard you were back."

Ruby turned to face June McGavin. Her late husband's mother wore an elegant black Western shirt embroidered with bright turquoise horseshoes, a full black skirt and shiny black boots. Her pale complexion showed only the slightest wrinkling in her cheeks and around her dark brown eyes. With a casual glance, she could have passed for a decade younger than her sixty years.

"Merry Christmas, June," Ruby said carefully. She still felt nervous as an alley cat whenever she was around June, despite the fact that since selling her portion of the ranch back to the family a year ago, she was no longer any kind of threat to her former mother-in-law.

June nodded, not returning the holiday greeting. "You didn't like Tennessee? I thought that's where your people were from."

My people, thought Ruby. What a strange remark. The only people she "had" were Nash, her fly-by-night dad and a mother she hadn't seen in almost twenty-three years. "It was fine. But it's good to be back in Cardinal."

"Really?" Her gaze was steady, unblinking. "I can't imagine what this town has to offer you." She raised one perfect eyebrow. "Or your brother. I heard he has a few . . . problems. You are aware our social services for the indigent are already quite overburdened in this county."

Anger flared up in Ruby's chest. "I can take care of my brother."

June gave a slow smile. "I'm sure you can. I was only trying to give you some advice. Maybe a larger city would fit his particular needs better."

Ruby bit the inside of her cheek, knowing that if she opened her mouth, she'd start screaming at this woman and embarrass herself. Lucas had warned her that his mom hadn't changed. Cole's death had seemed to make her only more brittle and angry.

Ruby walked around June without answering and headed for the buffet table.

Birch was ladling out a bowl of chili for Rodeo. The young girl wore a red peasant blouse and tight black jeans. Her shiny raven-colored hair was pulled into a French braid dotted with miniature red flowers.

"Cheddar cheese and onions," she instructed Birch. "That's how Nash likes it." She giggled, making her seem fifteen instead of the twenty-two-year-old college graduate that Ruby knew she was.

Birch arched her pale eyebrows. "He does, does he? Why, pray tell, isn't he fetching his own supper?"

"A tamale, too, please," Rodeo said, ignoring Birch's question. "Green chile cheese."

Birch's lips pressed together while she silently dished up the tamale.

"Thanks!" Rodeo flung over her shoulder as she scurried back to where Nash was still talking intently to Cassie's new boyfriend.

"I'm sorry," Ruby said, coming up beside Birch.

"For what, sweetie?"

Ruby nodded at her brother, who accepted the bowl of chili from Rodeo, granting her one of his brilliant smiles. "They met a couple of weeks ago at the Red Coyote. I think she has a crush."

"Not your fault some silly girl is attracted to your brother. He is a nice-looking boy." Birch shook her head. "Why do we women make such fools of ourselves over men? I'll never know." She picked up a ceramic bowl and started filling it with chili. "You look hungry. What's Senor Claus up to?"

"Busy listening to Christmas wishes." Ruby accepted the offered bowl from Birch. "Cheese only, please. No onions."

"No onions?" Birch's eyes squinted slightly with good humor. "Plan on spending some time under the mistletoe?"

Ruby gave a tight smile. "As if I don't have enough problems." She busied herself with doctoring her chili with sour cream and Maxie's famous sourdough croutons, pretending not to see the disappointed expression on Birch's face.

"Will you and Nash be coming by the house tomorrow?" Birch asked.

"Sure, but probably later in the day. I told Sueann we'd eat Christmas dinner at the café."

Birch stirred the chili. "Usually she and Cassie come by for leftovers in the evening after Cassie gets back from the ranch."

Ruby wondered if it bothered Birch that she and Bobby were still not welcome at the Circle MG ranch, where Birch had been born and raised. She knew Birch's father turned his back on his only daughter when Birch married Bobby and that when he died, her brother, Carson, continued the cruel tradition. Once Carson died, June made it clear they were still unwelcome. Lucas told Ruby all of this last year when she first came to Cardinal. Maybe, after all these years, it didn't matter to Birch. Maybe the ranch held too many bad memories and she wouldn't go back even if she could.

"You know," Birch said, "Lucas also comes by after his appearance at June's fancy-pants dinner. I think I actually enjoy Christmas night more than I do the big meal at noon. It's certainly more relaxing. Some of Bobby's family always sticks around, but mostly by then the whole clan has moved on to someone else's house." Bobby had aunts, uncles, first, second and third cousins and stepbrothers and sisters from Riverside to Reno. Birch said they'd never had the exact same bunch for Christmas, but it was always fun.

Last year Ruby hadn't known Birch and Bobby well enough to be invited to their house for Christmas leftovers. A sense of joy came from knowing she and Nash were included with Sueann, Cassie and Lucas. But it troubled her a little, too. When Birch and Lucas finally understood that a relationship between her and Lucas would never happen, would they react like Nash predicted and reject her? How would she be able to stand that?

"Thanks, Birch," she said. "We'd love to drop by." She held up her bowl. "After I eat this, I'll help you serve."

"As the kids say . . . no worries." Birch grinned as if she'd invented the saying herself. "Everything's under control."

"You are so hip," Ruby said, smiling. "And I think I just made myself less so by using the word *hip*."

"Who can keep up?" Birch said. "Enjoy your dinner and relax a little. You deserve a night off."

Ruby found a free chair in a corner. It sat partially hidden behind a large artificial blue spruce Christmas tree covered with shiny glass pinecone and cardinal bird ornaments. The spot gave her a panoramic view of the crowded room. She loved studying the hotel guests and townsfolk without them knowing. It was one of the things she'd enjoyed about being a waitress. As a server, she'd had an anonymity that caused people to talk as if she wasn't even there. Some servers found it insulting. Ruby always found it fascinating. It was like doing scientific research on wild animals who didn't realize you were observing them.

She watched the front doors open; frigid air rushed in, reaching her half-hidden perch. Lucas stepped over the threshold, followed by Ely. Both men stomped their feet and rubbed their ungloved hands together. Lucas's eyes searched the room, lingering a moment when he saw Nash with Cassie and her boyfriend. Ruby knew he was looking for her, but she wasn't ready to talk to him. She'd seen him a few times this week, but she'd worked so many hours at the bookstore that their encounters were only a few minutes long while both grabbed a quick meal at the Lone Pine Café's busy counter.

She was grateful they were both so busy, keeping them from being alone. Looking at Lucas's face, so physically similar to his oldest brother's, broke her heart. The holiday celebrations rekindled painful memories of Cole, reminding her that they hadn't experienced even one Christmas together. She and Cole met last January, married three months later and by October, he was dead. She wondered if she'd ever like Christmas again.

"Holidays are a psychiatrist's nightmare," a woman's voice said beside her.

Ruby looked up to see Dr. Collins standing next to her. She'd waited on the doctor at The Novel Experience this last week, helping her pick out some children's books for a friend's grandchildren and a book on old railroads to send to her uncle who lived in an assisted-living home in San Jose.

"I guess you'd know," she said, giving

the older woman a polite smile. Ely had told her that Margaret Collins was a retired psychiatrist.

"Maddie Collins, in case you don't remember me," she said, pulling up a chair and placing it next to Ruby. "Whew, that feels good. I love these shoes, but they aren't made for walking or standing." She lifted the edge of her long black skirt to reveal red four-inch pumps. "You helped me pick out books this week."

"I remember," Ruby said, thinking she should feel uncomfortable around this woman, considering her profession. However, the long-faced woman with the silver hair in a loose bun just seemed like someone's nice aunt. "Were you able to mail your books in time?"

Maddie nodded. "Sent them FedEx, which cost me a fortune, but at least they were guaranteed delivery by today." She gave Ruby a lop-sided smile. "The girls won't care. Their parents and grandparents probably bought them a stable of ponies for Christmas. But my uncle will be grateful."

"Good." Ruby looked back over the crowd, not certain what else to say.

"I love this town," Maddie said, giving a loud sigh. "But though it's my third year here and I've made some good friends, I still miss my late husband."

"How long have you been widowed?"

"Five years. This time of year, it is so easy to dwell in the idealistic past. It's not that my husband and I did much to celebrate Christmas. He wasn't very sentimental. It's the in-your-face expectations that the holidays always bring. I *know* I am being manipulated by the media and yet . . ." She touched one of her long silver earrings. "I still feel like I'm somehow missing the party." She chuckled. "Despite the fact I'm smack dab in the middle of a party!"

Ruby couldn't help smiling back at the woman. She liked her honesty. "I know what you mean. I should feel happy because I'm alive, I'm healthy and my brother is here with me, yet . . ."

"All you can think about is what might have been," Maddie said softly.

Ruby nodded.

"Just remember, dear," Maddie said, standing up. "It's only a few days out of a whole year. I'll tell you a professional secret." Her voice went low, like the purr of a large cat. "Everyone I've ever known who was honest with themselves feels the very same things you and I are feeling. Even . . . no, maybe especially . . . the ones who act the happiest."

She squeezed Ruby's shoulder. "I think I'll try some of that eggnog." She sailed away toward the buffet table, her fingers wiggling good-bye. "You'll do fine, dear. Most of us are stronger than we think and we all have more control than we realize. Thanks again for your help with my gifts."

"Thank you," Ruby whispered. Though what Maddie Collins had said was simple and obvious, it *had* made Ruby feel better. She was right; it was just a few days. The rest of the year and the next and the next spread out in front of her like a newly paved highway. Whatever this next year brought, she *would* do fine.

She stood up, brushed her hands down the front of her black jeans. She would go help Birch serve food, that great comforter in good times and bad. She would talk to people and wish them a happy holiday, a Merry Christmas, a peaceful New Year and she would mean it. She would not worry about her brother, whether he was finding any alcohol, whether she could make him happy, how long or if he would stay.

For a day or two, she'd try not to think about her mother and about whether she should call her, go see her, send her a letter or just leave her be. Ruby would just relax and let each day unfold.

And before she went to Sueann's tomorrow for Christmas dinner, she'd go by the cemetery and put flowers on Cole's grave. She had a bouquet of red tulips on her table at home. Then, just to cover all the bases, she would drive alone out to Clear Creek again, climb the fence and place a single flower at the foot of the huge old cottonwood tree that Cole had loved so much.

15

Lucas

"Can someone tell me where this year went?" the old man asked Lucas on New Year's Eve. The electric sign above Cardinal Valley Bank stated thirty-two degrees at nine forty-seven p.m. The line at Holy Grounds's free hot coffee and donut booth was the longest at the First Night celebration.

The man wore a puffy green ski jacket and a dirty Winnemucca Fly Fishing School cap. The strong scent of alcohol told anyone within ten feet that he had already started celebrating the New Year even though midnight was a little over two hours away. Cardinal First Night started as a way for the town to combat loud, out-of-control New Year's Eve parties and cut down on drunk-driving accidents. A half-mile stretch of Main Street was cordoned off and there was a huge block party, with food and craft booths, carnival games for the kids, mimes, clowns, magicians, trick ropers and even an Ask the Rabbi booth that was manned by a young Orthodox Jewish rabbi who liked to vacation with his family at the Tokopah Lodge. The local teenagers had initially tried to bait Rabbi Ben and found instead someone who was willing to talk and listen about subjects like tattoos, piercings, serving in the military and the eternal quest for the perfect bagel.

Lucas glanced over at Ruby, who was taking a shift at the coffeehouse's booth. She gave him an amused wink.

"How about you, young woman?" the old man said, pointing to the apple cider donuts with cream cheese frosting. "Can you tell me where this last year went? A large cup of that joe, please."

"I have no idea, sir," she said, using a white paper napkin to pick up two donuts and put them in a brown paper sack. "I swear Christmas was yesterday." She poured a paper cup of coffee.

"How much do I owe you?" he asked.

"It's free, though a donation to the Cardinal Valley Boys and Girls Club would be appreciated." She nodded at the jumbo pickle jar half filled with change and dollar bills.

"Good woman," he said, ignoring the jar and staggering off down the crowded Main Street. He bumped into a mime, snapped something at him, then kept going. Without the man realizing, the mime started following him, mimicking his inebriated walk. A few onlookers chuckled at the performance.

"Hope he eats those donuts soon," she commented to Lucas.

He smiled. "And drinks that coffee."

She pushed back a strand of hair and laughed. "Yes, we definitely want our drunks to stay wide awake. So, what have you been up to this last week of the year?"

"Just the same old thing. When is your shift up?"

Ruby looked at her black Timex watch. "I'm here for the duration, but I can take a break. I've been handing out donuts since six p.m."

"Are you hungry?"

"I've been craving a corn dog since they started frying them three hours ago."

"My treat."

She turned to the teenage girl next to her. "I'm taking a break, Lila. When Ely comes back, tell him I'll be back in an hour."

"No problem," the girl said. "We've got plenty of help."

"Ely keeps you on a short rope," Lucas said, regretting the words the instant he said them.

Ruby's face froze for a second. Her reprimanding gray eyes met his. "That was a remark worthy of your mother." Her tone was tart and annoyed, like a substitute teacher pushed too far. "I work for him, Lucas, but tonight is purely voluntary. No one has me on a rope."

Lucas ducked his head, his face hot.

"Shoot, I'm sorry, Ruby. You're right, that was a June McGavin remark if there ever was one. I don't know . . ."

"Forget it," she said, with an audible sigh.

Lucas touched the rim of his hat with two fingers. "My deepest apologies, ma'am."

"Oh, stop with the lame cowboy affectations." She bumped him with her shoulder. "That might work on your silly girlfriends, but it doesn't fly with me."

He almost said that there weren't any silly girlfriends, not any girlfriends at all, but for once, he kept the remark to himself. "I'll still buy you a corn dog."

"And I'll accept it."

At ten p.m., the street was shoulder to shoulder with, it seemed to Lucas, every citizen in Tokopah County. The Ask the Rabbi booth had a respectable six people in line. Ruby waved to the young man with the blue and silver yarmulke.

"Have you talked to Rabbi Ben yet?" Ruby asked while they stood in line for their corn dogs.

"His line's too long," Lucas said, glad that Ruby had chosen not to dwell on his

stupid remark about her and Ely. "Besides, I'd have no idea what to ask him."
He bought two corn dogs and two bottles of Coke. "Mustard?"

"Nope, I'm a purist." She took the corn dog and the Coke. "The curb okay for you?"

"I've eaten in worse places."

"What are you working on now?" Ruby asked after they sat down.

Lucas took a long drag of his Coke. "Made two sales at Cowtown Christmas, so I'm starting on the first of those. And I've been commissioned by Mustang Days again to do the All Around Cowboy and Cowgirl saddles. I'm cranking out some cell phone holders and some bracelets . . . both Cassie's ideas. I'm keeping busy."

"Do you ever miss being a lawyer?"

The question took him by surprise. He looked at her a minute before answering. "Sometimes. Why?"

She shrugged, took a small bite of her corn dog. "I guess it seems funny to me to spend so much time learning something, and then never use it."

"Funny?"

"Wrong word choice. Maybe sad . . . odd."

He looked down at the tips of his good Lucchese cowboy boots. The left toe had a large scrape in the leather. When had that happened? "Odd is so much better. Thanks."

She stretched out her legs, her face troubled. "I'm sorry, Lucas. I'm not saying at all what I mean. I'm in awe of anyone who could go through that much college, take the bar and all. I guess I don't understand how you can walk away from all that."

He stood up, tossing his mustard-smeared corn dog in the trash. "Guess who's sounding like June McGavin now?"

She stood up, keeping her corn dog in her hand. "You're right. I'm being horrible. I'm really sorry."

"Forget it. I think that's an exact quote from a good friend of mine."

"Sounds very wise," she said, giving him a tentative smile.

"How's Nash doing?" he asked, changing the subject. The last thing he wanted to talk about was his failed career as a lawyer.

She nibbled on her corn dog, giving herself time to consider her answer. "He's okay, I guess. He has a gig at the Rusty Dog tonight. It's on the road to Mammoth."

"I know the place. Are you going there later to listen to him?"

She shook her head. "He says he'd prefer I didn't. I just hope . . ." She let her voice trail off.

"He stays sober?"

She nodded, her gray eyes cloudy. "He hasn't been drinking since we moved here so I don't know why I'm worried."

Lucas looked down at his boots, afraid she would see the truth in his eyes. Yesterday, when he was filling up his truck with gas at the cheap station north of town, he had seen her brother buying a bottle of Seagram's in the station's minimart. Did she really think he'd stopped drinking? Could she possibly be that naïve?

Or, he thought, was it more likely that she was doing what humans have done since the beginning of time, seeing what she wanted so desperately to see rather than what was really there. Was it his place to force her into seeing the truth before she was ready? Besides, though he felt selfish and petty, he didn't want to be the person she equated with bad news.

These were the types of dilemmas that always confused Lucas. He'd often wondered why didn't they teach these kinds of things in high school. Instead of learning a few years of algebra and geometry, subjects he'd never had any reason to use and didn't even remember, they should teach kids a class called Life 101, show a person whether it was better to tell a friend her brother was still drinking or better letting her find out on her own. That was certainly more useful than the crap about two trains traveling at the same speed going in opposite directions.

"I should get back to the booth," Ruby said, finishing her Coke.

"Hey, Ruby. Lucas." Ely walked up to them, carrying three pink bakery boxes. His long black hair hung free from its customary braid. "Happy New Year."

Lucas glanced at his watch. "You're about two hours early."

"Hey, Ely," Ruby said. "I was just heading back to the donut booth."

Ely lifted one eyebrow at Lucas and shrugged under his faded flannel shirt. "I may not see you at the stroke of midnight, partner. Just getting my greetings in early."

"Very organized," Ruby said, laughing. "Very businesslike."

"I do my best, Miss Ruby."

She smiled and took the top bakery box without asking. "I'll help you carry these."

"Ha," Ely said. "You just want first pick."

"You're onto me," she said, bringing her nose to the box lid. "Do I smell cinnamon rolls? My favorite."

Ely grinned at Lucas. "The lady has the nose of a bloodhound."

"Donut hound," Ruby said, laughing.

"A Tokopah County donut hound," Ely said. "New up-and-coming breed. I hear they are the canines to beat this year at Westminster."

"Absolutely," Ruby said, peeking into the box.

Lucas knew he should join in the joking, but he couldn't. It was petty and childish and he'd cut off his right index finger before he'd admit it, but he was jealous of the easy words flowing between Ruby and Ely. Ely was his best friend and Ruby . . . well, Ruby was Ruby. He'd let himself fantasize too much this last year about what might happen if she came back. Nowhere in that imagined scenario was Ely anything but a secondary character.

"You okay?" Ruby asked.

It took Lucas a few seconds to realize she was talking to him.

"Yeah, fine. Just . . ." He waved his hand at her, never mind.

She laid a hand on his forearm. "I know, Lucas. I miss Cole, too."

"We all do," Ely said.

Lucas ducked his head, unable to look at either of them. "Think I'm getting a migraine. Catch you later." He turned abruptly and started walking away from Ruby and Ely.

"Feel better," he heard Ruby call over the crowd. Ely said something, but the words were lost to Lucas in the hum of the crowd.

Lucas raised his hand in reply, not turning around. As he walked through the throngs of people, his head actually started aching. Could a person talk himself into a migraine? By the time he reached the street that led to his apartment, he was already starting to feel that sick aura that came right before a headache sparked like a comet in his brain. He took the steps to his garage apartment two at a time, his head throbbing each time his boot hit wood. Without turning on the lights, he went to the medicine cabinet, found the bottle of migraine pills by feel and took two, dipping his head and drinking straight from the faucet. Back in his apartment's living room, he pulled off his boots and lay down on the sofa.

In the distance, he could still hear the animated voices of the crowd celebrating the coming New Year. Lucas pushed his head back into the sofa pillow, willing the pills to do their job and fight off the civil war taking place inside his skull. He didn't know how much time had passed, how many times he dozed and awoke, before he heard gunshots telling him the New Year had arrived. The sheriff was going to be pissed, his warnings ignored again. The headache was still there, a dull throb now, held cautiously at bay if he didn't move too quickly.

"Happy freakin' New Year," he whispered to the dark, thinking about Ruby, thinking about Cole, then, when the gunshots finally stopped, falling asleep and dreaming about nothing.

16

Birch

"There's money missing from petty cash again," Birch told Sueann on New Year's Day. They were in the back storage room of the Lone Pine Café. It was ten a.m. and the breakfast rush had been over for an hour. The lunch crowd wouldn't start trickling in for another hour and a half. Sueann was using the lull to check her supplies. Birch waited to elaborate while Sueann counted the large cans of peaches and fruit cocktail.

"Twelve," Sueann said under her breath, then looked up from her clipboard. "I'm so sorry, Birch. Do you think it's the new girl? What's her name . . . Roper? Stetson?" The warm room caused small curls to form around her freckled face.

Birch gave a weak smile. "Rodeo. I've been consciously not trying to think that."

Sueann grinned and tapped the clipboard twice with her yellow pencil. "That's right . . . Row-day-oh. Bada-bing. I was just kidding with you." She leaned back against the metal shelves, hugging the clipboard to her chest. "She is the newest employee and everyone else has been with you for years. It's kind of logical."

Birch stuck her hands into the pockets of her fleece jacket. Despite the warm room, her hands felt like ice cubes. "This time it's sixty dollars. With the other money missing, that makes it a hundred in the last month."

Sueann lifted one eyebrow. "How long has she worked there?"

Birch flexed her fingers inside her jacket, wondering if she should have just kept the theft to herself. "Two months. But she's such a sweet girl."

Sueann flipped her head, causing her

strawberry blond braid to flick like a whip. "So were Lizzie Borden and Ma Barker, I'm told."

Birch gave a rueful smile. "Thank you for at least putting the problem in perspective."

"My pleasure. Are you going to tell Bobby about this missing money?"

"Not yet," Birch said. "I'll just do some quiet checking on my own. Maybe it's a guest, which would be disappointing but preferable to Rodeo."

"No kidding. Say, have you seen Lucas today? He's usually here for breakfast—two scrambled eggs, two bacon strips crisp, sourdough toast with butter and three cups of coffee. Every day, rain or shine, he's planted in that third stool. Is he sick? Maybe celebrate a little too much New Year's last night?"

"Oh, dear, he's beginning to sound like a predictable old bachelor, isn't he?" Birch said. "No, I haven't seen him since early last night when he was perfectly sober. His truck was in the driveway, so I assume he's sleeping in."

"We have to find him a woman," Sueann said.

Birch cocked her head and didn't answer. Sueann was close to Lucas's age.

Sueann held up a protesting hand. "What you're thinking is written all over your face. I don't want anyone fixing me up, either. I'm happy being a cranky old divorcée whose child will soon be jetting out of the nest." She stuck her pencil behind her ear. "The difference is I really am okay with being alone. Lucas seems so lonely. I thought when Ruby got back . . ." She shrugged.

"You are preaching to the choir," Birch said, patting Sueann's shoulder. "I thought there might be something there, too. Lord knows I want it to come to pass, but Bobby keeps telling me that I'm way off, that Ruby and Lucas getting together would be disastrous."

"Maybe he's right. I mean, she was married to Cole. That would be a little weird."

"Have you and Ruby talked about it?" Birch assumed that because Sueann and Ruby were close in age, they'd discussed Ruby's possible interest in Lucas.

Sueann shook her head. "We've only

been able to get together twice for coffee since she's come back, what with the holidays and her moving and getting her brother settled. When we did talk, it was mostly about Cassie and Nash." Sueann's lips moved into a straight line. "I'm worried about that brother of hers. Ruby says he's sober, but he just doesn't look . . ." She paused a moment, then said, "I shouldn't be gossiping, but . . ."

"I know what you mean. She's trying so hard to make a life for them."

"It's understandable. She's the only real mother he's ever had."

Birch nodded. "I suppose all we can do is be there for her."

"To pick up the pieces?"

"Hopefully not that drastic," Birch said.

Sueann glanced at her watch and set her clipboard on a giant can of tomatoes. "It's almost eleven. The hungry hordes will soon be descending."

"I'd better get out there. Ruby's meeting me here for lunch."

The café was already three-quarters full. Sueann and Birch surveyed the room. In a corner booth, Ruby stood up and waved to them.

"There's my lunch date now," Birch said, turning to give Sueann a hug. "Thanks for letting me bend your ear."

"Anytime," Sueann said. "After all the whining about Cassie you've had to hear? I owe you about two thousand hours."

Birch moved through the crowded café, calling out greetings to half the room. She could not imagine what it would feel like to walk into a place and not see someone she knew. How did people survive in the city without dying of loneliness?

"Good morning, Birch," Ruby said, hugging her. "Or I guess it's almost afternoon. I slept until ten a.m. this morning, so I'm all thrown off."

"I know what you mean," Birch said, slipping into the bench seat across from her. "I only stayed out until twelve thirty, but I feel like a truck has run over me." She patted her short, gray curls. "And I didn't even drink one bit of the demon rum."

Ruby grinned at her. "Neither did I. Though I did have two donuts, a corn dog, one large cotton candy and a caramel apple."

"That could be an invitation to some powerful dreams."

Ruby laughed, her gray eyes clear and steady. "Fortunately, I had Pepcid at home. Slept like a baby. Didn't even hear Nash come in after his gig last night." She ducked her head to study the menu.

Their waitress walked up, a twenty-something woman who had just moved to town. Sueann told Birch that the girl's husband was a new sheriff's deputy. "What can I get y'all?"

"That sure sounds familiar," Ruby said to the girl whose nametag stated "Darla May." "My brother and I just moved here from Tennessee."

"Really?" Her smile widened. "I'm from Memphis."

"We're native Californians, but our mother was born in east Tennessee." Ruby looked down at the plastic menu. "We were living in Nashville because my brother was working there. Nash is a musician."

Darla May cocked her hip. "You mean Nash Stoddard? You're his sister? We heard him last night at the Rusty Dog. Man, his guitar playing is sick."

Ruby rested a hand on top of her menu. “Yes, he is very good.”

“He was rockin’ last night. Havin’ a good time, just like the rest of us. I’m, like, so thrashed this morning.” She looked behind her and lowered her voice. “Don’t tell Sueann. Only Excedrin and Red Bull is going to help me make it through this day. I can’t even imagine what your brother is feeling. *Everyone* was buying him shots last night.”

Birch watched Ruby’s face turn still as a deer in a hunter’s sight. Birch blurted out, “What are you having for lunch? Sueann says the fried chicken is a new recipe. I’m starving, though after all I ate last night I shouldn’t be.”

“The chicken is definitely killer,” Darla May said. “I think the new recipe is made with some kind of buttermilk and chili powder.”

Ruby bit her bottom lip and stared at her menu, a small frown wrinkling her brow. “After my junk-food fest last night, I think I’m going to stick with a salad. I’ll have the Santa Fe. Hold the tortilla strips.” She handed the menu back to the waitress. “And an iced tea.”

"The same for me," Birch said, wanting the girl to go away before the subject of Nash and his drinking came up again.

Once the waitress left, there were a few moments of awkward silence.

"All settled into your place?" Birch finally said.

Ruby smiled gratefully. "Yes, thank you again for finding us such a wonderful home. It reminds me a little of the house Cole and I rented in San Juan Capistrano." The skin around Ruby's eyes softened in memory. "Maybe that house reminded Cole of Cardinal."

"Have you been up to Clear Creek yet?" Birch asked.

"Yes, twice actually," she said, playing with a white sugar packet, flipping it over on the speckled Formica table. "Did you hear about June possibly selling the land next to Clear Creek?"

Birch picked up her water glass and took a sip. "I heard."

"That forty acres is the only thing that Lucas has ever asked of her," Ruby said. "Why does she want that one little piece out of all their land?"

"If I had to guess, it probably isn't complex. She needs money."

"There's no other land that she could sell?"

"None as valuable as Clear Creek. It's fairly close to the highway, has the creek and likely water for wells." Birch gave Ruby a sympathetic look. "It's always about the water, Ruby. Always."

"Part of Cole is up there," Ruby said. "Do you think if we told her that, she'd change her mind?"

Birch circled her water glass with both hands. "Probably not."

Ruby tightened her lips. "She's a horrible person. How can she live with herself?"

Birch nodded. "But sad, too. The older I get, I find her more pitiful than anything."

Ruby started to answer, but Darla May arrived with their iced teas and salads. When they were settled, Birch changed the subject. She was weary of discussing June McGavin. She'd spent too much of her life fretting about that woman. Bobby's near death last year had changed her, made her realize, more than she ever had, how life was so unpredictable. She didn't want to spend any more of her time with Ruby talking about June McGavin.

"Did you hear about Cassie's story jam project?" Birch said.

"Yes, she told me about it," Ruby said, picking up her paper napkin and unfolding it. "Sounds fun."

"It'll keep the kids busy," Birch said. "At least some of them. Sometimes I think that's the best thing to keep young people out of trouble, just keep them so busy that they have no time to think up mischief." Birch laughed, touching her chest. "I do sound like an old school-teacher, don't I? Truth is I know better than anyone that if a body truly wants to find trouble, nothing can stop them." Birch instantly regretted her words. Would Ruby think she was talking about Nash?

Ruby concentrated on her salad and didn't look up. "But I guess we have to try, don't we? I sometimes wonder if my mother . . ."

Before Ruby could finish her sentence, Darla May came back.

"I brought you a double chocolate brownie to split," she said. "Compliments of the boss. Sueann says it's bad luck to start the New Year without eating chocolate."

Ruby gave a small laugh. "I thought that was black-eyed peas."

"Your mama *is* from the South," Darla May said. "Sueann says this here's a long-time Western tradition." She lifted her shoulders.

Birch winked at Ruby. "She might be pulling your leg. It's more like a Sueann McGavin newly made-up tradition, but I say it's a keeper."

"I second that," Ruby said.

There were a few minutes of silence while they ate. Finally, Birch couldn't stand it any longer. "You were saying that you wondered something about your mother?"

Ruby took another bite, chewing before answering. "I was thinking that if my mother hadn't left when he was so young, maybe Nash wouldn't have started drinking." She contemplated her half-eaten salad. "That's all."

Birch reached over and touched the top of Ruby's hand. "My mother was there for Carson and me all our young lives. We were both grown-ups when she passed away. She was a wonderful, loving mother and my brother still drank too much. We never used the word *alcoholic*, but that's what he was. Daddy drank, too. And *his* mother never lived farther from him than five miles until she died at ninety-two. I'm not condoning what your mama did, deserting you two, but I don't know if her being around would have changed Nash."

Ruby dabbed her lips with her napkin. She carefully replaced it across her lap. "I'm thinking I might go see her."

Birch froze. The sound of the other diners' voices seemed to fade away, as if someone had turned a radio on very low.

"What do you think?" Ruby asked.

Birch wanted to say, *Don't go. Let the woman who deserted you wallow in her own selfishness. Stay here in Cardinal with me. She didn't want you. I would have wanted you. I would have never left. I would have loved you and Nash more than my own life. I would have protected you.*

"Do whatever your heart compels you to do," Birch finally said, hating her words even as she said them. What was it they always said? Act the part and the feelings will follow. She wasn't so sure about that.

Ruby's eyes filled with tears. She reached across the table and took Birch's hand. "Thank you. I just needed someone to . . . You are . . ." Ruby choked on her words and squeezed Birch's hand. "Thank you."

"You're welcome," Birch said, a cold thread of some emotion racing through the core of her.

Change my heart, she prayed, though she didn't mean it. She wanted to be angry, wanted to hold a grudge against the lot in life she'd been given.

They finished their meal without speaking of Etta Walker again. Instead, they talked about the story jam, the Western Film Museum's anniversary celebration, business at the bookstore and improvements they were planning for the lodge.

They finished their meal and read the fortune in their fortune cookies.

Birch's fortune read—"The best fortune is found within your heart."

"Oh, I like that," Ruby said. She broke open her cookie and pulled out the slip of paper. "'You can't ride in all directions at one time.'" She stared at the words for a moment, then crumpled it up. "Silly things."

"Keep me in the loop about your trip to Arizona," Birch said when they said good-bye in front of the café. She couldn't say the words—*visit your mother*. She lightly stomped her feet to keep warm.

"I will. But it will be a while. I don't know when I can get away. I don't want to take advantage of Ely. And, well, I still have to figure out what I want to say to her." Ruby shrugged. "Maybe I'll decide to just let things stay the way they are, not upset the apple cart."

Birch watched Ruby walk down the street until the cold compelled her to start moving. She started down Main Street toward the lodge, walking by Lucas's saddle shop, closed today. Not unusual since technically, today was a holiday. But Lucas didn't really pay attention to things like that. He usually worked every day.

After stopping by Holy Grounds and picking up a couple of vanilla bean scones for later when she and Bobby had their evening tea, she'd swing by the house and see if Lucas was still sleeping. Maybe he had gone out drinking last night and had a hangover. She'd known only one time in his life when he drank to excess. Then again, he lived and worked many years in San Francisco before coming back to Cardinal. She had no idea what his life had been like when he'd worked as a public defender and was married to that snippy girl who'd never appreciated Lucas's soft heart. If anything would drive a person to drink, it would be Lucas's first wife, who, as far as Birch could remember, never had a kind word to say about anything or anybody.

Every table was occupied at Holy Grounds with people seeking a warm spot to spend the first afternoon of the New Year. On the tiny stage was a middle-aged man with frizzy red hair whom she didn't recognize. He was playing an old Joan Baez song. Ely let dozens of musicians perform on the tiny stage in exchange for free food and all the tips they could finagle. During the weekends and holidays, the musicians did pretty well. Most tourists on their way to Mammoth to ski were in good moods, happy to be away from their own routines and were generous with their spare change and dollar bills. Ruby said that the first night Nash played there he made sixty-three dollars.

Though many of the old-timers in town grumbled about Holy Grounds since it tended to be where many of the town's young, less affluent and, sometimes, downright odd, people hung out, Birch had come to love the place. She never had to worry about running into one of her church lady friends here, that was for sure. It still had Linc Holyoke's special touch, a kind of kooky charm with its Southern-tinged outsider art on the walls showing yellow-eyed poodles playing pink and purple mandolins and old Pan Am Hawaii posters featuring stylized people and palm trees. The fifties-style dinettes in reds, yellows and grays made it feel like you were sitting down at your grandma's kitchen table.

She ordered the scones and a chai latte to keep her warm while she walked home. While the barista, a young girl with so many piercings Birch wondered how she would make it through airport security, prepared her drink, she walked down the hallway to Ely's office. The door was open, as it always seemed to be. Ely sat at Linc Holyoke's old wooden office desk, a toaster oven in parts in front of him. Ely hadn't changed the office at all, keeping the same travel posters on the wall showing Borneo, Alaska's majestic mountains and more fifties-era Hawaii posters. The bright red love seat sat in the same spot it was when Linc was alive. The only thing different was the man in the high-backed office chair.

"New career?" Birch said.

"Come on in," Ely replied, pointing over to an empty black and silver visitor's chair. Stacks of paper covered the red love seat. "I know I should just buy a new one, but something cheap in me wants to see if I can get this working and save the coffeehouse fifty bucks."

"Frugality is an admirable quality," she said, sitting down.

"*Gracias*, Senora Hernandez." His lips turned up in a half smile. "That's high praise coming from my favorite teacher. Of course, if the place burns down because I've crossed wires somewhere, it might not be such a wise idea."

"Life is not without risk."

"So I've discovered." He put down the flathead screwdriver. "How is the new year treating you so far?" He glanced up at a coffee cup–shaped electric clock on the paneled wall behind her. "It's been almost thirteen hours now."

She shifted in the cold vinyl chair. "Some good moments, some not so good."

He laughed and sat back in the tall leather chair. Next to his left ear, from a hole in the leather, a thumbnail of stuffing tried to escape. "What's not so good?"

Birch felt her face flush. Why had she said that? Why had she come back here to see Ely? For a brief second, she felt like young girl who'd blurted out the wrong answer in Sunday School. "I was just being facetious. Everything is wonderful. It's a beautiful day."

He just kept his gaze on her, his black eyes somehow conveying disbelief and understanding at the same time. For a brief, odd moment, she almost felt the calming presence of Lincoln Holyoke in the room. Before he died, he'd been there once for her when she'd broken down and needed a place to run to, a nonjudgmental place of comfort. Maybe that was why she felt compelled to come back to this room.

"I feel him, too," Ely said softly. "He's not really here, of course. Some cultures believe that when someone helps us through a troubled time or physically saves us, a part of them lives forever inside us."

Birch nodded without speaking. That was exactly what it felt like.

"You know, you were the only teacher who never judged me by my mother's actions."

"Oh, no," she protested, bringing a hand to her heart. "I'm sure . . ."

He held up a light brown palm. "Pardon me for interrupting you, but it's true. You were kind to me and I've never forgotten that. What you wrote to me a few days after that open house when my mom showed up drunk changed my life."

Birch sat still, staring at Ely with surprise. If someone held a gun to her temple, she could not have repeated what it was she wrote so long ago. She only remembered saving his painting of the horse, which she still had in her attic at home, in the trunk where she kept her mother's Bible and her grandfather's silver spurs. She'd had this vague idea that he might want it back someday.

"The next week you gave us the assignment to write a poem about something we loved. I wrote a page about how I didn't love anyone or anything." He looked away, staring at a "Celebrate Mardi Gras" poster for Houma, Louisiana. "I expected you to fail me. Instead, you gave me an A. You wrote something on my paper that has stayed with me my whole life. Linc said that God often speaks to us through other people. I used to repeat the words to myself when I was in prison." He looked down at his rough, scarred hands.

His voice was barely audible as he quoted the words he'd obviously memorized. "'Dear Ely, We cannot help the circumstances to which we are born, but we can make our own lives something that is fine and useful. You are a brave and good boy and I'm very proud of you.

You will find something to love someday. I promise. Always, Mrs. Hernandez.'"

Tears burned her eyelids. Now she remembered. She'd cried when she read his paper out loud to Bobby.

"You gave me hope," Ely said. "Is there something I can do for you?"

"It's Ruby," she blurted out. "I know she's going to eventually go see her mother and I'm so afraid I'm going to lose her."

17

Ruby

After saying good-bye to Birch, Ruby pulled her scarf tight around her neck and started walking the three long blocks to her new house. Darla May's remark about people buying Nash drinks only verified what Ruby already knew, that Nash was lying to her. He was drinking again. He'd probably never stopped.

She should have gone with him to that New Year's Eve gig. She could have stopped him. She could have kept all those people from buying him drinks. Her stomach felt queasy from the spicy salad.

Coming back to Cardinal was not turning out at all like she'd hoped it would.

Nash woke her early this morning, stumbling around and muttering to himself. It was something she'd heard many times when they'd lived in Nashville. She'd lie in bed and listen to his angry girlfriend's bitter words echoing through the thin apartment wall separating their bedrooms. Angela had scolded Nash, begged him and threatened him. She'd been his conscience and his nurse and his parent until she told Ruby late one night that she couldn't do it any longer.

"I'll always love Nash," Angie had said, her green eyes round as plates and glossy with tears. "But I don't want this life. My dad was an alcoholic and I swore I'd never marry one. I'm sorry, Ruby, but I can't do this any longer."

"I understand," Ruby replied. "You have to do what is right for you." *Please, don't leave him,* she wanted to say. *Please, don't leave* us.

This morning Ruby had walked quietly down the narrow hall decorated with the few family photos of her, Nash, their father and his wife, Prissy. Ruby hung the photos the first day they'd moved in, the photographs carefully placed in cheap wooden frames purchased at Kmart. A family gallery. Well, semi-family.

The door to Nash's bedroom was open and he was sprawled across the bed, on top of the red and black Pendleton blanket that Birch and Bobby had given him. Was that the tangy after-scent of alcohol? She tried to convince herself it wasn't. He *promised*. But he'd underestimated how hard it was to hide things in a small town like Cardinal. What a patsy she was. She closed his bedroom door hard, knowing it wouldn't even rouse him.

Minutes later she was walking down Main Street. She knew that she'd have to confront him today, knew that even when she did, it probably wouldn't make any difference. He'd alternately be angry, stubborn, depressed and belligerent. He'd swear up and down that he'd accepted the drinks, but hadn't drunk them. Addicts didn't change until something compelled them to change, something made them want to get sober.

Sometimes, according to the books she'd read during quiet moments at The

Novel Experience, an intervention might help. Maybe that was what Nash needed. Ruby could call their father and Prissy and arrange a family intervention. Would they agree? With his health the way it was, how the hepatitis had damaged his liver, something had to be done. Nash had to be shown that he was killing himself and that people cared and didn't want him to die.

Now that she knew where their mother was, maybe she should be included. The minute she formed the thought, Ruby dismissed it. Nash was right. Why would their mother even bother? No, the intervention had to come from people who knew Nash, who cared about him. The situation with her mother was an entirely different problem, one Ruby didn't have the time or energy for right now.

She passed Lucas's saddle shop and glanced at the windows. Inside, a light was on though the wooden door sign was turned to "Closed." She paused and considered knocking, wanting to talk to someone about her new plan. In ten seconds, she decided that was a bad idea and continued walking. Lucas wasn't the person she needed to talk to right now. He and Birch cared for her, but she was also beginning to wonder if the Ruby they were emotionally attached to was someone they had made up, a woman they had invented in the scant three weeks she'd stayed here last December. The woman in their imagination was likely not someone who came with the unruly baggage of a runaway mother, an uninvolved father and an alcoholic brother.

"Well, this is who I am," she muttered, a bit angry, not exactly knowing why. "Take it or leave it."

She kept walking, head ducked low as a light snow started dusting the sidewalk in front of her. Cardinal's downtown still held a festive air, though the window displays were beginning to wilt. Tomorrow everyone would begin the melancholy task of taking down holiday decorations.

She walked up and down the almost silent streets of Cardinal, any excuse not to go back to the house. Not much was open on New Year's Day and the cold was obviously keeping most people inside their houses. She liked imagining Cole as a teenager walking these streets, eating at the Dairy Queen with his friends, going to the movie theater to watch the week's attractions. She stood in front of Cardinal High School for a long time, gazing out at the long expanse of lawn, buried now under a fresh coat of snow. She looked at the steps leading up to the stone building, tried to picture a young and laughing Cole sitting there, joking around with friends, secure in his role as the high school's bright and shining football and rodeo star.

She eventually ended up back at Holy Grounds, one of the few places open today. The coffeehouse was crowded and loud and she immediately realized that this was not what she was looking for, either. She was almost out the door when she heard Ely call her name. She turned around slowly.

"What's up?" he asked, coming across the room toward her. He was dressed in his usual faded Wranglers, white waffle-knit undershirt and a plaid flannel shirt. Even though he was now one of the town's more affluent citizens since inheriting all of Linc's assets, he still dressed like the man who everyone called when their truck broke down and they needed quick, inexpensive repairs. His hair was in two braids today, emphasizing his mysterious Native American roots.

"Nothing," she said. "I was going to get a coffee, then changed my mind." She shrugged. "I'm a bit out of sorts today."

He rested his hands lightly on his hips. "Want to go for a drive?"

She looked around the crowded coffeehouse. "Don't you need to be here?"

He smiled and shook his head. "Just promoted George to assistant manager. He'll watch the place. Besides, my customers tend to police themselves."

She realized that was true. Like Linc before him, Ely somehow inspired the people who frequented his coffeehouse or bookstore to watch out for each other and for his interests. Any number of his customers, many who attended various AA meetings and NA meetings, would make sure that things stayed on an even keel at Holy Grounds.

"Let me tell him I'll be gone for a few hours," he said.

Before she could answer, he was at the

cash register talking to a sixtyish, tattooed Hispanic man who stood at least six-four. Seconds later, he grabbed his black parka hung on a hook near the door. "Where to, Ms. McGavin?"

They stepped out on the icy sidewalk.

"Clear Creek?"

"You got it. We'll take my truck."

He opened the door of his Dodge Ram pickup. It was a deep red, a few years old, not fancy, but had an engine that purred like a contented lion.

On the drive to Clear Creek, they didn't speak. But with Ely, it didn't feel awkward. In that way, he reminded her of Cole, who'd had that same ability to be silent yet still present. She understood now how they could be friends, why Cole had been the perfect AA sponsor for Ely. She had the feeling that Ely had understood Cole in a way that she wasn't sure his family or the town did.

At the turnoff, snow was piled in neat, muddy drifts from the snowplow. It was also the road to the McGavin ranch, so it was likely one of the first roads plowed. June's influence would have seen to that. The dirt road to the creek property hadn't been plowed, but the ruts on the road showed someone had been up here earlier.

She glanced over at Ely's profile. "I guess Lucas has already been here today to check on the horses."

"Appears so." She felt the tires slide on the icy road. Ely smoothly switched the truck into four-wheel drive.

Though she wasn't physically cold, Ruby shivered inside her wool-lined denim jacket and gazed out through the windshield. Around them, the snowdrifts looked like mounds of white sugar, untouched by any human or animal tracks. Above them in the leafless trees, a hawk bobbed in the afternoon wind, his mottled, feathered body seeming too heavy for the branch.

At the first gate, he put the truck in park and reached for the door.

"No, let me," Ruby said. "What's the combination?"

"Thirteen, three, forty-seven."

Ruby jumped down from the cab, twisted the dial on the lock and unhooked the chain. She swung open the long metal gate. He pulled through and she closed the gate behind him, fastening it and running back to the truck. "I've learned something about ranch life," she said, a little out of breath. "The passenger is supposed to open and close the gates."

"I'm impressed," Ely said, giving a small smile.

Inside the pasture, he pulled up close to the cottonwood tree. He turned off the truck, tossing the keys in the drink holder between them.

Ruby stepped down from the cab. She could see Lucas's rescue horses in the distance. They looked like toy horses placed by some giant child on the smooth white landscape.

"I like the new one, Chico." She shifted from one foot to the other. The snow crunched like cornflakes beneath her leather loafers. "Its coat, that's called buckskin, right?" She glanced down at her feet. "I should have worn better shoes. Maybe I need some boots."

"Yes," Ely said, coming up beside her. "I mean about the horse." He studied her shoes. "The boots, too, though."

She contemplated his words. "Nash got drunk last night."

Ely nodded silently. Across the pasture, the new horse whinnied. It was a sad, thin sound that made her want to cry. She remembered Lucas telling her about horses and their need for the herd, even if only a herd of two. Without it, they could die of loneliness.

"Is Chico fitting in?" she asked.

"He's doing okay. It's hard. The others had a rhythm. He threw it off. They'll adjust. Eventually one of the others will embrace him and the rest will follow. He'll find his place."

"What if they won't? What if he doesn't?"

Ely turned his head to look at her, his forearms resting on the fence. His face was kind, his black eyes unreadable. "Horses aren't people, Ruby."

"I think I'm disappointing everyone."

"Not everyone."

"Lucas and Birch, then. They have their ideas about what I should be. I don't think Nash and his problems were part of what they expected. But I can't desert him. He's my brother."

Ely looked back out at the horses, who were slowly ambling toward them.

"Look, even the horses can't stay away from you," Ruby said, her tone teasing.

He smiled but didn't turn his head. "They know I have treats."

"Is that the secret to winning friends and influencing people?"

"Just animals. And kids."

"Do you have anything for them?"

"In the truck. Always do."

"So dependable."

He laughed. "Not always. But in this, yes."

She turned away from the horses and looked out at the jagged Eastern Sierra Nevada Mountains in the distance. "I was thinking about calling my dad and Prissy, ask them to stage an intervention with me." She held her breath, waiting to hear what he thought. It was the first time she'd said it aloud.

"Interventions can work," he finally said, looking at his hands. "But . . ." Then he stopped. "I've heard they can work."

"What were you going to say?" she said, her breath coming out in white puffs. She could now hear the shushing sound of the horses' hooves in the snow, the whisper of their heavy breathing as they moved closer.

"It's not my business."

"It is if I'm asking your opinion."

He still didn't look at her. "Do you think an intervention is right for your brother? It's hard. It takes . . ." He stopped again. She could see that he was fighting something.

"I know my family is screwed up, Ely, but I'm desperate. I want to do something before Nash hurts himself." Or someone else, she thought. "You've been in AA."

"Still am."

"So you know. He needs help."

"AA is about admitting you need help, Ruby. You can't force a person to want help."

She threw her hands up, wanting to wail into the swaying treetops. "But he can't help himself. He . . ."

Before she could finish, her cell phone rang.

"I can't believe there is reception here," she said, hurrying toward the truck.

"They put in a tower," Ely called. "For the new houses they hope to build."

She had forgotten about that. She couldn't imagine houses out here in this pristine land. By the time she opened her purse, her phone had stopped ringing. She checked the screen. It was a New Mexico area code. Her father's number. He and Prissy kept a single-wide in an Albuquerque trailer park. Though they only spent a total of a month or two there all year, it was their home base.

Why would her father be calling her? To wish her a happy New Year? He never had before. He barely remembered Christmas, though he'd been better since he'd married Prissy. No, he wasn't better. *Prissy* remembered Christmas and made him call Ruby and Nash. She'd talked to him only a week ago. He and Prissy caught a run that ended in Las Vegas on New Year's Eve. Prissy told her they were going to spend the night at the MGM Grand and ring in the New Year at a downtown blackjack table.

She contemplated ignoring his call, not feeling like making small talk about the weather and how she'd spent New Year's Eve. She sat sideways in the truck's passenger seat, her long legs dangling. But if she wanted to have this intervention, she needed her father on her side. She dialed him back, determined to sound warm and loving, buttering him up for the difficult thing she might ask him to do in the next few weeks. She was surprised when Prissy's gravelly, smoke-harsh voice answered, "Hello."

"Prissy?" Ruby asked. "Dad just called me. Is everything okay?"

"It was me," Prissy said, her voice sounding wet now. A sob bounced through the lines, surprising Ruby. "It's not okay. Your daddy's had a stroke."

18

Lucas

"Why didn't you tell me about Ruby's father earlier?" Lucas asked Birch the next morning, standing next to the coffee machine, holding an empty mug. "This thing takes forever. When was the last time you cleaned it out?" He hated that such a huge event happened in Ruby's life and he was one of the last to know. Why hadn't Ruby called him?

"I just found out myself." Birch looked at the clock on the white stove. "She called from Las Vegas about two hours ago. She knows I get up early. I didn't want to wake you up at five a.m. There's not much any of us can do right now except pray."

"How is he?" Lucas asked, feeling ashamed at his childish response. Her father had had a stroke, for Pete's sake.

"He's in ICU. She said they aren't giving them much hope." She took a loaf of bread from the metal breadbox stenciled with red and yellow flowers. It had sat in that same spot on the tile counter for as long as Lucas could remember. "I have some raisin bread from Maxie's. Would you like a slice?"

He shook his head. "I wish she would have called yesterday. I hate to think of her driving to Las Vegas at night by herself."

Birch placed two slices of bread in the toaster and pushed down the lever. "She didn't. Ely went with her." She faced Lucas. "He was with her yesterday when she received the call from Joe's wife."

"Oh." Lucas poured himself a cup of coffee. "Well, good."

"Yes, I suppose it is," Birch said. Despite his attempt at nonchalance, it was apparent on his aunt's face that she understood what he was feeling. "Would you like some eggs?"

Lucas took a deep breath, then sipped his hot coffee. "No, thanks. I need to get to the shop and start working on those story jam notebooks." He'd been asked to donate three leather notebooks for the first, second and third place winners of the contest that would be voted on by the people attending the event.

"Thanks, sweetie," Birch said, patting his back. "You're a good kid."

"Guess we'll keep him," Bobby said, coming through the swinging kitchen door. "Top of the morning to you, *la familia.*"

"Hey, Uncle Bobby," Lucas said.

"Hear anything more about Joe Stoddard?" Bobby asked, hooking his silver-topped cane on the back of a kitchen chair. "That's a real shame. He's about our age, isn't he?" He sat down heavily, his face tightening slightly.

"Close," Birch said. "I think Ruby said he's sixty-seven. I haven't heard anything else since she called. I'm sure she'll let us know if anything changes."

"Or Ely will," Lucas said, trying to keep his voice light.

"Right," Birch said, glancing sideways with a sympathetic look.

"Glad Ruby isn't alone," Bobby said. "Is her brother with them?"

The toaster popped up and Birch placed the two pieces of toast on a clear glass plate. "You know, she didn't say." She buttered the toast and set it in front of Bobby, along with a prescription bottle of medication. "Coffee? Eggs?"

"Yes, love," he said, opening the bottle. "God bless pharmaceuticals. Or at least the people who discovered them."

Lucas sat his half-finished coffee down on the counter. "I'm going down to the shop. Call me if you hear anything."

"I will," Birch said. "And you do the same."

He kissed her cheek. "Yes, ma'am."

He was a block away from the saddle shop when his cell phone rang. He glanced at the screen. It was Ruby.

"Hey," he said. "How's Joe?" The crackly background noise sounded like she was in an airport lobby or a crowded mall.

"Hi, Lucas. So, you heard."

"Birch told me a few minutes ago."

"I would have called last night, but we got on the road the minute Prissy called and, well, I was so upset and distracted . . ."

"No worries," Lucas said. "I understand."

"I need your help, Lucas. I can't find Nash. I keep calling his cell phone, but he never answers. We don't have a landline. He doesn't know about Dad."

"Okay," Lucas said, carefully. "What can I do?"

"Could you go over to our house and see if he's there? If not . . ." She paused a moment. "He can't drive, so he can't be far."

"He can't drive?"

He heard her take a deep breath. "He's not supposed to drive. He lost his license for DUI in Nashville. So he can't have gone far."

Unless he talked someone else into taking him, Lucas thought. Or he took your car. He almost asked her where she kept a spare car key, but didn't. If she hadn't thought of that, there was no use worrying her further.

"I'll find him. I know this area pretty well. When I do, what should I tell him?"

She was quiet a moment. "I guess the truth. I'm sorry to dump this on you. There's no one else I can trust with this except Ely and he's with me."

Lucas made a noncommittal sound that he hoped she took as agreement. "I'll say he's real sick and that . . ." He floundered, not certain what he should tell her brother.

"Just tell him that Dad's in the hospital in Las Vegas and to call me. I'll take it from there."

"Got it. Maybe he's just sleeping real heavy or his cell is turned off." Or he's passed out.

"Right." The doubt in her voice told him she was likely thinking the same thing he was. "Either way, could you let me know if he's okay?"

"I'll go over to your house right now."

"Thank you, Lucas. You're a true friend. I have to go. Prissy is waving at me. I think the doctor is coming. Bye now."

She turned off her phone before he could reply.

He slipped his phone back into his shirt pocket. He quickened his pace, his boots slipping slightly on the icy street as he passed his saddlemaking shop and headed toward Ruby's house past the high school. It was nearly seven o'clock now and he found himself walking with bundled-up students hurrying to an early class, the first one after the long holiday. He remembered those seven a.m. classes, usually extra-credit projects to bring up his B-average grades.

How many times had he made this walk? When he was a young teenager, before he could drive, he often spent the night at his aunt Birch's house when an afterschool activity kept him in town after dark. He cherished those times. Birch and Bobby's warm and shabby house had been a refuge. The only thing he had missed at the ranch was Cole, and when he left, there wasn't much about the Circle MG that drew Lucas. He loved the land, but the ranch itself wasn't a place he connected with the word *home*. The Tokopah Lodge felt more like home than his family's hundred-year-old ranch house ever would.

Ruby's house on Maple Street boasted trees that he knew canopied the streets with shade during the spring and summer. This time of year, they looked like mottled gray fingers reaching to the clear blue sky, the shade they'd eventually cast appearing like dark cracks on the street. Ruby's Honda sat in front of the neat little house. That answered at least one question. Nash had obviously not taken her car. Or if he had, he managed to get it back home in one piece.

Lucas knocked on the door, then rang the doorbell. Its flat *pink-ponk* sound echoed inside the house. He knocked again, harder this time, then tried the doorknob. Locked. He should have asked Ruby if she kept a spare key hidden. Should he call her back?

He walked around the back of the house. Maybe he could tap on the window, wake Nash up. If he was there. The house looked deserted.

He climbed the three steps and tried the back door. It opened with a loud squeak. The hinges could use some oil.

Maybe he'd take care of that when everything was back to normal. He stuck his head inside the room, obviously a back bedroom. "Nash? You up? It's Lucas."

In the dim light, he could make out the human shape on the double bed. A bright red and black Pendleton blanket covered it. "Nash? Hey, it's Lucas."

No answer came from the shape. He stepped into the room and felt along the wall for a light switch. He flipped it on and gazed around the messy room. Clothes and crumpled fast-food bags littered the floor. Two guitars sat in a corner, propped up like brooms. A photo of Mount Whitney hung over the double bed. The only other furniture was a nightstand and a tall chest. It smelled stale and sweet, like grapes gone bad. The shape under the blanket erupted with a loud snort, then started snoring.

He strode across the room, his boots squeaking on the uneven wood floor covered with a worn Persian-style rug he remembered from one of the spare rooms at his aunt's house. He reached down and shook the figure. "Hey, Nash, wake up. It's Lucas."

It took almost five minutes to coerce Nash into waking. Who knew what time he had gotten in. Hadn't it even occurred to him that Ruby wasn't here? No, Lucas thought, remembering his father and his grandfather. When they were that drunk, no one existed except them and the bottle. They just assumed that those around them could take care of themselves. Lucas felt a sick revulsion looking at the bleary-eyed young man. Why was he stuck with this part of it? He should be in Las Vegas comforting Ruby. This was more Ely's area of expertise.

"What's goin' on?" Nash finally said. He slowly eased his body to a vertical position, swung his legs over the side of the bed. He rested his elbows on his knees, holding his head in his hands.

"Your dad is sick," Lucas said. "Get your shit together and call your sister. She needs you."

Nash looked up at Lucas, his blood-laced eyes trying to focus. "Dad? He's sick?"

"In Las Vegas. Ruby is there now. You need to call her."

Nash dropped his head, staring down

at his bare feet. "I'm so tired, man. I gotta . . . Let me just take a little nap and then I'll call her." He lay backward on the bed, his arm covering his eyes. "Man, I'm just so tired. Worked late last night." In less than a minute, he was back asleep.

Lucas looked down at him, tempted to kick him. But what would that accomplish? He was trying to help Ruby, and smacking her brother around, despite the fact that he needed it, wouldn't solve anything. He walked down the long hall to the living room and stood by the front window while he called Ruby. It went straight to voice mail, which told him she was probably somewhere in the hospital where there was bad coverage or her phone was turned off.

"Hey, Ruby. I'm at your house right now. Nash is here. He's . . . fine. I told him about your dad and he said he'd call you when he wakes up. He's pretty . . . tired. But he's okay. Call me when you can." He hung up, wondering if he could have worded that better. He concluded that there wasn't any good way to say, *Your brother is too damn hung- over to talk right now . . . try again later.* She's smart.

She'll read between the lines. At least she knows he's not in a ditch somewhere. One less thing for her to worry about.

On the walk back to his saddle shop, he attempted to put Ruby out of his mind, concentrate on the work waiting for him. He bought a large coffee and two maple bars from Maxie's Bakery and ate them in front of his small space heater while the shop's furnace did its best to warm the freestanding building. This summer he really needed to put in some kind of insulation. He was halfway finished with the second maple bar when the front door opened.

He set down his coffee and donut, wiped his hands down his Wranglers and walked around the half wall that separated the shop's small lobby from his work area.

"Hey, cowboy," the young, smiling woman said.

He stared at her a moment before it dawned on him. The waitress from Las Vegas. Marie-Sacheen. She was dressed in black roper boots, dark blue jeans, a yellow and white sweater with a vaguely Swedish pattern, and one of those silly ski hats with the dangly side strings. "Hello Sunshine!" was printed across the hat. She carried a black leather backpack that was so full it appeared to hold all her worldly possessions. "How's the Stetson doing?"

"Hey." He touched his stained gray Stetson. "Oh, the one you cleaned. It's at home. It's good. Still clean."

She grinned at him and pulled off her knitted hat. Her black braids were as shiny as her boots. She tossed her head and they flew back as if on command. "That one you're wearing looks like it could use a good cleaning."

He touched his hat again, feeling his neck turn warm. "It's my everyday hat. Doesn't matter. Marie, right?"

She nodded. "You remembered! I'm impressed." She gave him a wicked grin, telling him that, actually, she wasn't impressed at all. "Seriously, I could make that hat look like new. I once worked for a Western clothing store in Amarillo. That's where I learned how to clean cowboy hats. It's more complicated than you think. You use fine sandpaper if the stain is bad. It's all in your brushing technique."

"I thought it was your grandmother who taught you."

She jutted out one hip like she was posing for a photographer. "I lied."

"Oh." Now, there's a clever comeback, he thought.

"So," she said, shifting her leather backpack to the other shoulder. "Aren't you going to ask me what I'm doing here in your saddle shop?" She gave a quick look around. "It's pretty cool, by the way. I kinda thought you were just a wannabe. Get a lot of those in Vegas during NFR. But, here you are." She held her arms out. "The real thing."

"What are you doing in my saddle shop?" he asked, smiling.

"I'm in Cardinal visiting Grammy Eula. Decided to drop by and see how your hat was doing." She gazed down into his glass counter, which held some of his smaller leather creations—checkbook covers, business card holders, a notebook with a rearing mustang on the front, some of the bracelets Cassie suggested and a Paiute basket filled with carved key chains. "You have some nice stuff here. How many saddles do you make a year?"

He walked around the glass counter and stood in front of her. She was shorter than Ruby, maybe five-three or -four. He could see the vulnerable skin in the part of her hair. "How did you find me?" She didn't even know his name and how did she know he was a saddle maker?

She gave a quick laugh and set down her backpack. It hit the wooden floor with a thump. "You buy that hat from the same place as your rich-boy one?"

He nodded. The McGavins had bought their hats from Walt's Feed and Seed since Lucas could remember.

She held out her hand.

He removed his hat and gave it to her, feeling a little vulnerable with a bare head. She turned it over and pointed to the brim, where stamped in gold was "Walt's Feed and Seed, Cardinal, California."

He gave a rueful, half smile. "So, I still don't see how you found me here. I never told you what I do."

She shrugged. "There are no secrets in small towns, don't you know that? I went to Walt's, described you and the clerk there told me right where to find you. No big *CSI* moment."

"Still, I'm impressed." Mostly that she went to the trouble.

She waved away his comment. "I'm here for a few months," she said, answering a question he hadn't asked. "Decided that Las Vegas has no interesting stories and my grammy's feeling a little under the weather. Told Ma I'd stay with her awhile, give her a hand."

"Oh," he replied. "Well . . ." He glanced around, feeling as awkward as a fifteen-year-old. Was she flirting with him? How could he be in his midthirties and still not get what this young woman was trying to communicate?

She slapped the side of her leg and laughed. "Okay, you pried it out of me, you slick talker. They fired me for smarting off one too many times to a customer. He was a real dick, though, and deserved that pot of coffee I poured on his head."

Her revelation alarmed him. Was this woman some kind of nut?

She laughed again. "Relax, I was just kidding. I *wanted* to pour coffee on his head after he grabbed my ass, but I just knocked a glass of water in his lap."

Lucas couldn't help laughing. "Should

I believe you? You majored in creative writing."

"Good memory, cowboy. My fantasies are always more fun than the reality." Her dark eyes narrowed slightly, the laugh wrinkles turning to a furrowed brow. "But the water part is true. So is the part about my grammy. She really isn't doing that well. Mom's worried."

"Your mom lives here?"

She shook her head. "Bakersfield. She's a nurse practitioner. Works for a cool doctor dude. She, like, has her own patients and everything." She grimaced. "Ugh. I'm trying not to use the word *like* in that way. So high school."

"Like, for sure," Lucas said, smiling.

Her giggle made her sound like a teenager. "The cowboy cracks a joke. It's lame, but, hey, it's a start."

"I can be funny," Lucas said. "Though usually not on purpose."

"An honest white man. Wow, there's a concept."

Before he could think of a clever comeback, his cell phone rang. "I'm sorry, but I need to get this. A friend's father is ill . . ."

She waved a hand in acquiescence.

He glanced at the screen. It wasn't Ruby, but his mother.

"Hello," he said, his voice cautious.

"Where are you?" His mother's voice was loud enough for Marie to raise her eyebrows.

"Should I go?" she mouthed, pointing toward the door.

He shook his head. "My mother," he mouthed back.

She made an okay circle with her finger and thumb, walked right around him and started inspecting his saddlemaking tools. "Take your time," she murmured.

"I have a customer." He turned his back to Marie. "What do you want?"

"Did you look at the latest offer for the Clear Creek property? I don't think we can afford to say no to this one. This deal includes the property next to Clear Creek."

Lucas felt a throb in his left temple. Not a headache, but likely his blood pressure going up ten points. "I don't want to sell. We had an agreement. I get these forty acres. How many times do we have to go through this?"

Her voice grew sharper, the words like tiny blades. "You know that development for the property up north fell through. Have you looked at the stock market lately? Our investments are in the toilet. Do you realize how bad off the ranch is? We do not have much choice, Lucas. We—"

"I have a customer, Mom. I have to call you back." He hung up and tossed the phone on his workbench. It clattered against his tools and knocked over an empty Coke can.

"Whoa," Marie said, eyes wide. "Bad blood in the McGavin clan?"

"Sorry. Just some old family business."

Her smooth face turned thoughtful. "Want to talk about it?"

"No." He was beginning to get impatient. He was too old to be playing adolescent games. Why was she here?

"'Send in the Clowns' as your ringtone?" she finally said, pointing to his phone.

"My niece's idea. You have no idea how appropriate it is."

She shrugged. "I probably do. Everyone thinks their family is the nuttiest on earth. In reality, most of us are pretty much equal in that race."

"Surely there are some families somewhere who get along." He smiled at her. "I see them on Hallmark card commercials all the time."

"Sucker," she said, smiling back. "Hey, want to go out for a cup of coffee? We can discuss the blatantly predatory and unreliable aspects of modern commercialism over peppermint lattes."

He glanced back at his unfinished work, then thought, Why not?

"I'll buy," he said, grabbing his barn jacket. "If that doesn't offend any feminist feelings."

"Cowboy," she replied. "In my generation, starving artist trumps angry feminist any day of the week."

19

Ruby

Years later, when Ruby tried to recall those two long days in Las Vegas, they came to her in fragments, bite-sized moments of scent and sound, like a half-remembered dream. It troubled her that she could bring back only insignificant memories—the sound of machine-made coffee splashing into a plastic cup, the smell of a woman's magnolia perfume in the intensive care waiting room, the hum from the bluish light in the emergency room hallway, the rumbling murmur of Ely's voice talking to Prissy about, of all things, snow foxes. Why were they talking about snow foxes? Why would she remember that and not what her father's face looked like while he lay in the hospital bed hooked up to so many tubes and machines she wondered how in the world anyone could keep track.

He died the second day. He never even woke up to see that Ruby had come to him. She and Ely had left the room a half hour earlier, had gone down to the cafeteria to quickly eat. Rice pudding, she remembered, and ginger ale. They were the only things she could stomach.

Prissy was with Joe when he died, which made Ruby glad. Though her father had rarely been there for her and Nash, she did not want him to die alone. She would not wish that on anyone. It still caused her heart to seize like a trapped animal every time she thought about Cole spending his last few minutes on earth alone, lying at the bottom of that embankment, his battered face cradled only by his truck's air bag. No, she would never wish dying alone on anyone.

Prissy told her he wanted to be cremated. She and Joe had apparently discussed this subject on one of their long trips across the country.

"Since we don't really live anywhere full time," she said, her round blue eyes so swollen from crying she looked as if she'd been beaten up, "I'm thinking he'd want you to have half his ashes, honey. We didn't discuss that, but I think he would." They'd found out with one phone call that it was going to take a few days for his ashes to be ready.

"We could get rooms and wait for them," Ely said.

Ruby rested her eyes on his calm face for a moment, grateful for his presence. She looked down at her hands, studying her ragged nails. The thought of spending one more day here in this city almost stopped her breath.

"No need," Prissy said, giving a small hiccup. "I can send him to Cardinal. UPS or FedEx."

Her solution made Ruby want to laugh hysterically. Or burst into tears. This is what life ultimately came down to. Your boxed ashes shipped like a book from Amazon complete with a tracking number. At least when Cole was cremated, Ruby was there to pick him up, wrap his box carefully in his favorite afghan and drive him home to Cardinal.

"Whatever you think is right, Prissy." She put her arm around Prissy's soft shoulders. "Whatever makes you feel better. I can bury him next to Cole in Cardinal Cemetery."

The moment she said it, she realized that June would never allow that to happen. But Prissy didn't need to know that.

Prissy's swollen eyes started leaking tears again. They rolled silently down her shiny red cheeks. "Oh, honey, I'm going to miss your daddy. He was one of the good ones. I know he wasn't always there for you and your brother, but he loved you in his way." She wiped one cheek with the back of her hand. "He did the best he could. He just never really got over your mama, you know. And I understood that about him, because I loved my second husband, Lloyd, that way. There's some people you never get over, so you just go on, make yourself a life from the pieces they leave behind. That's what Joe and me did. We pieced ourselves a little quilt of a life." She dug through her huge red crocheted handbag for tissue. She held a tattered piece up to her shiny nose. "I like the idea of part of him being somewhere permanent, someplace where he has family to visit his grave on his birthday."

"Yes," Ruby said, even though she wasn't sure if Cardinal would end up being her permanent home. That was also something Prissy didn't need to hear right now. But, in a way, the town would always be sort of home to her. Ruby would always come back to visit Cole's grave. Perhaps having her father in the same place would be good. Practical, anyway. She let Prissy's words about her father's feelings for her mother rush past her, through her, like an unexpected cold wind. She couldn't think of her mother. Not right now. Eventually, she'd have to be told about Joe. Ruby didn't even want to imagine that phone call.

"What do you want to do?" Ely asked.

His hand rested against her upper arm and she looked up at his tired face. There was just the slightest hint of darkness under his almond-shaped eyes, hinting at his fatigue. They'd both been up over forty-eight hours, catching catnaps in the waiting room. Time had done that funny thing it did in crisis moments, become something outside of the rest of the world. If she were staring at a calendar right now, she couldn't even guess what day it was.

"Oh, Ely," she said, bringing a hand up to her cheek. "What about Holy Grounds? Who's been taking care of the book-store?"

"They're fine. I have good employees and friends who are covering for us. Don't worry." He squeezed her arm gently. "What do you want to do?"

She turned to Prissy. "Will you be okay? I don't want to leave you alone with all this."

Prissy sniffed wetly. "Don't worry about me. My sister's flying in from Tucson to-night. We'll stay at a motel until we get Joe settled. Then she'll ride in the truck back with me to Arizona." Prissy shook her head. "I'd been doing most of the driving these last couple of months, anyway. Joe had been real tired. He was due for his annual physical next month. I didn't realize. If I'd known . . ."

"You couldn't have known," Ruby said gently. "Don't blame yourself."

Prissy sighed. "It'll be good to get back to Arizona. My sister has a real nice guest room. She said I can stay as long as I want."

Arizona. The mention of the state caused Ruby to think of her mother again. Would Loretta—or Etta, as she apparently went by these days—even care that he'd died? Maybe. She had kept in touch with him even while ignoring her children.

"Okay," Ruby said, bending down to hug Prissy. "Thank you. I . . . Just thank you for being here. For calling me."

"Oh, honey," Prissy said, clutching Ruby tightly. Ruby could smell the tart, old scent of hairspray on the woman's curly hair. "He loved you. He did."

Ruby looked over the shorter woman's head at Ely, her face feeling like a block of ice. His dark eyes held hers for a long moment, communicating something that she couldn't comprehend. She closed her eyes briefly, thinking, only a little while longer and they would be in the truck heading back to Cardinal. For a moment, that seemed almost like a solution, even though what waited for her back there was only more problems. She understood what Lucas had been trying to say about Nash. He was drunk or hungover. But, still, it had been two days. Why hadn't Nash even called to find out how Dad was doing? She tried his cell phone a dozen times and it always went to voice mail. She pushed down the anger that roiled inside her. There was nothing she could do right now. She'd just tell him about Dad in person. She'd deal with her feelings then.

By eight p.m., they were on the road.

"Are you okay to drive?" she asked Ely. "I can do half if I can just sleep a few hours."

"I'm fine." He held up a red and silver can. "The nectar of the Red Bull tree will sustain me."

She gave a small smile. "That stuff tastes like cough syrup to me. Give me plain old coffee anytime." She settled back in her seat, pulling Ely's fleece-lined denim jacket close around her despite the fact the cab was warm. "Prissy wouldn't take any money from me to help with the expenses, so I told her I'd pay for Dad's cemetery plot. I'll have to look into that."

"Try to sleep," Ely said. "You can worry about that when we get home."

She nodded, leaning her head against the window. It was cold against her temple, a sensation that she thought would keep her awake. "I don't know how to tell Nash." She closed her eyes, relaxing as the heat started to warm the cab. "It might set him off. Don't let me sleep for longer than a half hour. I should be helping you stay awake."

"Close your eyes. I've made this drive a hundred times."

She could feel the truck shift as it started up an incline and then she remembered nothing until she woke to the sound of Ely changing a CD. She bolted up, eyes wide with that bright attentiveness you feign when awakened by a ringing phone. "Oh! How long have I . . . ?"

"Sorry," Ely said, pushing pause on the CD player. "I didn't mean to wake you. I was just putting in a CD because there isn't any radio signal." He scratched the side of his jaw with the back of his fingers.

"Where are we?" She stared out into the blackness. Except for a few distant oncoming headlights, there was no sign of civilization.

"We've got a few hours to go. You've been asleep for about three hours." He concentrated on the road, his face shadowed green and gray by the dashboard lights.

She looked at his stoic face and remembered a conversation she and Lucas once had about Ely's heritage. He appeared Indian in the way he dressed, wore his long black hair, the jewelry he sometimes wore, yet he never claimed a tribe. "May I ask you something?"

A smile twitched at the corner of his mouth. "You don't snore, if that's what is worrying you."

"It's kind of personal."

He gave a quick nod. "Shoot."

"What was it like in prison?" It wasn't what she really wanted to ask, but at the last minute, she avoided the question about his heritage, afraid it would, somehow, sound racist.

"Are you wondering about me or about Cole?"

She pulled out the seat belt crossing her chest, readjusting it. "Both, I guess."

He thought for a moment. She studied his profile, the strong nose, the sharp cheekbones, coppery skin that tempted her fingertips, even though she'd never thought of Ely that way. How could his jawline be so smooth? When had he shaved in the last few days?

"Well," he said, the wrist of his right hand resting on the steering wheel. The road ahead of them was so straight, his arm barely moved. "Think about a moment when you felt confined against your will, even for a few seconds, and times that by a hundred thousand. It's the most overwhelming feeling of panic I've ever known. I don't ever want to go back." He turned his head toward her. His wide-set eyes seemed to look through her into the darkness outside the truck, to a darkness she couldn't imagine. "I can't speak for Cole, but I imagine he felt the same way.

Unless you are a lifer, in which case I imagine there are a whole other set of mechanisms you acquired to cope, those of us with a time limit tried to figure how to last until our release date. The stupid ones lived day to day. They reacted emotionally to the guards, the other inmates, to their crazy emotions, generally behaving like teenage boys with no control. The smart ones did what I did and what I'm guessing Cole did."

"What is that?"

"Kept to yourself. Walked that fine line between the rules of the prison and the rules of the inmates. You kept your mouth shut, did your good time and, with luck, got out in one fairly undamaged piece."

She looked down at her hands, clenched tight in her lap. "I feel as if there are whole parts of Cole I never knew. The Cardinal Cole. The prison Cole. The alcoholic Cole. The depressed Cole. It's like all I got was one tiny section of him."

"Isn't that true of everyone to some degree?"

"Maybe."

"Cole wasn't easy to know. He was . . . reticent."

Her laugh was a small puff of air. "Yes, he was. But, you know, you're not the most gregarious man your own self."

He laughed, flipped on the truck's bright lights, illuminating the dark desert road ahead of them. "'Your own self'? Are you cultivating your inner Southern girl?"

A hand flew up to her mouth. "I can't believe I said that. I'm Southern only if you consider south California a Southern state."

"Your mother was from the South."

"Eastern Tennessee."

"Some psychologists say we pick up our speech patterns from our mothers and that they stay with us for the rest of our lives."

"Do you think that's true?"

"Don't know. I might argue that it makes more sense that we pick up our speech pattern from whoever taught us to talk."

She nodded. "I agree. Who taught you?"

"My mom, I guess, though she was gone a lot. We lived with my grandmother the first five years of my life and I spent most of my time with her, so you'd have to take that into account. She was the one who really taught me to talk."

Before she could ask where that was or anything about his grandmother, he said, "Back to Cole. He was reticent, but once he decided you were okay, he was as loyal as an elephant."

"Are elephants particularly loyal?"

"They are to those in their herd. Once you were Cole's friend, that was it. He'd go to the mat for you. I respect that in a man." He glanced over at her. "Pardon me, ma'am, in a *person.*"

"You're pardoned, sir," she said, smiling. "Good catch."

"Cole and I were never in prison together. I told you we met at a halfway house in Los Angeles. I can only tell you what he was like there. In some ways, he was different than the kid I knew growing up, in other ways, not at all."

"That's right. I always forget you were friends as children."

"We lived in the same town." His voice was matter-of-fact.

"Not the same thing. I'm sorry. I know that."

He waved her comment away. "We were both products of a typical small-town caste system."

"Who approached who? At the halfway house, I mean."

"He came up to me, introduced himself. I was pretty drunk the first time we talked." He shook his head, remembering. "Drinking was against house rules, of course. He took me out to a diner, bought me breakfast and reminded me we were from the same town."

"You didn't remember him?"

"I did, but pretended I didn't. He . . ." Ely flexed his fingers on the steering wheel. "Scared me, I guess."

"You? I didn't think you were afraid of anything."

He raised his eyebrows. "Seriously? I was a drunk, Ruby. That's all about being afraid. And I was still into playing the tough guy. Still hauling around my prison persona. None of that intimidated Cole. Over pancakes he started telling me about books he loved, what he'd read in prison, what he was reading that day. Loved books that had hidden meanings, convoluted symbolism and crazy metaphors."

"Yes, he did. Not a lot of people knew that about him."

"He got me started reading. He loved to talk about ideas, philosophy, how people coped. That was a big one with him. He used to tell me you can't choose your family, but you can choose your life. The first time he said that, it really hit home. It was almost exactly the same thing Birch told me when I was a kid in one of her classes."

"Birch was your teacher? I didn't know that. I'm jealous."

"It was weird and kind of cool, hearing those words and knowing where he probably learned them."

"I can imagine," she said, feeling warm inside, happy to be talking to someone who knew Cole, who understood him in the same way she had. "We used to talk about . . ."

She almost said *our families*, but that wasn't exactly true. They'd talked about her family, her runaway mother, her distant father, how disconnected she'd felt even toward Nash. "My family. He'd never mentioned his, of course. Well, he said they'd all died in a car crash." That still hurt, that he hadn't trusted her enough to tell her the truth about his family.

"He was still working it all out, Ruby," Ely said, reaching over to touch her hand. "I think he would have eventually told you the truth."

"Instead, he killed himself." She hated the bitter tone in her voice but was unable to quell it. "I'll never, never understand."

Ely made an almost imperceptible noise in the back of his throat. Agreement? She didn't know, but she felt it was. Every so often, a car or truck passed them on the other side and their faces were lit for a moment with bright, white light.

She turned her head to stare out at the dark desert landscape. "I guess it doesn't matter."

"It does. But it's just part of the mystery."

"What?"

"Of why we are here. Why we are born, why we die. Who's behind it all."

She turned to look at him, skeptical. "You mean God?"

He shrugged. "I don't mean to preach." He gave a small laugh. "Or maybe I do. Sometimes I think when Linc died, he not only left me all his property, but his . . ." He stopped, obviously struggling for the right word.

"Calling?"

He shook his head. "No, I think it's more like his *place*. It's as if he passed on the baton. Only I can't run the race near as good as he did."

"He tamed you," she said softly, almost to herself. "Like the little prince did the fox."

"Cole loved that book!"

Ruby laughed. "He did. He gave me an antique copy of it on our third date." Ely shifted in his seat. In the warmth of the cab, Ruby could smell his smoky, cottony scent.

"He had to explain that word to me," Ely said. "I didn't understand why the author used the word *tame* until Cole told me it meant more like committing to someone or something rather than controlling them. It was not like taming a lion, which is the only way I understood the word."

She sighed. "He and I used to talk for hours about things like that. He gave me *The Velveteen Rabbit* on the day he asked me to marry him. He said when he was with me, he finally felt real."

Ely nodded and didn't comment.

"You know," she said, "I think if they taught high school students nothing but those two books in their senior year, we'd have a lot less confused kids."

"You could be right. *The Velveteen Rabbit* teaches them about being authentic and being satisfied with who they are and *The Little Prince* teaches them to be responsible for their fellow human beings. Not bad lessons to start out life with."

"We are responsible forever for what we've tamed."

"For what or who we've loved."

"So, Cole was my fox? The one I tamed?"

"And you were his."

"But he left. I didn't do my job . . ."

"Yes, you did. His choice to leave was *his* failure, not yours. We can tame someone, but we can't *be* them."

"Touché, Professor Ely. So you can't be Linc."

He nodded. "You're right."

"You just have to be you. Do the things you feel led to do."

"And you need to accept the life that Cole wanted for you, the one he made possible."

She felt her insides grow cold. "I wanted a life with him."

He waited a moment before answering. "Okay, so maybe just like Linc gave me a purpose in Cardinal by leaving me Holy Grounds and the bookstore and all that came with it, Cole left you his Cardinal . . . Birch, Cassie, Lucas, the Circle MG."

"I sold my part of the ranch back to the McGavins."

"But you are still a part of their lives. Because of Cole . . . and because they want you to be. I think that Cole knew he could never live there again, it was just too much for him, but maybe he wanted you to have a life there."

"Without him." She didn't try to conceal the bitterness she felt.

He glanced at her, then back to the road. "We'll never know why he felt that he couldn't take this life anymore. But he knew Lucas's heart, Birch's, Bobby's,

Cassie's . . . and yours. I bet he felt like Cardinal was the home you wanted, maybe needed . . ."

"But why couldn't he come with me? Why wouldn't your great and mighty God fix *that*?"

He sighed. "Linc touched so many people, did so much good. Believe me, I wonder all the time why he died instead of me. He had so much more to give the world. That's the mystery, I guess. Part of it anyway. I don't have any answers for you. Linc could have answered you. What can I tell you or anyone? I'm an ex-con, an alcoholic, a car mechanic, a . . ."

"A philosopher," she said, softly. "A friend. A wise man."

He laughed. "A wiseass, maybe."

She laughed, too, feeling the ice block inside her crack a little. "That sounds like Cole. He would do that to me, make me laugh just when things got too heavy."

"He'll always be with us, Ruby."

"Because he tamed us. He tamed us both."

It was a little past two a.m. when they pulled into her driveway. The house was dark, and when Ruby unlocked the door and went inside, it was obvious that Nash wasn't there. She had tried calling him at eleven p.m. and his cell had once again gone straight to voice mail.

"Do you want me to wait with you?" Ely asked.

"Thank you, but I have no idea when he'll be home. I'm just going to go to bed. It's probably better I tell him about Dad when I'm more rested."

"Don't come to work tomorrow."

"I'll come in the minute I am awake and functioning."

"I mean it, Ruby. You need a few days off . . ."

She held up a hand. "Stop. I cannot even tell you how much I appreciate you coming with me to Las Vegas, supporting me, taking time from your own life. But, I know things aren't easy with either of your businesses and you can't afford to . . ."

He grabbed her hand, holding it tight for a moment before letting it go. "You can't dictate terms to your boss. What I say, goes." He softened his words with a wink.

She crossed her arms over her chest. “What about you? When are *you* going to sleep?”

“Sleep is for amateurs.”

“Ha, ha. Seriously, Ely, I’m worried about you.”

“Get some sleep. Come in when you want.”

“I’ll be there by ten a.m. We need to start inventory.”

“Sleep well. Call me if you need me.”

After he left, she leaned against the front door, listening to the sound of his truck engine fade into the distance. She glanced around the living room, lit only by a single lamp. She knew she should try to call Nash again. But what was the point? She’d left him at least a dozen voice mails in the last two days and he’d ignored all of them. Maybe she should have just blurted out that Dad died on the last message, see if that would jolt him into calling her back.

She lay down on the sofa, meaning to rest there a moment before going into her bedroom. In a few minutes, she was asleep. It was still dark when she heard the back door open. A few seconds later,

Nash called her name. She didn't answer, but listened to the footsteps come down the hallway, a hollow, wooden sound.

"Ruby?" he said, coming into the living room.

She opened her eyes and sat up. Her mouth felt dry, her tongue sticking to the roof of her mouth. Her brother's chagrined face seemed blurry; his gray eyes were bloodshot and tinged yellow.

He stuck his hands deep into the pockets of his jeans, tossed his long hair.

"Man, I'm sorry I didn't answer your calls. It's just, me and hospitals, we totally don't mix. They give me the willies. I—"

"Dad died," she blurted out. "His ashes will be delivered in a few days." She stood up, walked past him and into her bedroom. "I'm going to bed."

20

Birch

"Her car isn't here," Sueann said. "Are you sure she's home?" She shifted her fabric grocery bag from one hand to the other and leaned crookedly, trying to peer into Ruby's front window. There was no light shining around the closed blind.

"Where would she be?" Birch replied, setting her casserole dish down on the small round table next to Ruby's front door. She knocked harder, watching the needles drop from the pine wreath she'd hung weeks ago. "I called Ely at the bookstore to see if she was working. He'd told her to take the day off. When she never showed up to work, he assumed she listened to him." Birch glanced at her watch. "Maybe she went to get something to eat."

"Well, it sure looks like no one . . ." Before Sueann could finish, the front door opened. Ruby stood in front of them, blinking her eyes slowly. She wore navy sweatpants and a red and white Old Navy T-shirt.

"Oh," she said, bringing a hand to her tousled hair. "I wasn't expecting anyone."

Birch picked up her casserole dish. "We thought you and Nash might be hungry. We brought you supper."

Sueann held up her bag. "And enough provisions for a few days."

"Oh, no, what time is it?" Ruby's hand flew to her mouth. "I told Ely I'd come in to work."

Birch smiled. "Sweetie, that train has left the station. It's a little past five o'clock. We called there first and he told us you would likely still be sleeping. He's doing fine. It's never too busy during the first week of January."

A sudden wind shimmied the wind chimes on the porch. "Where are my manners?" Ruby said, stepping back and opening the door wider. "Come in. It's cold out there."

"We're so sorry about your daddy," Birch said, stepping inside the house. "How's Nash taking it?"

Birch watched Ruby's face travel through a week's worth of emotion—shock, sorrow, anger, despair, fatigue.

"Please, take the food to the kitchen," Ruby said, her voice still hoarse from sleep. "I'll see how he's doing."

She turned her back on them and abruptly went down the hallway, her sockless feet making a soft *thump, thump* on the wood floor.

"Let's heat up the casserole." Sueann's voice went low. "I bet neither of them has had a good meal for at least three days."

Birch nodded and followed Sueann into the kitchen though she wanted to follow Ruby down that hallway. The look on Ruby's face told Birch that either Ruby hadn't told her brother about their father dying . . . or she had and it hadn't gone well. In the kitchen, she and Sueann started setting the table.

"I hope he isn't drunk," Sueann whispered as they folded paper towels into napkins and searched the cupboards for glasses. "Or hung- over."

Birch didn't answer, her stomach as sick as if she'd been drinking herself. How many times had she done this same thing with her mother? Tiptoeing around, wondering if her father was going to come out of his room drunk or hungover or at some terrible angry place in between where he seemed to spend most of her childhood.

They were discussing whether to turn on the stove or wait and see if Ruby wanted a full supper or just a sandwich when she came running into the kitchen, her eyes wide and frantic.

"He's not there!"

Birch and Sueann glanced at each other, then back at the food they were preparing.

"Did he leave a note?" Birch asked, knowing the answer. Drunks never left notes. Her mother spent half her life wondering where her father was, when or if he'd come home.

Ruby shook her head, then tried to smooth back her hair. "Who am I kidding?

He's probably already out drinking." She dropped her head and stared at her bare feet. "What was I thinking bringing him here? Did I really think he could start over? He was perfectly happy living hand to mouth in Nashville." She inhaled a tiny sob. "I'm such an idiot."

"Oh, sweetie," Birch said, moving across the kitchen floor and pulling her in a hug. "You were just trying to be a good sister."

"Look, we all have family troubles," Sueann said. "You will get through this. You'll figure it out."

"Why don't you come eat something," Birch said. "Ely said you had a rough few days."

Before Ruby could answer, the phone rang.

"That's probably Nash now," Birch said.

Birch and Sueann kept fussing with the table setting while they blatantly eavesdropped on Ruby's conversation.

"Oh, hi," Ruby said. There was a long moment of silence, and then Ruby exclaimed, "What? What?" Her voice grew strident, hysterical. "Oh, no, no, no . . ."

Birch heard the phone drop and she ran into the living room.

Ruby stood staring at the phone, where a faraway voice was calling her name. She turned, ran down the hall to the bathroom, where Birch could hear the sounds of dry heaving.

"What's going on?" Sueann said, coming into the room. "Why is Ruby . . . ?"

Birch reached down and grabbed the phone. "Who is this?"

"Aunt Birch?"

The familiar voice stunned her. "Lucas? What's going on? Why is Ruby . . . ?"

"There's been an accident," he said, his voice sounding stiff and hollow.

"Who?" Her mind flashed to Nash. Oh, no, that poor girl . . .

"Mom," he said, his voice strangled. "It's Mom."

Birch froze silent for a moment. June? June had been in an accident? "Lucas, I'm sorry . . ." She shook her head. "But why . . . Ruby . . . ?"

She could hear his rapid breathing over the phone. "Mom's okay. I mean, she's not okay, she's in surgery with a broken leg, a few cracked ribs and some bruising . . . she'll be okay eventually, the doctor says." She could hear Derek saying something in the background, the angry timbre of his voice.

"It's Aunt Birch," she heard Lucas say. "I don't know why she's there. I'll . . . Just back off, Derek, I'll take care of it." He came back on the line. "There's no easy way to tell you. It's Nash. He has a few bumps and bruises, but he's fine. He's the one who hit Mom. He was driving Ruby's car and broadsided Mom at the intersection near the fairgrounds. He's under arrest."

21

Lucas

"Right now, he's in police custody here at the hospital," Lucas told Birch. "When the doctor releases him, he'll go to jail. Probably in the next twenty-four hours. His injuries weren't serious."

"I can't believe this," Birch said. "I don't know how much more Ruby can take."

"I know," Lucas said. "Just a minute, it's really noisy in here. Let me go outside." As he walked out of the waiting room he heard her give a quick report to Sueann. He could see in his mind's eye Sueann's mouth dropping open in shock. Once outside he said, "Sorry. Derek wouldn't shut up so I couldn't really talk. He's fit to be hog-tied. Or rather, that's what he wants to do to Ruby's brother. Mom will likely agree when she comes out of surgery."

"Oh, Lucas, this is a mess, isn't it?"

"Yes, it is. And I'm torn. You know how much I care about Ruby."

"We all do," Birch said.

"But this is bad. Gordon told me there's little doubt that it's Nash's fault. There are witnesses that said he ran a red light and . . ."

"He was drunk," Birch said, her voice low.

"There's *no* getting around that. The Breathalyzer put his blood alcohol at way past the legal limit."

"What can I do, Lucas?"

"Just stay with Ruby."

"I'm sure she's going to want to come right down to the hospital."

"No doubt. Most likely she'll have to make a decision about whether she wants to bail him out."

"She doesn't have the money," Birch said flatly. "And, frankly, that boy is better off in jail."

"I agree, but it's not up to us." He leaned against the cold concrete wall outside the emergency room.

"June?"

Lucas knew what she was asking without her having to say it. "You can bet she'll go after him with guns blazing. She won't turn the other cheek on this."

"What can she do?" Birch said. "I mean, she could take him to court . . ."

"Or sue Ruby. It was her car Nash was driving."

Birch was silent for a moment. "Well, Ruby doesn't have a pot to call her own, so what could June possibly get?"

"Whatever happens, this is not going to be pretty. You'd better start praying."

"I already have. I'll call Bobby, and then I will talk to Ruby about what she wants to do. We'll see you in a little while."

After he hung up, Lucas stood outside the Cardinal General Hospital emergency entrance and wished he smoked. At least it would give him something to do. He took in a deep breath of freezing air, then straightened his spine. Somehow, he would have to tread this fine line between Ruby and his mom. However, he knew, just as sure as he always knew that split second before a horse threw him, that something was going completely wrong, that he was going to end up on the hard ground. He doubted that even a Supreme Court justice could successfully mediate between these two women.

He looked up at the sky. A dense cloud cover hid any stars. "So, what should I do, big brother? You got some kind of cosmic answer for me down here in the trenches?"

He shook his head at his foolishness and went back inside the hospital, through the emergency room to the busy waiting room. Derek was nowhere in sight, so after checking with the front desk clerk and finding out his mom was still in surgery, he took a vacant seat in the corner of the waiting room. Ten minutes later, he saw Ely come through the sliding glass doors.

He stood and called Ely's name.

Ely walked over and they clasped hands. "How's your mom?"

Lucas pushed back his hat. "Still in pain, but the doctor says she'll probably be okay after some physical therapy. How did you hear?"

"You know this town. One of Gordon's deputies stopped by the Grounds for coffee and told me. How's Ruby?"

"Not good. I only talked to her a minute, but at least Birch and Sueann were at her house when I told her. They're bringing her down."

"Nash?"

Lucas gave a disgusted grunt. "Like most drunks who cause accidents, he only got bumps and bruises. He's under arrest."

Derek walked up before Ely could comment.

"Mom's still groggy from anesthesia," Derek said. "You know they're going to have to knock her out again once she hears who did this."

"Yeah, I know," Lucas said. "But I'm sure we can work something—"

Derek interrupted him with a cynical laugh. "Oh, little bro, you aren't serious? Work something out? Mom is going to go for this guy's jugular. He was drunk, man, and ran a stoplight. There are eyewitnesses. He broke her damn leg in three places."

The automatic hospital doors opened again and Ruby, Birch and Sueann entered. They started walking toward them with Ruby in the lead.

"Derek," Lucas said. "Now's not the time . . ."

"What do you mean?" he said, his voice booming. "Now's exactly the time. Mom is going to go after him with everything she's got, and probably Ruby, too. She'll nail them both to the wall." The timbre of his voice rose with the last sentence.

"Derek!" Lucas barked his name. He looked past his brother to Ruby, who had stopped abruptly, her face white and tear-stained. There was no doubt she heard Derek's last sentence.

Ruby turned and fled back out the front door. Birch and Sueann gaped at Derek.

Lucas moved swiftly past Birch, touching her shoulder briefly. "Don't worry, I'll talk to her."

Outside, he found her a few feet from the entrance, leaning against a large pine tree.

"Ruby," he said, walking toward her.

She held up her hand for him to stop. "I'm okay, Lucas. I just had to get out of there before I said anything I might regret. I know what a screwed-up mess this is and I know you are caught in the middle. I don't expect you to help me . . ."

"Stop it. Of course I'll help you."

She hugged her leather purse to her chest. "Oh, Lucas, don't you understand how this changes everything? We're on opposite sides now. There is no way you can straddle something like this. You have to be loyal to your family. And I have to be loyal to mine."

"But . . ." He stopped, not able to say what he was thinking. *You're my family.* Because, it wasn't true. He cared about her. She was once his sister-in-law. He might even be in love with her. But she was right. June was his family and Nash was hers. Nothing could change that.

"I still want to help," he said. "Cole would want me to help you."

"I understand, Lucas, but Cole is gone. June is your mother. Your *mother.*" She said it gently, pleading. "I cannot be the thing again that causes more of a rift between you and your mother."

"You can't make it any worse than it has been for years."

"Oh, Lucas." Her voice was weary.

"Then what are you going to do?"

She hitched her purse over her shoulder, her expression grim. "I've decided to go see our mother, see if she has money I can borrow."

"I can loan you money." He had no idea where he'd get it, but he'd figure that out later.

"Thank you," Ruby said. "But the Stoddards have taken enough from other people. Nash is her son, and if she has the means, she should help him. Besides, if he does get out, at some point, I'm thinking we should do an intervention. I want to see if she can . . . or will do that. Maybe seeing his mother . . ." She shrugged, her mouth turned down. "She's the only thing I've got at the moment."

"You're really going to call her?" Lucas said.

Ruby gave a cynical laugh. "So it gives her a chance to take off again? No way. I'm going to just show up on her doorstep."

"You know where she lives in Ajo?" Lucas said.

"I found her name and address in the Ajo white pages on the Internet."

"You can't drive to Arizona alone. I'll come with you."

"That's not a good idea. You need to be here for your mom and it's . . . it's awkward."

"It's dangerous for you to drive that far alone."

"She won't be," Ely said behind him. "I'll go with her."

Lucas turned to look at his friend, his chest tightening. Ely's face was open, concerned. He turned back to Ruby. The relief on her face as she looked at Ely made him want to punch the side of the building. "I can go." He bit the words off.

She touched his arm. "Lucas, that would be awkward under the circumstances." She turned to Ely. "Can you leave right away?"

"I can," he said. "Gas tank is full. It's probably about a ten-, eleven-hour drive. We can be there by breakfast."

"What about Nash?" she asked.

"He'll be in the hospital for a few more hours, then they'll likely keep him in jail until someone bails him out."

"Then he'll be safe," she said, her voice firm. "Without me to bail him out, he'll have to stay there."

"Do you want to let him know where you're going?" Ely said.

"No, because I don't know what she will do. She might just blow me off and I'll have to think of something else. Let me go tell Birch and we can leave."

"I'll call George and tell him to take care of the store and the coffeehouse." Ely pulled out a cell phone and walked out into the dark parking lot.

Ruby turned back to Lucas. "I'm so sorry Nash hurt your mom, that he's caused all these problems."

He wanted to be angry with her. He wanted to be angry at Ely, who was managing to be exactly what Ruby needed at every turn. But he couldn't really be angry with either of them. Everyone was just doing the best they could.

"Go find your mom," he said, softly. "Do what you have to do. Somehow, this will all work out."

"Thank you," she said, hugging him so quickly he couldn't unfold his arms and return her hug. "We'll call you when we reach Ajo and find out how Nash and June are. Please, I don't expect you to talk to him or anything like that, but could you just check on Nash?"

"No worries, Ruby," he said. "I'll be here. I'll always be here."

22

Etta

"Etta, I do believe you have acquired yourself an admirer," Dr. Beth said while she ran her hand over the stomach of the Border Patrol rescue dog that Etta had named Appy.

The small male dog barked and wiggled his speckled stump of a tail, his black, shiny eyes never leaving Etta's face.

"You hankering for a game of ball?" Etta said, holding his squirming body still for the examination. He'd had a horrible case of mange when he was brought in, but it was almost healed now.

He barked again, recognizing his favorite word.

"We should name you Gecko," Etta said, laughing. "You're as fast as a lizard." He'd already escaped his cage twice, though only getting as far as the outer, fenced yard. He didn't want to run away; he just wanted to get to the grass and play. "Now, quiet down while Dr. Beth checks you out." She touched the back of his head and he instantly sat down, his eyes still glued to Etta's face.

"You're the only person he'll listen to," Dr. Beth said. "And he's not the only one. I think you have some magical dog-whispering ability."

Etta felt a warm wash of embarrassed pleasure. It had been a long time since she had felt special, though her relationships with Dr. Beth and Father Tomas certainly counted as something. With them, though, it felt more as if she was a project, someone who needed help. And, Lord knows, that was true. She'd be the first to admit that.

All the dogs enjoyed her slow, careful touch and soothing words. She loved and worried over them all. When she washed the new rescues, she sent up a request for each one that the right person would come along to adopt them. Though she had been technically out of dialog with God for many years, since she wasn't even sure He was there, Father Tomas had assured her that He hadn't moved and to not hesitate to ask for anything. So she did. For the dogs. That was all she felt she deserved. For herself . . . well, that was just asking too much. She was grateful to be, for today, alive and safe and working and not drunk. Day at a time. That blessed sameness was all she dared hope for.

"He's much better," Dr. Beth said. "I think we've licked that nasty mange. In a few weeks, he can be put up on the website."

Appy licked Etta's hand, whined to be let down. His shiny, black eyes were miles better than the sad, dull ones that had stared up at her when the Border Patrol agent had brought him in. He had been so sick with mange and worms that he'd huddled in the back of his cage, his head hidden in the tattered blanket. He didn't look like the same dog that was rescued four weeks ago.

Etta lifted him down and attached the leash to his collar. "You know, I've been thinking . . ."

Dr. Beth smiled. "I agree. It's time a dog owned you. Whenever you're ready to take him home . . ." She turned back to Appy's chart and wrote something in it.

"Maybe tomorrow," Etta said, suddenly feeling nervous. It had been a long time since she'd been responsible for anyone but herself.

"Whenever you're ready," Dr. Beth said without turning around. "He's not going anywhere. I've got to drive to Tucson for medicine. Think you and Lupe can hold down the fort?"

"No problem," Etta said.

When Etta put Appy back in his run, he started howling.

"Sorry, little bud," she said, grabbing the long-handled pooper scooper, "but the ball will have to wait until later. I've got kennels to clean."

She was on the second row of kennel runs, filling their metal bowls with water, when Lupe, their sixteen-year-old volunteer receptionist, came back to find her.

"Hey, Etta," Lupe said. "Someone wants to talk to you out front."

Etta looked and nodded. "I'll be there in a minute. Two more bowls to fill." It was probably someone with a donation or maybe, if they were lucky, someone who wanted to adopt a dog. Usually people made appointments after seeing a dog that struck their fancy on the rescue's website, something else Lupe helped with. Occasionally they had a drop-in, a curious person from Phoenix or Tucson, looking for that special dog.

"Okay," Lupe said, nodding, fingering the red and black beaded necklace around her neck. It was one designed by her grandmother, Helen. Etta was taking a beading class from her and was still working on her first necklace. "It's a guy and a girl," Lupe called over her shoulder. "He's Indian, for sure, though he's not from around here."

Etta lifted a hand in acknowledgment. They were likely some young couple out for the day to take photos of Ajo's picturesque downtown square famous for its

Spanish colonial architecture. A few minutes later, she dried her hands, smoothed down her old red sweatshirt and tried to knock some dirt off the knees of her jeans. She glanced at a small mirror stuck on the wall next to the door leading to the reception area. She ran her fingers through her hair, damp from working. Oh, well, they weren't here to see her. They'd probably want to know if there were any puppies. People always wanted puppies.

She walked into the reception area and stood behind the counter where Lupe sat working on the computer. The man looked straight at her, his long black braids and coppery skin verifying what Lupe had said . . . he was almost certainly Native American. His face was neutral, though not unfriendly, an expression Etta was accustomed to seeing on the faces of Indian men around Ajo.

The woman had her back turned, studying the framed photos of All Good Dogs successful adoptions. It was Etta's job to clean the pictures, a task that always left her hopeful. All those happy endings.

"Can I help you?" Etta said.

The woman turned around and Etta froze. Her head exploded with a million buzzing bees.

"Ruby Lee," Etta said, holding her hand over her throbbing, grateful heart.

23

Ruby

Ruby had imagined this moment since she was thirteen years old. The day her father told her that Mama wanted a different life, that she was never coming home, remained as clear in Ruby's memory as this morning's breakfast. In Ruby's teenage years, the scenarios in her head of confronting her mother when she finally came crawling back were always dramatic and angry. In her twenties, Ruby imagined humiliating her mother with biting, sarcastic words, of seeing Loretta's pretty face melt under Ruby's clever, biting accusations.

On the drive to Ajo from Cardinal, she let herself briefly imagine herself addressing this Etta person with cool, calculating words, not allowing her mother to see that she had even been missed, that Ruby and Nash had a fine life without her, thank you very much. Except, of course, it wasn't true. No matter when it happened, Ruby had always believed she would have a lifetime of words for the woman who had so blithely walked out of their life so many years ago.

Instead, she was speechless. The woman who stood in front of Ruby was a stranger. The picture of her chain-smoking, raven-haired mother that Ruby had always carried in her head had been replaced by this painfully thin, sad-eyed woman wearing dirt-stained jeans and a faded red sweatshirt with "Ajo Red Raiders" in white lettering across the front.

"Ruby Lee," the woman whispered, holding both her hands over her chest. "How did you find me?" Her hair was short, spiky and streaked with gray. Then she lifted a single index finger to her pale lips, as if she were trying to keep herself from speaking.

Ruby's heart jumped at the familiar gesture. She stared at her mother, afraid if she opened her mouth, all that would come out was incoherent babbling. It angered and dismayed her that a tiny part of her wanted to fling herself into this woman's arms.

"I go by Ruby," she whispered. "We went by your house. Your neighbor said you worked here."

Her mother's dark gray eyes widened. "Oh, my Lord, it's Joe, isn't it?"

Ruby nodded silently. Behind her, she felt Ely's steady presence, his warm hand on her elbow.

"Mrs. Stoddard," he said, "I'm afraid we have bad news. Joe passed away January second."

Etta covered her mouth with her hand, her eyes shiny. "How?"

"He had a stroke on New Year's day," Ely said, his voice gentle. "Mrs. Stoddard, is there any way we can go somewhere and talk?"

"Of course," she said. "Please, call me Etta." She glanced quickly at Ruby, then over at the young receptionist. "Lupe, I'm going to be gone for a few hours. Could you let Dr. Beth know when she gets back from Tucson?"

Lupe nodded, her young face curious and excited by this unusual event. "Yes, ma'am. If there's an emergency . . . ?"

"You have my cell," Etta said, touching the back pocket of her jeans. "I won't be far."

Outside the concrete building, Ruby, Etta and Ely stood in the weak January sun looking at each other.

Etta turned to Ruby and held out a hand. "Thank you for coming to let me know. I hope you didn't have to drive far."

"Cardinal," Ruby said, pretending as if she didn't see her mother's gesture. "That's in California. Dad died in Las Vegas though. Prissy was with him."

"I only met her once, but she seemed like a real nice woman," Etta said, sticking her hand in a back pocket. "Your daddy seemed happy. She must be devastated."

Ruby bit her bottom lip, afraid to say more, afraid it would only start an avalanche of words she might regret.

"It's only eleven a.m.," Ely said. "But

Ruby and I ate breakfast at five. What do you both think about getting an early lunch?"

"Okay," Ruby said, thankful he was taking charge. She kept darting glances at her mother, wishing she could freeze time for a moment so she could study this woman unobserved. Nothing about this encounter had gone the way Ruby had imagined. Yes, she was still angry, but seeing this aging woman in place of the young vibrant one who left so many years ago made her father's death even more poignant and unfair. How had their family disintegrated so completely? Was it just her mother's desertion or had there been things going on before that, rips and tears in her parents' relationship that culminated in her mother's leaving?

"Ruby?" Ely said.

She shook her head, unaware that he'd asked her a question. "I'm sorry, what did you ask?"

"Is Mexican food okay with you?"

"Yes, sure. Whatever you two want."

"Marcela's is only a few blocks away," Etta said. "They have wonderful food."

On the walk over to the café, Ruby concentrated on the scenery, gratefully letting Ely chat with Etta. He asked about the dog rescue, what she did there every day, why Dr. Beth started the rescue, the history of Ajo and the copper mine. It was obvious, as Ruby noticed when she and Ely drove into town, that Ajo was, like many towns started and supported by an industry and then abandoned, a town past its heyday, a place with a raucous history, a complicated past and faint hints of a future. She listened while Etta told Ely that she rented her small house from Dr. Beth. It was one of the old company houses once owned by the Phelps Dodge copper mining company. They had eventually sold them dirt cheap to snowbirds from Michigan and Wisconsin and people like her boss, Dr. Beth.

"You're welcome to come back and see inside," Etta said, her voice shy, glancing over at Ruby.

Ruby didn't answer, uncomfortable with her mother's attempt to engage her. She knew they'd eventually have to talk about personal issues, about the past, but she couldn't do it yet.

They ate their lunch in silence. Ely finished first and set his fork and knife across his plate. "I'm going to take a walk. I think you two have things to talk about and you need to be alone." He leaned over and kissed Ruby on the cheek, surprising her. "Call me when you're ready to leave. Lunch is on me." He slipped a couple of twenties under his plate and left.

Ruby stared at her half-eaten enchilada plate for a few minutes. Though she didn't want him to leave, she knew he was right. She and Etta had things to discuss and they needed to do it alone.

Ruby pushed her plate aside and looked up at her mother. "Where do we start?"

Etta's eyes, a darker gray than Ruby's, stared back at her, wary now. She gave a slight shrug. "I guess the beginning is the most logical. Do you want to walk downtown? It's only a little over a mile. Sometimes it's easier to talk when you're walking."

"Okay," Ruby said, standing up.

They started down the road, where they could see Ely's figure a quarter of a mile ahead of them. "He seems like a nice man," Etta said. "Are you together?"

"No," Ruby said. "Not like that. He's a friend. A really good friend."

"You said you live in Cardinal? Isn't that up near Mammoth? In the mountains?"

"The foot of the Eastern Sierra Nevada Mountains. I live there now. So does Nash."

Etta's face lit up, causing Ruby to feel a pang of jealousy. "How is he? How did you both end up living in the same town? Last I heard from your father, Nash was in Knoxville playing in a band."

"That was years ago," Ruby said. "He's . . ." She didn't want to get into what was going on with Nash. Not right yet. "Don't you want to hear about Dad?"

Etta looked down as they walked, puffs of dirt kicking up around their feet. "Poor Joe. A stroke, you said?"

"Yes, as Ely told you, it happened on New Year's Eve. They were in Vegas and had just got off a run back east to deliver some batteries. He was taking a shower. They were going to go see Wayne Newton."

"He always hated Wayne Newton," Etta said.

Ruby shrugged. "People change. You ought to know that better than anyone." The minute she said the words, she wished she hadn't, even though she meant them.

"Yes," Etta said softly. "They do."

They were silent a moment, concentrating on walking. Occasionally a person came out of their peeling old wood frame house or singlewide trailer and waved to Etta, many calling her by name.

"You know a lot of people," Ruby said, trying to keep her voice neutral.

"I've lived here five years. It's a small town."

When they reached the Spanish colonial town square, Etta gave Ruby a quick history of Ajo, pointing out the red-tiled building that once was the train depot, the old company store, the movie theater. The theater was now a restaurant called the Oasis Café. Outside people sat around wrought iron tables, sipped café lattes and ate triple-decker sandwiches.

"It's pretty at Christmas," Etta said, pointing to a bench that faced the whitewashed Immaculate Conception Catholic

Church and the less ornate, but similar-styled Ajo Federated Church.

"The palm trees remind me of Orange County," Ruby said.

Etta nodded. "They put twinkly lights on the trunks of the ones here in the square. Southwest Christmases are different than the ones I grew up with in Tennessee. Sometimes I miss the snow."

They sat down on a bench facing the two whitewashed churches, leaving a polite distance between them. They stared straight ahead at the almost empty street. The sky was an unreal blue, like a computer-enhanced photograph, Ruby thought. Nothing felt real at this moment.

Ruby inhaled, then asked in a rush of words, "So, what happened? Where did you go? Why didn't you come back? Why didn't you even write or call? Why did you just abandon us?"

Etta clasped her hands together, her knuckles white. "All of those are good questions. I'll try to answer them as best I can. My life . . . It was complicated and . . ."

"Oh, please," Ruby said, trembling with

anger. "Everyone's life is complicated. Everyone's life is *hard.* Don't try to make excuses. You just left."

Now that she'd started, it was what she feared would happen; she wanted to spew all her hurt and anger and blanket her mother with it, drown her with it, kill her with it. "You left because you wanted to be some kind of famous singer. So, how did that work out for you? Oh, not so well, I guess, since I never saw you accepting any awards on television or signing your latest record at Walmart. I hope whatever it was that you left Nash and me for was worth it. I hope you got whatever it was you were looking for that we couldn't give you. I hope . . ."

Ruby choked on her words, turning her head away, not wanting Etta to see her tears. She stared at the cross atop the Catholic church, blurry and indistinct. Next to her, she could hear her mother's labored breathing. Don't look at her, she told herself. Let her hear all that, let it all sink in.

"Everything you say is true," Etta finally said. "And I can say I'm sorry until the day I die and it wouldn't be enough. Ruby, I don't know what to tell you. I don't know how I can even begin to make it up to you and Nash."

Ruby didn't answer. Her heart pounded like she'd run miles and miles, and right now she wished she'd never come. What good could possibly come of it? Etta was right; there was nothing she could say that would be enough. Ruby thought about what an impossible situation this was. She wanted to dial Ely's cell phone and scream at him to get the truck and drive them out of here as fast as he could.

But ignoring things wouldn't make them better. The truth was the only other person in this world who might care as much as Ruby did about Nash's life was sitting next to her. Maybe their mother was the only person who could get through to him. She inhaled deeply, taking in the dusty, old scent of the town.

She turned to look at Etta. "Did you know we were put in foster care? Dad was gone too often, and when I was seventeen and Nash was eleven, someone reported us. The county found out and put us in foster care. They split us up. Dad just kept on driving his truck."

Etta's face paled and her eyes filled with tears. "I had no idea. Joe never told me."

"Of course he wouldn't. Communication is not the Stoddard way."

"I'm sorry," Etta said again. "Ruby, I hope it wasn't bad. I'm . . ."

"My foster parents were nice people. I wasn't sexually molested, if that is what you're asking. Or physically abused. Nash, either. We were lucky, I guess. If you can call Nash being sent to six homes in seven years lucky. We survived. That's something else we Stoddards are good at, I guess."

After another few moments of silence, Etta said, "Okay, while I appreciate you coming to tell me about Joe and tell me what is going on with you and Nash, I have a feeling there's more to your visit than that. You could have sent me a letter or called."

Ruby stared at the Catholic church, the whitewashed walls brilliant in the midday sunlight. The heat felt good on the back of her neck. "You're right, but I have one more question."

Etta nervously picked at a hole in the knee of her jeans. "Yes?"

"Why, after you didn't make it as a singer, did you still not come back home? I mean, not to Dad. I understand that your marriage was over. But, why didn't you come back to Nash and me?" Ruby despised the soft hiccup at the end of her sentence, a held-back sob. She didn't want her mother to know how much it had hurt, how much power she still had over Ruby even after all these years.

Etta stared straight ahead. When she spoke, her voice lost all emotion. The only thing that Ruby could see that showed Etta felt anything at all was the slight tremble in her hands.

"It's a long story. All I can say right now is I fell in with a very bad man. He caused me to . . ." She stopped abruptly. "No, I *chose* to do the things, *allow* the things that happened to . . ." She shook her head. "I can't go into that right now. I was a foolish woman. I threw my life away. I did things that . . ." She turned her head and looked Ruby directly in the eyes. "I didn't come back because I didn't deserve to be a mother. I wanted to come back, but I couldn't. It would have been worse for you—"

"No!" Ruby said. "Nothing is worse than your mother deserting you."

Etta's mouth hardened. "There are worse things. I would have been worse. I was a drunk, Ruby. I did something . . . I would have been a horrible mother. You and Nash deserved better. I sent money when I could. I don't know if Joe told you . . ."

Ruby shook her head. "He didn't."

"It wasn't much. I guess . . . Well, I'm sorry. That's all I can say. I'm so very sorry." She unclasped her hands and held one out, hovering over Ruby's knee, not touching.

Ruby moved her leg just slightly, not wanting to let her mother even have one touch. She felt mean and ugly and childish, but there it was. She couldn't give in despite the pulling of her heart. She could not trust this woman. Yet, she was going to have to. There was no one else.

"You know what? I don't really want to talk about what you did or didn't do anymore," Ruby said, her voice crisp. "I did come for another reason. Believe me, if there had been anyone else in the world I could have asked, I would never have come to you. But there is only you. Nash is in trouble and I need your help."

24

Lucas

"Would you like to come to church with us?" Birch asked. She stood next to the idling car, her mitten-covered hand on the door handle. From inside the truck's steamy cab, Bobby fiddled with something in the glove box. "There's going to be a potluck afterward. Rumor has it that Mrs. Parker is making your favorite caramel spice cake."

"No, thanks," Lucas said. "I'm behind on the notebooks for the story jam and I need to start on the Beumerses' saddle. Got to put in a full day's work."

"Okay," Birch said, giving him a cheery

smile. "I'll save a piece for you and bring it by the shop." She opened the truck's passenger door and climbed up next to Bobby.

He shoved his hands in the pockets of his Carhartt barn jacket. It was still cold, even at ten a.m., and the pockets didn't provide much warmth. This winter was breaking all kinds of records. He thought about going back upstairs and fetching his gloves. He resisted, knowing he would be tempted to flip on the television and veg out all day. Most of yesterday he'd spent out at the ranch helping Derek build ramps so his mother would have an easier time getting around on crutches.

When he'd visited her last night at the hospital, Cassie was there helping June look through the Internet at motorized scooters. Great, he thought, the faster to get around and harass everyone. She was due to come home tomorrow and Derek had arranged for a full-time LVN to live there for the next few weeks. However, there was no doubt he and his brother would be running twelve hours a day to keep up with June's demands.

He rubbed a cold hand over his face, his palm scratching against his two-day beard. The story jam was rapidly approaching and he still had to finish those notebooks.

By the time he'd walked the ten minutes to his saddle shop, he regretted his decision to forgo gloves. His hands were stiff with cold now and it would take at least a half hour for the shop to heat up. While waiting for the room and his hands to warm up, he puttered around his bench, putting away tools, wiping down blades, throwing away old candy-bar wrappers and empty drink cups. The only trouble with doing this sort of mindless tidying up was it gave his mind too much time to think about the one thing he'd managed to not think about since Friday evening—Ruby and Ely driving to Ajo to talk to her mother. Though he knew it was emotional and a little crazy, he was still jealous and angry that she'd chosen Ely over him to accompany her on this important journey. Illogically, he felt like he was losing a best friend and a potential girlfriend in one fell swoop. Hadn't he and

Ruby started . . . something? Or had it all just been in his feverish imagination? He felt like he was fifteen, not thirty-five. What a lousy year this was starting out to be.

Though he knew he needed to work on the half-finished notebooks, after he'd straightened up the room, he decided to clean Cole's saddle. Though it legally belonged to Ruby, she'd asked Lucas to keep it here in the shop until she found a permanent place to live. Well, maybe she had now, unless, of course, she decided to move in with Ely. Man, if that happened, he'd seriously consider moving away from Cardinal, though he had absolutely no idea where he would go. Not to mention his aunt Birch would have the conniption fit of all time.

"My life is a mess," he said aloud as he wiped down Cole's saddle with a damp sponge, a clean cloth and some saddle soap. His brother had actually trained and worked as a saddle maker before Lucas was even out of high school. He'd taught Lucas the fundamentals when Lucas was a boy, long before Cole went to prison. When Lucas gave up the law and decided to come back to Cardinal, he'd apprenticed under an elderly local saddle maker, Jake Seligman, the same man who'd taught Cole. Many ranchers in the area still used one of Jake's or Cole's sturdy saddles. Some of Lucas's most steady business came from repairing those old saddles. It always felt good when one came in, despite the fact that repairing saddles wasn't near as pleasurable as building one from the tree up. He found himself talking in his head to either Jake or Cole, both gone now, when he repaired one of their saddles.

"So, maybe it is crazy to think I'm in love with your wife," Lucas said, wiping the thin layer of dust off Cole's saddle. It was probably the best saddle Cole had ever built. Lucas had been offered thousands of dollars for it, the last time by a plumbing-supply millionaire who still e-mailed him every so often asking if the "pineapple" saddle was for sale. Under the cantle, Cole had carved a pineapple rather than the normal flowers or vines.

"It's a symbol of friendship," Cole said, when Lucas asked him why. "Maybe someday I'll find a friend who deserves this saddle."

"Did you?" Lucas said to the empty room. He ran his fingers over the unusual carving. "Was Ely that to you? You were his sponsor. Were you friends? Good enough friends that you'd give him your wife?" He rubbed the cloth across the seat, thinking how utterly pathetic he was on all counts.

Behind him, he heard the front door slam open. Startled, he turned to catch a whoosh of cold air and a high, feminine giggle. It was his niece, Cassie.

"Who're you talking to, Uncle Lucas?" she said, unwrapping the pink and black scarf Birch had told Lucas to buy Cassie for Christmas. "This place is way cold. Is your heater broken again?"

He smiled at her. "Trust me, it's way better than when I first got here. Heater isn't broken, just old and undependable."

She grinned and flopped down on the love seat under the shop's front window. "Like you?"

Lucas leaned on the wooden counter.

"Hey, thirty-five ain't old. What's cookin', good lookin'?" There must be a God, because the one person who could almost always kid him out of a cranky mood was Cassie.

"I'm supposed to be taking some cinnamon rolls over to the church for the potluck, but church doesn't let out for another half hour so I thought I'd come by and say hi." She held his eyes for a moment, then looked casually around the room. "Is that a new clock? What happened to the Bowden Saddle Tree clock?"

Lucas raised his eyebrows. "Broke. Why else are you here?"

She grinned again. "I'm so not a good liar, am I?"

"Wouldn't even make the semifinals, chickadee."

She gave him a sly look. "Guess I'll never be a lawyer, then."

"Ha, ha. That's your one lawyer joke for the year and you've gone and used it up in January. What's on your mind?"

"Aunt Birch was worried about you, so she asked me to come by and cheer you up. Why're you all depressed?"

Thanks, Aunt Birch, he thought. *Do you really expect me to spill my guts to a high school senior?*

"Just got the New Year's blues."

"I hear you. I just visited Grandma June. Man, she is on the warpath. She wants to shoot death rays at Ruby's brother. What's going on with Ruby, anyway? Is Nash still in jail? Man, Rodeo is so down. She's, like, so into him."

Lucas hesitated, not certain Ruby would want Cassie to know that she was going to Arizona to find her mother. He decided to be as vague as possible, because he also knew if Cassie found out about Ruby visiting her mother before Sueann did, Lucas would never hear the end of it.

"Nash is still in jail," he said. "I'm not sure when Ruby is going to bail him out. She might not have the money."

"Besides, it's safer for him to stay there," Cassie said, nodding. "At least Ruby doesn't have to worry about him doing it again until she can, like, figure things out."

Lucas was a bit amazed at her quick

grasp of the situation. Kids now were so much more sophisticated than he was at that age. "You called that one right. I think she's just trying to figure out what her next step will be."

"I'm *so* glad I'm an only child," Cassie said. "What a pain. Hey, did Mom tell you I got acceptance letters from three colleges? I am so ready to blow this pop stand."

"She mentioned it. You still thinking about majoring in physical therapy?"

"Totally. I actually want to be able to get a job that pays money when I graduate. No freebie intern crap for me. Besides, I kind of like the idea of making people feel better. You know, adding to the world, not taking away."

"Such adorably noble albeit naïve aspirations from one so young."

A hurt expression colored her face. "Whoa, excuse me for trying to be optimistic."

Lucas felt like he'd stomped on a puppy's tail. "Oh, sweetheart, I'm sorry. Your uncle just fell off the wrong side of the saddle this morning." He came around the counter and stood in front of her, holding out a hand. "Forgive me?"

She took it and allowed him to pull her into a standing position. He hugged her and she hit him hard on the back. The flat of her gloved hand made a soft *whump*. "You *are* turning into a cranky old fart. Seriously, you need to get out and have some fun."

"Right," he said, tickling her side. He let her go and leaned against the front counter. "With who? I've dated about every eligible lady in this town and there just isn't any sparks. Weren't you the one who told me how important sparks are? Don't you have them with that new boyfriend of yours—what's his name?"

She rolled her eyes. "He's history. Always wanted back massages, like I was some kind of slave."

He chuckled. "Well, you are aspiring to be a physical therapist."

"Yeah, then he can darn well pay me a hundred bucks an hour." She sniffed and tossed her head. "I'm done with musicians. I think I'm swearing off guys for a while."

"Your mom will be happy to hear that."

"I still don't understand why you and mom never got together."

"I love your mom, you know that. And she loves me. Like siblings."

"Seriously, that would be cool if you could be my stepdad."

"Forget it. Our relationship is screwy enough. Besides, I don't ever want to do anything that would make your mama stop cooking for me, and marrying her would definitely do that."

Before Cassie could answer, the door opened and Marie Williams stepped over the threshold. Lucas felt a twinge of guilt. They'd had a really nice time five days ago when they went out for coffee and he'd taken her cell number. Then, with all that had happened with Ruby's father and brother, he'd forgotten to call her.

"Hey, cowboy," Marie said, glancing over at Cassie with a curious, but friendly look. "Hey."

"Hey," Cassie said back, cocking her head. "Who're you?"

"Marie Williams. Friend of Lucas McGavin. Who're you?"

"Cassie McGavin, niece of Lucas McGavin." She looked over at Lucas and grinned. "Well, we're actually half siblings. But that's a whole other tawdry story."

Marie raised her black eyebrows at Lucas. "Really? You left that tawdry story out of our getting-to-know-you coffee date last Tuesday, cowboy."

Cassie jumped up and down with a squeal. "Date! Uncle Lucas, you had a date? Wow, Mom is going to bust a gut when she hears."

Lucas felt his face warm. "We had a cup of coffee."

"And talked about ourselves," Marie said, obviously pleased that she'd put him on the spot. "Gave each other our histories. I told him about being half Paiute, half Hopi. He told me about being half saddle maker, half lawyer. We had two peppermint lattes apiece. With whipped cream." She paused for dramatic effect. "He *paid.*"

Cassie clapped her hands like a little girl. "A date! Uncle Lucas went on a date. I'm so proud of you." She turned to face Marie. "I like you already and I don't even know you. Anyone who can get Mr. Grumpy Pants there out on a date is number one in my book. Do you live in Cardinal?"

"My grammy Eula does. I'm staying with her for a while."

"Is she Eula Williams?"

"That's my grammy."

"She's so cool! She came to our art class a few months ago and talked to us about making baskets. She's amazing."

"Wait, you know her grandma?" Lucas asked.

"Uncle Lucas, she's totally famous for her baskets. She's been making them since she was, like, eight years old! She has two baskets in the Heard Museum in Phoenix. She's won tons of awards."

Marie's smile grew wider. "She makes a mean buttermilk biscuit, too. And you should taste her baked salmon."

Cassie turned back to Lucas. "So, when are you two going out again?"

Lucas stared at his niece. He couldn't believe what had happened in the last five minutes. "Uh . . ."

"He's free for lunch," Cassie said to Marie. "Are you?"

Marie glanced up at Lucas, her silvery eyes twinkling. "I am."

For the first time he noticed she wore a dress today. It was kind of a gauzy-type pumpkin-colored dress that fell below her knees with a jagged hem. Over it was a tan suede jacket with sixties-style fringe. Her worn leather boots were a slightly darker shade of brown and had elaborate, colorful stitching on the shanks. The beaded necklace she wore had the same rainbow of colors in it as the boots' stitching. Her hair was pulled back into a low ponytail and tied with a single strand of leather.

"So, you should totally take her out for lunch, Uncle Lucas. When did you have coffee?"

"Wednesday," Marie said, before Lucas could answer.

Cassie frowned at Lucas. "Five days? And you didn't text or call her right away? Not cool, Uncle Lucas."

"I . . . A friend had some problems . . ." he stammered, "and . . ."

"No worries," she told Marie. "He's free right now. And he's hungry, I can tell."

"You're hungry," Marie told him, laughing. "Your niece says so."

Lucas couldn't help laughing with her. "Then I must be."

They were being railroaded into going out again by his teenage niece, but neither of them was bothered by it. "Actually, I didn't have breakfast."

"Okay, get going, you two," Cassie said. She held out a hand to Marie. "We can get to know each other later. I can tell you then all you need to know about my uncle that he will not tell you. Don't worry, he's not a perv."

"Thanks loads," Lucas said.

Marie shook her hand solemnly. "I'm so glad to hear that. I'll look forward to talking to you."

"I'll close up the shop," Cassie said, handing Lucas his jacket.

Before he knew it, he and Marie were out on the sidewalk, the door of the saddle shop closed behind them.

"What just happened?" Lucas said.

"I think we were hijacked by a teenager with romantic illusions." For a moment, Marie's face looked hesitant and Lucas felt his heart twitch.

"Not hijacked," he said, holding out his arm. "I did mean to call you, but a friend of mine really did have a crisis. Remember I told you about my late brother's wife, Ruby?"

Marie nodded, her face still vulnerable.

"Her father died and her brother was in a car accident . . . in her car. His fault and he was drinking. He's in jail."

"Oh, man," Marie said softly. "Is he okay?"

"He's fine, but that's just half of it," he said. "The person he hit was my mother and she's in the hospital with a broken leg and a hankering to send him up the river."

"Wow, those are some soap-opera-level troubles."

He took her arm and they started walking up Cardinal's Main Street. The temperature on the electronic board above Cardinal Valley Bank read thirty-nine degrees. But her hand was warm and he liked how it felt in his.

"Oh, there's so much more," he said, suddenly very glad that Cassie manipulated this date. "There's a new steak place over on Vine Street. I've heard their rosemary-garlic twice-baked potatoes are incredible."

"Sounds wonderful. Maybe over dessert you can tell me how your niece can also be your half sibling."

He gave a half smile, feeling an almost unrecognizable twinge of optimism. "I think that can be arranged."

25

Ruby

The drive from Ajo to Cardinal on Sunday was one of the most awkward and uncomfortable of Ruby's life. After she told Etta about the trouble Nash was in, Etta hesitantly agreed to come back with them to see if she could help.

"I don't know if he will listen to me," she said. "There's no reason he would."

"That may be," Ruby replied, her voice tart. "But, as I said, I have nothing else." She didn't mention that she'd been hoping that maybe Etta might have the money to bail Nash out of jail, even pay for the attorney he would definitely need. But, after seeing where and how her mother lived, Ruby knew that was a pipe dream.

Ely drove the whole way, with Ruby squeezed in the middle of the truck's bench seat. Thankfully, he'd been wise enough to have a book on CD in his truck, and they listened to a story about a young woman raised on a farm in Africa.

When the book ended, Ruby managed to find talk radio stations where people debated red state–blue state issues or the latest troubles in the Iraq war. They stopped for refueling twice and a quick bite to eat in San Bernardino.

While Etta was in the restroom, Ruby rested her forehead on the trucker café's speckled Formica table. "I can't do this, Ely. I'm so tired. I wish I could just go to sleep and wake up when all of this is over."

She felt his warm hand rest on top of hers. "I know, Ruby. It will work out. I can't tell you how and whether it'll be exactly what you want. Only God knows that. But it will all work out and you'll be okay."

She lifted her head to look over at him sitting next to her. In the yellowish light of the café, he appeared as old and wise as Bobby Hernandez. She contemplated his calm face for a long moment. "Do you really believe that?"

"I do."

When Etta returned and slipped into the vinyl tuck-and-roll seat across from them, Ruby noticed for the first time how worn her mother looked. The last time she'd seen her, Etta had been only a few years younger than Ruby was now. In the twenty-three years that had passed, this sad-looking woman had taken the place of the one who would dab candy apple red lipstick to Ruby's eight-year-old lips and sing "Stand by Your Man."

"Who is the best country singer in the world?" she used to ask as Ruby watched her mother pull on her shiny black miniskirt and sparkly top for another night of serving drinks, dodging drunks and, if she was lucky, being allowed by the bar's owner to sing a few songs with the house band.

"You are, Mama," Ruby used to assure her, proud that her mother would ask her opinion. Nash would sit on the floor and play with the pots and pans, banging them together.

"That boy's going to be a drummer someday," she'd tell Ruby.

Ruby wondered if her mother ever sang anymore.

It was dark when they finally reached Cardinal and Ely dropped them off at Ruby's house.

"Don't worry about coming to work tomorrow," Ely said when she walked him out to his truck. "Do you want me to see about arranging bail?"

She reached over and placed a hand on Ely's icy cheek. He reached up and grabbed it, enclosing it in his own. "You are my hero, Ely Grey. But, no, I don't want you to spend your hard-earned money bailing my alcoholic brother out of jail."

"If you're going to stage an intervention, he needs to be out."

"I do not want you to risk your house or your businesses. He'll just have to stay there until . . ." She let her sentence dangle. "I'll figure something out."

He nodded. "He'll be treated well. It's

not pleasant, but it's not the federal pen, either. Let's talk about this again after you and Etta see him."

"We'll visit him tomorrow. After we . . . talk. I brought her here to help, but first I have to make sure she won't make things worse."

"Call me if you need me." He squeezed her hand, then, before she realized what was happening, leaned toward her and brushed a kiss across her lips. "I'm here if you need anything."

Before she could respond, he climbed into his truck. Her fingers resting on the lips he'd just kissed, she watched his taillights until they disappeared and the night settled dark and cold around her.

Troubled by the feelings his kiss stirred in her, she pushed them aside and turned back to go inside the house. She found Etta standing in the hallway, studying a photo of Nash, Joe and Ruby taken the first Christmas that Etta was gone. It had been snapped by their neighbor, Juana. She lived two doors down and worked as a motel maid. When she realized that Ruby and Nash's mother had left and their father was on the road for days at a time, she taught thirteen-year-old Ruby the rudiments of cooking, cleaning and laundry. Until social services discovered their predicament and placed them in foster care four years later, Juana was the person Ruby went to when Nash was feverish or constipated or had an earache. When Juana's own folk remedies didn't work, she called her cousin who was an LVN back in Mexico but couldn't get a license here because she was in the United States illegally.

"I'm so sorry," Etta whispered, touching the photo with her fingertip. "I should have been there."

"You can sleep in Nash's room," Ruby said, brushing past her mother and taking clean sheets from the small hallway closet. "I'm tired. We can talk tomorrow."

The next morning, the smell of coffee and the scent of frying bacon woke Ruby. For a split second, she was confused, thinking she was back in San Juan Capistrano, in the ranch house she and Cole had rented. He always made breakfast on Sunday mornings.

She climbed out of bed, slipped on her robe and went into the kitchen. Etta was dressed in faded jeans and another sweatshirt, this one advertising Ajo Country Club. Worn black suede moccasins covered her feet. As when Ruby first met her in the dog rescue, Etta wore no makeup. Her silver-streaked dark hair was neatly combed, a small cowlick peeking up from her crown.

The cowlick pricked Ruby's heart. She could remember her mother fighting with it, trying to get it to lie down, but no matter what products she tried, it valiantly grew its own merry way.

"You used to like French toast," Etta said, turning around and giving Ruby a shy smile. Then she clamped her lips shut, as if realizing those were loaded words.

"I still do." Ruby sat down at the set table, feeling as awkward as if she were taking tea with the Queen of England. "Uh, did you sleep okay?"

"Yes," Etta said. "It was strange being in Nash's room. But nice." She turned back to the frying bacon. "This will be done in a few minutes."

Ruby sipped the orange juice next to her plate, wondering what to do next.

Like so many times in her life, she felt like she had been thrown into the deep end of the pool with no instruction about how to swim to the side. She watched her mother plate the French toast and bacon.

"Thank you," she said when Etta slid the food in front of her.

"You're welcome," Etta replied, sitting down. She waited until Ruby took her first bite before she began eating.

The meal was in complete silence, with Ruby avoiding her mother's eyes as much as she was sure her mother was avoiding hers. They both knew what was coming and could likely agree on one thing: Neither of them was looking forward to it. Still, they had one thing in common. They cared about Nash. At least, Ruby assumed her mother cared a little. If she hadn't, wouldn't she have made some kind of excuse not to come with Ruby and Ely?

After they were finished, Ruby insisted on doing the dishes.

"It's only fair," she said. "You cooked, I'll clean. Go out on the porch and catch the morning sun. I'll come out as soon as I'm done and we can talk about Nash."

Ruby washed the dishes as slowly as she could, then meticulously dried each plate, cup, fork and knife, putting off joining her mother as long as possible. She wished that they could keep their talk strictly about Nash and how to help him, but Ruby knew that was impossible. Besides, this might be her only chance to find out the truth about why Etta never returned even though she didn't make it as a singer. Something had happened, apparently involving a man. She sighed, putting away the last spoon and turning around to survey the spotless kitchen. It always involved a man.

She went into her bedroom and quickly pulled on a pair of jeans and a thick navy cotton sweater. She ran a brush through her wild hair, then pulled it back with a red velvet scrunchie. Okay, she felt a little more like she could handle whatever Etta had to say. She splashed some cold water over her face and patted it dry.

Out on the porch, Etta was sitting still as a lizard basking in the sun. Her eyes were closed but snapped open the minute Ruby sat in the rocking chair next to her.

"This is a lovely porch," Etta said. "That's one thing I wish my little house in Ajo had, a decent front porch. I do have a nice patio in the back though."

Ruby folded her hands neatly in her lap, more to keep her mother from seeing them tremble than for anything else. "We need to go see Nash today."

Etta nodded.

"But, before we do, we need to figure what we can do to help him. He's an alcoholic. I don't know if an intervention would help and he definitely needs to go to rehab and I don't know how I'll pay for that, but getting him to admit he has a problem is the first hurdle. I read about interventions on the Internet. And in books. Maybe we could get him to go to AA. Maybe there are places in the city, in Los Angeles, where he could go. We are in the middle of nowhere here, but maybe we can figure something out." Ruby stopped talking and stared down at her clenched hands. She felt like an idiot, babbling on like that.

"This woman he hit," Etta said softly. "You said she is pressing charges? Maybe we could talk to her? Ask for mercy?"

Ruby looked up, her heart aching with the impossibility of Nash's situation. "I didn't tell you everything about that part. My husband, Cole. He died last year. Well, it's his mother."

Etta's face registered the tiniest bit of shock. "Your ex-mother-in-law?"

"Technically, former," Ruby said. "And she's never liked me."

Etta murmured what Ruby assumed was a consoling sound under her breath.

"It's a big mess," Ruby said, feeling like she could burst into tears any moment.

"What do you want me to do?" Etta said. "I'll help however I can."

Ruby studied her mother's face for a moment. "To be honest, knowing the details about why you never came back would help. Help me, anyway."

Etta's gaze didn't change, though Ruby thought she saw a glistening in her dark gray eyes.

"I told you in Ajo that I moved in with a bad man and finally, I got away. I was a drunk for a long, long time. You didn't miss anything by me not being there . . ."

"How can you say that?" Ruby said, her voice rising slightly. The sound startled a hummingbird feeding at an antique glass bottle feeder, causing it to dart into the blue white sky. "We missed . . . everything! At thirteen, I was raising a six-year-old boy because you and Dad had to live your own lives! What do you mean I didn't miss anything? I missed my whole damn childhood!" Ruby's heart beat so hard and fast in her chest it felt like she would keel over.

Etta's head dropped to her chest. "I can say I'm sorry a million times and it would never make it okay. But, trust me, I wouldn't have been a good mother to you and Nash, and once I got sober, well . . ." She slowly lifted her head and looked at Ruby, her eyes definitely filled with tears. "By that time, I didn't feel like I deserved to be a mother. I got back in contact with your dad and he just said you and Nash were doing fine. We just sort of agreed without words that I didn't want . . . I couldn't handle . . . the details. Joe said you both were doing good. So, I just didn't allow myself to come back and maybe mess things up again."

Ruby chewed her thumbnail while Etta talked, unable to understand her mother's convoluted logic. How could a mother think it was better not to come back to her children, no matter how long she'd been gone?

"Why?" Ruby finally asked. "I don't get what you are trying to say. Why didn't you think you deserved to be a mother?"

Etta's whisper was harsh, agonized. "Because I was a coward and a drunk and a fool. There is a mother out there who will never see her child again. What right do I have to be a mother, when I took that away from someone else?"

26

Birch

"Mrs. Hernandez," Bobby said, putting his hand on the back of Birch's neck. His hand felt warm and familiar. "We need to talk."

It was Monday morning and she sat in the small office behind Tokopah Lodge's knotty pine counter. The lodge's tattered, antique ledger books and a stack of bills covered the desktop. It was quiet as a funeral service in the lobby, devoid now of the towering Christmas tree and all its glorious decorations. A single person lounged by the crackly fire on one of the Pendleton sofas, a man in a red wool shirt reading the *Cardinal Valley Gazette*. The scarcity of midweek guests was common for the second week in January. Though they usually had plenty of visitors on the weekends, providing there was adequate snow in Mammoth, the weekdays were often quiet. Birch didn't mind. After all the hullabaloo of the holidays, quiet was nice. Still, she missed the cheery decorations.

"What's up, Chief?" she asked, looking up from the bank statement she'd just opened with her bone-handled letter opener.

He sat down in the padded visitor's chair. "It's about Rodeo." The misery on Bobby's face instantly set off Birch's internal alarm.

"What's wrong?" she said.

"I'm sending her back home. I don't have any choice."

Birch was sad but not shocked. "Why?"

"She's the one who has been stealing from petty cash." He looked down at his hands resting on his cane. "I feel horrible about this. She's my niece. She's family."

Birch patted her husband's knee in sympathy, touched as she always was by his generous spirit. Rodeo was actually his cousin's daughter. But to Bobby, all his relatives were nieces and nephews no matter how distantly connected they were. His big, open heart had always been his gift and his curse. For every five grateful relatives he had helped over the years, it seemed there was one who took advantage. She felt horrible about Rodeo, not glad that her and Sueann's suspicions were correct. The guests had adored Rodeo's chatty, upbeat personality.

"How did you find out it was her?" Birch asked.

His dark eyes were moist with sadness. "I caught her this morning. She didn't realize I was already here and I came around the corner just as she was taking money from the box and putting it in her pocket."

Birch squeezed Bobby's forearm. "Oh, honey, I'm so sorry. I know this is breaking your heart. Did she say why?"

He looked away, which made Birch's heart skip. When Bobby wouldn't look her in the eye, something was very wrong. "Bobby?" Her voice caught on his name and she gripped the pencil in her hand as if it was a lifeline. "Why was Rodeo stealing from us?"

His voice was a mumble, which made her lean closer. "First it was for herself. Then for Nash. He needed money and he was always asking her for it. She's been giving him money since the first night they met here at the lodge on Christmas Eve." He gave Birch a beseeching look. "I think he bewitched that girl."

Birch thought for a moment, adding up the days in her head. "But the first night we discovered money was missing was a week and a half before they met. So she didn't actually start stealing for him."

Bobby's faced hardened. "Maybe not. But he probably encouraged it once he used up all her money. That boy is nothing but trouble."

Birch didn't answer, knowing that Bobby was old-fashioned and had a tendency to make more excuses for females than males. It could sometimes be endearing in a chauvinistic kind of way. In fairness, Nash couldn't be entirely blamed for Rodeo's dishonesty. Ruby's brother was certainly proving to be a peck and a half of trouble. And now a relative of Bobby's was involved. That complicated things even further.

She felt sick about the whole situation. She wasn't surprised that Nash Stoddard was capable of manipulating a young, naïve girl like Rodeo. He was an alcoholic. Even worse, a charismatic one. She knew what someone like that could do. Images of her father's winning smile and glassy eyes came to her. Kitteridge McGavin always wore custom-tailored Western suits and a pristine white cowboy hat. He charmed men and women alike and could make you feel like you were the most important person on earth. Until you crossed him. As she had when she married Bobby. Her brother, her only sibling, Carson, had been cut from the same cowhide. Just as charismatic. Just as amoral. Just as deadly when he drank. By the time they died, both men had left a trail of tears a thousand miles behind them. Her heart ached for Ruby.

"Nash is certainly where he deserves to be," she said crisply. "I'm sorry Rodeo was deceived, but I guess every woman has to be burned by a bad man once in her life, sometimes by her choice, sometimes not."

Bobby, wisely, didn't respond. He'd known Birch since she was in her teens. He knew her family history as well as he did his own.

He rubbed his left knee, his face grimacing. "Are you going to tell Ruby?"

She set down the pencil she'd been twirling in her nervous fingers. "I don't know. You know she's down in Arizona looking for her mother. I think the plan is to bring her back, see if she can talk some sense into her son." Birch shook her head. "I don't think it can do anything except pour gasoline on an already raging fire, but I understand how desperate Ruby feels. I wish I could do something to help her."

"Familia," Bobby said, with a sigh.

Birch nodded, knowing that said it all. She stood up, closing up the ledger books. They'd still not put the lodge's books on a computer program. Rodeo had teased them about that. "I'll finish this later. When is Rodeo leaving?"

"She's pretty upset. She called her

brother. He said he'd be here by tonight. She's in her room, packing. And crying." He gave his wife a pointed look.

"I know I should go talk to her, tell her that her life isn't over and we all make stupid mistakes." It was something she wasn't sure she was up to doing right now. This was just one more sad thing to heap on all the other sad things happening to people she cared about.

Bobby stood up, pulled her into a hug. His thick, familiar body folded around her and felt like the warmest, most comforting overcoat in the universe. "Why don't you go talk to Sueann. That always makes you feel better. You can see Rodeo before she goes home."

"I'm not mad at her," Birch said into his shoulder. "Well, a little. I'm madder at Nash. He's older than she is. He should know better. He . . ."

"Is an alcoholic," Bobby finished. "Not an excuse, an explanation."

"I know." She clasped her arms around his thick middle and hugged him hard. "You're right. I'll see what Sueann thinks about whether I should or shouldn't tell Ruby about Rodeo."

"Bring me back a club sandwich?"

She tugged his long, gray braid before letting him go. "You bet, Chief."

On the walk to the Lone Pine, Birch wondered how Ruby's meeting with her mother went. Would the woman who'd so blithely abandoned her children even care about what was happening to them now? Surely if she had, she would have sought them out sometime in the last twenty-something years. What in the world would keep a mother away from her children? Maybe she was being naïve, but Birch felt, if she'd had children, if they were ever lost, physically or emotionally, she would have tracked them down to the ends of the earth, done anything to save them.

She hoped that Ruby's mother didn't horribly disappoint her and, at the same time, she selfishly hoped that this woman would turn Ruby away, tell her that she didn't want to have anything to do with Ruby or Nash. Then Birch could have Ruby for herself. She would help her figure out what to do with Nash. She would be the mother to Ruby that her real mother never was. She sighed, realizing that it wasn't that simple. Life was never that simple.

That troubling question that had plagued Birch throughout her life rose up inside her again. Why would God allow a woman like that to have children and deny Birch the one thing in life she'd always longed for?

God's plans were often a mystery was what she'd been told by the ministers and priests who'd come and gone in her life. She remembered Linc once told her, "Suffering results in wisdom and wisdom is always a blessing. But it takes time. It leads to wisdom in the long run. And the short time we suffer is well worth what we eventually receive, which is a heart that is a tiny bit closer to being as loving as God's." That was the best answer she'd had so far, though it only rarely made her feel better.

She trudged down the soggy street toward the café, wishing she felt a little more loving. Help me, Lord, she prayed, glancing up at the gray sky. Change my angry heart. Then she asked for forgiveness for not meaning her prayer. She really didn't want to change. She really didn't want to stop being angry with Ruby's mother.

The cowbell clanged when she opened the café's wooden door, announcing her entry. The café was more crowded than the hotel lobby because the Lone Pine was popular with the locals as well as tourists. With a quick glance around the almost full room, Birch could tell that most of the customers today were her neighbors and friends.

Sueann waved at her from behind the antique brass cash register. At the long counter, not a stool was free.

Birch walked over to Sueann. "I thought you might have a moment to chat, but I can see you're swamped. I'll just get something to go." It was obvious Sueann wouldn't be able to talk at least for an hour.

Sueann took one look at her beloved friend's face and knew something was wrong. She started to undo her apron, her freckled brow furrowed in concern. "Heck, all these folks can wait. Most of them could well afford to skip a lunch or two, truth be told. What's going on?"

"Now, stop," Birch said, putting her

hand on Sueann's forearm. "It's nothing that can't wait until after the lunch rush. I need to eat anyway. We can talk afterward." She glanced around the room. "But I may just have to order it to go unless you have a spare orange crate for me to sit on."

Sueann pointed to a table over by the window. "There's a chair free by Cassie." Birch's niece sat across from a young friend, a raven-haired Native American girl dressed in a red and white ski-style sweater, fuzzy white knitted cap, her faded blue jeans tucked into those ubiquitous flat-soled suede boots that always reminded Birch of elephant legs. There was, indeed, a chair free at the small square table.

Birch shook her head. "Cassie doesn't want her old aunt horning in on her girlfriend lunch."

"Oh, you'll want to horn in on this one," Sueann said, lowering her voice. "That isn't one of Cassie's high school girlfriends. It is a new friend, but she's also *Lucas's* new friend."

"What?" The emphasis Sueann put on the word *friend* told Birch volumes.

"Where did she come from? Where has she been? Lucas is dating her? Why don't I know about this?"

Sueann giggled behind her hand. "All very good questions. I just found out about her this morning. Cassie only met her yesterday. When Cassie came in and saw the girl—her name is Marie, by the way—sitting by herself, she gave me a quick explanation and made a beeline over there. I think she's likely giving her the third degree." Sueann grinned. "She was well trained in the art of friendly interrogation and I don't mean by little ole me."

"I'll pretend I didn't hear that," Birch said, smiling back at her. "So, our sneaky little Lucas has been holding out on us."

"Apparently. All Cassie could tell me was they met in Las Vegas during NFR and that Marie's grandmother lives here. I think you might know her. Eula May Williams."

"I do know Eula," Birch said. "She used to come to my classroom and talk to the kids about her baskets. They are beautiful."

"Marie's staying with her. Eula had a slight stroke a few weeks ago."

"Oh, dear." Birch's hand came up to her chest. "I didn't hear about that. She's not much older than me."

"Marie said it wasn't bad, but she needs help around the house. I only talked to her a few minutes, but, you know, if my daughter isn't exaggerating and Lucas and Marie are, indeed, an item, it appears he could do a lot worse."

"And has," Birch said, frowning.

"Yeah, that first wife of his was a catfish best thrown back into the muddy Mississippi, for sure. What was Lucas thinking when he married her?" Lucas's first wife had left him for his boss and both Sueann and Birch agreed they would hold a grudge against her forever.

"He wasn't thinking," Birch said. "At least not with his big brain."

Sueann giggled again. "Go over and see if you can help your niece find out some pertinent information about this young woman. Though I only spoke with her a moment, she seems really down-to-earth. She said she actually lived in Cardinal for a little while when she was a girl. It's almost like he's dating a hometown girl."

"Have they actually been on a date?"

Sueann turned and picked up the Bunn coffeepot. "Two. One coffee date and one lunch date. These days, that's practically engaged." She walked down the row of men sitting at the counter, filling empty coffee cups. "Report back ASAP," she called over her shoulder. "What would you like to eat?"

"Chicken salad sandwich and hot tea," Birch answered. She slowly weaved her way through the crowded café, dodging chairs and calling out greetings to five people before getting to Cassie and Marie. "Hi, girls. Is that seat taken?"

"Yes," Marie said, smiling up at her. "By you, I hope."

"Hey, Aunt Birch!" Cassie jumped up and hugged her. "I'm so glad you're here. This is Marie Williams. She's staying with her grandma Eula who makes baskets and also makes this awesome jewelry. Look!" She turned her head so Birch could inspect her dangly beaded earrings.

"Are those coyotes?" Birch said.

"Good eye," Marie said. "Yes, it's one of Grammy's favorite patterns. Sells really well."

"They're beautiful, even if coyotes can be wily little critters."

Marie laughed. "Yes, they can. Maybe that's why the pattern is so popular. We humans can relate."

"Amen to that," Birch said, sitting down.

"So," Cassie said, flopping down in her own chair. "This is Marie and she is going to marry Lucas and be my sister-in-law . . . or whatever. Anyway, we'll be related!"

"Cassie!" Marie said, her cheeks blushing under her amber skin. "I'm sorry, Mrs. Hernandez, but Cassie is getting ahead of herself. I just like your nephew a lot and I think he might like me a little back." She gazed directly into Birch's eyes, not challenging, but not hiding, either.

Birch instantly liked her. Lucas needed a no-nonsense, straightforward woman like this. Birch smiled at herself. She wasn't any better than Cassie was. "I can't imagine him *not* liking you." Birch continued to search the young woman's face. There was something vaguely familiar about her. Birch's brow furrowed, trying to place her. She knew Eula and she did resemble her . . . but it wasn't that.

"Nineteen eighty-six," Marie said, grinning. She picked up her glass of milk and sipped. "I was in your fourth grade class for half a year. I left after Christmas vacation."

"Heaven Marie Williams!" Birch exclaimed.

"What?" Cassie said, her face bright with curiosity.

Marie groaned. "My mother missed the hippie era by ten years and totally regretted it. So, even though I was born in 1977, she channeled Haight-Ashbury and named me Heaven. Heaven Marie Williams. I stopped going by Heaven when I turned twelve and threatened to seek emancipation if Mom didn't allow me to use my middle name."

"That is so cool," Cassie said. "A hippie name. I'm jealous."

"Don't be," Marie said. "You would *not* want to hear all the jokes I've had to endure once someone knows my full name."

"Does Lucas know?" Cassie asked.

"Not yet," Marie said. "We haven't gotten to the part where we reveal despised given names or embarrassing childhood moments."

Cassie and Birch caught each other's eye and laughed.

"I used to call him my Lucky Lukey when he was little boy," Birch said.

"He even has a belt buckle with *LL* on it that he used to love when he was six."

"Lucky Lukey, huh?" Marie's expression was mischievous. "I'll save that one for future reference. I guess now I'll have to be fair, though, and let Lucas spend some quality alone time with Grammy Eula."

"Only fair," Birch said, nodding. "Give her my best."

"I will. You'll probably see her at the story jam on Friday night."

"I'll look forward to seeing her again."

"Hey, look!" Cassie said, pointing out the window. "Isn't that Ruby driving Ely's truck?"

Birch leaned forward to see better out of the slightly steamy window. It was Ely's red truck driving slowly past the Lone Pine. Ruby was in the driver's seat. So, she and Ely were back from Arizona. Where was their mother? Probably at the house. The house that Birch had lovingly set up for Ruby and Nash. She felt tears start to form at the corners of her eyes.

Loretta Stoddard was here. Here to reclaim her children.

Birch sat back in her chair. An involuntary shudder darted down her spine, as if she'd been injected with a syringe of cold air. She waited for the anger, the bitterness to envelop her. And, like a tiny miracle, it didn't.

Help her, Birch thought, not exactly sure who she was praying for. She watched the truck's taillights until it turned the corner and was out of her sight. Ruby was probably on her way to the city jail. Oh, Lord, help her, help us all.

27

Ruby

Ruby stared at her mother, watched her struggle to start the story that Ruby had been waiting to hear for twenty-three years.

"I met Ronnie at a bar, of course," Etta said. She didn't turn her head, but continued to gaze out at the leafless elm tree in front of Ruby's house. She gave a soft sigh. "Right after I left your daddy, I found a better-paying job at a place outside of Modesto. It catered to truck drivers, people who worked on the roads, tourists on their way up north. Ronnie grew up in Nashville, said he played in a backup band for Merle Haggard for a while and he . . . well, impressed me, and kind of bowled me over. He also kind of reminded me of the boys back home. He encouraged my singing, something your daddy never did. I was flattered. But, of course, what he really wanted was just to get me in bed. Believe it or not, I was still pretty naïve and I'd never been with any man besides Joe . . ." Etta's voice trailed off.

She rubbed a hand down one arm of the rocking chair as if she were cleaning a spot. "Guess I was just floundering. I left you all and felt so guilty, but also relieved. I wanted to be a star so bad." She shrugged, a cynical expression moved over her face. "It didn't take me long to figure out Ronnie was nothing but a fancy talker. And a drunk. Instead of admitting that and coming back, trying to figure things out with your daddy or even just coming back and taking you kids and starting a new life, I stayed with Ronnie and started drinking to help me block out all the stupid choices I made."

She plucked at an imaginary piece of lint on the knee of her jeans. "It sounds like a bad country song now. We might have just continued on like that until our livers or our hearts gave out, but then Ronnie started using crack." She bit her chapped bottom lip. "His divorce became final when we first hooked up. He had a child, a baby. His ex-wife was always calling the house about the child support, wanting this and that, wanting him to be a dad to his son. Ronnie Jr. RJ, they called him."

She turned to look at Ruby, who hadn't said a word, hadn't even allowed her chair to rock, afraid to interrupt her mother's words.

"He'd agreed to watch RJ while his ex-wife went with her girlfriends to Vegas. RJ was eleven months old and Ronnie had probably taken care of him only a couple of times. I didn't live with Ronnie, but I spent a lot of nights at his place. He asked me to come over after work to help him. The bar closed at two a.m. and I was already pretty drunk by the time I got to his place. He'd been smoking crack and the baby . . ."

She put a trembling hand up to her

mouth. "RJ was lying in his bed, needing his diaper changed. He was a real good baby, never cried, never fussed, but that night . . . I don't know . . . maybe he missed his mama, maybe he wasn't feeling good, but he started crying and just wouldn't stop. I changed him, tried to feed him, did everything I knew. Finally, I just put him back in his crib in the bedroom where Ronnie was watching TV. I told Ronnie it was his job to watch his son, that I was too tired, that I'd been on my feet for twelve straight hours. The last thing I remember was lying on the sofa and hearing RJ cry and cry. I think I heard Ronnie yell at him to shut the hell up. Then I don't remember anything."

Ruby could see her mother's throat convulsed. The taste of that morning bacon rose up sour and sharp in the back of Ruby's throat. She didn't want to hear the rest. She wanted to put her hands over her ears and scream at her mother to stop.

"I must have passed out," Etta said, her voice hoarse. "When I woke up, the apartment was so quiet. The sun was shining through the windows and it felt warm on my face, like someone touching it. I sat up, called out Ronnie's name, and when he didn't answer, I went into the bedroom." A sob caught in the back of her throat.

"RJ looked like a doll on the floor," she whispered. "Like a little doll some kid had tossed aside. Ronnie was passed out on the bed. There was a football game on TV. I touched RJ's little cheek and it was so cold. There was this big bruise on the side of his head . . ." She brought both her hands to her lap, linked her fingers as if in prayer. "I called nine-one-one. The paramedics came fast but it was too late. Then the cops came and took us both down to the station."

Ruby stared at her mother, her own heart feeling like it had stopped inside her chest. "Did . . . ? What . . . ?" She didn't even know what to ask. The thought of that defenseless baby and these two irresponsible adults. She had never thought there'd be anything worse that her mother could have done than leaving her and Nash. Now she knew there was.

"He was eventually charged with second-degree murder. The cops got him to confess that he'd thrown his son against the wall because RJ wouldn't stop crying. They ended up letting me go with no charges."

"What?" Ruby was incredulous.

Etta bowed her head. "I should have been punished, too. I should have taken that baby out of there when I saw he was smoking crack. I shouldn't have been drinking. I should have called his ex-wife. I shouldn't have . . ." She stopped and unclasped her hands. "My defense lawyer explained to me that I wasn't legally liable. If I'd been actually living with him or had some sort of agreement with RJ's mother to care for him, I would have been just as responsible. But, I was only a bystander. There's no law that says a bystander has to get involved."

"I can't believe you'd do that," Ruby said softly.

She lifted her head and looked at Ruby. "I know it was wrong, Ruby. It's the most horrible thing anyone could do. You see why I didn't feel I had the right to be your mother? To be anyone's mother? How could I allow myself the joy of my own children when I robbed another woman of hers?"

Before Ruby could answer, the phone rang. It was Ely telling her she could pick up Nash.

"But his bail."

"I paid it."

"Thank you," Ruby said, feeling relieved and guilty. "You know you didn't have to do that. You've already done so much."

"Keep the truck until we can figure out what to do about getting you a vehicle," he said.

"No, I can't . . ." she started. Ely's truck was his pride and joy.

"Yes, you can."

"Would you like me to go with you?" Etta asked after Ruby told her what Ely had done.

Ruby thought for a moment, her mind still reeling from her mother's story. She needed some time alone to process it and, the truth was, she couldn't bear to look at her mother right now. "No, it would be better if I prepare him on the drive here. Besides, your reunion with him should be here, not in the lobby of a police station." She paused for a moment. "Do not, under any circumstances, tell him what you just told me. He's not ready to hear it yet."

Her mother's eyes filled with tears. "I won't," she whispered.

What Ruby wanted to do more than anything, even more than picking up her brother, was go to Ely and tell him the whole terrible, sad story and listen to his low, soothing voice explain how something like that could happen, how two human beings could be so evil.

On the drive over to the jail, Ruby thought about her request that Etta not tell Nash about her reason for staying away from them. She decided it was the right one. Seeing Etta might be the crucial thing that would convince Nash that he had a problem and needed rehab. But if Nash found out what their mother had done, who knew what would happen. Right now, getting Nash sober and his life together was the most important thing. Ruby would deal with her own feelings about her mother's past later.

Nash was waiting outside for her when she drove into the sheriff's parking lot. When he saw Ruby get out of Ely's truck, he walked quickly over to her.

"I'm hungry," he said, without even a greeting.

She stood there for a moment, clutching her purse. "Really," she finally said. "That's really the *first* thing you're going to say to me after . . ."

He held up a hand. "I'm sorry, Ruby. But I'm tired and I'm hungry and I just want to take a nap." He opened the truck's passenger door. "Can we drive through McDonald's on the way back home?"

She climbed into the driver's seat. "We've got food at home. Besides, there's stuff we need to talk about before you take a nap. Like—"

"Ah, Ruby, I know I'm in a shitload of trouble. But can't we talk about it later?" He buckled his seat belt and looked away from her, out the side window.

She bit her bottom lip, holding back the angry retort on the tip of her tongue. "We'll have a lot to talk about with this whole mess, but I agree we can do it later. That wasn't what I was going to tell you. I found our mother."

His head whipped around to stare at her. "No way. You went to Arizona? Was that why you didn't visit me in jail? Thanks a lot, by the way. If it hadn't been for Rodeo bringing me snacks, I'd have starved in there."

"No," she said firmly. "You wouldn't have starved. They feed prisoners."

"Who wants to eat that crap?"

She started the truck. "Right now we're going home. Etta is there and wants to see you."

He snorted. "Yeah, right."

"I'm dead serious, Nash."

He shrugged, suddenly the happy-go-lucky kid again. "Well, shoot. I'll talk to her. She give any great explanation why she took off on us? Hey, doesn't she, like, owe us a ton of back child support? Think we can cash in on that?"

Ruby didn't answer. Right now, all she wanted to do was drop him off at the house and go to the bookstore. She wanted to immerse herself in mindless work, counting inventory, unpacking books, dusting shelves . . . anything to stop thinking about her family.

"I'll be home later. I'm going to the bookstore," she told him when she pulled into the narrow driveway of their house. "Go get reacquainted with your mother."

"No problem." He hopped out of idling truck. "Hey, Mom, I'm home!" he called out. Ruby could hear the sarcasm in his voice.

Etta came out on the front porch and stood there, waiting for Nash to come up the steps. Ruby put the truck in reverse and backed out of the driveway. Driving away, she could see them standing inches apart, Etta's hand fluttering as she talked. Then Ruby turned the corner and they were out of her sight.

Though a part of her wished she was there when Nash and Etta first talked, she knew that just as she had her issues with their mother, Nash did, too. He deserved to get reacquainted with Etta in private, just as Ruby did. She glanced at her watch. It was a little after one p.m. and she wasn't actually scheduled to work at the bookstore. Though she was tempted to go in anyway, she was afraid all she would do was blurt out her pain and anger to Ely and she didn't want to do that. He was going to get sick of hearing her family drama and she didn't want to lose his friendship or respect. Instead, she drove up and down the streets of Cardinal, imagining again what Cole's life might have been like growing up here. She ended up at the railroad museum outside of town where she wandered through the exhibits, trying to keep her mind off what her mother and brother might be talking about. Finally, she couldn't stand it and headed back to town. She had to talk to someone and Ely was who she wanted to talk to.

It was five p.m. when she pulled into the parking lot in the back of The Novel Experience. She came through the back door and saw Ely behind the counter, counting out change to an elderly woman who'd bought three calendars and the latest Elizabeth Ann Scarborough fantasy novel.

"Thank you, Mr. Grey," the woman said. "I'm so glad you saved me one of the wolf calendars. I was afraid they'd be gone."

"My pleasure, Mrs. Gothe," Ely said, winking at Ruby. "I set one aside for you the minute they came in."

After a few more minutes of chitchat, Ely walked her to the door and locked it behind her, turning the sign to "Closed."

He turned and walked over to Ruby. "You look like you could use a cup of tea."

"Only if you spike it with whiskey." She grimaced and brought her arms around to hug herself. "Oh, forget I said that. After what Etta just told me, alcohol is the last thing I want. What I want is to talk to you."

"I'm free the rest of the night."

She glanced around the empty store. "Oh, Ely, I don't want you to close the store just to listen to me."

He went over to the light switch and turned off the store's overhead lights. "It's Monday. I always close early on Mondays."

"Thank you. How about I take you to dinner?"

"How about I make us dinner?" he replied. "I have a feeling we're going to need privacy, and that's hard to come by in this town."

She nodded. “Okay, but you have to let me help.”

After he locked the back door and set the alarm, she handed him back his keys.

“You can drive,” he said, going over to the passenger seat. “I’m not that macho.”

She laughed and climbed into the cab. “That’s the funniest thing I’ve ever heard you say.”

“What’s so funny about it?”

“You are about the most macho man I’ve ever met, next to Cole.”

Just the mention of his name caused Ely’s face to soften. “He was one of a kind.”

“Yes, he was,” she said, starting the truck. “But, you know, so are you.”

He turned his head away and she felt a twinge of regret for her flippant words. Had she insulted him? She didn’t ever want to hurt this man who had been so kind to her.

He looked back at her, a ghost of a smile on his face.

“I meant that in a good way,” she said. “Really, it’s a compliment . . .”

His smile was real now. “I know.”

As she drove out of the parking lot, she said, “Okay, you have to tell me which way to turn. I have no idea where you live.”

“Left on Main Street. Then keep going past Walt’s Feed and Seed and take the second left.”

They didn’t speak during the short drive to his house, which ended up being at the end of a street on the edge of town, about a mile from the bookstore. His backyard looked out over the White Mountains. The Sierra Nevada Mountains were visible from his deep front porch. It was one of Cardinal’s old wooden bungalows, built back in the ’20s when Cardinal was truly a small Western town. It was painted a dark green with white shutters. There was a huge pine tree in front with a tire swing.

“Who’s the swing for?” she asked, climbing down from the cab. Her shoes sank down into soggy grass.

He shrugged. “Neighbor kids like to use it. Came with the house and I didn’t have the heart to take it down.”

It was dark, though an automatic porch

light lit the way for them. He unlocked the front door and flipped on a light. "Welcome to my home."

She followed him inside, feeling odd and a little nervous about seeing where Ely lived. Though she'd worked for him almost a month and they'd just shared a trip to fetch her long lost mother, which was about as intimate a thing as she'd ever shared with anyone, she suddenly felt shy. Visiting someone's home, especially someone as reclusive as Ely, was a huge thing. She doubted that he invited many people to his house.

"It's lovely," she said, looking around at the cozy living room. There was an overstuffed distressed leather sofa and matching chair, odd wooden end tables that looked as if he'd picked them up at garage sales but somehow looked perfect with the sofa. The thin metal floor lamps were a burnished copper color, with shades that were curvy and tall, almost Victorian. A red, brown and blue braided rug lay over the shiny oak floors. Above the sofa was a painting of an Appaloosa horse that looked straight at the viewer. She stared at it a moment, mesmerized.

"It's called *Soul Catcher*," Ely said. "The artist is a Navajo friend who now lives on the rez in Arizona. He and I shared a cell."

"It's gorgeous." She gazed around the room. "It's so . . . warm." She started taking off her jacket.

"I can turn down the thermostat," he said, holding out his hand.

She smiled and handed him her jacket. "I didn't mean the house is physically warm. I mean the way you've decorated. It's warm. Welcoming."

"You are," he said, hanging her jacket on a wooden coat rack in the corner. "Welcome here, that is. Now I have a confession. I lied to you."

She felt her heart jump, feeling a little vulnerable. "About what?"

"I can't cook. Not even scrambled eggs. I do, however, have a special relationship with Daniello's Pizza. They normally don't deliver this far, but will for me." He grinned at her. "I give their grandpa Tony free caramel lattes and hot cross buns at the Grounds every day."

She laughed out loud, very glad at that moment that she accepted his invitation.

Later, after they'd finished off most of a large pepperoni and black olive pizza and she'd become comfortable enough to take off her shoes and sit back against the pillows on the sofa, she told him Etta's story. He sat in the leather chair across from her, listening in that quiet way she was becoming used to, his face not showing one bit of emotion. When she was finished, it felt like she'd run a marathon. Her heart beat so hard she wondered if he could see the movement under her shirt.

"This is the person," she said, "who is going to help me with Nash? Was I crazy to look her up?"

Ely thought a moment. "Who else could you ask? She's his mother."

"But . . . what she did. It's horrible, inhuman."

Ely nodded. "Yes, it is. Alcohol and drugs will do that to a person; make you do things you'd never do sober."

"It's no excuse," Ruby said, wanting to stay angry with her mother. "It's people's choice to drink or take drugs. If they go ahead and do that, they are stuck with the consequences. But so are the people they hurt." She looked down at her clenched hands, feeling embarrassed by her self-righteous words. Still, it was how she felt. She'd had a crappy life, too, but she'd never put a child in danger.

She looked up at Ely. His expression, gentle, nonjudging of her or, she guessed, even her mother, blurred in her eyesight. "Oh, Ely, I sound like such an idiot. But a baby died. A baby." The word caught in her throat.

Ely sat forward in his chair. "Ruby, everything you are saying and feeling is true. Anyone with a heart and a conscience would feel revulsion over what your mother did. But, it seems to me that she has paid for it, is continuing to pay for it and probably will for the rest of her life."

"I don't know if I can have a relationship with her," Ruby whispered.

"You don't have to decide that right this minute. All you and she want to do is make sure your brother doesn't end up killing himself or someone else. Put your feelings about her aside for now."

She took one of the needlepoint Indian chief pillows and wrapped her arms around it. "What kind of Indian are you? I mean, forgive me if that's the wrong way to ask, but what tribe are you?"

He tilted his head, taken aback by the abrupt change of subject.

"I'm sorry," she said, hugging the pillow. "I know it's rude, but I just can't talk about my mother anymore and you know so much about me and have seen so much of the crap in my life and I don't know anything about you . . ." She swallowed hard, tasting a lump of salt. "Oh, Ely, forgive me . . . No, I mean it . . . I want to know. And, please, don't give me one of your 'I'm a tough, silent Indian' looks. I have a right to know a *little* something about your life since you are so intimately involved with mine."

He suddenly let out a big laugh.

She stared at him, surprised.

He came over and sat next to her on the sofa. She moved her outstretched legs to make room.

"What's so funny?" she asked.

"Linc told me once that I'd know when I found the right woman for me when she called me out on my brooding-Indian act."

She pulled her legs up under her, still

clutching the pillow. In that moment, she realized, yes, there was something between them. What, she didn't have a clue, but she knew this: When she was with Ely, she felt calm and safe and happy.

"Please, tell me," she said, softly.

"I don't know what I am," he said. "My mother worked in a brothel up in Ely, Nevada. That's where she got my name. I have no idea who my father was. Neither did she. He could be any of dozens or hundreds of men."

"Oh, Ely."

He stared down at his hands. "Obviously, by my looks, he was likely Indian. But I'll never know. When she got pregnant with me, she left the brothel and moved to Ridgecrest, where we lived with her mother. When Grandma Lucy died when I was five years old, somehow we ended up in Cardinal. It's really the only home I've ever known. Still, growing up here was hard. I wasn't part of the Paiute-Shoshone tribe, but look at me." He held his hand out. "I obviously wasn't going to be accepted by the white kids, either. And the Mexicans knew I wasn't one of them, either."

"It's so unfair," Ruby said, reaching over, taking his hand. It felt good in hers, strong and warm and familiar. "You were just a little boy."

He put his other hand over hers. "Life isn't fair. You know that. However, here I am, the biggest mongrel loser of all, an ex-con, a former drunk, a bastard, with a life. A good life. Maybe the reason I understand your mom, Ruby, is because I have done a lot of things I've regretted. Most of them when I was so drunk I don't even remember what I did. But throughout my life, there were a few people who believed in me, cared about me, even if it was just a tiny bit. You know, it doesn't take much, just a few words or a hug or buying someone a meal. Sometimes that one tiny act of grace is the thing that God . . . or Higher Power, if you're more comfortable with that . . . uses to help save you. But you have to be willing to hold out your hand. Grace can't be forced on anyone."

"Nash may not accept our help," she said softly.

"Right, but the fact that your mom was willing to tell you all of that about her, the ugly truth, and that she came back to see if she could help with Nash. Isn't that something? Isn't that a start?"

She stared at Ely, thinking, How does a person get to a place like this, this place of compassion and wisdom, this place of love, when he started life with so little? She pulled her hand out of his, slid closer to him on the sofa, placing her palms on each side of his face. His skin was warm and pulsing under her hands. She looked into his black eyes and saw that they weren't perfectly black, but that when you peered really close, they were lit with tiny flecks of deep golden topaz. In those black and topaz eyes, she could see the lonely little boy he must have been and the incredible man he turned out to be.

"Mr. Grey," she said, "you really are one of a kind."

Then she gently pulled his face to hers and kissed him.

28

Lucas

"She'll never change her mind," Cassie said, rolling down the window of Lucas's truck and sticking out her mitten-covered hand. She hand-surfed, giggling when her hand was pushed back by the force of the cold wind.

"We have to try," Lucas said. "What good would it do for June to sue Nash when he doesn't own anything?" They were on their way to try to talk his mother into dropping the charges against Nash Stoddard.

"Maybe someone should tell her that Gandhi said an eye for an eye will only make the whole world blind. I learned that in world history class."

"Well, hurray for California public schools." He tilted his head to look up at the sky and scowled. "Close the dang window. You're letting out what little warmth this crappy heater generates."

"Whoa," she said, pulling in her arm and rolling up the window. "Someone totally needs to get laid."

He glared at her. "I can't believe you said that."

She flipped a hand. "It's so obvious, Uncle Lucas."

He looked back at the dark highway ahead of them and flexed his fingers on the steering wheel. "I refuse to discuss my sex life with my teenage niece."

"Your now legally adult eighteen-year-old niece who is totally grown up now and has had—"

"Stop!" he snapped. "Don't say one more word. I don't even want a hint of a picture of that in my head."

"Okay, but I'm just sayin' . . ."

"Can we please talk about something else?"

"Let's talk about Marie. She's totally

into you, you know. She's going to be here for at least six months to help her grandma. Seriously, you need to—"

"I seriously need to not be discussing my love life with my niece."

"Aha!" She pointed a nail-bitten finger. "So you admit, you have a love life and it includes Marie."

He narrowed his eyes. "You're getting more like your mama every day. I'm going to start calling you Sueann Jr."

"Below the belt! I'm not comparing you to *your* mother."

He turned off on the exit for the Circle MG. "That's because I'm not acting like her, Miss Nosey Pants. Whatever Marie and I are doing or not doing is none of your business."

She sat back in her seat, making a pouty face. "Whatever. I was just trying to help. Forget it. I won't say another word." She mimed zipping her lip.

He could see her feelings were hurt and he felt himself soften a little. "Look, I appreciate that you care. But, really, Cassie, I can do this. I have had a few relationships in my life."

"But not for a while."

"Cassie . . ."

She flipped her hand again. "Whatever. But she does like you." She gave him a sly, sideways look.

He laughed, teased out of his irritable mood. At least for the moment. Only Cassie could manage that. "She does, huh?"

"A lot."

"Well, I like her, too." He pulled the truck into the ranch house's circle driveway. "That'll have to do for now because we are at the wicked witch's house and need to gird our loins."

"Whatever that is, it sounds gross."

"Trust me, it's the perfect metaphor when dealing with your grandma."

June was holding court in the ranch house's grandiose family room. She was sitting in her favorite chair, her broken leg up on a pillow-topped footstool. Her chair was butter-colored leather that Lucas knew felt like sinking into a bed at the Ritz-Carlton. Like all the furniture in this Western-style room, she'd had the chair custom made and loved telling people its price—ten thousand dollars. Every time he saw that chair, he had to bite back a sarcastic remark about how she was always whining that the ranch was low on money. Somehow, June always managed to find the money for the things she wanted.

Her motorized wheelchair was parked discreetly in a corner of the room while June sipped tea and one of the ranch's ever-changing Mexican housekeepers fussed around her, adjusting her leg and asking if she wanted more tea or cookies or another lap quilt or perhaps some hot chocolate.

"Oh, stop hovering, Gabriela," June snapped. "Just fetch some cups for Lucas and Cassie. Honestly, I don't understand why you flutter about like a scared bird."

"*Lo siento*, Senora McGavin," the young woman said, blushing.

"English, Gabriela!" June demanded.

"I'm sorry," the girl stuttered.

"Oh, Grandma, chill out," Cassie said.

"Watch your mouth, young lady," June said to Cassie. Then she turned back to the young Hispanic woman. "Go now, get those cups. I'll ring if I need anything else." She picked up the silver bell sitting on the marble-topped table next to her chair and shook it. The sharp tinkling caused the girl to flinch. Lucas wondered how many times his mother had rung that bell in the last few days.

The young woman glanced up at Lucas and it pained him to see the fear in her eyes. She likely needed this job badly, what with the economy being so bad here in Cardinal, a microcosm of the state of California, and June probably never let her forget how "fortunate" she was to be employed.

"No hurry, Gabriela," he said. "We'll be here a while."

The housekeeper gave him a grateful look and scurried out.

"Honestly, I don't know why these people are so nervous all the time," June said, straightening the cashmere shawl draped around her shoulders.

Cassie looked at Lucas and rolled her eyes. "I'm going into the kitchen and see if I can score a sandwich. You want anything, Uncle Lucas?" She pointedly ignored her grandmother.

"I'm good," he said.

She flounced out of the room, leaving

her attitude behind to settle into the crevices of the fancy Western furniture.

June shook her head. "She's getting more disrespectful every day. But, what can you expect? Sueann always has had a smart remark for everything and never taught that girl to respect her elders."

Lucas knew the wisest thing to do was not answer. Especially since he was here to try to persuade his mother to do something he knew she would not like. He had thought bringing Cassie along might soften her. Once, that was possible. Once Cassie and her grandmother had a good relationship, but his mother managed to mess that up in the same way she'd messed up her relationships with all her sons, by being too controlling.

Forget about all that right now, he told himself. You have a mission and the only way to accomplish it is to finagle your way into Mom's good graces. A Herculean task, without a doubt. Still, he owed it to Ruby to try.

He sat in the love seat across from her and took off his hat.

"A gentleman would have taken off his

hat the minute he walked in the room," June said.

He sat his hat carefully down on the table in front of him, holding back the retort that was on his lips. "Mom, I want to talk about Nash Stoddard. I am asking you to not sue him. He needs help and we're going to try and get it for him. A lawsuit would just complicate things."

She looked at him silently for a moment, her brightly painted lips turned down. "And why," she finally said, "should I do that?"

He sat forward, trying to avoid glancing up at the painting of his father, Carson, over the fireplace. Why didn't she put that monstrosity in storage? How in the hell did Derek live with looking at it every day? "Look, Ruby has gone through enough—"

"When," she interrupted, "are you going to get over *that*?"

"What?"

"This embarrassing and juvenile crush you have on Cole's wife. Really, Lucas, you can do so much better. It's just a little sick, if you ask me."

"Stop it," he said, his voice low, angry. "There is nothing going on between Ruby and me. There never has been. This isn't about that. This is about having some compassion for someone who was your daughter-in-law, someone who didn't have a great start in life and has had a lot of crap to deal with. You should understand that. You should feel some kind of, I don't know, sisterhood with her, don't you think?"

He knew he was treading on thin ice here. His mother hated being reminded of her beginnings, of the poverty she'd grown up with in Bakersfield, how the only reason she was not still there was because Carson McGavin had plucked her out of a Miss California preliminary pageant, gotten her pregnant and decided she was pretty enough to marry and bring back to Cardinal. Ironically enough, they'd been perfect for each other. He wanted a trophy wife who would look the other way no matter how many women he bedded and she wanted an easy way out of poverty.

She stared at him a long moment. "Sisterhood? With a waitress? Oh, please. I may have humble beginnings, but I worked hard to make a life for you boys here in Cardinal. A good life. One you could be proud of." Her eyes glittered with some kind of emotion, though Lucas couldn't begin to guess what it was.

This wasn't going the way he'd intended. He'd hoped to be able to go to Ruby to tell her he'd taken care of the lawsuit, that he'd convinced his mother to let it go. He realized now how foolish his plan had been.

He picked up his hat and stood up. "I shouldn't have come here." He started for the kitchen to find Cassie. They could drive through Jack in the Box on the way back to town.

"Clear Creek," his mother said just as he reached the kitchen's swinging door. "I'll drop the suit if you let me do whatever I want with Clear Creek."

He turned slowly around, feeling like an idiot. "I guess I should have seen that coming."

She smiled at him, the ghost of that beauty queen still lingering in her perfectly made-up face. She still could turn men's heads. Lucas remembered how his dad used to beam at her at barbecues, barn dances and Saturday nights at the Cardinal Country Club. Not because Carson loved her, Lucas eventually figured out, but because all the other men in the room wanted her and all the women wanted to be her. For twenty years, Carson and June McGavin were truly Cardinal's golden couple. But with his dad dead, his memory disgraced and June alone except for the few old guard who remembered those halcyon days, all she had was this last bit of control. Lucas had always known it wasn't just the money she could get for Clear Creek; it was that she couldn't stand there being something she couldn't have, something one of her sons held back from her.

He thought of Ruby and the look on her face at the sheriff's department. Nash was her only family now, except for this missing mother, who may or may not help her. He would do it for Ruby. And for Cole. Because of Cole. It was the one big thing that he and Ruby had in common. They'd loved Cole. Just as sure as he was standing in this room, he knew what Cole would say if he were here.

"It's just dirt, little brother. It's not people. I love the Circle MG and land is important. But we have plenty of land. Always remember, people are more important. Just let her have that little piece of dirt."

Still, before he gave June the answer she wanted, he needed to talk to Ruby. Though she no longer owned any of the Circle MG, part of Cole's ashes were in that pasture. She had the right to have an opinion. But even if she protested, he knew what he was going to do. He would agree to sell it only if June gave them enough of the money for Nash's rehab. That would at least give Nash a chance to straighten out his life. But, he'd make June wait. He would not let her know she had won that easily.

"I'll think about it," he said, turning away, trying not to dwell on the smug expression settling on his mother's perfectly made-up face.

29

Etta

Talking to Nash had been easier than she thought it would be. Etta had always had an easier time relating to men. She didn't know why. Maybe it was because she'd grown up with three brothers and with a mother who was distant and distracted, disapproving of Etta's "crazy dreams" of being a singer.

"Why is it crazy?" she would ask Mama as they scrubbed Daddy's and the brothers' coal-stained clothes on scrub boards. "Loretta Lynn did it. So did Dolly Parton. And what about Tammy Wynette?"

Her mother didn't look up from her

scrubbing. Etta remembered how red and raw her mother's hands always were, how her knucklebones seemed ready to burst out of the skin, like too-ripe fruit. She never wanted to have hands like her mother.

"Those women have talent," her mother said, her voice flat, matter-of-fact. "Besides they got someone who helped 'em. Long as I can remember, ain't nobody ever helped a Walker, Loretta. We always had to help out ourselves."

Etta remembered how hot her face became, how she wanted so badly to take her washboard and slam it against the washhouse wall. "I can do it," she muttered into her chest, her thin T-shirt cold and wet from the dirty water.

So, on that fateful trip to Las Vegas with two girlfriends in 1967, a long-saved-for trip to celebrate Etta and the other girls turning twenty-one, she met Joe Stoddard. Joe, who pretended she sang like an angel, who fell in love with her soft Tennessee twang, who promised her he'd be the one who'd help her find her way to the *Grand Ole Opry*, who talked her, with the help of three Sloe Gin Fizzes, into his bed after knowing him only a few days. That was the moment when her life took a turn that culminated with her standing here with her son in this small town on the edge of the Sierra Nevada Mountains.

She stared down at her sleeping son sprawled out on the bed she'd slept in last night. They'd talked for over two hours. She answered his questions as best she could, leaving out the part about the baby. She'd promised Ruby and she could see that Ruby was right. It wasn't something he needed to deal with right now. The questions he asked weren't much different from Ruby's, but, somehow, she felt less judged. Not surprising there, considering her first words to him.

"Nash, I was a drunk for years and years. I lost more of my life than I want to think about. Please, I don't want that to happen to you. I am so sorry I was never there for you and I know it's late, but I'm here now. What can I do to help?"

For some reason, that struck something in him and he started crying. She led him inside the house and sat him down at the kitchen table, where he cried and cried and she just sat next to him, her hand on his head, silent tears flowing down into the crevices of her cheeks. When he was done, she fixed them bacon and eggs and buttered toast and they talked. Unlike Ruby, he didn't press about why she hadn't come back. They talked about what was going on now, the dilemma he was in, how much he wanted to run away.

"Ruby's friend, Ely, posted your bail because there was no way Ruby or I could," Etta said. "I hope you know that if you take off, you'll hurt him and so many other nice people. But most of all, you'll hurt your sister. And she loves you more than you can imagine."

He nodded. "I won't run, but I'm gonna be straight with you. I don't know if I can quit drinking. I don't know if I want to."

Etta sighed and looked down at her half-eaten eggs. "I understand, but know that by continuing, you'll be hurting a lot of good people."

"I know."

They finished the meal in silence, then he stood up. "I'm beat. Those cots at the jail are murder on your back. I'm going to take a nap."

"I'll clean up. We can talk more later."

After she finished cleaning the kitchen, she walked quietly down the hallway to Nash's bedroom. He'd lain down on top of the red and black Pendleton blanket and was softly snoring, his face made younger by ten years in sleep. In his relaxed features, she could see a ghost of the little boy she'd left so many years ago. She brought a fist up to her mouth to stifle the sob. She turned quickly and walked out of the house to sit on the porch, despite the fact that it was dark now and a frosty wind swayed the treetops. She forced herself to sit there in the bitter cold, a small penance for deserting her children, for all the bad decisions she'd made in her life, for that last drink that caused her to pass out and not hear the sounds that led up to the thump against the wall that ended RJ's young and innocent life.

She would not even allow herself the natural tendency to encircle herself with her arms to get warm. She forced herself to sit still in the cold, allowing it to creep into her feet and hands and bones. She wished it were cold enough to stop her heart, to stop the life that she didn't deserve to have.

But while she sat there, the words of those who'd rescued her seeped into her pounding head—her first sponsor, Rita Lee, a black, former Marine sergeant who'd served in Vietnam, Dr. Beth, Father Tomas. Their words intermingled with the tenets of AA, which she had memorized and repeated during moments when she felt like the only thing that would make everything all right was just one drink. *Grant me the serenity, grant me the serenity, grant me the serenity.*

Help him, she prayed to this god that Father Tomas swore was listening, the one he swore had forgiven her. I'm sorry. I'm sorry. I'm so, so sorry. Please, help my boy. Help my son. You know what it is like. Please. Help him. And, please, sir, bless my baby girl, too.

30

Ruby

When Ruby arrived home that night, Etta had already made a bed for herself on the sofa. Jay Leno was performing his monolog on television.

"You can have my room," Ruby said, feeling guilty.

Etta's face was neutral. "I'm fine here. Nash went to bed about an hour ago. He was pretty worn out." She switched off the television.

"The sound doesn't bother me," Ruby said.

"It's okay. It's been a long day. I need some extra sleep myself."

They looked at each other, the discomfort between them like a third person in the room.

"Well, good night," Ruby said.

"Good night, Ruby." Her mother's voice sounded tired and sad.

Ruby closed the bedroom door behind her with a soft click, then sat down on the bed. What had Etta and Nash talked about? Had she told him things she didn't tell Ruby? She touched her lips, remembering the kiss she'd given Ely, how it had turned into a deeper one so quickly and how oddly fine she felt about it. Good, even. How was it possible to feel passion and comfort with the same person? It was a combination of feelings that she'd never experienced. Then again, it was the first time she'd kissed a man who'd started out a friend, not a potential lover.

The next morning, the clanking of pots and pans woke her with a start. She pulled on sweatpants and a T-shirt and went into the kitchen. The clock over the stove read six fifty-five. Etta stood at the stove waiting for a pot of water to boil.

"I'm sorry," she said. "I was trying to be quiet. I woke at six and laid there until my legs starting aching. I'm so used to getting up and feeding the dogs that I can't sleep in even when I want to." She gestured at the Quaker Oats box. "I'm making oatmeal. Would you like some?"

"Yes, thank you," Ruby said, going to the coffeepot. She poured herself a cup and turned back to her mother. "How long have you worked at the shelter?"

"Five years. I got the job at the shelter a few days after I came to Ajo."

"Do they pay you?"

Etta measured out the cereal and poured it into the boiling water. "Dr. Beth pays me a little. But I also bartend at The Roadrunner Saloon on weekends and clean houses for some of the snowbirds. I don't make a lot of money, but enough to get by in a town like Ajo. Not much to spend money on there, which is a good thing."

Ruby sipped her coffee, wondering what else she and Etta could talk about. She wanted to ask her what she and Nash discussed, but she didn't have the nerve, especially when he could walk in any minute.

The phone rang, saving them from further uncomfortable conversation. It was Birch. Ruby felt her queasy stomach ease slightly.

"Oh, sweetie, did I wake you up?" Birch asked. "I did not even look at the clock when I dialed your number."

"No, it's okay. I've been up a few minutes."

"Can you help today with getting the museum ready for the story jam Friday night? Or does Ely have all your time sewn up at the bookstore?"

"I'd be happy to help. I'm scheduled to work until two. A Tuesday during January isn't likely to be a busy day and we haven't started inventory yet. What needs to be done?"

"It's not so much the museum itself. The docents do a great job keeping that spiffy. But the auditorium where we're holding it needs some light cleaning and we are going to have a few craft and food booths in the back parking lots, so we'll need to kind of spruce that up a little, pull a few weeds."

"What time do you need me there?"

"How about right after you get off at the bookstore?"

"Perfect. I'll be there about two thirty."

There was a short pause, then Birch asked, "How is Nash doing?"

"Good," Ruby said. "He came home last night. Ely paid his bail. He and Etta . . ." She looked at her mother's thin back as she stirred the bubbling oatmeal. "They talked."

"She's right there," Birch said.

"Yes."

"Okay, we can talk later. Try not to worry. We'll figure out this thing with your brother."

"Thank you, Birch. See you later."

After she hung up, she went over to the cupboard and pulled down three bowls, three glasses and three spoons. It felt strange to her, setting the table like this when she had been alone so much of her life.

"That was Birch Hernandez," Etta said, turning off the fire under the oatmeal. "Your husband's aunt."

"Yes," Ruby said, putting paper napkins at each place. "His father's sister. She's been very kind to me."

"She . . ." Etta started to say, then stopped.

"What?" Ruby asked.

Etta shook her head. "I'm glad you have someone like her in your life. Maybe I can meet her before I go back home."

A few seconds later, Nash wandered into the kitchen, rubbing his eyes as if he were five years old. "Hey, Ruby. Hey, Mom. Oatmeal? Seriously, is there anything else? That's all they served at the jail."

"I can make you some scrambled eggs," Etta said, standing up.

"Cool, thanks," he said, sitting down at the place set for him as if this was the most natural thing on earth. "Man, I slept like a brick last night."

Ruby stared at him, wanting to get up and shake his shoulders, scream at him—Mom? Really? You give her that title back so easily? You forgive her that quickly? When you were the one who didn't even want to go see her? And, by the way, do you have any idea what kind of mess you are in? She glanced over at Etta, who was busy cracking eggs into a ceramic bowl.

"I told Ely I'd come to work early," she lied. "Then I'll be at the Western Museum for a few hours."

"Do you need any help?" Etta asked, pulling a whisk from the large red Folgers coffee can that Ruby used to hold her utensils.

"No, thank you," she said. "But tonight, we need to talk about . . ."

Nash looked up at her. "What a screwed-up mess I've made of my life."

"Nash, it's not that bad," Etta said.

Ruby felt herself go still, her heart pounding so hard she could hear it in her ears. "You're wrong, Etta. It is bad."

Nash looked from his sister to his mother, then back at Ruby. "I'm sorry, Ruby. But I told you it wasn't a good idea for me to come out here. I should have stayed in Nashville."

"Right, so I could come back here and wait for the phone call from the police department telling me you'd either killed somebody while driving drunk or to identify your body after you died from alcohol poisoning."

She hated how angry her words

sounded, wished she could have said them with the love for him she truly felt in her heart. But at this moment, as much as she loved her brother, she wanted to pierce him with her words, hoping to stun or shame him into changing his life.

He answered her with an almost imperceptible shrug, then turned to Etta. "With some cheese if there is any."

Ruby turned and went into her bedroom, dressing in less than five minutes. She left without saying good-bye, slamming the wooden screen door behind her.

In the five minutes it took her to drive to the bookstore, she was already heartsick about her outburst. It was only eight o'clock and the bookstore wouldn't be open for two hours. Besides, she'd left without eating most of her breakfast. Her stomach grumbled in protest. She sat in the cold truck and contemplated what she should do. She could not bear to go to the Lone Pine Café. Sueann would immediately see her distress and demand all the gory details. Ruby didn't think she was up to that this early.

Holy Grounds and Maxie's Bakery were

both open. She would go to Holy Grounds in support of Ely and, she had to admit to herself, she was partly hoping that he would be there.

Inside the warm coffeehouse, the morning chatter was like a balm to her ears. She ordered a mocha latte and a strawberry scone. When her order came, she surveyed the room with dismay. Not one chair was free.

"Hey, Ruby."

She turned to face the morning barista, Marcus. "Yes?"

"Ely's back in his office. Bet there's a chair in there."

She nodded her thanks, picked up her coffee and scone, then went down the hallway to his office. He was sitting in his beat-up leather executive chair reading the *Atlantic* monthly.

"Hey," she said softly, standing in the doorway. "Marcus told me there's a free chair back here."

He looked over the magazine at her, his rimless eyeglasses perched on his nose. He gave her the biggest smile she'd ever seen from him. "Good morning, Ruby."

"I didn't know you wear glasses," she said.

He gestured at the visitor chair in front of his desk. "We're all getting old. I only need them for reading."

She sat her mocha and scone down on his messy desk, then pulled the metal chair closer. "So, what's new?"

He sat the magazine down, stood up and came around the desk. He pulled her up and into his arms, encircling her with his corded forearms. "Hard night?" he whispered. His breath was warm against the top of her head.

She nodded, resting her head against his chest, thankful for his ability to assess situations so quickly. "I acted like a real bitch to my brother this morning."

"Understandable, considering the circumstances. Though nagging someone into sobriety has been scientifically proven to be of no use."

"It's just that, I felt so . . . out of place. He and Etta, they seem to be getting along fine. He called her Mom." That last sentence came out almost in a hiccup.

"I'm sorry."

She pulled out of his arms with reluctance. What she didn't want this relationship to become was something where he always had to comfort her, always had to deal with her problems. "No, I'm sorry, Ely. I really don't know why in the world you would even want to have any kind of relationship with someone with as many problems as I lug around."

He held onto her shoulders, ducking his head to kiss her gently on the lips, then under one eye, then under the other, in those vulnerable places where tears first fall. She stood still as a rabbit, not wanting the moment to end.

"Why in the world," he repeated softly, "would you want to start a relationship with an ex-con, bastard, half-breed alcoholic with a reputation for breaking women's hearts?"

"Because, he's good man," she said, looking into his black and golden eyes. "Because he's one of the best men I've ever known."

"You'll get through this, Ruby." He brought his hands to her face, caressing her cheek. "We'll get through this." He kissed her again. "Now, eat your breakfast. I hear you've got a whip-cracking boss who has a very hard shift for you today."

She smiled at him, feeling relaxed for the first time since she left him last night. "Ha, he's a cupcake. Easiest guy in the world to manipulate. After I'm off at the bookstore, I'm going over to help Birch and some others get the museum auditorium ready for the story jam." She sat down and picked up her latte.

He grinned at her. "Yes, I know. A very persuasive Senora Hernandez also roped me into helping. My shift starts at ten. Think you'll be okay for a few hours?"

"Yes," she said. "It's probably better that I give them a little space."

"Good idea," Ely said. "You have some time to figure things out. He's not going anywhere and I have a feeling he'll dial back on his drinking while your mother is here."

"I sure hope you're right," she said.

The official name of the museum was the Beverly and Jim Rogers Cardinal Valley Western Film History Museum. But everyone in Cardinal just called it the Western Museum. Some kids had, in keeping with their tendency to shorten everything as if it were a text message, started calling it WeeMu. That, of course, drove the old-timers crazy, which made the kids use it more. The Rogerses had given a generous sum to build the museum as well as donated many of the items in the museum from their private collection of Western memorabilia, which made the ten-thousand-square-foot museum with its eighty-five-seat movie theater and popular gift shop possible.

The building's design resembled one of the many old-fashioned movie theaters that once graced the main street of almost every small American town. The museum's collection included hats, guns and costumes of many Western stars, such as Roy Rogers, Gene Autry, Barbara Stanwyck, John Wayne and even Errol Flynn. Silver-ladened saddles designed by Bohlin and Ted Flowers always drew people's admiration. Eventually, the museum became a gathering place for the community, something that held them together, something uniquely theirs.

The parking lot was three-quarters full when Ruby arrived. Obviously, Birch and the other docents had convinced quite a few people to help. She could hear laughing and talking from behind the building, so the outside contingent was already working. It was cool today, in the high fifties, actually the perfect weather for outside work.

Inside, the first person she ran into was Cassie, who was setting up a display of Western-themed books. Another young woman was helping her, a pretty, dark-haired girl who appeared about ten years older than Cassie. They both wore jeans, gray sweatshirts and high-topped Ugg boots. Cassie's boots were a bright pink, a Christmas gift from her mom. Ruby had been there when Sueann was wrapping them.

"Hey, Cassie," Ruby said. "Need any help?"

"We're good," Cassie said. "Besides, you need to check in with General Hernandez. She has a list a mile long and is very specific about what she wants people to do. Thank goodness we have two more days after this to complete her list. We're going to need the time."

The young woman handing books to Cassie from the open box chuckled. "Some things never change."

Cassie laughed with her. Ruby looked at the young woman curiously. "Hi, I'm Ruby McGavin."

"Oh, sorry," Cassie said, straightening up. "This is Marie Williams. She's helping her grandma who's been sick. And she's Lucas's girlfriend."

"Cassie!" Marie said, her cheeks flushing deeper.

"Well, aren't you?"

"We're not going there right now." She held out her hand to Ruby. "Nice to meet you. I had Mrs. Hernandez as a teacher for half a year when I lived with Grammy back in the day."

Ruby smiled and shook her hand. Lucas's girlfriend? Apparently, a few things had happened since she and he last talked. "Oh, so you know how it's always best to do whatever she wants without argument."

"Oh, Heaven knows that," Cassie said, giggling.

Marie's cheeks turned rosy and she slapped at Cassie's thigh. "Shut up, girl.

I told you I didn't want to ever hear you say that."

Ruby tilted her head, confused.

"It's her first name," Cassie said gleefully. "Heaven Marie. Isn't that the coolest name? Her mom was, like, a total hippie. But she's a nurse now for people who are dying."

"Actually, she was a hippie wannabe. She's a nurse who specializes in end-of-life care," Marie said. "In Bakersfield."

"I understand your pain a little," Ruby said. "I've always been teased about my name."

Marie nodded. "I think parents should let kids name themselves."

Ruby laughed. "It's a thought, but what would they call them until they were old enough to decide?"

"Numbers," Cassie said. "They ought to just give us numbers."

"Think of how many number ones there would be, though," Marie said.

"I'll leave you two to figure that dilemma out," Ruby said. "Where is the general?"

"In the auditorium, last I saw," Cassie said.

Ruby walked through the museum to the auditorium, greeting a few people as she did. Even working at the bookstore the short time she had, she had fallen back into the rhythm of Cardinal, something that she treasured and missed the year she'd lived in Nashville. In the apartment complex where Nash lived, Ruby barely got to know someone only to find out they were moving in a few weeks. She finally gave up and contented herself with interacting only with the people at the café where she cooked. During those three weeks last year in Cardinal, and since she'd come back, she realized that she was a small-town woman at heart.

Inside the auditorium, Birch was on stage directing the placement of some floral arrangements donated by Cassie's part-time employer. They were autumn-colored flowers—mums, scarlet Gerber daisies and pine boughs and appropriately themed with physical touches of cowboy, Indian and mining cultures—old rusty horseshoes, pockmarked mining pans, pickaxes, some pseudo-Indian baskets and beadwork and pictures of famous Western stars like Audie Murphy, Hoot Gibson, Rory Calhoun and Vera Ralston.

"Need any help?" Ruby asked, walking down the carpeted side aisle.

"Hi, Ruby," Birch said, turning around. She came down the stage steps and met her with a warm hug. "How are you doing?"

"Okay," Ruby said, hugging her back. "It's awkward. Nash and Etta seem to talk easier than she and I can."

Birch patted her gently on the back. "Sometimes men are able to move on quicker. Not because they've figured things out, but because they are more willing to stuff it down and pretend like nothing happened. It only delays the problem, in my opinion." She touched her chest, looking a little embarrassed. "Not that it's any of my business."

"No, it is. I'm always glad to get your opinion. I'm a horrible person. So unforgiving. Linc would have a field day with me." She gave a rueful half smile.

"Linc would be the first person to tell you to go easy on yourself," Birch said. "We each have our own paths to walk and our own time to walk them in." She laughed. "Oh, my, that was not a sentence I'd give an A."

"You're so right," Ruby said. "Not about the sentence, but the other. I'll attempt to cut my brother and mother a little slack."

"And yourself even more," Birch said, wagging a finger at her. "That's the point I was making, young lady."

Ruby smiled at her. "Point taken, Senora Hernandez. What do you need me to do?"

"I've got plenty of help in here, but I think Lucas might need some help outside. He just brought a load of drinks and snacks they'll be selling at one of the booths on Friday."

"I'll go find him. See you later." She started to walk away, then turned back. "Question. In the lobby, I saw Cassie and met Marie. Cassie said she and Lucas are . . . seeing each other?"

Birch nodded. "I haven't had a chance to chat with you in the last few days, so much has happened, but, yes, the official word is they are dating." She gave Ruby a curious look.

"I'm happy for him," Ruby said. "She seems like a really nice lady."

"Yes, she does. She was a smart little girl, I remember. Loved to read."

"That alone makes me like her."

She found Lucas on the side of the museum where a crew was setting up booths, tables and chairs and portable heating lamps.

"Hey, saddle man," she said, waving at him. He was standing next to his old truck, looking over a bed filled with cases of soda and bottled water.

"Hey, Ruby," he called back. He walked across the gravel parking lot to Ruby. "When did you get here?"

"A few minutes ago. Birch said you needed help."

"I do. I need someone to count the cases of soda and make sure it matches the order." He nodded over at the two teenage boys unloading the cases. "They're great for brawn, but I'd rather have your brains doing the counting."

"No problem."

They stood there an awkward moment, the cool breeze ruffling their hair. Finally Lucas said, "How's Nash doing?"

"Okay. He got out last night. He's at home with Etta."

"How's that working out?"

She tightened her lips. "They seem to be talking."

"I have some news for you. From June."

Ruby felt her stomach tighten. Here it was, the final swing of the axe.

"She's agreed to drop the lawsuit if I give her the right to do whatever she wants with Clear Creek."

"Oh, Lucas," Ruby said, bringing her hand to her mouth. "That's . . . that's awful. Of course you said no."

"I told her I'd think about it. I wanted to talk to you."

"Absolutely not. I could never allow you to do that. That land is . . . well, sacred. Where would you keep your horses? How could she ask that? Part of her son is there! How could . . . ?"

He held up his hand. "In her defense—something I never thought I'd ever say—she doesn't know about us sprinkling part of Cole's ashes there."

"Do you think it would change her mind?"

He shrugged. "Probably not."

"Look, why don't I just let her sue me and Nash?" Ruby said rashly. "What is she going to get?"

"Letting her have Clear Creek is not just to avoid a lawsuit," Lucas said. "I'm going to stipulate that some of the money she makes selling it will be used for Nash's rehab. You do realize how expensive that is? If you don't send him to a private place, he could be on a list somewhere with the county for months, maybe years. That money would get him in right away. Just from a legal standpoint, telling the judge that he is going into rehab will make it appear he's really trying."

Ruby dropped her head, her eyes burning with tears. How had all of this gone so wrong so quickly? Any hope she'd had, any dreams she'd imagined, of a good life here in Cardinal seemed impossible. The leaden sadness that had descended upon her from the phone call telling her of Cole's death almost two years ago came back. She felt like she weighed a thousand pounds.

She felt the touch of Lucas's hand on her shoulder. "Ruby, don't cry. It's just a piece of land. The McGavins have lots of land and I can pasture the horses somewhere else. Clear Creek is beautiful, but in the end, it's just dirt. My dad would kill me for saying that, but it is just dirt. People are more important. He's your brother, Ruby. Please, just say yes."

She slowly lifted her head and looked into his troubled face. It was like seeing a small part of Cole still on this earth. She realized in that moment how very much she loved this man. Was not in love with him, but loved him like he was her brother, like she did Nash. And she did love Nash. Tonight, she would tell him so. After she was finished at the museum, she'd go home and hug him and tell him how much she loved him, that she'd be there for him no matter how long it took.

She smiled at Lucas. He was Cole's little brother and she knew their mutual love for Cole would always be the steel thread that connected them.

"Yes," she said, gratefully taking his hand in hers. "Thank you. Yes."

31

Birch

"It's crazy busy," Sueann said to Birch on Friday. It was four o'clock, an hour after the anniversary celebration for the Western Museum officially started. They were working in the gift shop.

"Stop running!" she called to three kids playing tag around a display of horseshoe sculptures made by a local artisan. "Did every family with out-of-control kids decide to come tonight?"

Birch gave her a sympathetic look. "They've likely been inside all day and their parents were looking for something to do. The bowling alley and McDonald's playground are probably filled to capacity."

A winter storm blew down from Alaska late yesterday afternoon, surprising everyone, including the weatherman, with its intensity. It had snowed off and on all night and into Friday morning. Fortunately, it had stopped by noon, leaving a beautiful white landscape and treacherous road conditions. Highway 395 ran right in front of the museum and they'd watched through the front window the constant line of SUVs and fancy trucks barreling down the two-lane road headed for Mammoth's ski slopes.

"What's the four-one-one on the outside booths?" Sueann asked.

"We'll move the craftspeople in here tonight. There were only a couple of them, so that's not a problem. The hot dogs and tri-tip . . ." She frowned, pulling the stack of dollar bills from the register and started rearranging them so George Washington faced the same way. "Since it's not currently snowing, we'll go ahead and have them cook the food and hope people buy something to eat. We had to put away the tables and chairs, so folks will have to eat in their cars or take it home. Hopefully, we'll be able to put everything back outside tomorrow."

"Great," Sueann said, glaring at the kids who finally heeded her and ran out of the gift shop into the museum, where they'd probably torture some poor docent. "That means we'll be telling people all evening that they can't come inside the museum with food. This is a disaster. I hate to point this out, but what a crazy time for an anniversary celebration."

"It is what it is," Birch said. "This is when the museum officially opened, and you know how some people are a stickler for those kinds of things. I voted to wait, but I was outvoted. Don't worry, everything will work out." She said it with more certainty than she felt. Bobby limped over to the gift shop from his post by the door where he was taking tickets.

"How's it going, ladies?" He leaned against his "dress" cane, an ebony cane hand painted with sacred white buffaloes.

"I think we should charge double instead of half for kids," Sueann grumbled.

"It is a little lively in here," Bobby said,

smiling at her. “But, it’s better to have it like this than three old folks and a service dog in the audience.”

Birch laughed, came around the counter and gave him a hug. “How are ticket sales?”

“Sold out for the story jam,” Bobby said. “But at least we’re getting folks in the door to see the museum. If we’d known the story jam would be this popular, we could have had it in the high school gym.”

“Maybe next year,” Birch said. “Besides, it might be a fluke because of the weather. Have you seen Ruby and her . . . family?”

Bobby gazed at his wife with understanding eyes. “They came in about a half hour ago.”

Birch tried to hide her disappointment. “I thought she’d at least come over and say hello.”

He placed a hand on his wife’s shoulder. “She’s got a lot on her plate right now. I’m sure it’s not personal.”

Birch nodded, knowing what he said was true. But, somehow, she felt pushed aside. She knew how petty that was, but there you go, she was human.

Whatever you intend, Lord, she thought. I will try to accept whatever you intend.

"I'd better hobble back to my perch," Bobby said, nodding over at the door, where a group was waiting for someone to take their tickets. "See you at the jam." He kissed his wife's cheek and limped over to the door, calling out to the guests a warm greeting.

For the next forty-five minutes, the gift shop was busy. Birch was grateful because it kept her from worrying about anything except making the right change and giving people their receipts.

One of their long-time docents, Kit, came up to the counter. "Fifteen minutes to showtime. I know you both want to see Cassie, so I'll take it from here."

"Thanks, Kit," Birch said. She finished wrapping up a novel set in Cardinal Valley written by a woman who used to vacation in Tokopah County as a child. She had mentioned the Lone Pine Café and the Tokopah Lodge, which had tickled them all. The museum hosted a signing for her a few months ago. "Enjoy it," she told the man buying the autographed novel. "Rumor has it that she's working on a sequel."

"Did you save us seats?" Sueann asked as they hurried toward the auditorium.

"Yes, I put reserved signs on them and, no doubt, we'll hear about that from a few cranky souls."

"So what," Sueann said. "You put a lot of work in this and so did I. We deserve a little special treatment."

There was a backup at the door to the auditorium. Sueann craned her neck to see what the holdup was. "Oh, for cryin' in a bucket."

"What?" Birch said.

"It's June and her motorized wheelchair blocking the aisle. Of course any holdup would include her."

Sure enough, when the crowd broke up, Birch could see June McGavin down at the front of the auditorium, her chair right in front, though at the side so she wasn't blocking anyone else's view. Birch saw with dismay that her own seat, the left aisle seat in the front row would be right next to her sister-in-law. Oh, well, they wouldn't really have to chat. The story jam would be starting soon and then Birch would make some excuse about getting back to the gift shop.

"Hello, June," she said, taking her aisle seat. Sueann sat next to her and ignored her former mother-in-law. "Hope you're feeling better."

"I feel like crap," June said. "I wouldn't even be here except I want to see my granddaughter's performance." She touched a red fingernail to matching lips. "I can't believe that woman and her brother have the nerve to show up here."

Birch looked over to where her sister-in-law had fixed her gaze. Ruby, Nash and Etta were taking seats on the other side of the auditorium near the front exit. She tried to catch Ruby's eye, but she was busy saying something to Nash, who was laughing. Etta looked peaceful, her tanned face still. Birch couldn't help feeling a little envious.

Now, stop it, she scolded herself. You

should feel happy for Ruby that she's having a nice moment with her brother and mother.

"They have as much a right to be here as anyone," Birch said to June evenly.

"Huh," June said. "I think not. Not after all the havoc he's created."

Sueann rolled her eyes at Birch.

"Oh, stop it, Sueann," June said. "You look possessed."

Sueann pointedly ignored June and said to Birch, "I think I'll go backstage and see how Cassie is doing."

"Good idea," Birch said, not feeling like mediating between these two right now.

It was a little past seven p.m. when all the seats were finally filled. Though it was technically against the fire code, Birch noticed that there were people standing in the back, obviously begging and pleading their way past Bobby. Not a hard thing to do, she knew, especially if they had kids in the production. Sueann had come back and sat back down, pointedly ignoring June.

"Cassie is nervous as an alley cat," Sueann said. "But they're ready."

Maddie Collins stepped onto the stage.

She was dressed in a red velvet broom skirt and a black velvet top with red flowers embroidered around the neckline. She wore one of her Indian-inspired necklaces made of red and black stones and long earrings made of feathers. She made a few announcements, thanking the different sponsors and the various committee members for their help.

"Okay, that's it with the announcements from the old broad. You're all here to listen to some of the wonderful and unique stories these kids have collected for this event. If you'll look behind me"—without turning around, she pointed to the movie screen automatically coming down—"you will see a photo of the person whose story is being presented. Some of these folks are still alive and might be sitting right next to you and some are dead and let's hope they are *not* sitting next to you." She allowed the laughter to ripple through the audience before continuing. "These kids have worked hard on this, the first annual Cardinal Valley Story Jam, so all I have to say now is, let the stories begin!" The lights dimmed and the audience grew quiet.

The first person up was a young Indian man in his middle teens. He wore small, square glasses, baggy jeans and a black T-shirt. A bone and bead necklace hung around his neck. Behind him was the black-and-white photo of a very old Paiute woman sitting on a log, holding a small basket in her lap.

"My name is Johnny Cardenas. This is my great-grandmother Nonnie Cardenas. This is a story she used to tell my father when he was a little boy and then he told it to my sisters and me. It's about how the North Star began.

"A long time ago when the earth was a child, the People of the Sky were so restless that they made trails in the heavens. When we watch the sky today, we can see those trails and they tell us which way to go. But there is one star that doesn't ever travel. That is the North Star."

He paused, his Adam's apple convulsing in his thin neck.

"You can do it, Johnny," Birch murmured, the teacher in her never far from the surface.

Johnny cleared his throat and continued. “So, the North Star was first called Na-gah, the mountain sheep. His dad was Shinoh. Na-gah loved to climb mountains and he climbed them every day.” He gave a big grin. “My great-grandma Nonnie used to call me Crazy Na-gah because I was always climbing on the roof of our house.”

The audience laughed at his personal comment, causing him to relax a little. “So, Na-gah started climbing the biggest mountain in the valley because he wanted to know what was on the very top. He traveled round and round, looking for a trail, but he never found one. He didn’t want to come home without reaching the top because he thought his dad would be ashamed of him. So he kept climbing. Pretty soon, it got dark and he couldn’t see his way and he fell on some loose rocks and started falling toward this big, black hole. He got really scared, but he didn’t give up. He finally realized that all the rocks he was slipping on had filled up the hole. He had only one way to go now and that was up. So he started climbing again in the darkness until he saw a tiny light above him. When he reached it, he saw it was the peak of the mountain and he could see the whole world from there. All this time his dad was looking for him, but he couldn't find him. Eventually, he saw him up on the peak with no way for Na-gah to come down. So Shinoh decided to turn his son into a star so he could be a guide to everyone on the earth who was lost. Other mountain sheep eventually became stars, but they were never like Na-gah because they would move in the night sky. Na-gah, the North Star, is always in the same place so he can show us the way home."

He then gave a short biography of his grandma, Nonnie Cardenas, how she would make his favorite hot chocolate with a touch of nutmeg in it and how she taught him how to quilt.

One by one, the students came up, telling stories, some in poems, some as songs, some in the words of the person they had interviewed. There were stories of great-great-grandfathers who had worked the gold mines that had started the town, shopkeepers who'd served the miners, a story about a girl's grandmother who was a ski instructor in Mammoth before it became a tourist mecca and more Native American stories about Coyote and his wily ways, and the California Big Trees and how anyone who cuts down the trees or shoots an owl will bring onto themselves much bad luck.

Birch glanced at her program and saw that Cassie was next. She nudged Sueann and pointed to Cassie's name. Next to it, it just said—"Local Hero."

"I know, she's the last one before intermission," Sueann whispered. "Then there are five more. I saw the dress rehearsal a few days ago."

"So, you know who she is talking about?"

Sueann nodded and grinned at her. "She's telling a story about Cole. She said she wanted people to remember the good stuff he did in this town, not just that he killed his father."

When Cassie came to the stage, she was dressed in Wranglers, her old Roper boots, stained leather chaps and a well-worn straw cowboy hat. Behind her appeared a photo of Cole McGavin. He was standing next to the pineapple saddle that Lucas kept in his shop. She started telling the story of the time when he was sixteen when he pulled a young pregnant woman from a burning car wreck on the highway up near the Circle MG. He had been out riding and seen the smoke from the crash.

"I totally forgot about that!" Birch whispered.

She glanced over at Ruby to see how she was reacting. At some point, her brother, Nash, must have left, because it was only Ruby and Etta sitting there, an empty seat between them. Ruby sat forward in her seat, listening intently to Cassie. Her face seemed lit from inside.

Cassie was halfway through the story when one of the docents tapped Birch on the shoulder. "There's a problem in the lobby. Please, hurry."

"What's wrong?" Sueann said.

"I don't know," Birch whispered. "You stay and watch Cassie. I'm sure it's nothing."

"I'm coming with you," Sueann said. "I've seen this speech about a million times. Besides, it's being filmed."

Birch walked quickly up the aisle with Sueann close on her heels. Out in the lobby, next to the entrance to the gift shop, a young woman was crying hysterically. Bobby was talking on the museum's phone.

"What's wrong?" Birch said.

"It's her little girl. She's missing."

Birch's heart froze in her chest. Was there any worse moment of fear than that exact second when a child couldn't be found? In all her years of teaching, it had happened only twice. Both times, she thought she would die from the terror.

"How old is she?" Birch asked. "Where was she last seen? What's her name?"

"Sheriff is on his way," Bobby said, putting down the phone. "Her name is Riley. She's four years old and she's been gone approximately fifteen minutes. We've looked outside already and checked every hiding place here in the museum. There are people outside looking for her. Lucas and Ely are out there."

"I told her to sit there on the chair in the bathroom while I was in the stall," the young mother wailed. "Riley's a good girl. She's never done anything like this before. Why did she leave?"

Birch glanced over at Sueann, exchanging a silent dialog. What in the world was this young woman thinking telling a four-year-old to stay put while she used the restroom? You never let them out of your sight at that age.

“She’s wearing a dark blue puffy jacket and a dark blue hat with red trim,” Bobby said.

“Let’s go back outside,” Birch said. “The more people looking the better.”

“Should we stop the show?” Sueann said.

“The sheriff said not to,” Bobby said. “With this many people here, it could make it worse, everyone panicking and all. Gordon and his men will be here soon. But, we’ve got another problem. It’s started to snow again.”

“Oh, no,” Birch said.

Birch and Sueann followed Bobby outside and stood in the parking lot. Birch could hear voices yelling Riley’s name. She walked to the edge of the parking lot and watched the traffic speed by. The thought of all these cars and trucks speeding past carrying who knows what kind of predator caused her to shiver. She prayed that Riley was just lost and that she'd be found before it got much colder. The museum was on the edge of town. Past it was the vast, dark high desert plain. But, really, how far could she have gotten? She was only four years old.

Across the road was an empty lot that once was a truck repair shop. She could see the men with flashlights looking through the piles of old tires and trying the shed doors. She saw out of the corner of her eye the flash of a match at the end of the museum's parking lot. She peered into the darkness. When she saw who it was, she tsked under her breath.

"Who is it?" Sueann asked.

"Nash. Smoking a cigarette, it appears."

"Huh," Sueann said. "I didn't realize he smoked."

"Neither did I." Birch turned back to watch the searching men, wondering if it would help or hinder if she tried to help.

"There's the sheriff's department now," Sueann said. They could see the red and blue flashing lights in the distance.

"Riley, Riley," Bobby called out, sending his flashlight out into the darkness. The cars and trucks kept coming at a steady pace.

"Shouldn't we stop traffic or something?" Birch said. "Set up a roadblock?"

"Gordon will have to do that," Bobby said. "We don't have the authority and . . ." Before he could finish, a Tokopah County Sheriff's vehicle drove up, followed by two similar vehicles. One said "K-9 Officer" on the side.

"Maybe the dog will find her," Sueann said.

They all started toward the cars. Gordon Vieira, the chief deputy, stepped out of the first one. "Where's the mother?" he asked.

A Highway Patrol officer arrived a few seconds later. By this time, people had started coming out of the museum, asking what was happening, had there been an accident.

Ruby and Etta rushed over to Birch. "What's going on? We heard there was a little girl missing."

"We need to get control of this area right now," Gordon said. He turned to his deputies. "Get everyone back into the museum and keep them there until we set up a perimeter." He walked over to the Highway Patrol officer. "I need to talk to the mother . . ."

"Look!" Birch heard a young man yell. "I think that's her."

Everyone turned to look across the street at the little girl crawling out from under a thick bush. The men must have walked by it ten times in the last few minutes, but her dark clothing and the snow flurries had hidden her. Birch guessed the little girl had been too afraid to call out.

"Riley!" the young woman yelled, her voice screaming with relief.

"Mama!" The girl started running toward her mother.

A white pickup truck barreled down the highway.

"No!" A million voices screamed.

When she remembered it later, Birch saw it like a series of old Kodachrome slides—*click, click, click*—snow, darkness, the white truck, the crying child, a rushing black figure, screeching brakes, men cursing and the horrible smell of burning rubber. Though she wanted to close her eyes, she couldn't.

"Help," she prayed while barbed wire seemed to squeeze her heart.

"Oh," Ruby whispered beside her. "Oh, no."

In seconds, there was bedlam—the truck flipped on its side, people rushing across the street, police officers stopping traffic and, above it all, the wonderful cry of a child.

"She's okay," one of the deputies yelled. "But we need an ambulance."

"What happened?" Birch said, straining to see. She turned to Bobby, who had somehow materialized by her side. "The girl, she's okay?"

"You didn't see?" Bobby said. "Someone pushed her out of the way." He glanced over at Ruby. "It was Nash. He was the closest and he pushed her out of the way. But he was hit."

Behind them, a wounded animal cry pierced the dark, snowy night. Etta was running across the street, pushing her way through the crowd.

When someone tried to hold her back,

Birch heard her scream, "Let me through. He's my son. He's my *son*."

Ruby stood frozen, looking at Bobby, then at Birch. "Nash?" Her voice sounded like a little girl's. "Nash saved her?"

"Let's go, sweetie," Birch said, taking her arm. "We have to go help your mother."

They pushed their way through the crowd and found Nash lying on the side of the road, his head twisted at an unnatural angle. His eyes were open and snow softly fell on his face. Etta kneeled by his side, clutching his hand, a keening sound radiating from deep inside her, floating up and into the night sky.

"Nash," Ruby said, clutching Birch's hand so tight that Birch's rings cut into her palm. "I can't . . . I'm . . ." She collapsed against Birch, tears flowing down her cheeks.

"Bobby!" Birch yelled, catching Ruby's weight. "Somebody. Help!"

From behind her, Bobby and Ely appeared, helping her hold Ruby upright.

"It'll be okay, sweetie," Birch murmured in her ear, even though she knew it wasn't true. She encircled Ruby with her arms, willing warmth into her cold, trembling body, as they watched Etta move closer to Nash, cradling him in her arms.

"I've got you, baby," Etta said, tears shining on her cheeks. "Hold on now. Mama's here. I've got you."

From a distance, Birch could hear more sirens and all she could think was how much it sounded like *too late, too late, too late*.

32

Lucas

Bobby and Ely beat Lucas to the hospital. They were standing in the emergency room waiting area talking in low voices when he walked in.

"He died on the way to the hospital," Bobby told Lucas. "His mother was with him. Birch is with Ruby and Etta." Lucas hugged his uncle, the fragility of his uncle's bones made him feel like all their lives were on a bullet train to this unavoidable destination.

"I'm so sorry for Ruby," Lucas said. "And for his mother."

Bobby rubbed small circles on his back

as he had when Lucas was a boy. "He saved that little girl's life. No matter what that boy did in his life, he ended it with something noble."

Lucas glanced over his uncle's shoulder at Ely and their eyes locked for a moment. This was something they'd no doubt discuss someday. Ely had become that for Lucas, the person with whom he pondered these life questions.

Lucas thought about Cole and the people he touched in his life, the sacrifices he had made for others, yet he died what many considered a dishonorable death. Nash Stoddard had been a drunk and an addict and caused his family and friends no end of heartache, yet he died a hero. Does one act truly define the essence of a person's life? Is our last act before we die our legacy forever?

Lucas broke away, clasped hands with Ely. Yes, Ely's eyes told him, we will talk all about this, partner, for many years to come.

"What about the people in the truck?" Lucas asked.

"They had some cuts and bruises, but they're okay. The driver isn't going to be cited because they weren't speeding. Just in the wrong place at the wrong time. They did their best to avoid hitting the girl."

Lucas followed Bobby over to one of the blue vinyl sofas in the crowded emergency room waiting area. Because of the storm, the traffic and the precarious road conditions, it was a busy night. But, so far, the only fatality had been Nash Stoddard. The three men settled in, preparing for a long night. They would all wait for the women, to see what else they could do to help.

They would bury Nash on Wednesday. At Etta's request, it would be a graveside service. Nash's act had made him a minor celebrity in Cardinal, a permanent part of the town's history. Every year when they celebrated the Western Museum's anniversary, this story would be told. Enough donations came in to buy a plot for Nash and to pay for his funeral.

It was an ironic and sobering coincidence that his father's ashes arrived by FedEx on Monday morning. Ruby and

Etta decided to hold a double funeral. Ely bought the plot next to Nash's for Joe Stoddard so he and his son could rest side by side.

Over the next few days, Lucas only saw Ruby and Etta a few times. Birch had kept him busy with errands pertaining to the funerals and the dinner at their house afterward. Each time he saw her, Ruby seemed thinner, more fragile. She walked hesitantly, her eyes swollen from crying. Her mother was always the same, stoic and solid as a block of old wood. She reminded Lucas of a bristlecone pine, one of those trees that was thousands of years old. They had seen so much come and go in this world. One more death was just another dandelion puff blown into the wind. But Lucas knew Etta was suffering, too. He remembered the sound of her keening that night, bent over her dying son, wailing like one of those black-clad old women he'd seen on some *National Geographic* special. She was mourning in her way.

Ely seemed to be everywhere. He and Birch worked efficiently together, taking care of the details, comforting people, patiently telling the story over and over as people tried to process what happened. Ely was constantly at Ruby's side, his arm around her, whispering in her ear. Lucas could see how much he loved her.

A few weeks ago, Lucas would have been jealous of Ely. But how could he be angry with this man—his friend—who would also sit with him at the Red Coyote until one a.m. discussing life, why they were all here, what all of this meant, what really did define a man at the end of his life. Ely was his friend. His best friend. The best one he would ever have. And he knew that his realization a few days ago was right. He had never actually been in love with Ruby. He had mixed his feelings for her up with his love for Cole, his loneliness and his desire to change the past. Lucas loved Ruby as his beloved brother's wife. As his sister. As his friend. Ely was in love with her. Ely loved her.

It was sunny and cold the day they buried the Stoddard men. Hundreds of people showed up at the cemetery, some out of curiosity, but many out of respect for what Nash did. The biggest spray of flowers, a huge standing cross that was covered with white gladioli and purple irises, were from the little girl's family. A bannered ribbon across it said simply—"Thank You." A large picture of Nash stood on an easel next to his casket. His guitar lay on a table in front of it. It was a long day that ended at Birch and Bobby's house with only the family. Marie came to the funeral and Lucas asked her to come with him to Birch's for the meal.

"Are you sure?" Marie said, her face hesitant. "Isn't that just for family? Won't it make them uncomfortable having a stranger there?"

"Heavens, no," he said, smiling at her.

"Oh, great," she said, smiling back. "That's the first of about a million jokes about my name, right?"

He slipped his arm around her shoulders, thinking how natural it felt. "Only if I'm lucky."

33

Etta

“I’m sorry, but I have to go back to Ajo,” Etta said to Ruby the next Saturday, three days after they buried Nash. “Dr. Beth is running out of people she can beg to cover for me.” She had been gone only thirteen days. It felt so much longer and, yet, it was a heartbeat. Oh, Nash, she thought. My dear son. My beloved child.

“I know,” Ruby said. They were sitting on her front porch, watching a chattering mockingbird chase off a persistent crow. The crow had been eying a half-empty French fry bag tossed aside by some school kid. The mockingbird was not sympathetic to the crow's hunger and was determined to protect its territory.

Etta was silent, waiting for her daughter to speak. Since Nash's funeral, they had both run on automatic pilot, getting through that day with help from Birch and Bobby, Lucas and Sueann. And Ely. Lord, how would they have made it without his comforting presence? She'd never met Cole, Ruby's first husband, though she liked his family a lot.

At least some of them. That June was someone she hoped Ruby made a wide path around. June McGavin was a woman who had too much hurt and too much anger inside her. Etta suspected she was the type who relieved her pain by throwing it onto someone else. She said a quick prayer for her. A thought to whomever watches out for fools and drunks and sinners. Help her turn that pain to good.

Yes, Birch and Lucas and the others were good for Ruby. Kind of like a family. The family she'd never really had. They would help her through the grief of losing Nash.

And Ely Grey. He was something special. She hoped that Ruby could see how much that man loved her and how hard that kind of love was to come by. Etta had long given up the idea that she'd ever be loved like that. But to know that her daughter was loved made her happy. It didn't make up for Etta running away from her children or for how she failed them, but her daughter finding love and a home, well, that was just flat-out grace. The grace Father Tomas always said was hers if she would just ask for it. Etta made a vow to his god that she would light candles for Ruby and Ely every Sunday of her life and say a prayer for their happiness.

"Will you be okay?" Etta asked. Then she waved her hand. "Forget I asked that. Of course you will be. You have good people here watching out for you."

Ruby turned to look at her. The strained expression that Etta had seen on her daughter's face in the shelter's lobby almost two weeks ago was gone. Nash's death had done that. It had cracked the wall between them. At the funeral, she and Ruby had held each other and cried. They hadn't even done that the night Nash died, too much in shock to comfort each other. Nash's funeral was the first time Etta had hugged her daughter since she was thirteen years old.

"Yes, they are good people," Ruby said. "And, though I haven't met them, it sounds like you have some good people waiting for you in Ajo."

"I don't deserve them, but I do." Etta rocked her chair slowly back and forth. "I called Dr. Beth this morning. I'll take the Greyhound to Phoenix and she'll pick me up."

Ruby stopped rocking, her face concerned. "You don't have to do that. We can take you home."

Etta smiled, liking that Ruby so easily said *we*. There would be a wedding soon. She could feel it in her bones. "Thank you, but I already bought the ticket. It's no problem. Dr. Beth has to go to Phoenix for supplies anyway. The bus ride will give me time to think."

"I understand," Ruby said.

They rocked silently together for a long time before speaking again. The mockingbird finally won and the crow flew off in defeat, cawing his loud protests.

"Wonder if he'll come back," Etta commented.

"Guess it depends on how bad he wants those fries."

Etta nodded. "It always comes back to that." She stopped rocking and stood up. "My bus leaves at two p.m. I'd better get packed."

Ruby followed her into the house. "Do you need any money? I know you weren't expecting to stay this long. I . . ."

"Thank you, but I have enough to get me home."

She didn't tell her that Ely had already asked her the same question yesterday. She'd admitted to him that she had only twenty dollars left, not enough for her ticket home. He bought it and handed her a fifty-dollar bill.

"I'll send it back to you," she had said, knowing she should be embarrassed. Almost sixty years old and having to take money from someone who could be her son.

"Forget it," he had replied. "Practically everything I own was given to me. I'm just passing it on." He'd hugged her and said in his low, melodious voice, "Don't worry, Etta. I'll take care of Ruby."

"Thank you," she'd whispered.

"I have something for you," Etta said, reaching into the pocket of her worn jeans.

Ruby turned to her and smiled. Etta wondered if her daughter realized that was the first time she'd smiled at Etta since she was a girl. "What is it?"

Etta held out her hand. In her palm was a gold wedding band carved with tiny flowers. Ruby stared at it, her expression perplexed.

"It was my mother's," Etta said. "Throughout my life, it was the only thing I kept no matter what. When my life was particularly crazy, I sent it to your father to keep safe for me. He knew how much it meant to me and knew I'd be devastated if I ever pawned it or lost it when I was drunk." She pushed her hand closer to Ruby. Ruby slipped the ring over the tip of her forefinger, studying the carved gold.

"He sent it to me when I was one year sober," Etta said, "right after I'd moved to Ajo. Mama never took it off, but she told me that when she died, she wanted me to have it. It's engraved inside."

Ruby pulled the ring off her finger and looked inside. "'Love never ends.'"

"That's from the Bible. The love chapter in Corinthians. It was Mama's favorite. I want you to have it. You're a lot like her, you know. Good. Tough. Loyal. She would have adored you." Etta tilted her head to one side. "Mama and Daddy were married for thirty-nine years before the black lung took him. I want you to know that love can last."

Ruby hesitated, then slipped it on her left ring finger. It slid on without a hitch. "Look," she said, her voice amazed. "It fits."

"I never had any doubt," Etta said.

Epilogue

Ruby

Six months later

"I love having actual seasons," Ruby said, leaning back against Ely. It was early summer. Blue lupine bloomed and kill-deer called out their own name. They were at Clear Creek watching the horses gallop around the brilliant green grass, nipping at each other like colts. Even shy Greta kicked up her heels a time or two. The new horse, Chico, was part of the herd now. Greta and he were fast friends.

"In Southern California, you barely knew when it was when the seasons changed," Ruby said with a sigh. "Everything always looked the same. I wish I could run out there and do just what those horses are doing."

Ely's breath was warm against the back of her head. "You can. But I won't promise it won't be the talk of the town."

She turned to look up at him. "I suppose that is one downside of a small town, you can't hide your eccentricities."

"On the other hand, you don't have to. We kinda revel in them."

She laughed, kissed the edge of his jaw and turned back around to observe the horses. "Do you think the new horse Dr. Beth is sending us will take long to fit in? Greta adopted Chico so quickly, but I wonder if she'll open her heart to another one."

He tightened his arms around her, telling her he understood the subtext of her question. "We'll have to see."

Ruby had received a call from Etta a week ago. The Border Patrol had found a half-starved palomino gelding in an abandoned house on the edge of the Tohono O'odham reservation. Their first call was to Dr. Beth.

"I don't have a permanent place for him here," she told the officers. "But I do have a connection to a wonderful horse sanctuary in California."

So Lucas had acquired yet another horse. At the bookstore, Ely and Ruby started a jar for the gelding, who the Border Patrol officers had named Lucky. Despite the hard times, people had already donated three hundred forty-seven dollars. Cassie and her friends were planning a fund-raiser over the Fourth of July weekend during Wild Mustang Days.

Ely offered to go get Lucky using one of the Circle MG's horse trailers.

"You should go with him," Lucas told Ruby when they had breakfast together at the Lone Pine. "Visit your mother."

"He's right," Marie said, stealing the strawberry off the top of his pancakes.

"Hey, I was going to eat that." He grabbed at her side, tickling her.

"You snooze, you lose, counselor," she said, popping it into her mouth and winking at Ruby. "He's pathetic." But her eyes told Ruby how much she adored him.

"Can't take you kids anywhere," Ruby had said, laughing. Oh, Cole, she thought.

Look how happy your brother is. He's in love and she's such a wonderful woman. And he'd been invited by a local attorney to join the practice part time.

"A lawyer who is a part-time saddle maker," he said to Ruby.

"A saddle maker who is a part-time lawyer," she corrected, laughing.

"At any rate, I'll actually be able to make a living wage. I can support a family now." He grinned at her, telling her in those words exactly what Marie meant to him.

"What time did you tell people to come to the party?" she asked Ely. At Cassie's request, they were having her high school graduation party at Clear Creek. Ruby and Ely came early to set up the barbecue, the portable chairs and tables, lay out the tablecloths and plastic cups.

"Eleven. I figured we could leave about four or five. Later, if we have to. I told Etta we'd likely not be in Ajo until the early morning. She said she'd leave the door unlocked, to just come on in." Ely liked to drive at night and Ruby agreed.

"It'll be nice to see her," Ruby said. Over the last six months, since Nash was killed, Ruby had made an effort to call Etta once a week. Etta, in turn, wrote Ruby long letters, telling her about daily life at the shelter, in Ajo, the squabbles among the artists at the art center and revealing, little by little, her own stories about Tennessee, about the town Etta had grown up in, her parents and brothers. In April, with Ruby's encouragement, she contacted her brother, Burr. A month later, Burr's wife died from a brain aneurysm. He asked Etta to come to the funeral.

Etta's first response was to call Ruby and ask her if she thought she should go. It flattered Ruby that her mother would value her opinion and they decided it would be good for Burr and for Etta. She took the Greyhound bus back home. Her brother was waiting for her at the station, tears streaming down his cheeks.

"I'm glad I went," Etta said.

"Me, too," Ruby said. "Maybe I'll go back there with you someday. I'd like to see where you grew up."

Her mother was silent for a moment. "That would be real nice."

Cassie graduated last Thursday night.

She'd been accepted by Northern Arizona University in Flagstaff and would be leaving Cardinal in August. Sueann kept telling everyone how long she'd waited for this day, how excited she was to finally have the bathroom to herself, but when she was alone with Ruby, the truth came out.

"What am I going to do?" she wailed while Ruby fixed her a cup of tea. "I'm going to miss her so much. That little stinker. How dare she kidnap my heart." The tears in her pale green eyes looked like little jewels.

"You'll be fine," Ruby said. "I'll keep you busy. There are so many places who need volunteers and you have the café. You've wanted to redesign and change up the menu, there's that herb garden you've talked about planting since I've known you, the yoga classes you always wanted to try. Then there's the museum and Wild Mustang Days coming up and . . ."

"Okay, okay," she said, holding up her hand and laughing. "I get your point. I need to get a life."

"Right and there's plenty of life to get

here in Cardinal. There's that new veterinarian who I hear is a widow . . ."

"No way," Sueann said. "I'm not ready to date."

"It's now or never, sister," Ruby teased. "Shoot, maybe you and I should take a cruise to see Alaska. We'll take Birch! Pig out at the buffet. Take photos of glaciers. Look for whales. Or we could take one of those Mississippi River cruises and pretend we're Huck Finn and Tom Sawyer. I've always wanted to float down the Mississippi."

"Travel," Sueann said, resting her hand on her chin. "Gosh, that sounds fun."

"See, a whole new life awaits you. And since you don't have to worry about paying for Cassie's college, you can save all your extra money for your own selfish pleasure."

"At least June is good for something. That was nice of her to have put that money away for Cassie's college."

"Not to mention she is paying for this graduation party." Sueann looked at Ruby and they both burst into giggles.

"Oh, for pity's sake," June had said about Cassie's party choice, according to Derek. "Will I never hear the end of that place?"

After Nash was killed, Lucas had, with Ruby's blessing, gone to his mother and said she could have Clear Creek.

"I don't want to fight about it anymore," he'd said. "If the ranch needs the money, then we have to sell. It's for the greater good."

June, delighted, had put the land up for sale. But, the economy was already starting to turn bad and suddenly anybody who'd been looking to build ski condos the year before was too afraid to invest the money in such an expensive chunk of land no matter how beautiful it was.

"I can't help but wonder if there was a little divine intervention," Lucas said to Ruby and Ely.

"Who knows, partner," Ely said.

The first to arrive after Ruby and Ely were Lucas and Marie.

"We've got the steaks!" Marie called. "And firewood."

"I'll go help Lucas carry the wood," Ely said.

Before long, Birch and Bobby had arrived and Sueann's brother, John, and his family, a dozen or so of Cassie's closest friends and Carlos, the Lone Pine's cook, and his wife and four kids who'd known Cassie since she was a little girl. June drove up in her new Escalade, driven by Walt Creston, bringing the cake. She had the cake custom made with a realistic icing photo of a grinning five-year-old Cassie in a tiny cap and gown at her kindergarten graduation.

"Oh, that's wonderful," Birch said. "I love it."

"Gee, thanks, Grandma," Cassie said, blushing with embarrassment.

"Actually, it is really cute," Sueann said, in a side comment to Ruby. "I can't believe June did something nice."

"Are she and Walt still an item?" Ruby asked Sueann as they set out salt and pepper shakers and bottles of Tabasco and Tapatio Hot Sauce.

Sueann shrugged, straightened out one corner of a tablecloth. "Who else in this town would date her? Or him, for that matter."

"Guess there's someone for everyone," Ruby said. "Now about that vet . . ."

Sueann playfully pushed her. "Mind your own beeswax, sister."

Everyone brought a side dish or two, and soon the long tables were covered with black beans and salsa, corn pudding and potato salad, Greek salad and cheese-stuffed jalapeños, homemade tortillas and fresh guacamole.

Ely and Lucas manned the barbecue, brandishing their barbecue forks, good-naturedly fending off teasing suggestions and advice from the older men.

"No respect," Bobby said to Carlos, settling back in his lounge chair and grinning. "This younger generation just has no respect."

After they'd eaten and cut the cake and Cassie had opened her presents, Ruby climbed over the fence that separated the rescue horses from the party and walked toward them, carrots in hand. All of them, even Greta, started ambling toward her.

"Need some help?" Ely said behind her.

She turned to smile at him and handed him half the carrots. "What's mine is yours."

"And what's ours is theirs," he said, nodding at the horses.

"I don't mind."

"Which is one of the many reasons why I love you." His cool hand rested on the back of her neck. "So, when do you want to tell them?"

She broke a carrot in half and held it out to Muddy Waters. He gently scooped it up, tickling her palm with his lips.

She turned to look up at him. "When we get back from Ajo. Let's make dinner for Sueann, Cassie, Lucas, Bobby and Birch. We can tell them then. Today is Cassie's day."

He broke his five carrots in half all at once. The horses crowded around him, pushing to get their share.

"Everyone loves Ely," she said, laughing.

"Everyone loves the man with the snacks."

"I love you even when you don't have snacks."

He gifted her with a brilliant white smile.

"I'm glad you talked me out of Vegas," he said.

When, a few weeks ago, while sitting in front of a fire at his house, Ely asked her to marry him, she'd not hesitated one second before saying yes. Whenever, wherever he wanted.

"We can leave for Las Vegas right now," he said, kissing her hard. "We can be married by midnight."

She almost agreed, then said, "No. I take back what I said."

His expression froze, his eyes hesitant.

She touched his scarred cheek. "Oh, Ely, I mean I do want to marry you. But, I take back the whenever or wherever part. Unless you are totally against it, I think we should have a wedding. Here in Cardinal. In front of all our friends and family. I want Birch there. I want Etta there. I want Bobby to walk me down the aisle."

"Okay," he said slowly. "Why the change?"

She took his hands in hers. "Running away, keeping to ourselves, not sharing our lives with others . . . that's what we both did for so many years. Not any longer. We have friends here and family and they care about us. We *are* a part of Cardinal, of this life we've made. We need to show that to everyone, but mostly, we need to show it to ourselves."

He nodded, his face fluid with emotion. "You are absolutely right."

She had brought his hand up to her lips and kissed the top of it. "Besides, do you really think Birch would let us get away with eloping to Vegas? We would end up having another wedding anyway. Might as well go whole-hog the first time."

"Should we tell your mother when we pick up Lucky?" Ely said. "Do you think that'll hurt Birch's feelings?"

Ruby thought for a moment. "Maybe a little. But Birch will get to plan the whole thing and I'll gladly let her. She knows how special she is to me, how she is truly the mother I never had. Lucas can walk both of them down the aisle and they can sit together or one on each side. They are both our mothers, really. We won't have a bride and groom's side of the church. We'll tell everyone to sit where they want."

"You, future Mrs. Grey," he said, "are one smart woman."

"Oh, no, I just realized, my name will be Ruby Grey! It sounds like a color for granite tile."

"Not to me. To me it sounds like the most beautiful thing I've ever heard." Greta nudged him with her nose. "I'm all out of carrots," he told her. "You are getting downright pushy for someone who used to be an outcast."

"I sure hope Lucky will fit in," Ruby said.

"He'll be fine. I'm going to help Lucas break down the barbecue so we can get on the road."

"Okay," she said. "I'll be there in a minute. I just want to go say good-bye to Cole."

"Give him my best," Ely said, touching her cheek.

The horses followed her partway to the huge cottonwood in the middle of the pasture, until they realized that there were no more treats. The air was starting to cool down, the real heat of a Cardinal Valley summer only days away. The sky had turned that dusky purple blue that signaled the end of the day. It had been a good one and tomorrow would be, too. She was looking forward to the long drive to Ajo with Ely, listening to late-night talk radio, laughing at the local commercials, watching the stars turn the inky sky into a beautiful, sparkling tapestry.

"He's a good man, Cole," she said, leaning against the cottonwood tree's solid trunk. "But you knew that, didn't you?" She ran her hand over the scratchy wood, the roughness reminding her of Cole's face first thing in the morning. She used to feel silly talking aloud to him, but now she didn't. She didn't really believe he could hear her. When she told Ely about it, a bit embarrassed, he didn't laugh.

"The way I see it," he said, "you're just getting used to praying. Maybe someday you'll feel like talking to the Big Guy himself."

"Maybe," she'd replied. Years ago, a remark like that would have made her angry. Now, it just made her think. Maybe Ely was right. Maybe not. But she was willing to open her heart and consider it.

She remembered something Cole told her once when they talked about how they met.

"I don't believe in accidents," he said. "There's a plan, a reason to why we met at this particular time in our lives."

"Really," she'd said, laughing. "And who had this great plan?"

He had shrugged, trying to save his dignity. "God, I guess. Whatever. I know, it sounds stupid."

"Nothing you say sounds stupid," she'd said, kissing him.

She realized now that he'd believed in God, in this Higher Power talked about in AA. She hadn't known that part of him then, didn't know what he was trying to tell her.

"Was this *your* plan, Cole?" she asked. It tore at her heart to think that, in a way, by arranging for her and Ely to come to Cardinal, he'd given them both the life he knew he'd never be able to have in this town. Had Cole done that consciously? Or was there really a bigger plan? She felt her heart soften. "Whatever, whoever planned this, please, take good care of Cole. Take care of Daddy and Nash. Please, let me see them all again someday." Tears welled in her eyes, tracked down her dry cheeks. "And thank you," she whispered. "Thank you."

She gazed across the field at the people cleaning up Cassie's party, all those good people who were her friends, her family. Ely lifted the grill and slid it into Lucas's truck bed. He turned and looked in her direction, searching. She moved out of the tree's shadows and held up her hand, willing him to see her. The minute he did, she could see the anxiety melt from his face. Then she took a careful step over one of the cottonwood tree's solid roots and started walking across the wide green pasture toward him.